THE HORSE TAMERS

Previous Books by RLB Hartmann

I Rode with Cullen Baker
Floyd and the Traveling Yard Sale

୫

Previous Volumes in the Cordero saga
Tierra del Oro

Book One: *Forty Grains of Black Powder*

Book Two: *Legend of the Sierra Madre*

Book Three: *Los Pobres*

Book Four: *La Puerta del Sol*

Book Five: *A Lion Against the Wind*

Book Six: *Bitter Victory*

Book Seven: *Tierra y Libertad*

The Horse Tamers

Book Eight of the Cordero Saga
Tierra del Oro

RLB Hartmann

Catawba River Press
Morganton, North Carolina
2012

The Horse Tamers

First Edition

ISBN-13: 978-0615433004

ISBN-10: 0615433006

Cover design by RLB Hartmann
Flying Hawk logo by Tom Stine
Los Nuestros photos by Ed Treverton
The typeface chosen for the Tierra del Oro saga is
Centaur

Chapter One

Los Dos Corazones. 1915

Anita, Mamá, and Tereza stood in the chill dawn to see them off, arms loosely around each other's waist. Ramón was groggy from being awake most of the night. First, making love, and afterward, thinking about his sons, and Mamá, and Luis.

The stubborn boy had refused to ride with them almost until the last minute. Then, hair wet from sobering up by dunking in water, head swathed in his sarape to keep out the cold, Luis rode up and said, "Forgive me, Patrón. I have been acting like a loco."

"Sí, you have. It's a trait common to men in love."

Diego and he had made arrangements to load their horses and supplies into boxcars, and on the train south the band of mustangers filled their coach with cigarette smoke and laughter, reminiscences and plans. Martín, though having no connection with the legendary Sierra Madre hunt, was the best vaquero in three villages, and had been his chief horse handler in the cavalry.

Seven hombres del campo, men of the wild country, out for adventure. Disregarding news that Obregón and Villa forces were shedding blood along the route between Guadalajara and the capital city, they pushed out of their thoughts further reports which told of sporadic fights still occurring between the Calles and Maytorena factions in the north. It was easy to ignore the stir over Carranza's moving the seat of government to Veracruz; squabbling over where and when to hold the convention at which everything was supposed to have been settled, but wasn't; even the matter of who was actually acting as Presidente de la República.

"I wish Mano had come along." Ramón was drowsy and full of lunch. He would be glad when they left the monotony of the train and were on the trails into the Cordillera.

Martín said, "He and María are expecting another child."

Luis's head jerked around. "I didn't know that."

Strange, how people form and lose ties with each other. Once Mano had been his best friend; now they seemed hardly to speak. Only a few months ago, he had believed he could never let Anita out of his sight again; now he was hurtling away from her—and Mamá, and Sereno—as fast as this locomotive could take him.

"It's too much for me." He slid down on his backbone and covered his face with his sarape, preparatory to sleep.

They stayed one night in Culiacán, to enjoy as lavish a supper as possible before the coming weeks of camp food, and see a cinematográfica. It included indecently-clad white women parading about and batting their eyes. Domingo sat erect, unmoving. Just as Ramón was about to cut the boy's education short, the scene shifted to something less exciting. He dreaded questions, but as they walked under the street lamps back to the hotel, Domingo remained silent.

They shared a room with Luis. Undressing in the dark, they crowded into the same bed and tossed about for awhile, trying to adjust the space. When Luis was faintly snoring, he felt Domingo lean above his ear and whisper, "Jefe, are you asleep?"

"No, but you should be."

"I keep thinking."

"¡Sin duda!" Without doubt.

"About babies."

"Dios divino," he groaned softly. "I thought the soldados told you everything while I was in Mérida."

"Well, maybe not everything. It's all a tangle again."

The boy's warm breath tickled his ear, recalling the night he'd found Sereno at last, and the child lay sleeping on his arm, sweet and alive. Perhaps his younger son and Domingo were building that close relationship he had hoped for. Perhaps naming it was, as Anita had suggested, of little consequence, so long as the bond was there.

"What is tangled?"

"Luis. Paz. Mariano."

"How the hell did Mariano get into this?"

"He was with Paz."

"What do you mean, with her?"

"He went in the carriage, the night she left. And I think he didn't come home until the morning."

He felt his neck muscles stiffen. He couldn't hear Luis snoring any more. "Hush," he said softly into Domingo's ear. "We'll finish this talk later."

"But—"

"Silencio." He laid his fingers against the boy's lips. He wished Domingo had chosen to keep quiet until morning, for now sleep was far from him.

Leaving the city behind, they cantered southeasterly, across a region of neglected plantations where native grasses were already taking over once-productive fields. The guide

Diego hired in Culiacán was called Lobo, a wiry young Seri with Indian-straight hair and knowing eyes.

Ramón felt more relaxed than he had in years, secure in the assurance that his family were guarded, well-fed, and, if not completely happy because of his decision to leave them, at least content in their new friendships.

Rice and cane fields gave way to rolling foothills covered in shrub oaks, where great jagged outcroppings rose into cliffs. Hawks soared overhead, hunting for quail, and when the horses flushed a covey, rifles came unshucked as rapidly as if Villistas had appeared. The mustangers took enough for supper, and hung that many more on the pack saddles for morning.

Domingo complained, "If I had a rifle, I bet I could have hit a few, too."

"If you had a rifle, none of us would be safe," Luis said, laughing.

Glad to see his young friend recovering from the misery of unreturned love, Ramón said, "I remember one time when you set out to shoot a wildcat with my rifle. We ate goat for a week."

"Jefe! That cabrito jumped in front of my bullet. It was not my fault. But, didn't he make a good stew."

Laughter rang against the sun-gilded hills.

Ever climbing, Lobo routed them along narrow packtrain trails which wound up the sides of bluffs and clung to edges of arroyos. Evergreens contrasted with the gray background of leafless thorn forest. Kapoks and cacti, limberbush and ancient higueras, shared the slopes, and as the Cordillera grew wilder, undergrowth thinned. Crossing parklands, hooves muffled by carpets of pine needles, it was easy to imagine spirits lurking in the high canopy, waiting for a false move on the part of the intruders.

February dusk came early in the cañons, bringing a sharp wind, so before the first camp they were unpacking jackets to wear beneath sarapes. Lobo chose a level place shielded by rocks from weather and enemies, and they divided up tasks.

Luis and Domingo, skilled in feeding soldados, offered to cook the quail. Sliced camotes fried in its grease, crumbled piloncillo making a sugary glaze. Strong coffee tempered with goat's milk, tortillas made yesterday at Dos Corazones and reheated. The food satisfied, though they had no music, as there was ever danger of bronco Indios, deserters from both armies, or bandidos of some sort plotting to rob travelers.

"In the days of the Rurales this was not so," Diego mused. "At least Porfirio kept the peace."

Ramón steered the talk onto a safer subject. "I wish we could have found García. He seems quite a character."

"Sí—un malo tipo," Francisco agreed. "Talk of your bandits, Señor García was one of them."

Diego blew a thin stream of cigarette smoke into the air and turned to Ramón. "Did your mother never tell you about him?"

"Not much. Only that he became a mustanger because he thought my father possessed a treasure, and he wanted it."

Francisco made an impatient noise. "I remember, when you were growing up, you believed it, too."

He pressed his lips together to keep from shouting, *Dammit, there is a treasure! I found the map!* His long-ago promise to Trouble's spirit bound him to silence. But he couldn't help asking, "Do you believe the dead return, to guide us?"

All of the men nodded, giving assent in greater or lesser degree. Gregorio told them, "My father said he thought the bruja who rescued Trouble that time was a fantasma. If all the stories told about her are true, she would have been over a hundred and fifty years old, even then."

"Maybe there's more than one," Domingo suggested.

Gregorio shook his head. "There are many brujas, of course, but this one about whom the legends are told has the magical power to remain young and beautiful."

Domingo turned to him. "And your father saw her? She saved his life?"

"So Mamá said, and she does not lie."

"Maybe we shall see her. The bruja, I mean."

Diego tossed the spent end of his cigarette at their small campfire. "Not in Sinaloa. She's una hija de Sonora, and if you hope to see her, you must go to the northern mountains, around Arizpe."

"Does Sinaloa not have such a bruja?" Domingo persisted.

"None that I have heard of. Lobo, ¿qué piensa usted? Is there a bruja who rewards the pure-hearted, and puts curses on those who do evil?"

Lobo gave a little self-conscious laugh. "No sé, señor. One hears much. Quizá sí, quizá no. ¿Quién sabe?"

Mariano and Martín were called in from guard duty, to warm themselves for sleep, and Diego and Lobo took the first watch. The rest found places away from the fire to avoid being blinded by its glow in case of attack. Domingo spread his blankets between him and Luis. "Thank you for letting me come along, Jefe," the boy said sleepily.

"De nada," he answered, happy from a sense of well-being.

Just before departure, he had managed to find time alone with Mamá. Letters had never seemed the way to tell her about Trouble, but with her soft hand in his and her presence inviting confidences, he'd said, "When I had been away from home for nearly a year, I woke once before dawn high in the Sierras northeast of Los Pobres, and saw my father, and he spoke to me. Returning to our empty casita hurt most because I could not share this experience with you, while it was still fresh."

Mamá was silent a long while, finally saying, on a sigh, "Francisco's business was bringing in little, and I had neglected my own mother for many years. Had we not gone when we did, I would have missed seeing her alive again, for she died in my arms only a few days after we arrived. My sisters had deserted her. After that, I couldn't face returning to the hillside where I had known so much happiness, and so much pain. We thought you were dead, as we never heard different. It was as though you had vanished from the earth, and nothing was left there for me."

"That is how I felt when I came home from Tía Sofía's deathbed and found my family taken by soldiers."

Mamá clasped his hand. "Dios is good to us, mijo, to give us back loved ones."

"Sí," he said. "And to allow opportunities to make right those things which haunt us."

"You speak of Francisco."

"Yes. I was young and stupid."

"Young, of course; stupid—maybe, a little." She laughed, to show it was supposed to be a joke.

Curious, he asked, "Did you ever see my father, after he was gone?"

"No.... Not like that. But I always saw him in you." She stared across the compound, to one of the corrals, where Domingo had just roped his caballo for a morning ride. "And, I see Trouble in him. They share an aloofness that you never had. Your heart is more tender."

"Anita says the war has changed me."

"On the outside, perhaps. Not inside. Guard against being hurt, Ramoncito. He has the power to hurt you."

"Don't worry, Mamá. I'm tougher than you think. Besides, I have Anita and Sereno, and you and Francisco. I am rich."

"Sí, you are. But after the hunt, Francisco and I go back to California. We have obligations, and our home is there. Even if we visit often, God willing, Sonora is your tierra, and you would never be happy anywhere else."

"Sonora is your tierra, and Francisco's, too."

"After the children are grown, we shall return. For now, they have a better life where they are."

"I wish to start a school. When the revolution is over—" So much would be possible, if only the fighting stopped.

There was a little silence. Then Mamá said softly, "Someday, I would like to know about his mother."

Another silence. "I loved her."

Mamá had turned her serene smile on him. "Of course you did."

Lying wrapped in a wool blanket on the side of a mountain east of Culiacán, his canteen against his ribs to keep ice from forming in the water, he dreamed of Serafina, laughingly alive in her house in La Puerta del Sol. Dreamed, too, of Anita, her kisses enflaming his youthful blood so that even the yoke of marriage no longer felt restraining to him.

When Martín shook him awake to stand watch, however, it was Paz whose hands were unbuttoning his clothes and sending thrills of anticipation through him.

"There is more coffee," the domador said, motioning at the pot in the edge of thick coals.

"Gracias." He took a cup to his post, high on the western slope, the starlit dome of sky exactly like the one he remembered from a year ago. He and Paz had spent a night like this in an abandoned house in Culiacán, after he broke the news of Joaquín's ill-fated patrol. Nothing intimate had passed between them then, nor later in the mountain village of Cosalá, where he told her Joaquín was found alive.

They had shared a few hot kisses in Guadalajara. Only the vision of Anita, appearing in the doorway, had halted him from surrendering to her desire. He wondered what would come of Mariano's interest in Paz.

Gregorio was on the same watch, on the other side of camp. They were well off the trail and no travelers were likely to pass, not even those intent on robbery, but occasional rustlings in fallen oak leaves traced the ramblings of night creatures.

In the distance downriver, el Tecolote, the owl, called a soft echoing query into the darkness. It sent a shiver along his spine even though he considered himself much less superstitious than were his companions. Gregorio would be swathed in his sarape, huddled in as small a crevice as he could find, gun cocked, alert for any danger.

Owl cries portended death, and a man never knew from what quarter it might come.

They paused at a place where the Río San Lorenzo branched to their left under the shoulder of mountains, and another river forked east. Lobo said, "The village of Los Remedios lies in that direction." He pointed vaguely. "Beyond is the great city of Durango. So I am told."

"I've been there," Domingo said, next to him. "How far is it?"

Lobo shrugged. "¿Quién sabe? A long way."

"We shall camp at Los Remedios tonight," don Diego said. "And learn if anyone has seen mustangs."

They reined their mounts along the riverbank.

Domingo kept watching for terrain that looked familiar, but any of the narrow canyons leading crookedly into the brushy hills could be the one taken the night he and Paz fled those bandidos. They had not gone through Los Remedios.

He rode near Ramón. "I think we're too far east," he said, nervous that another day of travel would cause them to miss the right valley.

"What makes you think so?"

"A feeling, only." It was possible they had already passed by the village in the dark without knowing it was there. "We went south to get to Cosalá. Mountains were all around, but there was a pass."

"Due south?"

He tried to remember where had been the position of the sun. "Southeast, I guess."

They rode in silence for a while, the others in front. "You and Sereno—" Ramón began, and he gave the major a guarded glance. "You seem to be making friends."

He hesitated, unwilling to admit how jealous he felt every time he saw them together, especially when Ramón gave his son a hug or kissed the pretty cheek, or ruffled the light brown hair. "He and Teo like each other very much."

"I didn't ask about Teo. I asked about you."

Resisting the impulse to spur his mount ahead and avoid answering, he said tightly, "We don't fight anymore."

Ramón made a face of wry acknowledgment. "That is a start."

It took all his strength not to cry out, Must we become brothers, to earn your respect? And, yes, your love. He felt both love and respect for this man riding beside him. None of the other soldados had shown Ramón's concern, nor attempted to discipline him when he'd been disobedient. Only Ramón had given him the attention of a father. Until Sereno came.

"I can't be friends with him," he said, driven.

Ramón laid a hand on his horse's rein and stirrups collided as their mounts jostled to a halt. He expected anger and was unprepared for the expression on the man's face. Mamá always looked like that when he had tormented Teo over possession of a favored toy.

"You can try," the major said.

Something was demanded of him, though the words he longed to shout stuck in his throat: I can never be friends with someone who has the place I want, the place which was almost mine. At last he said hoarsely, "I will try."

Ramón released his bridle and nodded for him to ride ahead. Kicking his heels into his horse's flanks, he caught up to the others.

Villagers living at Los Remedios had seen mustangs. "¿Cómo no, señores? The hills are full of them."

Drinks available in the candle-lit cantina were mezcal or aguardiente, which Ramón refused to allow him to have. The niño serving tables offered to milk a goat and when he brought a clay mug, held out a hand into which Luis placed a centavo.

Wedged between the major and Luis on a crude bench, Domingo stopped listening to talk of Villistas terrorizing the mountain towns and began thinking about Luis and the girl in the choza at Los Dos Corazones. He wondered whether they had made a baby. Stealing a look, he saw a young man still jaded from disappointment but starting to recover enough to laugh at jokes.

He thought about Paz, lost with him in these very mountains, sleeping entwined inside all their bedding to keep from freezing. What had taken place the night she left Dos Corazones with Mariano? He thought about Tereza. While they were at work on the burro piñata, he had noticed womanly changes from the beautiful but childish girl she had been ten months ago, when he first met her.

If he caught a clean-limbed filly with the reata which Ramón had given him, he could present it to her as a gift. Maybe, to show her appreciation, she would kiss him—when her father wasn't looking. He thought about kissing her mouth, the way he had seen Ramón and Anita kiss when they thought they were alone. A warm, tingling sensation filled him.   For a moment he feared he had been picking up Luis's glass by mistake and was getting drunk.

"Luis."

"¿Sí, chico?"

"Could a girl as young as Tereza have a baby?"

Luis leaned away to stare at him as if he'd suddenly grown horns. "Why does that concern you?"

He felt his cheeks grow hot. "No reason. I was just thinking about things."

"Pues, think about this. If Ramón did not kill you, Diego would."

"¡Hombre! I never —"

Laying a friendly arm around his shoulders, Luis said into his ear, "Domingo, niño, there will be plenty of time for women when you are older. I thought I had the years to know my heart, but I was wrong. Don't let your heart—or that other part—lead you into making a fool of yourself, the way I did."

Rising unsteadily from the bench where they were seated, Luis went out into the night. The gathering was breaking up. Ramón stayed behind, slowly moving his glass in a tight circle with the thumb and forefinger of one hand. His chin was propped in the other.

"Jefe. Is something the matter?"

The major heaved a sigh, stood up, found his hat. "Someday, Domingo, I'll give you the answer you deserve."

"Why not now?"

The man startled him with a rough, quick hug. "Don't ask."

The campsite lay south of town, only cigarette tips guiding them to their compañeros. He took off his boots, leaving them inside the blankets along with his canteen. Like everyone else, he slept with his bridle, so the bit would be warm when morning came, making his mount accept it more readily. He hoped to dream pleasurably of Tereza.

Waking, he remembered images of being back in the Valle de Los Mesteños. He and Ramón were riding side by side through a meadow of billowing yellow grass, and the major was about to tell him something important, a big secret, which would change his whole life.

"Do you think it is safe to split up?" Gregorio asked, his forehead furrowed.

Ramón suspected that fear of evil spirits more than any chance meeting with outlaws prompted the question. "Are you not the one who once laughed at Coyote when he was warning us about brujos and the dark forces which they control?"

"If I laughed, it was only because I doubted Coyote, not the spirits themselves."

Mariano said, "None of the villages north of the Río Piaxtla has been raided by anyone. The region is too remote to be of interest to either soldiers or renegades."

"Tell that to Domingo," he said mildly.

"The situation has changed," Diego said. "Last year Culiacán was a vital military center, drawing thieves who stole goods and horses easily sold. Now the land has no more to offer. I think it is safe to split up. It's the quickest way to find mustangs, which is why we came."

"Then, let us pair off," Francisco suggested. "I shall feel safer if someone is watching my back."

Ramón chose Domingo.

The plan was to fan out, and then work back to meet where the San Lorenzo was said to join a branch known as San José. With his hunting knife, Lobo sketched the spines of the fan in the dirt, assigning the northern route to them.

Stopping Domingo's objections with a hand on the boy's arm, Ramón said, "Be patient."

They crossed the river and rode among hills covered in chaparral and boulders. Deer trails, and an occasional wider path used by people, led among thorn thickets. They climbed gentle slopes that soon wound into a needle-strewn parkland of pines, oaks, and hardwoods he didn't recognize, they came upon an old road.

"Lobo said the village of Santa María lies in that direction." He nodded eastward. "This is probably the road between there and Cosalá."

"Then, let us turn south now."

"If we turn too soon, we'll miss the rendezvous point."

"Jefe, does this look like a place to find mustangs?"

He had to laugh. "You're right. We'll follow the road for a while to rest the horses."

Trotting beneath overhanging bare branches, he was awed by the silence around them, as though no other living thing existed save the various birds flitting among sunlight-dappled chaparral.

"That story Lobo told us," Domingo said. "Do you believe it?"

"Which one?" Lobo's campfire stories rivaled any he had heard.

"About the lost mine. El Naranjal. According to him, it is somewhere in these mountains."

"That's an old story, like the bruja legend."

"You doubt that the beautiful bruja saved your father's life?"

"I think that a woman, a curandera, found him and healed his injuries with herbs. I no longer believe she was a famous witch, one hundred and fifty years old."

"Did you, once?"

He conquered a smile at the boy's insistence, and admitted, "Sí, once."

"If we found a gold mine, we would be rich."

"Finding it is one thing. Getting out the gold is a different thing. Besides, such a mine wouldn't belong to us."

"El Naranjal would. Lobo says it began with the Spaniards long ago in the days of his great-great-great grandfather."

"And has been lost almost as long."

"Lobo knows a man who saw the hacienda buildings. Did you not hear him say that?"

"I heard. It's a pretty story. All those orange trees, and a white casa grande shining in the sun far below in a valley, with no trail down from the cliffs."

"Bueno, the thing is," Domingo said, "one must approach from the other side. There must have been a road as wide as this, at one time, for the people living there to travel on."

Ramón's thoughts drifted to the map he had taken from his bandit grandfather's safe when he was younger than Domingo. Was there a treasure at La Nariz? Francisco had never believed it. His lips parted to relate how he had carried the map and the dream, until his promise to Trouble made him discard the scrap of paper. The location, however, remained in his memory. As far from here as his old life in Los Pobres.

Then they emerged from timberland onto a grassy slope leading among chaparral-covered hills, pale brown bluffs in the near distance to the east, the blue haze of mountains rising beyond.

"See those cliffs, Jefe? I bet if we were up there, we could see that lost hacienda."

Ramón pointed far across the rolling grassy plains, cut by arroyos and patched by forests. "Mira. There are cliffs, also."

Picking their way downslope, they lost sight of both ranges, as the old road wound among brush and rocks where rabbits scurried and lizards sunned themselves. In a few minutes the road forked.

They drew to a halt, unstoppered canteens and drank. No column of smoke marked rancho, town, or hungry traveler. It was good to be here, away from the chaos of battle.

"Al derecho," he decided, repositioning his hat. To the right. "At least we shall have shade."

This part of the road, hardly more than a cleared space meandering among trees, seemed not to have been used for a long time. Littered with windfall limbs, it was undisturbed by track of beast or wagon. Out of the corner of his eye he glimpsed a wolf deeper in the woods, and later they startled two deer drinking at a spring sheltered by a crag. Filling canteens and watering their mounts, he showed Domingo many raccoon and panther tracks in the mud surrounding the basin.

"Sí. I know those, from when Mamá hired the Indio guide who kept Teo from dying after the snake bit him."

"A snake really bit Teo? You were not making it up?"

"It was when we were crossing these mountains."

Domingo closed his lips as though there were more to say, but he preferred not to continue.

Eighteen months had passed since Serafina's death. It seemed like eighteen years to him. How did that passing of time feel to the boy? He couldn't guess.

"My hunger tells me not to dawdle here," he said, and they mounted up and rode on. In less than half an hour he could see a break in the trees, just ahead. He lifted the gelding into a relaxed lope and Domingo followed.

Coming to the woods edge, he drew rein, not entirely surprised by an iron carriage gate set in the high rock wall of an hacienda. Because of Lobo's story of El Naranjal, prickles raised the hair on the back of his neck.

"Dios, Jefe," Domingo whispered. "Maybe this is it."

"My luck would have to turn for that."

"It's open," the boy said hopefully.

He unholstered his pistol. Nudging with his heels, he rode forward and, swinging aside the half-gate, passed through, Domingo right behind.

Chapter Two

Ahead, in a level clearing strewn with storm-cast leaves and bits of branches, was a casa grande. Two stories, with a kitchen patio facing them. Whitewashed plaster had crumbled away in places, revealing rock, yet the ancient tile roofs appeared sound.

Lower windows were barred but unshuttered, the darkness inside screened by dingy white curtains. The wing to the right formed a corner where household herbs straggled in a wild state. Tuffs of grass sprouted here and there in less-packed earth.

Within shouting distance, across a wide road that curved downslope, three well-built—but long neglected— structures might once have housed fine carriages, harness, tools, and stores of grain. At the rim of a clearing, behind which rose great trees, were more hacienda buildings, one belonging to a blacksmith; his bellows and anvil waited beneath a sagging ramada.

A rock fence bordering the road was obscured by old-growth bougainvillea. Inside the fence was a winter-brown yard cut by gravel paths.

Domingo walked his horse toward the front of the house. "Cuidado," Ramón called, wishing he had given him the pistol.

Domingo waved that he heard.

In the back patio, where he dismounted, ears straining for sounds, there was only the February wind murmuring in the corners, the hiss of dry brown oak leaves scudding across unglazed tiles. Not lowering his guard, he pushed open the plain wooden door, and found himself in a stone-floored hallway.

He peered into the cocina, where one smoky wall bore shapes of utensils that once hung ready for the cook's hand. A large table and the adobe ovens were all that remained. Opposite were three store rooms, two with nothing in them. The door of the third was stuck tight.

The hallway led into a stone-floored patio graced with columns but no fountain. Through an archway lay a long room, empty except for the chair-less mahogany banquet table.

Passing into another corredor, he found a staircase leading upward and wide wooden doors that gave access to a sala still furnished with things too heavy to be stolen—a thick rug, bulky Spanish tables and benches, a large stuffed sofa with a curving back and lion's feet.

At one end of the central hall was a small room with glass doors opening beneath the balcony. At the other end, a carved door with glass panes set in the upper half let him onto a paved terrace. Six posts supported its roof. To his right lay a chest-high outer wall, backed by ancient trees covered in thick vines. To his left, uncut grass stretched to a lower wall topped with an ornamental fence. Ahead, Domingo had dismounted and now motioned him forward. "Look, Jefe. A mirador."

Running the width of the yard, the overlook was a waist high retaining wall that made him dizzy to lean over.

Below, the ground sloped sharply before leveling beneath wide-branching trees. Their stark gray limbs stood out among evergreens whose tops resembled a piece of mottled green cloth flung upon the earth by an ageless god. The glitter of a river winked here and there, winding toward the horizon, banded by rugged mountains of misty blue. High white clouds filled the sunlit sky.

Across the rutted road lay fields, roughly plowed but never replanted, and about half a kilometre down the road, more than a dozen, maybe twenty, roofless adobes indicated an abandoned village. Trails and foot paths led past jagged outcroppings of rock and into the woods, likely to estancias belonging to the estate.

Domingo said, "No one has lived here for a very long time."

They turned back to the casa grande. A band of blue, painted two hand-spans from the foundation, girdled the house, and beside the entry a carefully rendered cross guarded the home against evil spirits.

Gazing about, the boy mused, "I wonder why they left."

Ramón paused with a hand on one of the peeled posts. His heartbeat quickened. The tilled earth was dark and fertile. Unlike Casa Vásquez, with fields tamed by two generations of peones, where mere cactus and chaparral threatened to overtake the land, where acacias, huisaches, and other hardy trees were planted for shade, here were wild forests of pine and thick-boled oaks, rampant flowering vines, the tangy fragrance of leaf-mold.

It wasn't jungle, rank and hot like the mangroves of the coast, but deeply mysterious, with valleys, cliffs, streams, endless woods, and prowling beasts just beyond the hacienda walls. Would Anita and Sereno like living here, or be afraid?

Domingo's little frown tokened intense thought before he said softly, "It gives me almost the same feeling as did El Valle de Los Mesteños."

"A good feeling."

"Sí."

They watched a hawk circling in the middle distance. Presently he remembered, "You haven't been inside."

At the stairs the boy stopped at the ebony post which had been fashioned by a master carver into the forequarters of a maned lion. "There was one much like this in our house in Monterrey." He touched the fangs of the snarling mouth. "Papá said this kind of león lives in a place called Africa." He looked up. "Sometimes, it feels like I shall wake, and be in my room, with the sunlight coming through the window to make a block on the floor, and see Meme grooming herself in the warmth."

Papá. Pablo, of course. His throat tightened almost too much for speech, but he managed to ask, "Meme was the cat?"

"Sí. I miss her."

"Domingo——" He had taken a step, ready to confess, to explain, to promise to make amends, when a shout came from the corredor.

"¡Hola! Ramón! Hombre, are you here?"

"Sí, we are here," Domingo called back.

Gregorio passed beneath the arches of the front patio, Martín at his heels. "We were getting worried about you."

Holding out an unsteady hand for one of Martín's cigarettes, Ramón said, "I forgot the time."

"No importa. Everyone is together. Diego picked up your trail easily."

"Did you find the mustangs?" Domingo held out his hand to Martín, who slapped the outstretched palm.

"Alas, no. But there were plenty of tracks to the west."

"See! I knew we were too far east. Did you also find my beautiful valley?"

The mustangers laughed, and Gregorio said, "Ten valleys, each more beautiful than the last."

"Stop joking," Domingo said. "And give me a cigarette."

"Not now." Gregorio glanced at Ramón.

"He doesn't care, do you, Jefe?"

Martín saved him from having to answer. "Smoking tobacco makes one cough in the mornings. You should guard against starting such a bad habit."

"Then, give me one of yours." Domingo laughed.

"Not a chance." Martín guarded his marijuana cigarettes with a hand over his pocket. "That is an even worse habit."

"Damn. Sometimes I wonder why I even bothered to come along."

Ramón laid an arm across the boy's shoulders and they walked out together to where the others milled around in the courtyard.

Diego gestured toward unused pens between the casa grande and the village huts. "Those corrals are sturdy and of a good size to hold small groups. It will be easier than running the band until they're exhausted, and safer than roping them one at a time."

Domingo asked, "What would we have done if the hacienda had not been here?"

"With this much timber, construct corrals of our own, though doing so would have meant extra days, which we can now use to find and gentle the manada."

Partly out of respect for the absent owners, mostly to avoid confinement in the house, they decided to remain outside. Lobo built a fire in the wagon yard and turned their mounts into the nearest pen. Martín and Francisco tended the stock, with Domingo's help, until Luis cried, "¡Ven qué comer, hombres!"

Roasted venison, along with steaming coffee and beans, was welcome after a morning of riding rough country. He tried to guess what Diego's cook was serving at Los Dos Corazones. When he thought of the comfortable bedroom and Anita, he felt a stirring of desire and sought distraction in the conversation around him.

"Could this be the casa grande of El Naranjal?" Domingo questioned Lobo. "These main buildings were whitewashed, and Jefe agrees it has been abandonada for a long time."

Lobo gave an uncertain shake of his head. "It could be. But where are the orange trees?"

"Perhaps they died," Gregorio suggested.

Mariano held a match to his father's cigarillo. "Only last year someone in Culiacán claimed to have found little oranges floating in the Río Tamazule during the rainy season."

"¡Caray!" Domingo cried. "Paz said she found a twig of orange blossoms when she was washing clothes in that river. It came past and she caught it."

Francisco smiled. "I thought we were hunting mustangs, not oranges."

"Not oranges," Domingo declared. "The lost mine, El Naranjal, named for the oranges."

Everyone laughed with affection, and, after a last draw on a cigarette, a last gulp of cooling coffee, they sought bedrolls for an hour's sleep before the afternoon hunt.

Ramón lay awake, tracing in his mind the rooms he had seen earlier. The casa was larger than any he had been in, including the Mérida townhouse of El General. There was not the elegance, of course, nor the clean simplicity of his own Casa Vásquez. This place had been built like a fortress, perhaps as much as three hundred years ago. Newer buildings had been added, but even those were old, belonging to a time when the country was wilder and more remote than now, and men shut themselves and loved ones in the compound at first dark, not daring to sit in the moonlit patio and sing until time for bed.

Weathered tile roofs peaked over wings and ells, the brilliance of midday sky making a pleasant backdrop. Letting his gaze wander from balcony to azotea to galería, he felt drawn to climb the stone steps to the second story windows and fling open those casements.

Cleaning the years of use and neglect from rooms, stalls, and store houses would require as much work as he had intended to put into Casa Vásquez; yet the structures were sound, and the land would produce. He could run cattle along the river bottoms, without the worry that they might die of drought.

He made up his mind to check municipal records in Culiacán, to determine what he could about the owner. Perhaps Domingo was right in wanting to believe this was El Naranjal. "But there are no orange trees," he muttered.

"¿Qué, Patrón?" Luis lifted his head, squinting groggily.

He feigned sleep so he wouldn't have to answer.

The mesteñeros rode from beneath the canopy of pines, crossed a rocky space, dismounted near a precipice. Domingo ventured as near the edge as he dared, noting that, besides their bootsteps, the only sounds were the jingle of bits and the slap of mane when someone's mount shook its head.

He surveyed the rolling grassland below, the sinuous line of cottonwoods marking a stream. Craggy hills rose in broken shades of crimson, tan, and brown. Far to the southwest was a break in the cañon wall, through which he glimpsed a distant range, purple in the late afternoon.

Across the dome of blue sailed a hawk, its cry silenced by the crystal expanse separating them.

"Madre de Dios," he whispered, and, louder, "That is my valley. We have found it."

Ramón was standing beside him, and he willed the man to experience the thrum of his heart, the thrill of belonging, without having to find words. The major's eyes met his, and something in them answered.

"Mira," Francisco said, pointing.

Over a faraway rise a bobbing mass fragmented into separate specks which fanned out and eventually became a remuda of perhaps thirty mustangs.

"Sweet," Martín said.

"Money." Gregorio grinned.

"Work," Mariano added.

Luis was silent, awed.

"We shall camp farther along," Diego told them. "Where the winds won't be so cold."

It was Lobo's task to find the route. He had hung back with the stock, content to await instructions, and now took the lead.

Winding down the slope, Domingo trusted his mount to find its footing. He could hardly wait to reach the herd, to choose a horse that would belong to him alone, a stallion— well, a young colt, which he could train—that he would name…something special. And, of course, a filly, for Tereza.

"See that break in the hills there, to the north?" he said to Ramón when the trail permitted riding beside each other. "That is where Paz and I came out. And—" He pointed to the pass in the south. "—that is the way to Cosalá."

"And, there," Ramón gestured toward the basin, "are your mustangs."

The billowing grass was cut by shallow streams draining into a rivulet which he had already named Río Poco. A dozen mares and half a dozen grown colts grazed on the far bank of one branch. As the wind carried scent to them, they flung up finely shaped heads to watch the riders approach.

"How are we going to get them up that cliff we came down?" he asked.

"I don't think we can," Martín said.

"Then, the corrals at the hacienda are of no use."

"We can drive them toward Cosala," Gregorio suggested. "Pick up the main road near Elota."

"It would be out of our way," Francisco objected. "We ought to keep them headed north, or northwest, if we expect to entrain them in Culiacán."

"I wouldn't enjoy trying to put wild horses on a train," Diego said, "without penning them for at least a week."

"Will driving them all the way to Culiacán not make them tame?"

"No," Ramón answered. "That would only make them tired. To be truly gentled takes human contact."

Satisfied that the riders posed no immediate danger, the manada resumed eating. Domingo could see little difference in quality, all being sound and graceful. He wanted to go closer, but Diego said, "Why don't we camp upstream and get some sleep. In the morning we will likely find the rest of them."

Between bites of warmed tortillas stuffed with black beans, he mused, "We are so close to the old casa grande, do you suppose this is a part of that hacienda?"

Mariano pondered. "Sí, I think so. We crossed no boundary walls. Although that's not a sure sign."

"There is a broken one, far to the west, beyond the pass," he remembered.

"This valley must cover fifty hectáreas," Ramón said. "A worthy range. Exploring it would take a week." He gazed into his tin cup of hot coffee, and Domingo thought he sounded wistful.

Deserted as the country seemed, there was some danger of Villista patrols, and always danger of mountain lions or bears. He and Luis took the first watch, one on either side of the camp. Wrapped in a sarape over his jacket, his back to the firelight, Domingo saw the stars come out, and imagined himself riding a swift, dappled stallion over this verdant land, and in his dreaming, it all belonged to him.

"Tierra del Oro," he whispered.

He was disappointed that the mustangers didn't intend to chase the horses and rope them with flair and excitement. He had been practicing the deft flick of the wrist, elbow tucked close to the ribs, and had long ago mastered tying the hondo in such a way that it slipped easily.

He knew how to fasten the end of his reata snug to the saddle horn, how to keep the coils untangled, the amount of loop needed to clear a mustang's head, the spot just behind the ears to land it so the horse would quickly choke down and become docile. Now, he wasn't allowed to use any of that knowledge, but must herd these fine caballos as though they were cattle.

Counting the yearlings and two-year-olds, this band numbered thirty-five. Riding to one side of the manada, he kept watching for the stallion, half afraid yet almost hoping it would appear, snorting and pawing the earth like a bull, its challenging neigh ringing across the valley.

Though the men claimed they would shoot the caballo padre rather than risk a fight, he suspected that not one of them could resist trying to capture it. But the stallion didn't show itself all morning, and the manada drifted northward over the grassland toward the break in the hills. Lobo guessed that this stream bed would connect to the river which crossed the lower pastures of the hacienda, making a convenient route to the pens. Passage would take at least three days.

Diego had early informed them that it was desirable to deny wild horses water for a day or two, but that was impossible in a spring-fed valley such as this. Their best hope was to keep moving.

Though the mares were skittish and readily gave way when a rider nudged them from straying or stopping, only half a dozen showed fear. He had narrowed his favorites to four or five sleek bays with white faces and stockings.

"¡Muchacho!" called Francisco, ahead of him. "Are you having a good time?"

"Sí, you bet!" His answer was muffled by a bandana over his nose and mouth to keep out dust. They all looked like thieves, a notion which made him giggle nervously. What if the owner of the hacienda came back and caught them taking horses from his range? Cutting across the rear of the manada, he rode close to Ramón and said, "Jefe, how long does a patrón's stock have to be abandonado to be considered wild?"

"Unfortunately, I've never read a law concerning that. I think, in a revolution, those laws do not apply."

He peered at the major's eyes—all of the face he could see because he also wore a bandana—and realized the man was smiling.

"You remember, all of my stock was stolen from Casa Vásquez, except the few my men saved. This doesn't bother my conscience."

He thought of trampled fields and empty grazing land, broken boundary walls, and a ravaged casa grande. Last year Ramón had tried to send him to the estate in Sonora, to keep him from following Obregón's troops. Even then, the north was unsafe, and the men decided to save what they could—a dozen horses, hidden in peones' huts from Villistas and brought south in boxcars to grow fat on land belonging to Los Dos Corazones.

"True, Jefe. If we didn't take them, some damned Villista traitors would."

Ramón's laugh was cut short by having to spur after a straying colt. It was one of the ones Domingo had his eye on, so he joined in the chase. A mild sort of chase, with no yelling or waving of hats or reatas to frighten high-strung mesteños.

"We don't want any broken legs," the domador had cautioned. "Theirs—or ours."

By late afternoon they had crossed the basin and were at the entrance to the cañon which they hoped would lead back to the corrals. An angry, ringing call came echoing out of the valley, causing his neck hair to prickle.

"I didn't think we could get away with it," Diego said without alarm.

"The caballo padre has come home and found his women stolen." Martín grinned. "I bet he has brought new ones with him."

"Better not wait to find out." Ramón tightened his cinch and stepped into his stirrup. "Stay out of his way, Domingo."

"I want to see him!"

"You'll see him," Lobo promised.

The horsemen took up positions between the yeguas and their stallion, and used hats, reatas, and shouts to block any return to the basin.

Domingo patrolled his sector avidly, racing back and forth, edging the mustangs toward the cañon mouth. Dust clouds swirled so thick at times that it was hard to see. One determined mare whirled and dodged until Diego and Martín settled their ropes. Pressure cutting off her wind finally conquered stiff-legged resistance. He was watching them when the shrill whistle of the stallion behind him nearly stopped his heart.

His gelding pivoted, though not to fight. Over the receding drum of more than a hundred hooves, he heard anxious whickerings issue from his mount. Whatever was communicated, the dappled stallion seemed to dismiss them as unworthy of more than a shake of the mane and passing snap of teeth.

He kicked the horse's flanks to pursue, and found himself astride a balky horse. Frantic that he would miss whatever excitement lay just ahead, he gouged in the spurs, his Día de Los Reyes gift from Ramón. The gelding gave a startled leap forward.

When he caught up to the herd, the stallion was in the center of milling horseflesh, biting at the mare Diego and Martín had snared. Shouts of confusion, someone down—he couldn't tell who—a pistolshot that made his stomach cramp, jostling of horses turning or trying to turn—and then the mare broke free, trailing lengths of frayed reata, chewed through by the stallion's sharp teeth.

Trembling so he could scarcely grasp the coils, Domingo shook out a small loop and urged his mount after her. The chase couldn't have lasted more than a minute before they came alongside. When her head bobbed so near he could see slobber dribbling from her lips, he made the cast. And missed. Gathering for another try, he glimpsed Ramón coming up on her other flank, heard a shout but no words, and threw this loop harder to compensate for the wind.

She ran her nose right into it, giving him the surprise of his life. With Ramón shouldering her to the left, he kneed his mount in a wide circle, using enough pull on the reata to urge her along. It was then that he saw half the herd also making the turn, and realized she was the lead mare.

At the mouth of the pass, the stallion rushed about, trying to force his band of confused yeguas back onto the grazing land. Mustangers kept heading them off.

As he and Ramón swept past, the rest of the herd raggedly fell in behind them, galloping upstream along the sandy banks, through chaparral, winding among boulders, and leaping over rocks. It was not what Diego had planned, but Domingo couldn't deny the thrill.

In several places the cañon walls were so close and the herd so bunched that his right leg suffered bruises from being bumped between his horse and the mare. He let out more rope and allowed her to lead.

Gradually the pace slackened. Glancing over his shoulder, he hoped to see what was happening in the rear, where the irate stallion might be giving trouble; but now the yeguada was too strung out. Within sight were Ramón, working on the far side of the stream, and Gregorio, a quarter-league behind him. It dawned on him that, though the pass was the one which he and Paz had taken, he was out ahead of the others, with no idea where he was going.

He searched for Lobo and at last located the guide making his way to the front. Presently the lean, grinning face was close enough for conversation. "¡Caballero! You are damn good with a reata. And one muy valiente, muy bravo muchacho, to go for that lead mare. I would have thought the padre would take you apart for doing that."

"I didn't want her to get away." He decided not to reveal that when he began the chase, he hadn't guessed her importance. Nor confess that sheer luck—or maybe one of those saints Luis talked about—had put his rope where he wanted it. Anticipation of praise from Ramón excited him. "Shall we rest soon?"

"If this cañon runs as I think it does, there is a place an hour distant which offers graze, and a narrow passage we can defend from the padre."

"Is he still back there?" He turned, but dust, brush, and bends in the stream cut off his view.

Lobo shrugged. "If someone has not stopped him."

"I heard one shot. Who was down? Who fired the gun?"

Lobo shrugged again. "No sé. Not I."

Chafing at not knowing, he reined to one side and watched the yeguada trotting past. He couldn't wait another hour for answers. Mariano soon appeared and they fell into step. "What of the stallion? Your father didn't shoot it, did he?"

"No—I fired to make them scatter so we might rescue Luis before he could be trampled."

"Is he hurt?"

"Only his pride."

At Lobo's campsite, Domingo had finished salving his bruises when Luis stepped off his jaded mount. His friend had lost skin over one eyebrow, limped, and wore his bandana around one hand. "Ay, compadre, ¿qué te pasa?"

Luis gave an embarrassed laugh. "That damned gitano of mine fell down when he saw the caballo grande, and I happened to be under him."

"You were lucky not to be killed."

"I am going to have to think long about that."

While the yeguada scattered out to fill their bellies on the winter-cured grass, the horsemen lay on blankets, and Martín and Mariano prepared supper. Ramón and Diego remained to guard the passage.

Gunshots at dusk made him fidget, unable to eat. He didn't want to believe either of them capable of killing the stallion, but .... Had not Ramón once executed Federal prisoners, after the fight at La Puerta del Sol?

Luis broke into his thoughts. "Is that liniment I smell? I could use some."

He handed Luis the bottle, glad his amigo couldn't see the bruises on his leg, which were becoming tender. "Would Jefe shoot the stallion, to keep from bothering with it?"

Luis was a long time in answering. "Ramón does those things which he must do. Sooner or later."

When the second guard left, Domingo was still awake, but exhaustion overcame him. When he opened his eyes, coyotes were calling back and forth among the hills and Luis was laying fuel on the breakfast fire.

The stallion continued to follow peacefully, so talk of shooting it ceased. He relaxed, riding proudly beside the major. The praise he'd wanted from Ramón came, belatedly and tempered with a rebuke: "If you ever do anything so dangerous again, I swear I will punish you."

He had heard those threats before, every time he went against orders. Yet, Luis's words *Sooner or later* burned through his mind. One day, he would do something bad enough to merit real punishment. He felt uneasy about the form it might take.

"If I had not caught her," he pointed out, "we might have lost a day's work, and be there still."

"One of us would have brought her around. It didn't have to be you."

"Jealous, Major?" he asked, half angry, half teasing.

Ramón's eyes flashed at his boldness; then he broke into a laugh. "Cachito, don't you know—"

A streak of dappled hide, an echoing command to the lead mare, and the padre was in the yeguada, kicking and biting, creating a terrible and beautiful chaos. Ramón's reata whizzed past Domingo's ear and landed with breathtaking precision on the stallion's throat.

Clinging with his knees, he circled the mustang and made a bad throw. "Sonofabitch!"

Reeling in the loop, he jockeyed for another chance. The second was worse, almost catching in a clump of chaparral. Now, both Diego and Martín were in the picture, arms extended, neat little nooses hovering.

Reining in front of the plunging mustang, he jerked his mount's head out of the way with one hand and placed his rope with the other, barely escaping the snapping teeth on the way in, barely missing being kicked on the way out.

Cries of "¡Viva! ¡Viva!"all around him mingled with more than one "¡Olé!" and even though other men added their reatas for security, everyone knew this catch belonged to him and Major Cordero.

Feeling pressure from all sides, the stallion lowered its head, bowed its back, and became quiet. As dust drifted away, the herd stopped running one by one and began searching for clumps of vegetation.

"Now what, Jefe?"

"Good question. What do you suggest, Diego?"

"Tie him up for a day or so, with a guard to keep the leones de montaña from chewing on him, and I think you might have a stud. I might even pay for his use. Mi Rojo is getting old, and those you brought from Casa Vásquez are too fat and lazy to breed."

"A nice offer, and an insult!" Ramón cried, yet both men were laughing.

"I'll stand guard," Domingo volunteered.

Martín and Lobo stayed as well, while the others finished taking the herd to the corrals.

Unable to sleep after his watch ended, he crept out of his blanket, put on his boots and walked to where the mustang was tethered. Wrapped in his sarape against the night wind, he sat down out of reach of teeth or hooves.

"I have been thinking, caballo grande. Maybe you are sad to leave this place. If I were a mesteño, with plenty of fine grass and streams and a family, this is where I should wish to be."

In the moonlight he saw the horse's ears prick forward, and went on. "If I could trust you to go back to El Valle de

Los Mesteños instead of making more difficulties for us, I would take off your ropes this minute."

The stallion made an answering noise deep in its chest.

"Perhaps you can learn to be happy at Dos Corazones." His thoughts drifted to the few months he had spent there. While any move depended on the course of the revolution, residence at the household of don Diego was not permanent.

It seemed he had not enjoyed the safety of a home for a long, long time.

Chapter Three

By the third day he was begging Martín to give the stallion a drink. "Just look at him, hombre. All his ribs are showing. His eyes are feverish. See how he hangs his head? If he gets sick, if he dies, Jefe will be muy *muy* enojado."

Martín laughed. "If we make him strong with water, and he gets away from us, will the major be less enojado?"

"I will be responsible. After all, I helped capture him. He is half mine. Give my half a drink of water, por favor."

Lobo winked at Martín. "Maybe his half is tame, ¿quién sabe? Domingo, why don't you go ride your half? You can take him to the stream and let him fill up the half of his belly which is yours."

"You think I'm afraid to do that? Pues, bien, mire."

He rummaged in his saddle pack for the rope halter Mariano had helped him make one evening when they sat talking in the courtyard at Dos Corazones. Filling one of the hide buckets, he carried it past his amigos and set it before the stallion. While the horse was drinking, he slid the halter on.

He heard but ignored the varied shouts behind him. Working for months with the cavalry mounts as well as stock on the haciendas had given him knowledge and confidence. During the last two nights, long conversations established trust. He also had breathed into this mustang's nostrils, as did Indio horsemen. The much-needed water sealed the bond. He stroked the dappled face. "I named him Cimarrón."

Lobo grinned. "I think Major Cordero is going to be very surprised to find that his prized stud has become a sugar-eater."

"Sugar—a good idea. Do we have some?" He petted the caballo padre a little more before joining his friends at the campsite, relieved that he wasn't expected to make good the rest of his boast.

Martín slapped his own thigh lightly with his quirt. "I think we taught you more than we meant to."

The other mustangers had been busy during their absence. New cedar poles gleamed in the fencing. Mares in foal, those unbred, yearlings, and two-year-olds were all in separate corrals.

In an isolated pen, several three-year-old fillies jogged restlessly back and forth. As soon as they spotted the stallion, an agitated chorus rose, and Cimarrón, riderless at Martín's insistence, lunged so hard he broke one reata. Lobo's knife cut him free before he could injure anyone, and he sailed over the top rail, to begin inspecting the females.

"¡Caray!" Gregorio rose from tending a fire upslope. "He has been lonely."

The rest of the men came forward to exchange news. "Did he give you any problems?" Ramón asked.

"Who?" Martín countered, with a grin. "Ah, el caballo padre—no, he behaved well. This one—" He gathered the nape of Domingo's shirt in a fist. "—he nearly gave me susto."

Ramón said drily, "You can tell me about it over coffee."

Seated with a plate of roasted venison straight off the fire, Domingo said, between bites, "It was nothing, Jefe. I simply made friends with Cimarrón."

"A friend like that," Francisco observed, "will desert you every time."

"You didn't try to ride him, I hope."

He swallowed a half-chewed bite. "Not yet. But I stroked his face, and" He gestured toward the corral. "I put on that jáquima he is wearing."

Ramón shook his head in mild exasperation. "Do you think, before you do these things? He could have bitten off your hand."

"I think all the time, but not about that."

"¡Sí, claro! Do you also think you're capable of breaking him?"

"He should not be broken."

"Correct. Nor ridden. He has one purpose, and it is not to be a pet."

"But, Jefe—"

A raised palm, signifying enough.

After a moment, however, he was compelled to say, "Not broken. Tamed. I can do that."

Martín held his plate for another helping and Lobo sliced off a chunk for each of them. "You have experience with tame horses, muchacho. Those cavalry geldings, a few yeguas. But even jinetes—experts—handle a stallion such as your Cimarrón with much caution."

"I can be cautious. You saw."

Ramón told him, "You stay away from that padre."

"Else, what?"

"Don't make me show you."

Obeying Ramón wasn't difficult. The colts which had been gelded were recovering from the shock and Martín kept him busy helping fit them with bozalillos, the light hackamores used in training. He selected a dark bay with two white stockings, and branded it with the Cordero mark: the letter *R* enclosed in a *C*.

He also picked a light bay filly to give Tereza and put don Diego's double heart brand on its rump. That caused some eye-rolling between the old horseman and the major, who must have guessed his intention; neither said anything.

Cimarrón knocked down bars of his corral the third night and took the unbred mares with him.

"Good riddance," Francisco said. "He's too old and set in his ways to keep. We should have left a colt uncut, for seed."

"Andemos." Diego took them into the long rock stable which had largely gone unnoticed, being at the outskirts of the village. In one of the stalls stood a long-legged dapple of about three years, its dark eyes intelligent, nostrils questing as visitors crowded the aisle and gawked.

"Madre mía," breathed Martín. "Where did he come from?"

"Did anyone see him in the manada?" Gregorio asked.

Disappointment filled Domingo's chest. This beauty was one of his first choices, but in the excitement of catching Cimarrón, he'd forgotten. Now, it was too late to make a claim.

"Here is your caballo," Diego said to Ramón.

"Gracias," Jefe answered, "for the use of so fine a stud."

"Not use, only. Tuyo."

More polite refusals seemed eminent, so Domingo urgently pinched Ramón in the back, and what Jefe said was, "Gracias—mil gracias. But—don't you want him? He is worth a lot of money."

Diego leaned on the stall. "Giving him to you is easier than watching you and Francisco fight over him."

"Hell," Francisco said. "What would I do with a little padre like that? I plan to take only good memories back to California."

Feeling more rested after that surprise than he had in months, Domingo spent the next days halter-breaking the dapple colt. At Dos Corazones, under the supervision of Martín, Diego, and sometimes Ramón, he had practiced on quebrantados, caballos already partially broken, and he knew all the steps and methods of training. The big difference in having this young stallion on the end of the workline was an intensity of emotional interaction which both exhilarated and exhausted him.

"Aguzado," everyone said, in passing. Be ready. On your toes. El caballo padre could return at any moment, to steal away more of his yeguada or fight his youthful rival.

He had his hands full, too, with his new gelding, which he named Valiente, and Tereza's filly, left unnamed but requiring as much gentling as time allowed before they must leave. Diego was usually at his side, offering encouragement and suggestions, while the rest of the mesteñeros worked to accustom the other stock to being around men.

Domingo felt as though he had always lived here. Every contour of the sloping land, the changing angle of sunlight casting indigo shadows throughout the day, the very air sustaining his body, were familiar. Without entering the huts that once housed peones and their families, or going back inside the casa grande, he felt he knew the history of this place, the lives once led by people he had never met but with whom he felt kinship. The sheds, stable, corrals, meals around a campfire with compañeros, work with the horses, all filled his spirit with a sense of completeness, so that only a small chink here and there still held longing for something he couldn't name.

Both Ramón and Francisco grew restless and began hinting that the trail to Culiacán would finish taking off any rough edges, and if they dawdled here much longer the stallion would return, or foals would start dropping before they could reach Dos Corazones.

"They wouldn't survive a day in a boxcar," Francisco warned.

"Besides," the major said, tossing coffee grounds at the supper fire, "I have business to attend to in Culiacán."

"You would never join the revolution again, would you, Patrón?" Luis asked, his face tense in the flickering light.

"¡Dios me libre! Have I been acting loco, to make you ask that? No. It is something else."

Those on first watch took the remaining coffee in their cups, and Lobo kicked up the fire to ward off wild animals. Domingo didn't concern himself with the major's business, so long as things between them stayed the same. Drowsy, warm in his blankets and feet toward the blaze, he listened idly to low voices in the darkness.

"Each day," Francisco was saying, "as you grew into manhood, you became more and more like him, until I couldn't bear to look at you, and remember."

Ramón answered, "I know now, that it was your pain I was feeling, as much as my own. It was easier for me to leave."

"I'm grateful you asked me to come on this hunt. At first, the idea made me afraid. I thought it would be like I was back in that time, and he had never been killed, but my mind would know he had, while my heart would break again."

The question was soft. "Did it? When you saw me?"

Domingo held his breath, but had to inhale before Francisco answered.

"You were you. Like him— ¡Dios, sí! —but yourself. And you made it possible for me to remain me. Does any of this make sense?"

"Yes," Ramón said.

The stallion did not return, but two of the mares were judged too near to foaling and were released to make their way back to El Valle de Los Mesteños. Domingo packed his saddlebags and mochila, gathered his gear, took up the filly's lead rope, and swung aboard Valiente.

He gave a final lingering survey over the fields and corrals, past the silent village, toward the great empty house. Vowing to return when he was able to survive on his own, he fell into place, riding point.

Diego and Lobo led at a relaxed pace, Mariano and Francisco teaming behind them. Across the backs of docile caballos, he waved to Ramón. If he looked over his shoulder, he could see Gregorio and Luis trailing, the occasional use of coiled reatas encouraging stragglers to keep up.

His mind wandered to that first sight of Cimarrón Grande. The memory still had the power to make his neck hair rise. Ramón had agonized over whether to snub the young stallion to his saddle, or trust Little Cimarrón to come of his own accord. In the end, he put on the rope. Domingo could see them jogging along, and felt proud that his training had made this possible.

In the afternoon, Diego rode back to tell them, "There's a fork ahead, and the northern branch is more level, for we can see fields in the distance."

Everyone agreed to try the new route, even though to him the land appeared no more level than what they had covered, and the fields soon vanished behind timbered hills. In the higher mountains there had been rain in the night; now a cold wind brought fresh wet clouds from the west, making them stop to unpack ponchos.

"I'll be glad," Luis complained, "when we reach the foothills again. I miss the hot deserts of Sonora."

Domingo found the brisk winds invigorating. The rumble of thunder, the thrashing of pine branches high overhead. They were climbing again, and when he fell back to request a cigarette, Gregorio remarked, "Maybe there will be snow."

None of them had ever seen snow, but soldados from the mountains had described how white, how cold, how deep it could get. "Dios, I hope not," Luis wailed. "I don't even like rain."

The sky grew darker, the wind sharper. There was no rain where they were, but across a gorge they could see sheets of it coming down. On the ridge, they were above the tree line.

Then the trail began to descend. In another half hour they were on the sheltered side of the mountain, working up a lather trying to keep the heaviest mares on the easiest terrain. Four days in, a week or more out, Diego had figured. And the hunt would be over.

They entered a parkland of straight-boled pines, the twilight of storm and forest creating an illusion of dusk rather than the middle of an afternoon. The geldings and yearlings, frisky at the start of the drive, now huddled with the mares, casting sidelong glances as if they sensed predators in the occasional thickets and among tumbled boulders.

"These trees make me nervous," Luis said, riding a little apart from him. "See how some of them have fallen."

The land began to tilt up on either side, forming an ancient arroyo thickly covered in pine needles and oak leaves. Ahead, Mariano and Diego were gesturing as they did when discussing some grand plan. Francisco drifted back to say something to Ramón, and Domingo had started forward, leaving the other men to take their turn at the rear, when Valiente began to tremble.

Immediately he feared a mountain lion and looked overhead at the branches, but none was large enough to hold the weight of a gato grande. Riders ahead of him were having similar problems. The caballada, scattering in panic, began climbing the lower side of the arroyo. Cimarrón gave a sharp neigh of alarm, Ramón cried out, "¿Qué pasa?" and the faint rumble which he'd thought was thunder became a continuous roar.

"¡Temblor!" shouted Diego, and just as he and Mariano whirled their horses, the high timbered ridge above them gave way, pines toppling, and a wall of water broke through.

Valiente pivoted to run but the flood was upon them, hitting Domingo in the back hard enough to knock out his breath, and sweeping the gelding into the current like a stick thrown into a river. He lost both stirrups and was half out of the saddle when the torrent flung Valiente against some obstruction with enough force to dislodge him. In the water, almost blinded, strangling, he clung to the mane and tried to avoid the thrashing hooves as the gelding fought to gain its footing.

Something huge and black bore down upon them—the blunt end of a broken tree trunk—submerging the horse and him with it. Unable to swim, unable to breathe, he had one clear thought: Mamá's face the last time he saw her alive, and her words, *Be good to Teo. He is young.*

Then he was heels over head, suspended by rough strong arms, on a slope just above the churning river, freezing cold, vomiting up limitless amounts of muddy water. Wet moss against his cheek, Ramón's voice, hoarse and strained and passionate, close above him. "Breathe, mijo, breathe. I won't let you die. Fight, mijo! Live!"

Hands beat him between the shoulder blades, and a rush of air into his lungs cut like Lobo's knife, making him cough and gag. His teeth chattered and he was trembling all over.

Ramón wrapped a drenched sarape close about him and held him tight, the bearded cheek scratchy against his. Held him the way Papá did the time he fell down the stairs. He couldn't have been more than three or four years old. Before Teo was born. Before Papá had Teo to love.

"Can you speak? Are you hurt?"

He shook his head. Numb from shock and the icy water, he couldn't tell whether he was hurt or not. The sound of the flood rushing by made him shudder. "I am all right," he said, though the violent shivering wouldn't stop, and he remembered Valiente. "My horse—"

Ramón loosened his embrace enough to look about. On the far side of the arroyo, Domingo saw half a dozen mares, and Lobo and Gregorio stripping off packs and gear from the saddle horses and pack animals that had managed to climb out. Valiente was one of them.

On their side, downslope, too far to call to, Luis and Martín were hauling on two geldings they had roped and were attempting to pull to safety. Upslope, Francisco and Mariano knelt over Diego.

"Diosito mío," Ramón breathed, dread in his tone.

"Is he dead?" Domingo's shivering increased.

The glance Ramón gave him was not reassuring. They stood up, but the major told him, "You stay here."

Watching him trudge toward the little group, his wool sarape, heavy with water, seeming to weigh him down, Domingo felt sick again. He had forgotten that the old horse tamer suffered from some illness. Others came up behind him, their manner concerned and awkward.

Gregorio said, "He was not strong enough to fight the water."

"Maybe he is only hurt." Doubt and hope mingled in Lobo's voice.

"Ay, no. Look at Mariano's face."

What Domingo saw there brought a rush of sorrow—for Diego, Mariano, Tereza, yes; but after months of holding back, he could no longer keep at bay images of Mamá's house in La Puerta del Sol, of being summoned before dawn by Major Cordero, Teo's crying, the walk across the field to where her coffin lay upon a crude bier, the loss of that final goodbye. On his knees, face in his arms, harsh sobs poured out like the muddy floodwaters.

He was aware of boots making uncertain steps nearby, the compañeros helpless to do anything, for him or for the hacendado. He tried to remember if Tereza's filly were one of the safe ones. Still his weeping went on, out of control, until those strong arms returned to gather him into an embrace. His chest heaved, striving for calm. Nobody else was making such a display of feeling, not even Mariano, who sat holding his father's hand, but without tears.

"Grieve, Domingo," Ramón murmured. "You must grieve, to be whole again."

"Mamá—" he gasped, torn by unutterable pain.

"Sí, yo sé, mijo, yo sé."

Yes, I know, my son, I know. The words in his ear, repeated softly over and over, gradually soothed him into that stage when only a jerky breath now and then gave evidence of spent emotion.

When he was able to raise his head, his tear-swollen eyes saw that the mustangers had built a fire close to Diego, and the injured horseman was propped on someone's saddle padded with a couple of blankets. More blankets warmed him, but his face, wan though it was, remained uncovered. "He's still alive," he whispered.

Self-consciously he and Ramón disengaged from each other. Gently, Jefe said, "He is broken inside. There is no hope, and he knows it."

How terrible, to know death was near, and be powerless. In Monterrey, for the festive celebrations of El Día de Los Muertos, families renewed flowers on the graves of their loved ones and held picnics in the campo santos among the tombstones. Candles lit the dusk and special foods were prepared. He and Teo always bickered over how many sugar skulls the other had eaten.

This was different. Different, too, from the nameless ones killed on the battlefield. None of the men he had come to know well had died in the revolution, though each time one was wounded, Ramón especially, he'd felt dread. In Diego's place, he knew he would be helpless with terror.

"Jefe, isn't he afraid?"

There was no hint of teasing. "I thought you told me you believe in Dios."

"Sí, of course. I learned about Jesucristo from Mamá and the padre in Monterrey. If the revolution had not come, there would have been a confirmation and the bishop—"

When he faltered to a stop, Ramón said, "Diego long ago made peace with Dios. It is something everyone must do."

The bitterness would not remain hidden any longer. "Dios let Mamá die, when I needed her."

Major Cordero gave him a long stare. Then, quietly, he said, "Did you?"

The blunt question left him speechless. How could he not need her? She was Mamá. Yet ... He had survived. With the help of Major Cordero.

"Sometimes," Jefe went on in the same tone, "we are mistaken about what we need."

Diego was conscious, for his lips moved as he talked with Mariano. The young man nodded slightly, still holding the hand in both of his, leaning forward at what must be an uncomfortable angle to hear those last things his father would say to him.

Now that Teo was Sereno's compadre, shutting him out, Domingo chafed to remember Mamá's bidding, and how thoroughly he had ignored it.

Late afternoon dragged into evening, and though nothing was done toward preparing a meal, they kept the fire going to dry out their clothing and rescued supplies. One by one, the mesteñeros went over to speak to Diego. "How can they do that?" he asked, stomach knotting from tension and lack of food. "How do they know what to say?"

"Whatever you say, Diego will understand," Ramón reassured him.

Then, duty could not be postponed any more. The rest of the men went to bring in as many of the manada as they could find before dark, yet Mariano remained, holding his father in his arms. Ramón knelt and took don Diego's hand. "Padrino, what do you wish of me?"

Dios, Domingo thought. *Exactly right.* But he could not mimic the sentiment without feeling stupid.

Diego's drawn face was familiar, yet ghastly in the dimming daylight, grotesquely orange from the flickering glow cast by the fire. "It will be too difficult to take my body home," he said. "Bury me here."

"No!" Mariano cried. "You must not lie in unhallowed ground."

The eyes closed, too tired to argue, but the voice went on doggedly, "It's better if Tereza—"

"She deserves having you where she can visit, and honor with Mother's flowers fresh every day."

"Hear him?" Diego gave a little laugh. "Sometimes he can be quite unreasonable. Like Angelita. Promise me, Ramón."

"Are you sure—? There is material at the old hacienda, for a travois—"

"For a coffin," the hacendado amended, his dry humor unfailing. "It's too far, and the trail is too rough."

Mariano insisted, "You and Mother belong together."

Diego loosed his hand from Ramón's grasp and laid his palm against his son's cheek. "Your mother and I shall be together." Then he began coughing, and the handkerchief Mariano used to wipe his lips came away stained with blood. "Promise, Ramón."

"Sí— Te lo juro."

Mariano's objections had to wait. His father said, "I always loved you, mijo," and the answering words, "I love you, too, Papá," were barely out of the young man's mouth before the horse tamer's breathing became labored and then stopped.

The stillness was broken by distant intermittent calls and whistles of the mustangers to the horses they were bringing in. Tenderly Mariano laid his father against the blankets. Then he whirled, temper flaring, his words wrathy. "Damn you, Ramón! Why did you do that?"

Both men jumped up ready to fight. Domingo scooted out of their way.

"Because he asked me to." Fists clenched, Ramón sounded just as angry.

"He was only being considerate. That is not what he wanted, I am sure of it."

"Considerate or not, he made me promise, and you know I honor my vows."

Mariano was trembling. "Maybe you need to think less of yourself and more of other people, before making such vows."

"I am thinking, of all of you. Your father was right. The trip is too difficult and too long. He must be buried here."

Domingo took hold of Ramón's arm. Determination flowed through the firm muscles into his hands, and he feared there was no preventing an exchange of blows. "Jefe! What about the campo santo at the hacienda abandonada? That must be hallowed ground."

The arm relaxed. "Sí. It would be."

The men stood eyeing each other until at last Mariano said, "Have it your way," and strode off into the night-dark woods.

Ramón drew a long breath and blew it out. Squatting beside Diego, arms resting on knees, he said, "Adiós, friend of my father."

Kneeling, Domingo murmured, "Adiós, don Diego," silently adding, "Adiós, Mamá."

Two or three moments passed, while the clop of unshod hooves came nearer the camp. Ramón turned his head. "You shall see them again."

Not for the first time, the major had read his thoughts. "En Paraíso." In Heaven, Paradise. "If I die well." He felt the swift water closing over his head, and shuddered.

Ramón nodded at the motionless body. "He died well."

The food prepared by Martín and Luis stuck in Domingo's throat. He tried not to think of the burial ahead, or how his gift to Tereza was spoiled because now her heart would be broken, unable to appreciate the beautiful filly or care about it. When Ramón gave him a friendly pat on the back, he flinched.

"What—are you angry with me, too?"

"I guess something in the water left a bruise."

The major was applying liniment to the injured shoulder when Mariano returned.

"It was not an earthquake." He hunkered and poured himself a cup of coffee, and everyone waited for more. Mud-splashed and draggled, he went on unemotionally, "The wall of the arroyo which gave way was holding back water channeled from a big river—" He waved an arm northward, beyond the ridge. "It was an earthen dam that had gone neglected."

He drank the cooling coffee.

For a long minute no one said anything. Then Gregorio voiced what they all must have been thinking. "If that damned thing had not been built, this would never have happened."

"He would have died at home with his family," Mariano said harshly.

Ramón seemed to struggle to keep silent, but at last had to say, "I don't believe he wanted that. I know you don't agree—"

Mariano threw down his cup and left the group.

Presently, Francisco said, "I think you're right, Ramón," and a warm glance passed between them.

Chapter Four

Before daylight the mustangers were on the trail, don Diego's body wrapped in his ground sheet and carried on a saddle platform such as they had often used to transport wounded rebels.

Chewing a strip of jerked meat, Domingo rode in front so he wouldn't have to watch Mariano and Francisco sweating to keep the burdened horse from falling on the slopes. Ramón had offered, but his help was refused.

It was one of the longest days of his life, exceeded only by three others, beginning with the morning after Papá failed to come home. Second was when he had to ride away and leave Mamá in La Puerta del Sol. Then, those endless hours as Ramón lay in a field hospital, with a medical student gathering courage to risk a transfusion of Mariano's blood.

"Jefe," he began, taking the opportunity of a wide place to draw alongside the major, "Mariano will be friends again, won't he? When this is all over."

"Sí, claro. He's upset now. Grief, responsibility. He dreads facing Tereza. She and their father were close." There was a pause. "You must try to help her."

He shrank from the idea. "She will cry, and I won't know what to do." It had taken him a year and a half to be able to accept the major's sympathy. What if Tereza felt that way?

Then the trail narrowed, forcing them apart.

Timbered ridges, stormwinds, and gullies behind them, they passed through fields of tall brown grass and patches of stark woodland. At last, about sundown, they emerged at the forest edge and drew rein. The casa grande, with its stables, sheds, corrals, and silent village, had not changed. Only the blackened earth and ashes of their campfires and branding fires showed that anyone had disturbed the solitude.

"El campo santo es por allí," Martín said, pointing.

A gravel path led to a clearing in the woods. He was struck by the sight of an iron fence separating two sections of the grave yard. "What does this mean?" he asked Luis, walking beside him.

"The hacendado and his family could not be buried with the peones." Luis took off his hat, and his elbow made Domingo do the same.

"Why not?"

"Burro. Because they were the hacendado, and his family."

Lobo and Martín had found shovels and dug until they gave out. Casting each other a wary look, Mariano and Ramón relieved them.

In his turn, Domingo labored beside Francisco. "When I first rode with the cavalry," he told the older man between shovelfuls of earth, "I helped Gregorio bury his brother." He leaned on the handle to catch his breath. "The pain is too much, when two are close. It does not pay."

"Verdad," Francisco agreed. "Yet, hearts cannot always choose."

"I choose," he said, grim.

Ramón came to the edge of the pit and looked down. "Give me your hand, and I'll hoist you out. It's deep enough."

Hurrying despite fatigue, the mustangers left behind most of the horses they'd worked so hard to capture, bringing out only remounts, Tereza's filly, and Valiente. Tears in his eyes, he obeyed Ramón and freed Little Cimarrón at the foot of the mirador, and watched the horse graze farther and farther away.

Up on the hill, the major leaned his arms on the retaining wall before being called away by someone. With don Diego gone, they all looked to Major Cordero for leadership.

Two camps later, they rode down out of the Sierra Madre, each pondering thoughts he couldn't share. The electric lights of Culiacán twinkled in the moonless distance. Murmurs of relief and plans for a hot bath and hotel food ran among the men. He said, "Luis, I want to sleep in your room."

The reason for his request wasn't lost on his friend, who said, "He was right, muchacho. Soon you must forgive him."

"But Cimarroncito was supposed to make much money with his offspring."

"Pues, he was Ramón's stallion."

He sensed Luis's careless shrug. "Entonces, vayas el diablo," he answered, spurring his horse. Then, go to the devil. Of all the men, he'd expected Luis to side with him.

While Martín and Lobo made arrangements to load their saddle horses and remounts in a boxcar, Ramón checked civil records and found maps and papers relating to the abandoned hacienda. Dated in the last century. One of the older clerks knew a bit of its history.

"Hombre, that parcel is too rugged to produce anything of value. The family Salinas y Cortés tried stock fifty years ago, but Indios and wild animals killed the herds. Floods carried away crops, and the mountains are so steep and cold, nothing will grow."

"You have seen the land?"

"No, but my son's wife lived in Cosalá, and my wife's uncle lives in Canelas. Arturo, here, was born in Vegas. Those villages were a part of the hacienda. Long ago."

"Gracias." A little daunted, but not convinced. The tierra was situated where flooding was impossible, and the weather was such that crops should flourish. Why no one had lived on the hacienda for a generation baffled him. *Perhaps it's haunted.* He smiled.

The maps showed holdings as vast as Casa Vásquez. "Los Nuestros," he whispered. Ours. That end was what he cherished in his heart when he made Domingo leave the stallion. To avoid disappointment, he had decided not to tell anyone his plan until all was legal.

Better not to risk a broken leg or broken spirit in a boxcar; rather, have the caballo padre here and ready for service when they returned.

At the train station, he experienced a shock. With help from several of the mustangers, Mariano was loading a coffin into a second boxcar. Judging by the way they were handling it, it was obviously weighted.

Domingo stood to one side, elbows crooked, and the rest of the men were in the car, pulling.

"What the hell is he doing?" he asked.

Before the boy could answer, Mariano came to them. "I am giving Tereza the funeral she deserves."

"¡Loco! That is sacrilege. What if she finds out?"

Mariano's dark eyes were defiant. "I'm keeping your secret, Ramón. Now you must keep mine."

"Cuate, think this over—"

"Think? That's all I've been doing for three days. If you have any love for me, brother, you will be quiet."

Biting the inside of his lower lip, Ramón shook his head. If Mamá had given birth to this young man, he could not have felt closer. Besides their brotherhood of battle, the friendship of their fathers counted for much.

"Bueno," he said at last. "But I think you are wrong."

In Hermosillo Ramón helped load the black-draped casket into a wagon. Lobo, who had chosen to come to Dos Corazones, drove the mules. Mariano rode ahead, to prepare his sister for her tragedy.

He joined Domingo at the end of the procession, far enough back to avoid the dust. Neither spoke. The boy was still angry over the loss of Little Cimarrón, and aside from revealing his intentions concerning the hacienda, there was nothing he could say. The rhythm of the walking horses, coupled with afternoon warmth, should have made him sleepy, but his thoughts were churning. He longed to take Anita into their room at Los Dos, and close the door.

Slanting sunlight painted the hills surrounding don Diego's casa grande red and gold, bronzing the faces of the people who waited in the yard. Everyone from both villages had come to pay their respects, standing with hats doffed, women swathed in black rebozos. Younger niños perched like crows along the corral rails, also motionless on this solemn occasion.

When the wagon bearing their patrón's coffin passed the main gate, a wailing rose, a lament that continued as Mariano came out of the house and supervised the transfer of his father's body into the sala.

None of the house women was present, not even Jesusita, who was likely giving what comfort she could to the niña. Except for Francisco, the other mustangers, ill at ease in the home of the hacendado, mumbled and crossed themselves and escaped outside. In the shadows of an unlit hallway, Ramón glimpsed Sereno and Teo, eyes wide, awed by death. Domingo pushed them toward their room. Mariano bowed upon the casket, almost as if he believed it contained Diego's corpse.

Francisco said, "Get some rest. I'll stay with him."

"I shall relieve you at midnight."

He paused at the door behind which Mamá must be waiting. He knocked and her voice answered, "Pase."

She had been crying. "Oh, mijo, how sad—"

Hugging her, he said, "Francisco is in the sala."

"I'll go there, in a moment."

"Unless García yet lives, he is the only one left."

"I know. Pobre Teresita."

"Mamá—"

"¿Sí?"

He looked into her eyes, and decided to keep his promise to Mariano. "Don't stay up if you grow tired."

"Diego was kind to me when I was a girl without friends. I can sacrifice a little sleep in his honor."

He kissed her forehead.

Anita met him in the hallway and threw her arms around him. "Querido, thank God you're safe."

He guided her into the unlit room and shut the door, already fumbling with buttons, hungry for her kisses. "Comfort me," he urged softly.

II

Stepping down from the stage in the plaza major, Pablo Valente shielded his eyes against the sun and noted that little had changed in the years since he lived here.

Great trees cast blue shadows over pleasant walkways and iron benches, where people of all classes mingled to rest, eat something bought from one of the cart-vendors, read a paper, visit with friends.

Not so many young men as before. Buildings were now pockmarked from shells; he'd become accustomed to seeing that.

Carrying his valise to an unoccupied seat, he waited at a street car stop. Heat, and an excitement that threatened to overwhelm him, dampened his palms and caused his hands to tremble. He fumbled for his handkerchief.

The trip across the highlands had been more difficult and taken longer than he'd anticipated. In spite of the unanswered telegrams, he had a lingering hope that Serafina would be here. What did she think of him? That he had deserted his family. That whatever excuse he used, the thing which had parted them was his cowardliness rather than . . . What?

Ill luck? Ignorance? Destino? Face to face, would she listen? *She has to be here,* he thought. The hope of reunion with her and his son—sons—and his belief that Dios would preserve his life, had given him the will to endure.

A rapid clop of hooves on pavement set his heart to racing. Two mule cars pulled to a halt in the street. Neither was bound for Serafina's neighborhood, but only a few minutes went by before the arrival of one which was.

Grabbing up his bag, he pushed onto the crowded car and was given space by an abuela who took a niño on her lap.

Serafina's casita had changed little. Whitewashed adobe, curtained windows, sunny patio, ancient acacias in the dooryard. The ramada over the front door actually seemed in better repair than he remembered. The door was open to admit stray breezes, and when he leaned to peer inside he could hear a woman singing, in the next room, the cocina. It was not Serafina's voice.

In Monterrey, she had become accustomed to having girls work for her. The singer no doubt was a criada, and he had a swift image of Serafina hovering over the girl's shoulder to taste the stew he could smell simmering over a brasero.

"¡Hola!" he called, setting down the valise and trying to ready himself for either an emotional greeting or cold accusations.

A young Indian girl, barefoot, her long black hair plaited in a single tail, appeared in the doorway between the rooms. Wide black eyes showed surprise and enough fright that he knew she was alone. "¿Sí? ¿Qué quiere, señor?"

He took off his hat. "My wife, doña Serafina Villanova once lived here. I thought she might have returned."

A male child under two years old, clad only in a stained camisa, hung onto her faded skirt. She picked him up and, still watching Pablo, called over her shoulder in her dialect.

"Sí, Mamá," answered another niño. Bare feet ran down the back steps.

"He will bring my husband," she said. "Does it please you to wait outside?" She edged out of the room.

Going back to the packed earth which served as an entry under the ramada, he set down his bag and wiped his forehead.

A boy about the age Domingo would be now hurried across the field stretching southward from Serafina's house to the Río Sonora.

The line of trees bordering the river was unchanged. In the middle distance stood the shack belonging to the old goatherder Jesús, who must be long dead. Slightly beyond, a maze of gray forms, goats, grazing. The boy blended into them, and in moments a larger dark form emerged, becoming a young man on a horse as he rode across the field and into the yard.

Narrowed eyes and a wary manner put Pablo on the defensive. This couple obviously had taken over the house and were trespassing. He opened his mouth, intending to assert a claim, but as the man swung down from the saddle, words were postponed by the sight of an empty trouser leg.

Using a crude crutch, the rider came forward, and Pablo could tell that only the foot was missing, the trouser leg neatly sewed across the bottom.

"Hola," the young man said, propping on the crutch. "You are Señor Valente, no?"

He hid his surprise at hearing his name spoken. "If you remember me, you must know this casa belongs to my wife."

"I am aware of that."

"Then perhaps you can tell me where she is."

The response was soft. "Sí, I know where she is."

Something in his face chilled Pablo's heart. Had she married again, thinking he was dead? "Where? Take me there, or direct me—"

The young man eyed his shoes. "It is not far, but a long walk for a city man. Do you care to ride my horse?"

It would be a long walk for a man with one foot. "No—I have recently recovered from an illness. If I don't hurry, walking would be better." He couldn't bring himself to admit to this rough mestizo, undoubtedly an insurrecto wounded in the revolution, that he had never been a skilled rider.

"As you wish." Mounting from the off side, the man turned his horse in the direction he had come. Looking back, he said, "Venga usted, si por favor."

The sun beat on Pablo's shoulders, dampness gathered under his hatband, hummocks of brittle grass tripped him. Maybe the scoundrel meant to rob him. It would be easy to stick a knife between his ribs and toss his body into the river. He thought of the unprotected valise left at the casa, and imagined the Indian girl rummaging through it. His money, however, he carried beneath his coat.

When they came to a place where the river made a wide arc toward the west, his guide reined in.

Pablo glanced around. Near, to his right, shallow water rushed endlessly over smooth rocks, sparkling in the sunlight, contrasting with shadows along the tree-lined banks. A little way to the left, goats grazed under the care of two dogs and the messenger boy. A line of distant brown hills bordered the horizon.

"I don't understand."

His guide stepped down. His words were matter-of-fact. "There was a battle here, more than a year ago, between the Huertista dogs and the troops of my capitán. Doña Serafina was accidentally killed, and rests there—" He lifted his hand to gesture.

The first sharp pain felt like that knife he had just pictured. He wanted to walk toward the spot but his legs seemed detached and incapable of carrying him. Gazing at the grass, he noticed bare, black patches mingled with lusher, sun-cured clumps, as if there had been a fire. Certainly not a place that was remembered, or cared for. Never raked, trimmed, nor planted with marigolds.

"You lie," he murmured. "Why did you bring me here?"

Anger flashed in the eyes, in the voice. "I don't lie. She came back here with mi capitán, and was killed, as I told you."

Whirling, he demanded, "Who is your capitán? And where are the children?"

A long stare, a tightening of the jaw. Then, "Teo is at the home of doña Gloria Herrera, in Hermosillo. Ramón took Domingo with him."

Ramón! He began to shake, unsure whether from fury or the onset of another malaria attack.

I should have known. They must have kept in touch, somehow, all the time we were married. And as soon as I am out of the way, she goes to him.

He looked at the unkempt grave. She had always loved Ramón. Drawing a deep breath to steady himself, he said with pity, "See where it ended."

"Do you wish some time alone?"

"No." He put on his hat. This time tomorrow, he could be in Hermosillo.

The dusty lane led between a series of low adobe buildings, meandered past a corral and modest homes with ocotillo fencing, and turned the corner of an old wall too high to see over.

Inside, big trees inside seemed asleep, burdened by masses of vines awaiting the first rains, their dry leaves motionless in the heat. In the wall was set an iron gate.

Pablo leaped back as a huge brindle dog lunged against the bars, snarling and barking, froth flecking the dark muzzle. A pretty, blonde woman came to the doorway. "Zapata! ¡Silencio! ¡Abajo, perro!" The dog left off and trotted to a favored spot where it sprinkled the adobe.

"You may enter," the woman said. "But keep in mind that he is not tied."

Her Spanish showed long years of use, and though she dressed in the clothing of a countrywoman, she clearly was an Americana. He cautiously went into the tiny courtyard. "Is Teo Valente here?"

One hand pressed against her heart and the distress in her face alarmed him. He dropped the bag and grabbed her wrist. "Is he hurt? Dead?"

She wet her lips, swallowed, wet them again. "Don't be fearful. I'm sure Teo is well. Please come inside. There is lemonade, or beer, if you prefer it."

"He isn't here? I was told—"

The sight of a man seated at the small table in Gloria Herrera's front room shocked him more than not finding his son. "¡Estrada!"

The hated Protestante who had delivered Serafina's first baby gave him an ironic smile. "Well, don Pablo, so you have finally turned up. I was convinced you were dead."

"I almost was, if hearing it makes you happy."

"Not at all. But I'd be interested to learn the whole story."

He noticed that the médico's blue eyes and sandy hair had lost much of their youthful lustre, and the fair skin was sunburned as if he'd traded his practice for a saddle.

"Does San Juan de Ulua mean anything to you?"

A change came over Estrada's features. He could almost believe there was concern.

"My God, is that where they took you? I'm amazed you lived through it."

"If we had not been set free when we were, none of us would have lived. As it was, I spent eight months in a military hospital." He accepted a chair and a bottle of Monterrey beer. He studied the label. "When I went home, of course there was nothing left but the house, and restoring it will take years of work, and money I probably no longer have."

Estrada drew a long sigh and expelled it. "You are looking for Serafina—?"

"No." He filled a glass which doña Gloria had set on the table. Holding it up, he regarded the amber liquid. "I found her." He drank.

Estrada sighed again, as if his chest hurt. "I tried to take her to safety, across the border. Your niece and tía are living in Texas, but she jumped off the train, the boys with her, and by the time I was able to return, they had disappeared."

He stared into the pale eyes, wondering what had attracted Serafina to this man. He remembered being jealous, insisting that she stop Estrada's visits to their home shortly after Domingo was born. Teo had been delivered by the Valente family doctor, five years later, after Estrada left Monterrey. "Where did you go? She wanted you, when our son was born."

"I was—working." Estrada avoided his stare.

"Revolutionario."

"Does it matter?"

"It does if you were behind my imprisonment."

"You believe that?"

"I know you were in love with my wife." He hadn't been positive, but the look on Estrada's face confirmed it. "Is that why you're here? You thought you had a chance, with me out of the way?"

The young man's lips trembled. Then he lifted his chin, a mild denial. "You said you found her. In La Puerta del Sol?"

"Yes. But there is no need for you to make that journey."

"I know. Doña Gloria told me."

"Do you also know where my son is?"

Estrada's eyes darted to Gloria.

She had been silent, gripping the sides of the adobe asiento on which she sat. "He lived with me for a year," she said, faintly. "Then Ramón took him."

He had not hated Ramón even after discovering they were lovers, not even when she had the child. He'd felt other emotions. Envy, jealousy, anger, fear.

But not hatred. Until now. "He had no right."

Again the locking of eyes between Gloria and the doctor. So, they knew. Had Ramón told the children? Whether or not, he meant to have them both. Domingo had grown up in his house, bearing his name. If he returned to Monterrey without the boy whom his friends believed was his firstborn, explanations—or more lies—would have to be given.

If municipal and church records in Monterrey remained intact after years of strife, he had those to back up his legal claims. Though his attorney had fled to Laredo, in the United

States, money would entice him back. Miramón had died; unfortunately, Estrada had not.

"Where's Ramón now?"

"Just what I was asking," Estrada remarked, "when you arrived."

Gloria sat, head bowed, clearly finding the information hard to surrender.

"What is it to you?" he demanded of the doctor. "She is dead."

"But Ramón Cordero can tell me how she died."

"That's your only motive for seeking him?"

"Don Pablo, I admit I loved your wife. But she asked me to keep secret the truth of Domingo's blood, and I intend to honor her by doing that."

Practicality outweighed dislike. Still experiencing periods of weakness, he could use a traveling companion, one whose destination was his own and a medical man besides. Their reason for fighting each other was gone. She lay in an untidy grave beside the Río Sonora. And her sons were with Ramón. "Señora Herrera, we will find him sooner or later. You might as well tell us."

She raised her head, looking from one to the other. "He took them to the hacienda Los Dos Corazones."

It was nearing the end of siesta when the carriage pulled up in front of a massive gate with an iron grid set in the top. "Wait," Estrada said, stepping down into the billowing dust. He called "¡Hola, celador!" and a guard yelled from among the rocks above, "No one enters! The casa grande is closed to visitors."

"We are not visitors. We have business with a man named Ramón Cordero, who is staying here."

"He's not here."

"I wish to see for myself."

"You see this, hombre?" A different man spoke. The glint of a rifle barrel came through the bars. "There are many more like it, and we have a warehouse full of ammunition."

Estrada leaned to the carriage window. "What now? Any ideas?"

"Have him send word to Ramón to come to us."

The message relayed, the first guard answered, "I told you, señor, the man you seek is not here. He left months ago. The house is closed."

Estrada leaned in again. "I think he's telling the truth."

Pablo stuck his head out of the other coach window. "Can you tell us where to find him?"

There was a mumble of voices behind the heavy gate. Finally someone shouted, "Casa Vásquez."

"Where is that?" Estrada asked them.

"¿Quién sabe?" He could almost see the man shrug. "In the north, somewhere."

Estrada got back into the coach. "Where the hell in the north?" he muttered.

"Casa Vásquez," Pablo repeated thoughtfully.

III

Beyond the firelight, coyotes wailed. Ramón had lain awake all night, questioning but not regretting—yet—his decision to bring his household, and anyone else who desired to come, to Los Nuestros.

Anita's body, curved in sleep, nestled close to him in the wagon, blankets providing warmth and comfort. This was the last camp before reaching the casa grande. He could not explain the urgency which drove him to leave the safety of Diego's—no, Mariano's, now—hacienda and set out to reclaim the abandoned estate without first sending in a regiment to ready the house for occupancy.

"Don't worry, Jefe," Domingo had said. "There's enough of us to make everything shine in a day."

Hardly, though there were a dozen families from Casa Vásquez whose men had followed him in battle since the days of Madero, and nearly a hundred people of Los Pobres and Blanca Rosa. "I can't pay wages," he'd told the headman. "But everyone can plant crops and raise goats or some cattle."

One of the wagons was filled with barrels of plaster and whitewash, brushes, wallpaper, and thick rugs bought cheaply in Hermosillo. Another carried foods and kitchen supplies. Pack mules brought tools, ammunition, rifles. Everyone had added items to his list, and contributed handfuls of varied paper money, some of which was refused by store owners. Mariano gave him a fiber sack of silver pesos. "You need this more than I."

Anger over the hacendado's funeral had vanished as soon as the weighted coffin was safely beneath Dos Corazones soil. Tereza's black veil and mourning dress, the monotone of the priest whose presence until that moment had been kept secret because of rebel sentiment against the established Church, the fiesta held in Diego's honor—all over now, except as images in Ramón's mind. Francisco and Mamá, with abrazos, tears, and promises to visit Los Nuestros next year, had returned home to California.

He felt that an old part of his life was gone forever, and a new phase was beginning.

Against his back, Sereno began to stir. Crosswise at their feet, blanket securely over his head, Teo resembled a sack of grain. Domingo's bedroll was beyond the central campfire.

With the coming of dawn, ex-rebels, muleteers, and niños adjusted hats and sarapes. Stock had to be tended, harnessed or saddled. Packs had to be checked and lashed onto mules. Sentries came in from their watch. Women built campfires and warmed beans and tortillas, and made coffee. Pulque jugs were lifted by aged hands to dry lips.

For someone who shunned responsibility, he thought, he had bitten off an almost unmanageable chunk. "Aiiiy de mí," he cried, half in horror, half in jest. "What have I gotten myself into?"

Anita's warm hand slid around his ribs, drawing him close for a kiss. "Well, we cannot go on living with friends forever, and if this place is as beautiful as you—"

Domingo appeared at the side of the wagon. "Jefe, Martín says he has found a short-cut, and do you wish to take it?"

"Hell, no. The last time we did that, Diego paid with his life."

After the message was on its way, Anita said gently, "He would have died anyway."

"Sí, but some of the rest of us came close as well. If Tonio had not taught me to swim, all those years ago, Domingo would have drowned."

He woke the younger boys, who scrambled out of the wagon to oversee the saddling of their horses and to wolf down a few tamales and coffee before the caravan began its final day of travel.

Once there, former cavalrymen and herdsmen settled the stock, and Martín placed the Cordero stallions in the choicest accommodations. Cleaning the ancient casa grande turned out to be less of a job than he'd expected. Inside and out, plaster needed numerous but minor repairs, and the ovens in the cocina required simply the removal of rats' nests before laying the tinder and striking the match. Women from Los Pobres scrubbed floors, cajoling husbands and brothers to paint and rehang shutters, and old tíos helped niños unload the wagons.

Three furniture makers got busy replacing stolen tables and chairs, bed frames, and chests for clothing. Crews fell to re-laying stones which had fallen from the walls surrounding the casa grande proper, and vaqueros scoured long-neglected stables.

Downslope the silent village became noisy with laughter and friendly orders bouncing back and forth. Thatch, tile, whitewash, charcoal braziers, petates, and ollas found places in the huts of the long-dead estate workers who had built them. Indio families drew lots, though the headman made sure those with more children received larger quarters.

From one end of the compound to the other, Ramón supervised what was done. Coming here was his idea, and he had been chosen boss for the community.

"See, Jefe?" Domingo joked. "I knew what to call you, didn't I?"

He swallowed back the temptation to say, *I want to hear you call me Papá.* The time for telling Domingo had passed, his last opportunity slipping away on the banks of the arroyo as Diego lay dying.

For their bedroom, Anita picked the largest on the second story, overlooking the mirador. Each boy chose a room, with two left over. Sereno stood in his empty cubicle, slowly turning round, lower lip pushed out. "I wish I had all those toys which we left in Mérida."

"You're too old for such juguetes, mijo," Anita said. "Besides, you and Teo would likely fight over them."

Insofar as he could tell, Sereno and Teo didn't fight over anything. Yet he wondered whether life could ever reach a point when memories of Mérida no longer tainted the most ordinary situations.

Their first meal in the large dining room was served on the mahogany table. Benches rather than chairs, at least for now, still smelled of the ax and plane. Linen from Dos Corazones. Candlelit dishes prepared by the cook from Casa Vásquez. Besides his family, he was able to persuade only Luis, who used to eat with them in the casita in Los Pobres, to accept an invitation.

"Dammit, I am *not* the hacendado," he cried, aiming his remarks at Gregorio and Martín especially. "Why do you think I named this place Los Nuestros? It's ours, hombres, and we are all responsible for its success—or failure."

Lobo, hanging about at the edge of the corral, said mildly, "Major, some of us don't care to be landowners."

He thought of those dead ones whose blood sanctified General Obregón's route all the way from the northern border to the City of México. "Then what has this revolution been for?"

There was an uneasy silence, the men shifting from one booted foot to the other. At last Gregorio said, "To give us the freedom, Ramón. I came with you willingly because Los

Pobres is gone, no longer a village, even. Who could make a living there? I don't want to work in the mines, or for the rail road. Can you see me in an office in Guadalajara? Hell, I'm a horseman. It's what I want to be, and I can be that here."

Martín, and others, murmured assent. "We don't care if you live in the big house. That way," the domador added, grinning, "you are the one who pays the taxes."

Chapter Five

Los Nuestros. 1916

He was worrying over the account book, with Luis's help, in his office downstairs, when a niño announced a visitor at the little gate. Distracted by unexplained expenditures— some merely unrecorded, such as the furnishings of this room, including his pigeon-hole desk, bought in Hermosillo to replace the one he remembered from Casa Vásquez—he trusted the guards to screen anyone allowed inside the walls. "Bien, bring him to me."

Sitting back in his swivel chair, he thought of Manuelo and the meticulous records the wiry little segundo had kept. Distant shouts of the boys playing a ball game on the grassy field wafted through glass doors that opened onto the balcony-shaded porch. In three months, Los Nuestros felt like home. He idly wondered if the visitor might be Mano, friend of his youth, who had been invited to live here but because of his wife, declined.

"Has María had her baby yet?" he asked, and Luis looked up from a sheaf of bills.

"Sí, a girl."

"You never think of living with them in Hermosillo?"

"No, Patrón."

The niño came to the doorway again. "Señor Valente," he announced, and withdrew.

Ramón's heart gave a lurch. Stiff with surprise, he leaned forward, laid his palms on the desk, and whispered, "It is you," staring at the man he had not seen for more than a dozen years.

Pablo stood motionless, a narrow-brim hat grasped in front of him. He was almost gaunt, his thin dark hair streaked with gray. Once-tolerant eyes glinted with ruthlessness, once-soft lips thinned from enduring some hardship.

Ramón dared not let the panic he felt show on his face, or Luis would run for armed men without waiting for explanation. "Bienvenido, Pablo," he said, offering his hand, but his voice was raspy.

Pablo advanced and took a chair on the opposite side of the desk without greeting. Settling the hat on one knee, he gave a motion of his head which dismissed Luis.

The young man's eyebrows went up, questioning. At Ramón's nod, he left them, closing the door.

What to say? Serafina is gone. I want my son, even if he does not know who I am. Get out, Pablo. You're supposed to be dead. He said nothing, only waited for Pablo to speak.

The man looked tired, but his voice was strong. "I know about the battle at La Puerta del Sol," he began. "I have talked with Señora Herrera. Thank you for taking care of the boys when I was unable. I was in San Juan de Ulúa."

"The prison at Vera Cruz? Dios mío, how terrible!" He couldn't help staring. Pablo must be. . . mid-forties. Once prosperous, an easygoing merchant who had allowed Serafina her indiscretions and married her anyway. *He is more of a man than I thought.*

"Terrible, sí. I heard of your rise in the military."

"Rise?" He gave a short laugh. "Perhaps." He turned to a shelf on which were two glasses and a decanter of white wine. "Drink?"

"No. Prison food ruins a man's stomach."

"Lo siento." He wanted a drink, as much to keep his hands still as for any effect the wine might have. He clasped his fingers in his lap. "I know why you're here. Let's stop playing. What kind of terms are you willing to consider?"

"No terms. I'm prepared to take them today."

He leaned back, studied Pablo's face. Did he even know? He must. The look in those eyes. *He hates me now. He never did, before, even after he found out I was sleeping with the woman he loved.* "There's no difficulty about Teo. While I love him, I believe he will be happy with you."

Pablo's jaw tensed. He seemed to be forcing himself to remain civil. "They were both happy with me. Call them in, now. I want to see my boys."

"They are not your boys," he said, calm but ready for a fight, or whatever reaction Pablo might have. "Domingo is mine."

Pablo's stony face didn't flinch. So he did know.

"Records in Monterrey say different."

"Why would you want him? To hurt me?"

"No. I don't want you hurting him."

Ramón made a wide gesture at Los Nuestros. "Does this look like I am hurting him? From all reports, Villa has occupied Monterrey, and taking him there would be insane."

"Villa and Obregón can kill each other if they wish. What I do is none of your business."

Sensing that any argument would be useless, he stalled, "Give me a few more days—"

Pablo's face lit up and he laughed out loud. "Ah, Ramón, you haven't changed. I knew you would never find the right time for such honesty."

The truth cut, doubly so as he realized the weapon he had just given this man. They regarded each other in silence until he had to look away in defeat. Standing on shaky legs, palms sweaty, he said, "Let me prepare them. They believe you're dead."

Pablo changed his hat to the other knee. "Do that. I shall wait here."

Ramón went through the house, wanting to share his turmoil with Anita, before remembering she hadn't felt well and would be upstairs, lying down.

On the porch, he could see the ball game in progress between those from the casa grande and those in the village, heard bursts of shouting as team members raced about the field, making or preventing a score.

Vaulting the low wall bordering the road, he walked to the shade of trees where spectators lounged. It was Sunday. Everyone was resting from all except necessary chores. He leaned against a thornless trunk, returning the pleasantries of villagers, smoking a cigarette. His mind refused to think past the coldness inside, and the end of the game came too soon.

Boys jogged off the field, panting from exertion, and fresh teams ran out, tossing the ball and shouting.

"Teo," he called, and both Teo and Sereno came to him, Domingo following, damp hair plastered to dust-streaked foreheads. The sleeve of Sereno's shirt was torn at the shoulder, and their chests heaved like healthy young colts. "Rough game?"

"We won."

Leading Teo aside, he said, "There's a wonderful surprise waiting for you in my office." He had to restrain the eager departure. "It's someone you have not seen for a long time, and thought you would never see again." He put his fingers over the parted lips. "Whatever you're thinking, please don't say anything, and do me the favor of staying with him in my office until I return."

"All right, Jefe," Teo nodded, and ran away.

Sereno started after him. "No!" Ramón said. "Not this time, hijo."

Giving him a puzzled frown, the boy changed his course toward the olla for a drink of water.

Domingo was putting back the dipper. When he raised his eyes, Ramón said, "Come with me."

Together they sauntered toward the corrals. "Where did Teo go in such a hurry?"

Words which had come so easily a moment before stuck in his throat. Reaching the grassy pen where Valiente and half a dozen other geldings were frolicking, he leaned his arms on the top pole, and Domingo leaned beside him. The boy was nearly fourteen. Not as much difference in their heights as there had been two years ago. He'd been through horrors and grown strong. Tough.

Strong enough? Tough enough? Adult enough to understand the youthful desires and self-will that had created him . . . .

Moistening his lips, unable to take a deep breath, Ramón plunged in, trusting Diosito to make it come out right. "There is a thing which I have wanted to tell you from the start, but did not know how."

In the pause, Domingo's attention remained on the horses, his expression unrevealing.

"Your mother and I— We knew each other in La Puerta del Sol, before she married Pablo."

Domingo's voice was steady. "I know, Jefe. When she saw you at the station, she said, 'Thank God I've found you,' so she didn't have to tell me why we came across all of México." The dark eyes turned to consider him. "When I almost drowned, do you know what you said to me? You said, 'Mijo.' I thought about it later."

He had thought about it, too. Hijo could be used by any well-known older man. Not mijo. My son. Claiming him, inadvertently acknowledging shared blood. "It's true," he said softly, and for long moments they searched each other's face.

"I'm glad." Domingo smiled.

Ramón couldn't keep tears or relief from spilling over. He stepped back, taking a deep breath at last, and blurted, "Pablo is not dead. He's here."

Domingo looked stunned. "Papá is here? I'm sorry— that's what I always called him—"

"I understand—" Before he could think what else to do, the boy ran to the gate and swung it wide. Leaping onto Valiente's bare back, he kicked the flanks and was gone.

"¡Domingo!"

Standing in the swirling dust, he watched the rest of the horses find the opening and trot to freedom.

Sereno left his mother's room assured that her illness was not serious. Dawdling on the stairs, he heard voices in his father's office, where the door was ajar. Giving a passing caress to the ebony lion carved into the lowest post, he crept across the wide hall and peered through the narrow opening.

He could see Teo leaning back against an older gentleman in a business suit, held in the man's arms in the same way Papá often held him.

Moving to the right, despite the risk of exposing his presence, he saw that his father, facing them—but not too close—looked unhappy.

The visitor was saying, ". . .won't make any difference. You might as well have kept your secret."

Teo craned his neck up at the man who held him. "Why did he run away? Doesn't he like us anymore?"

Sereno strained for a better look. Teo's papá. A man come back from the dead. A thrill shot through him. Now he wouldn't have to share his parents with the other boys.

"Your papá is not Domingo's father. I am."

Those words caused his mouth to drop open. There was no doubt who had said them.

He felt his knees buckle. *His* Papá, Domingo's father? Why, that made— He reeled away from the office door, clung to the banister. That made Domingo his brother.

His brother, not Teo's.

Stumbling, pulling himself along, he ran up to the balcony and leaned over the stone parapet, sick and dizzy.

Water and an undigested dulce surged, landing as vomit on the paving tiles below.

An exclamation—a criada, Josefa probably—made him duck back to avoid being seen. He heard the swish of a wet broom and wished she could scour out his insides, which felt knotted and dirty. Fragments of thoughts ran around in his head like the squirrel old Jerónimo had kept in a wire cage until Domingo freed it. "¡Domingo!"

He spat into a maceta where tender shoots of a flowering vine of some sort broke through the dirt. So that was why Papá tried so hard to make them be friends. Why Domingo got a better saddle and more pesos to spend. Why Papá let Domingo go on the hunt, and not him!

His fury grew. Domingo was older, and as the elder brother would always be favored, given the best. Had not he heard vaqueros at Dos Corazones discussing Mariano's great fortune in being the only son? He hated Papá for not telling him.

Did Mamá know? Dios, did she? And had not told him? Complete betrayal.

He wanted to hate Mamá, too, but couldn't bring himself to go that far. She was all he had now to lean on. Too, maybe she'd been ignorant of the secret, this secreto malo.

He hoped Domingo had run away, never to return to Los Nuestros. Or, if he did return, after a few minutes, perhaps the strange man in whose home Domingo had been born would force him to leave with them.

Then, the worst thought: Domingo had known, all along. That was why he did as he pleased, and that was why he ran. He knew he belonged here and meant to stay.

Crouching beside the openwork of the balcony, cheeks hot, teeth clenched, Sereno heard his father calling him.

Swiftly he stood up, thought of hiding, then answered, "Here, Papá," in a voice weak and childish.

From the dim interior, his father approached and stopped in the doorway. "Son—"

He stepped back, bumped into stone, desperate to escape. Instead, he flung himself into arms that enfolded him.

Immediately pulling away, he landed blows against his father's chest with both fists. "I heard you! I heard—"

Clasped hard against Papá, he sobbed in spite of himself, fearing every moment that people would be drawn by the noise and come to stare.

"What did you hear?" Papá asked gently.

"D—Domingo—" Fresh sobs cut off speech, and he hated his lack of control. "Why didn't—you—tell me?"

"I kept hoping," the quiet voice said, "that a time would come when you would love each other as you and Teo do."

"That time shall never come," he declared, and wrenched away from the loosened embrace.

Slowly Ramón stood up, watching his younger son race down the stone steps and across the yard toward the ball field, where another game was in progress. He felt deeply disappointed, for he'd assumed, since there had lately been no outbreaks of temper from either boy, that the thing he so wanted was taking place.

Knocking lightly at Anita's door, he was relieved to find her sitting up in bed, reading. "Feeling better?"

"Sí— I just needed some extra sleep."

She propped his pillow beside hers and he joined her. He took one of her hands and began pushing the new wedding ring around and around her finger.

Leaning to peer into his face, she said, "Bad news?"

"I don't know where to start." He gave a sigh, trying to order his thoughts. "I finally told Domingo."

Her attention was focused now. "What did he say?"

The memory made him smile. "He said, 'I am glad.'"

She clasped his hands, her face alight. "How wonderful."

"The rest is not so wonderful." Her mood grew more and more despondent as he explained. "I had to. Pablo is downstairs. He wants to take them both with him. Today." She made a little sound of alarm. "Sereno heard us talking. When I found him, he was crying. He hit me. He said he and Domingo can never be friends."

"Of course they can. That's just boy-talk. Now that they know, they'll try harder." She laid her arms around his shoulders and kissed his cheek above the beard line. "It'll all work out. Although I shall certainly miss Teo. He's such a sweet child."

He couldn't help voicing his fear. "What if Domingo decides to go with them?"

"Why would he do that? You said he was glad. He will want to live with you. With us."

"Not with Sereno."

She nestled her face in the curve of his neck. "You make too much of this rivalry. I think they enjoy it."

Her words were comforting, but he didn't believe them.

Luis was in the office, laboring over the sheaf of papers. "They went to say goodbye to Teo's amigos." He jerked his chin in the general direction of the village.

"Just like that."

"I'm sorry, Patrón."

"Domingo hasn't come back?"

"Not to my knowledge."

The young geldings had been returned to the pen, but Valiente was not among them. He saddled up.

Following the shod hooves was easy. For a kilometre, the tracks stayed on the road. Then they'd led up a low bank and into the woods. Everything had leafed out with the rains, making pockets of underbrush where a regiment could hide.

He slowed, vigilant for enemies, for disturbed turf and broken sticks. Shadows already stretched long, and when the sun dropped behind the mountains there would be no moon. Domingo had left without coat, sarape, or blanket—not even a saddle, only the training halter Valiente still wore with its short lead rope.

Ramón had brought blankets, matches, and a canteen, along with his rifle and belt gun. When he crossed over the ridge, circling with the trail of his quarry, he realized where he was: below lay El Valle de Los Mesteños.

Closer to the casa grande than he'd thought. Another short-cut. He'd never entered from this side, and paused to scan the billowing grass for mustangs or a willful boy. A caballada numbering about fifteen grazed far across the valley, a smaller band to the east. Valiente's tracks led at an angle downhill toward El Valle.

Riding along the treeless ridge, he called at intervals and listened for a response. The sky was turning pink and gold, full of clouds shot through with beams of sunlight, but already the forest had taken on a gloomy aspect.

In about ten minutes he halted. Either the herds had moved, or he couldn't see them in the near-dark.

"¡Domingo!" he called, and was mocked by an echo. Fears he'd managed to keep subdued sprang out to dance before his mind's eye. Vivid pictures of the boy lying thrown, perhaps trampled, or mauled. The basin was home to stalking cats as well as less dangerous creatures.

His heels touched his gelding's flank and he was reining around to descend the slope and go back, when a quiet voice behind him said, "Here I am."

When Domingo raced out of the corral on Valiente, there was no thought, only an overpowering fear that the man he had once loved in Monterrey would take him away from Los Nuestros.

Since those minutes on the bank of the arroyo, while he was still confused from nearly drowning, Ramón's fervent words had haunted him. Had he heard correctly? Was it true? If so, many things became clear.

Yet—After Mamá's death, why had the major not revealed who he was? They had only each other—before Anita and Sereno were found—and how much easier every disappointment and tragedy would have been, if only he'd had the security of a blood bond. Watching the major and his family these last months, he had repeatedly doubted what he'd heard.

Even when he was positive the word *Mijo* had been spoken, more than once, other facts tortured him. Sereno was the favored one. Loved and recognized as the heir to whatever Ramón built of Los Nuestros. He, Domingo, was unworthy, maybe loved as an amigo, but not valued as a son.

He reined in, flung himself on the rocky ground, and sobbed like a tonto. Ramón had not thought highly enough of him to claim him until Papá—no, not his papá. Pablo, now—until a man came back from the dead and forced out the truth. Valente was not his name. He had no name.

Presently, spent from the storm of his anger, he sat up and looked around, a bit fearful, for he had given Valiente his head and had no idea where he was.

The gelding had wandered down a rocky slope. From the crest of the timbered ridge where they'd halted, he could see the horse half a kilometre away, grazing. Below, stretching to a border of hills backed by mountains, was his valley.

Vast, rolling uplands, new tallgrass bending in the first whisperings of a night wind. Darkly distant moving dots which he knew were mustangs. Somewhere in the lengthening shadows, Cimarrón Grande kept watch.

Somewhere downwind, Little Cimarrón would be waiting for a chance to steal mares for his own use. If they met and clashed, there would be a hell of a fight. Domingo shuddered.

Sooner or later, he had to go back. Face everyone, people who by now would know—

What? That he was the bastard son of the major. In the families of soldados, Indios, vaqueros, peons, lower classes of all sorts, having children without being married was common, especially if the man and woman lived together in the same home. More than half the villagers in Los Pobres and similar towns had never married because of the fees charged by priests and municipal registrars.

But in families of his class— He thought of the fine old townhouse with the iron gate which bore the scrolled crest of Sarria-Ortiz y Valente. That was the heritage handed down from Pablo. He sensed that visitors there would have shunned and gossiped about women who had children by a man not their husband, and those children were never invited to saint's day celebrations in the better neighborhoods.

Chilled, he realized he was completely ignorant of Mamá's family. Would a man like Pablo have married her if she had been a common person? His thoughts took a knotty turn. He was five years older than Teo. Their mother and Ramón must have been together—in an intimate way—before that, in La Puerta del Sol. Obviously they had never been married, for she married Pablo Valente.

Loosing a cry half of rage, half of frustration, he leaped to his feet and ran stumbling up a rocky slope that tripped and bruised and showered him with pebbles and dust. He found himself in a high meadow overlooking the valley.

A crescent-shaped grassy space banked by tall trees, a smaller canopy of flowering trees between, and over it all the tender lilac haze of evening. "Rincón," he named it in a whisper. "My secret place."

He shivered, more from intense excitement than the freshening wind. If only he'd brought food and blankets, he would stay here. A gun and ammunition, for hunting. An ax, with which to build shelter. Matches, to light a fire for cooking and keeping away predators.

Then he heard...Ramón...calling him.

"Here I am," he said, going forward.

He waited for explanations, excuses, suggestions about what to do when they came face to face with their visitor; but the major—his father, he had to start thinking of him that way—laid a soft Mayo blanket around him, saying, "You might need this."

Domingo whistled to his horse and mounted up without speaking.

It was full dark before they rode through the gate, and the guard closed it. The lower floor of the casa grande was softly lit, and in the courtyard lanterns glowed. Beyond, torches illumined the road to the village, where the open doors of the huts were rectangles of pale orange, and the smoke of many supper fires spiced the air. His heartbeat quickened with love for this place.

They dismounted to brown hands that took away the horses. They walked together across the paving, down the hall, and into the dining room. Two Opata criadas had readied the table with linen, glassware, and place settings, and were lighting candles in silver holders at each end. "Buenas tardes," the women murmured.

"We shall eat now," Ramón said to them, tossing his hat and sarape over a rack in one corner.

Domingo shed his blanket and went to stand behind his own chair, feeling awkward. Was it his chair now? Was this his home?

In a minute Anita entered from the hallway with Teo. And Pablo Valente.

"Sereno didn't feel hungry," she said.

He looked into the lean face and remembered balmy days in the patio when he and Teo used to wait for this man to come home from his shop, carrying a newspaper, dulces or a small toy for each of them in a coat pocket. He could almost hear city traffic in the streets outside, other birds twittering in established trees, other criadas calling back and forth as they brought out fragrant dishes. He saw again the Monterrey lamps glowing, and breathed in the sweet cured aroma of cut grass wafting through other open doors.

Against his will, his feet moved, taking him around the end of the table and toward Pablo. He was prepared for the abrazo. Not for, "Hola, hijo. Thank God I've found you boys at last."

Panicky, his gaze sought Ramón's. "Does he not know?"

A look of annoyance crossed the bearded face. "Of course he does. Why don't we all sit down, before the food grows cold."

Steaming bowls of tender beef, spiced vegetables, salsas, fresh flour tortillas, pastries, frothy hot chocolate, coffee, flan, frijoles. He ate without tasting any of it. Whenever he could do so unobserved, he looked at Pablo.

He recalled how when he was very small this man had often held him on his lap, reading aloud items from the paper until sleep made his young eyelids too heavy to lift. According to custom, boys kissed their father's hand when saying good night. He could still feel the texture of Pablo's skin against his lips.

This man seemed too old. His jowls sagged, once-kind brown eyes had become hooded. Hair which Domingo remembered as black but thinning, now made a heavily-gray fringe over his ears and around the back of his head, and the mustache matched.

Teo was the only one in the mood to talk. Beside Pablo, he chattered on and on about the ball games, the horses, dozens of major and minor events. Pablo responded with encouraging questions, casting satisfied glances at the rest of them, and both ate with evident pleasure.

Presently Anita excused herself, leaving Teo behind for a change. Ramón also stood up. "Cigarette, Pablo?"

Domingo wanted one badly, but now realized why the ex-rebels had always been nervous about his smoking in Ramón's presence. Not that the habit fouled his breath and might ruin his health. It was considered insulting for a son to smoke in the company of his father. Mariano never indulged while don Diego was in the same room, or even near him in the horse camps. So the others knew, too, even Martín. Luis. Luis should have told him.

He dawdled with his empty chocolate mug, hoping a criada would come and fill it, to give him something to do besides sit like a loco, waiting for whatever had to happen.

"I asked for terms, earlier," Ramón said, blowing out a stream of smoke as casually as if they discussed a cattle deal or the price of a caballo padre. "I've decided you don't have a case. So I make the terms." He leaned his elbows on the table. "Domingo stays with me." The shortest of pauses. "If that is what he wants." He rose and half filled two short fat glasses from a decanter on a chest where silverware was kept.

Pablo looked across the cluttered linen cloth at him. "Domingo. Do you remember our home in Monterrey? Comfortable, clean. It will be that way again. And you'll have Teo and the friends you knew. School, the Church. When you're old enough, a share in my business."

Handing Pablo a drink, Ramón said, "Have you been in Monterrey lately? Tell him the truth."

Anger flashed. "Truth? If I were not a guest here I would call you what you are."

Domingo could see beads of sweat on his forehead. On Ramón's, too.

"Monterrey is in control of the Villistas. You might not have a house left, nor a business, nor funds. And those legal records you used as a threat might not exist." He sat down and crossed one ankle over the other knee.

"There is a house." Pablo loosened his collar. "Most of the money, it is true, I left for Serafina. Who knows what happened to it. Some funds should be in Texas with relatives. Enough for a new start."

"This country isn't ready for a new start. Obregón will have to whip Villa's ass before anybody is safe."

"Obregón might wish he had chosen Pancho instead of Carranza."

Ramón smiled a little. "¿Verdad? I'd have taken you for a Carranza man. What did happen, Pablo? Why did you leave Serafina with no alternative but to find me?"

"She had alternatives. Estrada—" He halted, and took a gulp of the liquor.

"Who is Estrada?"

"You'll find out, in a day or two. He's coming to see you. I persuaded him to let me finish first."

Domingo cleared his throat. "Estrada was the one who warned us that night. Don't you remember, Jefe, I thought I told you. He said we had to leave, so we got on the train, but Mamá jumped off and we took another one."

Pacing about the softly-lit room, carrying his glass, Ramón said, "Why is Estrada coming here?"

Pablo turned to follow his movements as if he didn't trust anyone behind his back. Teo, dozing against his shoulder, joggled awake and declared, "I wish to go to bed."

Would Teo remember the customary kiss?

He did, and gave his father a hug around the neck, and a kiss on the cheek. "Good night, Papá."

Domingo's fingers ached from being in a tight fist. Pablo looked at him as if to say, You can do that, too.

What he said was to Ramón. "Stop derailing the subject. I want this settled tonight."

Ramón set down his glass. "I told you, it's not up to me. Domingo is man enough to make his own decisions."

"Is he man enough to live with his own mistakes?"

That was the question which gnawed at him now. With Pablo, there would be all those things he'd offered. The family name, fine home—when restored—a brother he could tolerate, even like on occasion. A promise of wealth and security when the war ended. Boyhood friends. A future.

With Ramón came Sereno.

"You were my son once," said the sad-faced man. "I gave you my name, when I didn't have to, because I loved your mother. We had a good life, a good home. You and I have shared memories, Domingo. You can be that boy again, and enjoy all the heritage to which my name entitles you."

Ramón said nothing. He lit another cigarette, face turned away. Didn't he care?

Tempted to drain the half-filled liquor glass within reach, Domingo ached to shout, Would you watch me leave, with no move to stop me? But he feared the major's answer. Finally words came, without planning.

"Lo siento mucho, Papá. There is a warm feeling in my heart for you and the home you made for me when I was little." He couldn't help glancing at Ramón, who didn't look around. "But now home is here, with my true father. Besides," he faltered, not knowing what the clenching of Pablo's jaw meant, "you still have Teo."

He heard both men let out pent-up breath. Looking from one to the other, he couldn't read any emotion on either face except great weariness.

"Sí," Pablo said gently. "I have Teo." He stood up. Walking as if movement required effort, he disappeared down the dimly lit hall.

Domingo hurt in almost the same way as he had when he understood the news of Pablo's first disappearance, the same dull pain as when he knew Mamá was never coming back.

Ramón poured a few spoonfuls from the decanter. "Here," he said. "It will help you sleep."

He felt as though he could never sleep again. He wanted to run out to the corral and leap on Valiente and race back to his secret place, his rincón, and shout for happiness. He wanted to rush up to the room where Sereno was sleeping so peacefully and pound him until the boy cried. Sipping the liquid, which burned his lips and was probably brandy, he waited for Ramón to speak; but the major only rested his rear on the edge of the table and sipped his own drink.

After awhile, he asked, "Why didn't you tell me sooner?"

"Once," Ramón answered as if feeling his way along a dark path, "I had a dozen reasons. None of them makes any sense now, but I suppose I thought you couldn't understand."

"I guess I wouldn't have, then," he said. "Before I found out about—things. Jefe—" He felt his cheeks flush, from self-consciousness, and the brandy. "What shall I call you?"

The major gave him a probing stare. At last he said, "Whatever feels right to you."

97

He bit his lower lip, trying out terms of address in his head. "Maybe it better stay Jefe, for a while." He set down the empty glass. "How— How old were you, when— When— You know."

Ramón's expression softened, thoughts moving into the past, and the hint of a smile touched the corners of his mouth. "Seventeen."

Chapter Six

Teo's departure, amid abrazos and goodbyes from friends who gathered in the courtyard, seemed unreal to Domingo, as if they would vanish like a dream before the hired coach could take the younger boy away. Earlier, criadas had brought the customary breakfast trays of pan dulce and chocolate to each room, and while he was eating, he heard the chatter and footsteps of the younger boys in the hall.

He had dressed and gone out, and was swept into the bustle of finding clean handkerchiefs, a misplaced hat, and lost toys Teo wanted to take with him.

"Where's Jefe?" he asked Anita, who seemed pale and distracted as she came into the patio with a small basket containing lunches for the travelers.

"He already said farewell. There was some emergency in the village . . . " She drifted onto the patio.

Sereno and Teo were giving each other a tight hug at the edge of the paving.

Beyond, in the driveway, Pablo tossed up traveling bags and the cochero caught them. The coche door stood open, ready to receive them for the start of the long journey to Monterrey.

Anita knelt to kiss Teo. Sereno ran upstairs, promising a special last-minute gift.

When she stood up, blotting tears, and moved away, Teo looked around and saw him loitering against a patio column. "Hermano, are you not going to wish me a buen viaje?"

His throat closed with unexpected emotion. They met and clung to each other for several moments.

"Write to me," Teo said. "I read very well now."

"I will," he promised. "And send you photos, after I buy a camera."

"That will be nice. If the Villistas don't steal them out of the mail."

"Don't be afraid of any damned Villistas, hermanito. Dios will take care of you."

"That's what you said to Mamá," Teo told him. "On the train. Remember?"

"Hardly. I'm surprised you do."

"I remember a lot, Mingo. I wish you were coming with us."

"Someday, you'll understand."

"I understand already some of it. That Papá is not your papá, and Jefe is. But you and I are still brothers."

They hugged each other again. "Sí, we'll always be brothers."

"Take care of Volador for me," Teo called as he hurried to the waiting man who lifted him into the coach, climbed in after him, and shut the door.

The driver's whip cracked, the mules lunged into their harness, the wheels began to turn.

"I will," he said softly.

Sereno ran out of the house, halted, and began jumping up and down in a frenzy. "He left! He left without my present!"

Grabbing a tiny package from the waving hand, Domingo cut down across the yard, scaled the corral, and whistled for Valiente. The gelding expected a morning treat, so came at once. "Open the damn gate," he ordered a niño who was lounging about, and the boy sprang to obey.

The coach was farther along than he'd expected from so unlikely a vehicle, but he soon overtook it, waiting only for a widening in the road to allow him to draw alongside. "Hola, en el coche!" he cried, and fingers fumbled at the canvas curtain, a surprised look on Pablo's face as if he expected a robbery. The man's relief at seeing him, however, twisted his heart, for in that instant he knew there was a surge of hope that he'd changed his mind. "Here. A present from Sereno." He thrust the package into Pablo's hand. "¡Vaya con Dios!"

He sat watching until the coach dipped out of sight, leaving the road empty except for a set of tracks which would be washed away by this afternoon's rain.

After he'd treated the colts to sugarcane from Señora Rojas's bin, he turned Valiente into the corral and mounted Teo's pony. A few minutes of exercise in the yard of the mirador cut Anita's prized turf, but the view over the wall was worth a scolding.

The sun and breeze and the gamy smell of horsehair rising to his nostrils gave him that sense of belonging which he'd felt the day he and Ramón first stood here, together. He leaned and stroked the dappled neck. "I am glad."

On a fitful wind, almost masked by wagons, hooves, the clang of a hammer on the anvil as someone made horseshoes, and the nearby noises of ranch people working and visiting, he heard the faint notes of a mournful tune.

Peering down, he saw no one but located the area from which the music was coming. Walking Volador to the corner, where grassland met the forest, he looked over the wall and could just discern the beginnings of a path. Someone— Sereno, of course—was using this route to some secret spot.

He could let the pony graze while he followed the trail to find where the boy was, and perhaps jump out at him with a startling cry.

Then he thought of Rincón. "If you did that to me," he murmured, "I would bloody your nose."

Later, in the patio hammock, resting from work with colts under Martín's supervision, he spotted the blond head easing up over the wall until the eyes showed. Pretending to be asleep, he watched Sereno put the flute between his teeth and clamber onto the surface like a lizard; then he dropped to the ground and ran hard along the house side of the wall.

Light boot steps approached from the far end of the porch, and Sereno asked, "Are you asleep?"

He sat up as if groggy. "Can anyone sleep when you tramp about and shout like a mule packer?"

Sereno flopped into a cushioned wicker chair and batted at a flowering vine which hung past his head. It was clear something was on his mind.

Domingo waited, swinging the hammock slightly with his toe, wondering what it was.

"Thank you for taking my gift to Teo."

"How can you be sure I didn't just throw it into the woods?" He turned his head in time to glimpse Sereno's dismay. A pause. "I was hoping it was that damned flute."

"I don't play it around you anymore," Sereno said stoutly. "Hadn't you noticed?"

"No." Another longer pause. Curiosity got the better of him. "What did you give him?"

"My silver saint's medal. For a safe journey."

"The one your mother gave you?"

"She said I could. She will get another for me. It was the best thing I had."

Domingo's fingers crept to the crucifix he wore always, on its chain of beads around his neck. Ramón had given it to him with a minimum of ceremony. It belonged to your mother, Jefe had said. She would want you to have it. Now he understood the significance of Ramón's possession of that crucifix.

"These things cannot protect anybody." He felt ashamed that his voice quivered.

"Mamá says they are symbols to remind us of God's love." Forgetting that his music was not appreciated, Sereno lifted the flute and blew a few soft notes.

"Play," Domingo suggested. "Let's see if you are getting any better."

"Teo liked this one." With only a few mistakes here and there, he played 'La Llorona,' the ancient melody about the crying fantasma who haunts the streets at midnight, looking for her lost children.

After hearing that twice, Domingo begged, "Dios mío, give us something cheerful."

Sereno launched into 'El Tecolote.'

He made a swipe to snatch away the instrument, nearly tipping himself out of the hammock. "You call that cheerful?"

Evading him, eyes gleaming with zeal, Sereno cried, "Wait! Here is the good part," and played to the end.

Then he said, "I heard an owl last night."

"The Opatas believe Tecolote announces a death."

Sereno remained undisturbed. "The Mayas believe the owl can give a person ojo, because its eyes are fixed."

"Jerónimo captured a little owl and put it in that same cage where the squirrel was."

"Did you let it go free, as you did the squirrel?"

He shook his head. "He wouldn't let me. It died."

"In Mérida—" Sereno stopped, glanced at him, found him listening, and went on, "El General kept a parrot, which also has fixed eyes. It was named Párajo, Bird, and the Mayan servants were frightened that if they disobeyed or tried to run away, Párajo would put the Evil Eye on them."

"Is that why Anita was afraid?"

"No. The guard at the front door had a gun. That was why we didn't run away."

"But you did. You said you traveled for days on trains by yourself, and joined Zapata's camp, where Jefe found you."

Sereno's voice grew wistful. "Had I not been playing my little cane whistle, he never would have known I was there. I might still be there."

"The whistle I threw over the ship's railing."

"Sí."

He made an abrupt gesture toward the new flute. "At least some good came of it."

The younger boy sighed. "Nicer, to have both."

Scowling, he snapped, "Be glad I did not throw you over instead."

"Papá wouldn't have stood for that." Sereno met his gaze. "Even from you."

Ramón dreaded the visit from Estrada, whoever the hell he was. He spent two days tending to ranch duties, commending Martín and Domingo for the progress of the colts, watching the farrier fit shoes on the three-year-olds.

He postponed a ride into the hills with old Jerónimo and his helpers to find materials with which to stuff new panniers. The mules were left in a cul-de-sac where fresh green mingled with winter-brown grass. His cattle from Dos Corazones were settled on a sweeping pastureland visible from the far side of the village, with a wide stream for a fence and cottonwood bosques for shelter. The stallion Bandera, named for the saddle horse lost in a battle after Guadalajara, enjoyed his brood mares in a small valley to the east, where Gregorio and Tío Agustín had dynamited all exits and put up a high gate for access from the ranch.

Life was good, and he resented anyone who might threaten it.

On the third day after Pablo left, and there was no sign of the mysterious Estrada, he said to the boys, "An estate this size has estancias. The boundary walls must be found and repaired. I would like help in searching for them."

This plan was revealed at supper, and Anita appeared less than thrilled. He realized he should have told her first. Being married again took some getting used to, even when it was to the same woman. "Of course, I can send out riders," he amended.

His sons looked at each other, gravely, as they had done that time on the steamer when he made them apologize for fighting. Then Domingo said, "When do we go?"

"In a few days," he said, and was rewarded by Anita's sigh of relief.

As soon as the meal was over and the boys went out to their own pursuits, she said, "There's something to tell you."

He felt in his pocket but had left his cigarettes in his dirty shirt. The lavandera's sweetheart would be happy. "Something good, I hope."

She stood, offering her hand. "Come into our room. It's a private thing."

Going upstairs, he anticipated a pleasant interlude before having to reprimand the Opata headman for not settling a dispute over pasturage for a couple of goat herds.

In the light, cool room, she shut the door and hugged him long and hard. When he began unfastening her dress, she said, "Not that, silly. Not yet—"

"What, then?" He landed a playful kiss on her lips.

Leaning back in his arms, she gave him an earnest look. "I didn't want to tell you until I was really sure. Now I am." She moved one of his palms to her belly. "There is going to be another child."

He didn't know why he should feel shock, except that the news was so unexpected. "Mine."

"¡Hombre! Of course yours." She laughed, sounding a bit uncertain, and slapped him on the chest.

"No— I mean, *mine*. I had forgotten—" Forgotten the helpless, happy, confused ecstasy he'd known when Sereno was born. His thoughts traced back through the years to that night, Mano and Luis giving him what comfort they could.

He had not been there for Serafina. Pablo had been the one to sit on the bed afterward and caress her hand, to peer into the tiny face and wonder what the future held for so tender a being. *He could not have guessed. Neither could I.*

"When you said you felt sick—"

"It was easy, before. I don't recall being ill, with Sereno."

"There are midwives in the village. Maybe even the girl who helped you then."

A shadow passed over her face. "That one was taken by the soldiers."

"Yo lo siento."

"Yo, también."

As they stood holding each other, he sensed her mistrust of those who remained. "Is there something you're not telling me?"

Moving to look through the open glass doors, to where Domingo was riding his colt back and forth at the foot of the slope bordered by the mirador, she said, "I wish he would not do that."

He strode onto the balcony and shouted, "Domingo! Take your work to the corrals or fields." Then he turned and gently demanded, "What's the matter? You want this child, don't you?"

She came into his arms again. "Sí, I have prayed for this. Only— The parteras agree that there could be difficulty. But if they know why, they won't tell me."

"Are they asking for money?"

"No more than customary." She looked away.

"You fear they're right."

Nodding, she laid her face against his chest, and from the balcony he watched the guards at the gate admit a man on a black horse.

Anita stayed in their room, lying on the bed and wishing Ramón's mother had remained in México. She felt strange, having no other women of her class within days of difficult travel. A girl even as young as Tereza to confide in would have lessened her concern. Briefly she considered going to Dos Corazones for the period of her confinement. There was an experienced mestiza midwife, and the hacienda was only an hour by carriage from doctors in Hermosillo.

The Inditas were skilled in herbs, true; the girl who had eased Sereno into the world had been Opata. Yet they were ready to accept a baby's death as God's will. She wished she were in Los Pobres, living in the casita where she and Ramón had been happy. She wished she still trusted village women to deliver a healthy baby.

Dozing, she scarcely heard the footfalls enter and come to stand near the bed. Eyes shut, she knew it was Sereno. He used to creep into the room at El General's like that, when she was crying inside for all they had lost and didn't feel like going downstairs. If she lay still as though asleep, he would watch her awhile and then leave. She let her eyelids flutter open.

They smiled at each other.

"Hola, gatito," she said. Little cat. It was what she often called him, for the silent way he could enter or leave.

"Did I wake you, Mamá?"

"I was only thinking." She patted the bed, and he perched on the side, the flute in his hands. "Play for me, mijo."

The tune was unfamiliar, its haunting melody no doubt learned in the village. When he had played it twice, he gave her that smile again. Someday he would break hearts. How was he going to take the news of a baby? Bonds of love and trust had been damaged, whether temporary or deep, by having to accept Domingo as a medio hermano.

"Play 'La Llorona.'" She lay back, one arm crooked over her eyes to keep out the shaft of morning sunlight. If she kept still, perhaps the blanquillos and tortillas would stay down.

Ramón met Estrada in his office, standing, with no offers of brandy or cigarillo.

"Yo soy Antonio Estrada, de Monterrey—"

"Pablo said you would come. He didn't say why."

In other circumstances, he would have found the respect in Estrada's shrewd eyes flattering. The Spanish features were weathered. An officer? Huertista?

Estrada gripped the brim of a new felt hat and raised hopeful eyebrows. "This will be easier if you can believe I am not your enemy."

He pulled his swivel chair closer and pretended to relax into it. "I prefer to make my own judgments."

"I have waited a long time to see the man Serafina really loved."

"Who are you?" he snapped, angry to have the past brought to him again, by a stranger, one who sat in the chair Pablo had occupied five days earlier.

Estrada sighed, leaned forward. "I loved her, too."

Not sure what response was expected, he gave none, only stared into the man's blue eyes. They resembled those of his stepfather, who also had light-colored hair. However, Estrada didn't appear much older than himself.

"I delivered Domingo. I believe she would have died, had I not arrived when I did."

He swallowed. How fragile life was. How close he had come to losing the boy without even knowing. "Then—I must thank you."

A weary smile. "You're welcome. I saw him in the corral, on the colt. If you fear I shall tell him, be assur—"

"He knows." Ramón got up and poured them drinks from a wine bottle. "So. You came to look at us? See if we are alike? Or, is there more?"

"There is more. I wish to know how she died."

"In an insignificant skirmish. She came to where the damned Huertistas had us pinned in a hollow, and they killed her. She is buried beside my father, near the Río Sonora." He gulped his wine, set down the empty glass.

Softly, "Did you love her?"

Another searching look exchanged. "Yes."

Estrada savored a mouthful of wine before saying, "I was afraid Pablo would somehow manage to take them both. Now I can see my concern was useless."

"You didn't see him after he left here?"

"No. I was in La Puerta del Sol."

"Saying good bye."

"Yes. Your friend Joaquín lives in her house."

"Thank God. We had lost track of him." He leaned back, his mind starting to work again. "You delivered Domingo. You are a médico, then."

"Yes."

"You were never Huertista?"

"Never."

"Domingo said you tried to put them on a train."

"I knew Carrancistas would try for Monterrey. Pablo's wealth and connections made his home a target, though his politics later proved sound."

"San Juan de Ulúa."

"The prison—sí. He was taken in one of Huerta's round-ups. ¿Ironico, no?"

"We were surprised to see him alive. I neglected to learn how he found this place."

"It wasn't easy. Guards at Los Dos Corazones told us you had gone to Casa Vásquez."

"You were with him."

"For a short time. We found someone at the military headquarters in Hermosillo, who telegraphed someone else in Culiacán, to finally locate you."

"You both went to a great deal of trouble."

"He gained his son."

"He wanted more. Do you?"

"If that is all you're willing to tell me, I must content myself."

On close examination, he decided the man would have been attractive when Serafina knew him. Had she loved him? For saving her life? He possessed traces of a vibrancy such as Mariano used on women; an appeal which Ramón suspected was latent in Domingo and would give them all headaches in a few years. He wondered what Estrada could tell him, if he asked.

The doctor stood up, glanced about the room. "If it is no bother, I would enjoy seeing the rest of your home, and perhaps have a short siesta, before starting back."

Downstairs, Opata women were mopping the already shining floor. Going out by the kitchen patio, they nodded to other criadas whose lithe brown hands patted tortillas or prepared meat and vegetables for the next meal.

At the corrals, until Domingo spotted them and began showing off, they watched him put one of the wilder geldings through its workout on the reata.

"Where did he learn to handle horses like that?"

"In the cavalry."

Martín held a mare being shod. The farrier dunked a hot iron in a pail of water. The sizzle made him think of chorizos cooking over a campfire, which thought led to the camping trip ahead, which reminded him of Anita's revelation. He began weighing the risk he took in keeping old wounds open by asking Estrada to remain here at Los Nuestros, against having skilled care if she needed it when the baby came.

Village boys and Sereno were playing on the ball field. He pointed. "My younger son."

"Handsome."

"He is the image of his mother."

They resumed walking, through the village.

"How do they get along?"

"Like brothers who have just found out about each other."

"It is to be expected."

"Sí." They came to a rock wall crotch high, and sat in the shade of a couple of trees, overlooking the grazing cattle. "If you had taken Serafina to safety—" He fished in his pockets before remembering he didn't have any cigarettes. "—would you have married her?"

"Naturally. We thought Pablo must be dead."

"And raised my son."

Estrada's lips parted, then closed, and he looked away in sudden nervousness. Finally, "Yes."

They were silent for some moments.

"A dozen years had passed," Ramón told him, "when she came to me."

"Years between, for me, also. There was much to be done, to change the country. Yet I could not forget her."

"You didn't marry?"

Estrada shook his head. "I came close a few times. But—no."

"Then, you have no responsibilities?"

"Only to the revolution." He grinned. "As soon as I decide which leader to follow now."

They started back upslope to the casa grande. "I have an idea for you. My wife is expecting another child. Your skill might be needed. Will you stay here and deliver this one? That way, you can delay your decision."

"And let the wrong man run the country? Again?"

"Who is the wrong man, hombre?"

Estrada laughed and gave a shrug. "¿Quién sabe, amigo?"

At supper, Anita was introduced to Señor Estrada and learned that the güero man with blue eyes was the doctor who had brought Domingo into the world, and he would be living with them until this new baby was born; but little else. When Ramón got into bed beside her, she snuggled in his arms and demanded, "Bien, where did you find him so quickly?"

"Diosito sent him. ¿Cómo no?"

She couldn't tell whether or not he spoke in complete seriousness, but she did know there was much more behind this man's sudden arrival than either of them had admitted. "He must be connected to Teo's father, since he delivered Domingo."

"Well, yes, they were both looking for me."

At last she had to ask. "Why?"

Ramón's words were matter-of-fact. "Estrada was once in love with Serafina, and desired to know how she died."

A little silence, while she worked up courage to continue. In a whisper, she said, "Ramoncito…how did she die?"

The muscles of his arm beneath her hand tensed, but after a moment he said in the same even tone, "She came to where my patrol was defending against the Huertistas, and was hit by the machine gunner's fire."

She shivered. "How terrible." He had been there. Had been with Serafina, when she died. Before she died. It required all her will power to stop herself from asking the thing she most needed to know.

He answered, anyway. "No," he said softly, and kissed her. "I didn't sleep with her, not then. Only before I met you."

There was a short silence. Through the open glass doors she heard the faint cry of an owl deep in the forest.

Then he said, "A long time ago…you promised never to lie to me. I guess I never made that promise to you, but I do so now."

She moved to kiss his cheek—shaved only this morning, newly strange—but he pulled away. "What?" She was more puzzled than alarmed.

His voice tightened on the words. "There is something I've been keeping from you."

A long wait. "What?" she whispered.

"When I thought you were dead—and had no hope we would be together again— Serafina was buried— Domingo, sent away—the whole damned world like a nightmare— I did—only once—never again—try to find comfort with someone else."

Now there was a new question she lacked the courage to ask; this time he did not answer it. Both knew he didn't need to. She guessed it was Paz, the girl who had traveled with the rebels and whose disdain had bruised Luis's heart. But it didn't matter who the someone was.

The owl came closer, into the trees at the edge of the mirador. Anita shook off a chill of superstition. "Thank you for telling me," she said softly.

Domingo was up at dawn the day they were to depart for the camping trip. He readied Valiente and Volador for himself, while Jefe and Sereno prepared other geldings and one pack mule.

Anita stood at the top of the mirador, swathed in her rebozo against the damp of a mountain morning, waving until they passed through the village and out of view. Despite knowing about Jefe and Mamá almost from the start, she had always been kind to him, and his respect for her ran deep.

He missed having Luis or Martín or Lobo with them. Jefe must have some reason for not bringing the customary help to do camp chores. As they rode side by side across the pastureland toward the north, he stole a glance at the shaven cheeks, finding the man younger than he had realized. Stealthy looks into the ornate mirrors brought from Culiacán to adorn the casa sala had shown him their resemblance. No wonder everyone guessed, no matter how hard Ramón had tried to keep his secret.

Sereno's skill with horses had improved since coming to Los Nuestros. And, ¡gracias a Dios! he had been persuaded to leave behind that flute. When they made camp, however, and sat with full bellies near the fire, Jefe's rifle close at hand in case of enemy or any four-footed threat, he missed the songs Sereno might have played; and when he was drifting off to sleep with his feet to the warmth, he could hear the lonely tunes in his head.

The first estancia, a day's ride from the main house and in much worse repair, consisted of corrals, a shed for tools, and a three-room log casita with wooden shakes for the roof. An uncovered trash heap at the rear of the building drew in scavengers.

Wild cattle broke out of the chaparral near a stream and trotted off in several directions. There was a spring. Evidence of past habitation in weathered or broken implements. But the contour of the land was pleasing. Rolling grasslands ringed by low mountains, and bosques of hardwoods just leafing out.

Dismounting, they removed saddles and the pack mule's pannier so the animals could roll. They would spend the night here. Sereno took one look through the front door and turned away to scratch at something in the dust which proved to be a silver peso.

"Dios, you attract money like piloncillo does flies," he said in disgust. The silver from the unfortunate don Miguel had been put away in a safe, but Sereno was given a sack of centavos whenever they were in any place coins could be spent. Domingo had little use for money besides what he needed to buy gifts for his new family. It was the principle of the thing that galled him.

"I keep both eyes open," Sereno answered, kicking about for more.

Jefe came from surveying the stream, and they led the horses down to drink.

Domingo remained at the spring, emptying their canteens of stale water and refilling them. A movement in the dense branches of an evergreen shrub made his mouth go dry, as it was not the startled flight of some bird, but clearly an animal on the ground, less than a stone's throw from him.

Jefe's rifle was in its scabbard on the saddle, his belt gun riding as always on his hip. Both were at the stream, out of reach.

"Ay, damn," he said, as the bushes parted.

Chapter Seven

The hair on the back of his neck prickled, his heart thrummed, and he was unable to run. Unable to move, or breathe—

A little buff-and-white spotted head appeared, the baby mouth opened in a silent appeal, and a puma kit tottered out into the clearing. Thin to the bones, fur matted and dirty, fluid streaking down from each eye, it ran toward him with faint cries of desperation, and he picked it up.

Even as he did so, he knew the danger if the mother were nearby. "Pobrecito," he murmured into the furry ear, trying to hold a squirming creature larger than his mother cat Meme had been, and more needy. "What has happened to you, little one?" *Abandonado* flashed through his mind and his fears abated at once.

He lifted the upper lip with his thumb. "Milk teeth," he muttered. "You must be starved. Are you hungry, niño?" He checked to determine whether it was male, and repeated the question, already walking toward the supply pack.

Breaking off bits of a cold tortilla, he stuffed them into his own mouth and chewed. The kit sniffed, then turned away from the soggy mass he spit into his palm, but he had succeeded in poking some of it in and was watching the little thing greedily swallow when Sereno and Ramón appeared over the rise.

"¿Qué piensa?" Sereno cried. "We found la madre del gato by the stream, dead from— ¡ah! ¿qué es ésto?"

"Don't frighten him," Domingo warned sharply, moving the kit to his other side so it couldn't see the people and stock coming at it.

Sereno hunkered almost in his face, reaching across his lap to stroke the spotted back. "¡Qué bonito!" Seeing the chewed tortilla in Domingo's hand, he pretended to gag. Then he said, "If those cows were not so wild, we could milk one for him."

"Go do that." He pushed Sereno with an elbow. "He was eating fine before you scared him."

"He doesn't look scared."

Ramón had tied the horses and now came to them. "One of the cows must have gored the mother a few days ago. Sereno, why don't you look about, you might find another one." Squatting on his heels, Ramón watched him feed the rest of the bread to the kit. "He probably would prefer meat."

"How old is he?"

Looking into the mouth as he had done, Ramón said, "I'd guess a couple of months." He explored with a fingertip and added, "Maybe three. Feel."

Behind milk teeth, he could feel the fangs just pushing through the gums.

Sereno was coming back already, face downcast. "I found one. Dead."

They watched the kit stagger off across the grassy space and then return to Domingo. He scratched behind its ears the way he used to do Meme. He knew what the answer would be before he asked, yet heard himself asking. "Jefe, may I keep him? He will die too, if I don't."

Ramón stood, resting hands on his hips in the pose which always meant he was about to do or say something unpleasant.

"Please. I'll take care of him, and—"

"And in less than a year he will be as big as you are, and have a taste for little goats."

The spotted face turned up to his and their eyes met. The mouth opened for a sound, not quite a meow, but equally entreating. Tears started and he felt himself trembling.

He'd had to abandon Meme the night Estrada came and made them leave Monterrey. As soon as he had learned the identity of the man now living in their home, eating at their table, all of those wrenching memories resurfaced, making him deeply thankful for this trip, so he wouldn't have to deal with overwhelming emotions.

But he still missed his pet, and in a measure this helpless creature would fill the hole left by their separation.

"Please, Jefe." He couldn't keep the longing out of his voice, though he hated letting Sereno hear him beg.

"You have Valiente," Ramón said, turning away. "And now Volador. Be content."

Sereno went with him to help start supper.

Domingo remained on his knees, watching the kit sniff the pannier. It showed the aloof alertness of a cat, the friendly sense of fun of a dog. But it was too young to kill anything larger than a grasshopper or small rodent, if it had learned how.

He unwrapped their supply of jerky and began soaking pieces in a pan of water. After he'd cared for his stock, he offered the food to the kit and was heartened by its appetite. He wondered what he would name it, if Jefe relented. It wasn't afraid of the fire, but avoided getting too close. Wasn't afraid of them or the horses or the dark. "Bravo," he said with satisfaction. "Fearless."

"Here, Bravo," Sereno called to the wandering kit, and held out his hand. "Come, Bravito."

Jealous, he watched Bravo hurry over and accept the younger boy's caresses.

"Don't get too fond of it," Ramón warned. "It will try to follow us."

That didn't sound promising.

The first watch was Sereno's, who stationed himself against the dark side of the casita, where fire light would interfere less with his night vision.

"Buenas noches, hijos." Ramón said, but Domingo pretended to be asleep.

He was still awake about an hour later, when Bravito crept into the shelter of his blanket and cuddled in his arms the way Meme used to do after Mamá had put out his light.

"Dammit," Ramón said, irritation thick in his voice, "I told you that gatito is not coming with us."

They turned in their saddles. Bravo was trotting along the backtrail, eyes and ears on the move for sounds of birds and the flit of butterflies. When he saw that they had stopped, he halted and gave them a clearly questioning look.

"See how intelligent he is, Jefe," Domingo said. "I bet I could train him to herd stock just like the dogs do."

Their laughter made him feel foolish. But Ramón's words weren't cruel. "We have days of riding ahead, over rough country, and I don't think Jorge packed enough food for four."

"He can have part of mine," he insisted.

"And your ribs will begin to stick out as his do."

"Then, shoot a deer. Damn jerky is no good anyway."

To his horror, Ramón dismounted and walked toward him. Old threats of being whipped came to mind, despite his belief that the man would never lay a hand on him.

"Get down," Jefe said gently.

He did so. Leaving their mounts drop-reined, and Sereno silenced with wonder, he followed Ramón a little way into the woods. *Ay, Dios,* he thought. *I am going to get a beating.*

And for what? Much less than he had frequently done in the past. Did Ramón's new authority give him this right? Not many Mexican men, and no Indios that he knew, ever struck children. He wavered. He wasn't exactly a child.

Out of hearing, Ramón stopped and they stood facing each other, an arm's length apart. "So much to say to you." His eyes were friendly. "First, to get it out of the way, I understand that you have lived with vaqueros and soldados whose speech is often crude. I, myself, have used these words, and worse. But this is not a good habit, and it would please me if you tried to break it."

Astonished, he blurted, "You bring me out here to say I use bad words?"

Ramón bit his lip, fighting a smile, and grew serious. "That was First. Second, I don't want a gato grande on my hands, ever. You have never heard about how my pony, Mío, died? Luis is remiss. I thought it would have been one of his best campfire stories."

He racked his memory. He'd heard that Mío died tragically, but no details came forward. "No, Jefe. Tell me."

Staring into the distance, Ramón swallowed a couple of times before he could steady his voice enough to continue. "Mano—you know him, Luis's older brother—was my best friend. Well, they had a middle brother, Fernando."

"I have heard his name. Only that, and hushed stuff I couldn't hear, or don't remember."

"Anita had to shoot him."

The mystery and scandal, then, had basis. He tried to picture the gentle Anita shooting anyone. "She must have had great cause."

"Sí. He was loco from peyote. And he had killed my Mío. Everyone thought it was a gato grande—the wounds were like those from claws and teeth."

"But if it was Fernando who really killed Mío—"

"There was a gato grande. Fernando—or a wild night shot from some villager, more likely—did kill it. The thing which sticks in my mind, and makes me crazy, is the image of him wearing that stinking skin, head and claws and tail, and attacking my wife." He leaned one hand on a tree, and laid his forehead on his arm.

Domingo was silent, aware of the pain. At last he said softly, "I'm sorry, Jefe. But none of that is Bravo's fault."

Raising his head, Ramón opened his mouth as if to argue, but something behind Domingo brought different words. "Mira, hijo, he is tired of walking."

Turning, he saw the kit had leaped onto the pannier and clung to it, making the pack mule prance, eyes rimmed in white and teeth snapping uselessly at paws anchored out of reach. The horses snorted and moved away, but Sereno controlled them.

"Or," Ramón amended, "he's hungry. If that pack were not between him and the mule's hide, you would see why I want him left behind."

"Give him a chance. I will tame him."

"He is not a horse."

"He loves me already."

"He loves the promise of your tasty insides."

"Jefe! Don't jest."

"Who jests? We've said enough for now. Let's go."

"Bravo, too?"

Already down to the trail, Ramón called back over his shoulder, "I don't know of any way to prevent it, short of shooting him."

Even when opportunity came, Sereno didn't ask what they had talked about. He wondered whether Ramón told him in private, and hoped not.

Several times during the week, Bravito forayed into the brush and was gone an hour or more; but always reappeared on the trail behind—or ahead—and was present for meals. Whether under Domingo's blanket or resting in the open doorway of an estancia house, the kit remained with them and woke him by nosing in his face.

The stock, especially Viento and the pack mule, shied at the cat's approach and kicked at him but never landed a blow. He learned to keep away from them, keeping clear of Ramón as well.

"He knows how much you don't like him, Jefe. See how intelligent he is? I can train him, easily."

"We'll see how he acts when you have to tie him or put him in a pen. He is not going to run loose when we get home."

"But he's a wild creature and that will make him sad."

"Exactly," Ramón said drily.

Three more estancias rimmed the boundary in a great circle which took another week to cover. The dry-laid rock walls were in better condition than feared, and two or three men at each station would be enough to handle the job. Domingo considered volunteering for the work and thus keep Bravito with him until the kit learned to obey him.

When he suggested that, Ramón said, "Too dangerous. We don't know what the Villistas are doing. If they ever intend to take back Durango, Los Nuestros will be in their path."

Sereno complained, "I thought Villa was one of the rebel generals, Papá."

"He was—and is. Now that Carranza and Obregón have become the government, they are the Federales, and anyone against them is now a rebel."

"Who are you for, Jefe?"

"I am for Los Nuestros, and any fighting I do will be in defense of my own."

"Me, too, Papá," Sereno said.

Biting the inside of his lower lip, Domingo wondered if a day would ever come when he would feel comfortable calling Ramón *Papá*.

Ramón insisted that Bravito be tied with several varas of rope, and that Domingo carry him across the front of his saddle for the last two days before they reached home territory, to accustom the kit to being controlled.

They had explored much ground, slept little, eaten light, and were drawn closer by shared experiences on the trail. Yet he knew the boys were civil to each other only because he expected it. Sereno surprised him by being capable of handling Viento as well as his share of camp duties. Domingo's hands, he noted, were so light on the rein that it seemed Valiente read his mind rather than taking direction from the bit. Diego would be proud.

In their circuit of Los Nuestros property, they rode along the south border of Domingo's valley, and Sereno saw it for the first time.

"Look hard," Domingo said, standing in the stirrups, "and you might see Cimarrón el Grande."

Sereno examined the wide expanse of grass. From their vantage point, not a mustang was visible.

"When we ride out here again," Ramón promised, "I'll remember to bring the field glass."

The last half day's travel was by a wide road, leaving the northwestern quarter of the boundary uncharted; but they had been away long enough, and he wanted a bath, food, and Anita, not necessarily in that order.

The guard at the main gate drew back in horror when he realized what cargo Domingo carried across his lap. Making a swift cross over his face, he muttered, "¡Ay de mí, muchacho!"

Out of hearing, Ramón said, "Something we don't need is to have people think you are a brujo."

The boy's rare smile flashed at him. "What is wrong with that, Jefe? Then they'll leave Bravito alone."

"Sí—but will he leave them alone?"

The excitement of the gatito's arrival dissipated when it was secured in a strong wooden pen built to hold hogs. Fed, clean, and in Anita's arms, he complained, "I hope we don't wake up tomorrow morning and find that the entire village has deserted."

Her lips smiled against his cheek. "You worry too much."

"For one who hates responsibility as I do, it seems there's no end to choices and decisions. Damn Villa, for if not for him, we would be in Los Pobres, making a garden and raising a few goats."

"Or at Casa Vásquez, doing what you do now."

"True. Are you sorry we couldn't go there?"

The movement she made against his shoulder could have been a shake of her head or only snuggling, but she didn't say anything.

"It's easier making crops where there is more rainfall," he pointed out. "Also, don't you feel better with Estrada here? How is he fitting in?"

She drew a long breath, expelled it in a sigh. "I like him."

"Has— Has he said anything about—whether it will be hard for you, when the baby comes?"

Her silence sent a pang through him, but her words brought a measure of calm. "He made a list of foods I am to eat, and those to avoid, and I must take long walks every day." She leaned away to look up at him. "Will you walk with me, sometimes? I have an idea for making gravel paths—" His mind wandered and he grew drowsy. She sounded happy.

At cena, Estrada caught them up on what was happening in the country. "Since the Convention at Aguascalientes," he said between bites, "Carranza and Obregón have joined on one side, Villa and Zapata on the other. This is dangerous, as Obregón mustered out so many of his troops after taking the City of México."

Ramón squirmed, feeling guilty of shirking. He liked Obregón and didn't care to see Villa whip him. "Can Pancho take over the government? If that happens, maybe we shall have to move to California."

Estrada glanced at those present—Anita, Luis, and the two boys—before speaking. "Rumor says Carranza is displeased because Obregón was willing for him to resign as the provisional presidente. So not only does Obregón have an alliance between Villa and Zapata to worry about, he must guard his back against his own commander."

126

"And Villa still has troops in Guadalajara," Luis told them. "Lobo has a brother fighting with him, who sent a message, somehow."

That *somehow* bothered Ramón, and from Estrada's guarded look, sat ill with him as well. Were they harboring a spy? They had, after all, picked up Lobo in the city, to guide the mustangers, and knew nothing about him.

"It's time I myself went into Culiacán," he said, making little crescents in the surface of his flan with a spoon. "Things here seem to be in good hands."

Anita didn't want him going alone, Sereno had decided to stay home and play his flute, and Domingo was busy with the baby puma, so he took Gregorio and Lobo.

Riding with men again, he was able to relax authority if not vigilance. He noticed that his two compañeros had reached the joking stage of friendship, and as soon as he had a chance, he asked Gregorio, "Do you trust that one? Luis says his hermano rides for Villa."

Shrugging, Gregorio answered, "¿Y qué? So does my own brother Carlos, last I heard."

"But Villa has turned against us."

"Us, Ramón? You mean, against El Premier Jefe don Venus Carranza and General Obregón. And who are they? The First Chief was an hacendado, and one of Díaz's men himself, not so long ago, and mi general grows chickpeas on a rancho grande."

"Well, hell, if it comes to that, what am I but an hacendado? Is that what you had against Diego, that you refused to eat in his house?"

His friend's face registered pain. "I had nothing against don Diego—"

"See? Even the way you speak of him. I'm surprised you all haven't started calling me don Ramón behind my back."

Gregorio laughed suddenly. "Who says we haven't?"

Unsure whether he should take that seriously, he warned, "If I catch anyone doing so, I'll turn over the whole operation to him. How did I ever get chosen for this job, anyway?"

"Easy. You found the casa grande, and have experience in bossing people around."

Joining Gregorio in a grin, he was conscious of the major's insignia on his jacket, worn because his first stop was rebel headquarters, to glean information unavailable elsewhere.

The soldiers lounging about had to take second looks to recognize him without the beard, and after greetings, they filled him with news: General Obregón was wearing a beard now, and was whipping Villa soundly at Celaya.

They expected the telegraph to rattle into life any minute with details of the campaign. Though both generals had drawn troops from rebel-held Guadalajara, Villistas had destroyed bridges from Colima to Zapotlán. "It is turning out to be a hell of a fight," Joél said.

"What of those in the north? Will Maytorena's men join in? And come past here?"

"Word is, if they do, they will take the quickest route. Through Chihuahua. Villa territory."

The only mail awaiting him was a letter from Mamá expressing pleasure at having finally visited, and vague plans for the next trip. He put it in his pocket for Anita to answer.

While Gregorio and Lobo sampled the delights of Culiacán, he sat in the plaza and read a pamphlet picked up at headquarters. It was young Calles' *Tierra y Libros Para Todos.* Land and books for all. It jogged his intention to begin a school at Los Nuestros, and he sought out a junior officer to track down suitable books. "Send them to me by Joél. He knows where to find me." He left a considerable wad of old Carrancista bills which he hoped were still acceptable on the west coast.

He'd eaten a chicken tamal and was finishing a bottle of unidentifiable fruit juice, thinking of starting back home, when his compañeros ran across the plaza in some excitement.

"Villa's army is retreating toward Irapuato." Gregorio hunkered beside the bench where he sat, and reached for the drink. Lobo added, "Obregón shot one hundred of Pancho's officers, and many others have joined him. This is the end of Villa."

"And the beginning of what?" He frowned at the empty bottle Gregorio returned to him.

His friends shrugged. "¿Quién sabe?"

He could have sworn he heard the unspoken Who cares? that followed. "Do you not worry that people you love might have been killed already because of Villa's stubbornness?"

"Sí, claro, Jefe," Lobo said. "But they are grown men, and make up their own minds. If they believe so much in Pancho, so be it."

A couple of weeks later, Estrada returned from his own visit to the city and described in private the devastation at Celaya. "Villa's cavalry broke through some of that barbed wire, and much of the killing was done with pistols. It must have been one of the bloodiest battles yet."

Domingo, overhearing when he was supposed to be in bed, blurted, "Horses shouldn't be used that way."

"Cordero horses won't be," Ramón promised. "Any army that gets my stock will have to steal it."

The first week in July, a young Seri arrived with a cart load of books and announced himself as Lobo's younger brother. "Silvestre, a sus órdens, señor. The commandante in Culiacán says to tell you that your General Obregón was wounded at León—"

"Not dead?" Ramón braced himself.

"Almost, he was dead, but only his arm was lost."

"Who is in command?"

"General Benjamín Hill. Pancho Villa is defeated."

"We've thought so before. You are not the one who rode with Villa?"

Silvestre shook his head. "No, señor, that was our older brother, Matías. Killed a month ago in another battle for Celaya."

"Lobo does not know yet."

"No, señor. That is one reason I came, and to deliver the books." He glanced about at the sala, where the portero had left him. "Are you going to start a school?"

"Yes. Would you like to attend?"

"I cannot. There are little ones and my mother at home."

"Bring them. There is room in the village, and classes will last only a few months. I guess what we needed, more than books, was paper and ink and pens." He leafed through the volumes, seeing at once that they were too difficult. "Maybe I shall have to write the lessons." If Calles could publish a printed treatise, putting together a few sentences for beginners should be simple.

Sereno threw himself into the project with surprising agility. "I remember how Mamá taught me." He rounded up his own paper and pens, as well as a tin of watercolors. He drew cattle, horses, pigs, and other familiar objects, and embellished them with splashes of paint. Then he wrote descriptive stories to accompany the pictures.

When he had finished and showed the effort, it was all Ramón could do to keep a straight face as he said, "Now, make thirty more like this, so everyone will have a copy."

Sereno's jaw dropped. Then he retorted, "Why, Papá, part of the lesson is to have each pupil make his own book, like mine."

"¡Qué buena idea! That is just what we can do."

Throughout the summer, villagers and ex-soldados worked the stock and land, while he and the boys taught their children. Estrada helped with the lessons, and when Anita felt well enough, she and the smallest ones filled the air with merry counting songs. Messengers from Culiacán brought news of every Villista defeat. Obregón returned to his command with his right sleeve pinned up, and stories about the event began to circulate.

"They say he was going to shoot himself in the head," Gregorio informed them one afternoon, "but his gun was empty and someone prevented him from reloading. Then he was rushed to the médico."

Lobo gleefully told about Obregón's arm, which had been severed by a shell and lost in the confusion of the battlefield. "You know how they found the right one, Jefe? A soldado carried a gold coin around the area, asking, '¿Alvaro, dónde estás?' and the arm that leaped up and grabbed it belonged to our Obregón."

People in cities, especially capitals and places where fighting had been heavy, were suffering the effects of high prices and no crops. "I feel guilty, having so much," Anita said as they were served vegetables and meats from their own land. "Can we not send some to relieve the poor?"

"And start a flood which cannot be stopped?" He thought of the man who had sold him blue hair ribbons, and later followed him, trying to make further sales, offering to guide him to sights in Guadalajara. In the back and forth occupation of that city by Villistas and Carrancistas, what had become of such people? It didn't bear dwelling upon. "Rains and crops are abundant this year, but we have no guarantee of the next. Building another store house is high on my list of things to do."

Nevertheless, making rounds with Anita's suggestion buzzing in his head, he instructed the Opata headman, whose name he belatedly learned was Josefino, to apportion more of everything to each family. When he was honest, he had to admit that seeing the villagers living in chozas bothered him, as most of them had left better housing in Los Pobres and Blanca Rosa. Yet, they greeted him cordially and seemed grateful for his efforts at the school.

He recalled that when he first took over Casa Vásquez, his excuse was, 'Somebody has to be the boss.' Sometimes, he wished it didn't have to be him.

Threats of further intervention by the United States was a sore point between him and Francisco, who saw it as a means to stop the war before the nation's resources were completely destroyed. It was easier to argue with Francisco by letter than face to face. He enlisted Anita to read the pages of his replies before they were sent, and to remove anything too harsh or likely to cause real hurt.

In their bedroom on long evenings after a customary stroll, distant noises from the village drifting in through the open balcony doors always filled him with a bittersweet sensation. He and Serafina used to watch dusk fall, as aromas of bougainvillea and orchids mingled with the pungency of decaying scraps thrown out by neighbors, while the soft air carried faint shouts of children playing in the next street.

Here, he smelled new grass, many flowering vines in the patios, and, occasionally, the heavy scents from corrals, if the breeze was from the north. Villagers stayed up later than his household, lamps glowing softly through the fringe of trees, tunes from guitars playing corridos of the revolution. Despite everything he believed, and all he could do, he felt himself apart from them.

"Are we fooling ourselves, to think wars or laws of governments can ever make life the same for everyone?"

Anita laid aside her hairbrush and joined him on the bed. Leaning against pillows cushioning the headboard, they watched lights and shadows flicker on the walls. "I don't know, Ramoncito. Look how hard it is to make life the same for our sons."

Our. . . separate sons? Or was Domingo becoming one of them? He didn't dare ask.

Occasional thoughts of Serafina, even stray ones like remembering what it was like to sit on her little porch in the evenings, gave him a sense of betraying Anita's love. He held her close. "Mi vida, te amo. I thank Dios every moment for you."

Battlefields formerly taken were re-fought. Encarnación, Aguascalientes, Zacatecas, San Luis Potosí, León, Celaya, Querétero, San Juan del Río, Tula, Pachuca. First the Obregonistas were winning, then Fierro, who guarded the rear of his chief, Villa, retreating into Chihuahua.

As the Dorados of the North fled, Obregón's forces flowed in behind them, reoccupying cities and towns. Rumors said Villa's once-trusted segundo Urbina had stolen funds meant for munitions, and was at his hacienda in Durango.

"That is getting close," Ramón muttered, when he heard. "I'll wire Joaquín in La Puerta del Sol and find out how things stand there. If the fighting comes our way, it would be a good place for you to go with the boys until the baby is born." He saw her shiver at the thought of living in Serafina's house, which rightfully belonged to Domingo.

Wording the telegram proved difficult, but he finally rode to the rebel headquarters and sent one which said simply

> Am glad to find you.
> Send news. If unsafe,
> welcome here.

He waited around in town, hoping for a swift answer. Just before he stepped into his stirrup for the return ride, a niño ran out of the telegraph office with a paper. "Para usted, señor." He paid a few centavos for it, and read

> Safe here. Married. How is Paz?

Torn between answering at once or getting to his new way-station before dark, he hurried back and dashed off a message.

Paz in Hermosillo in January.
Anita with me. Letter follows.

Then he was faced with writing. At his desk, brooding beneath the lamplight while Luis went over the accounts, he thought up several fine schemes, from putting in his own telegraph line—an extravagance that might fall prey to wild animals or bandits—to dreaming of having a telephone such as the one Francisco had told them about. "I like it here," he said, and Luis looked up in anticipation of what would follow. "But it's damned isolated."

"You are worried about Anita?"

"Not so much as before. But she might be safer in La Puerta del Sol."

"Where Joaquín is."

"Yes. Serafina had a house there."

He pondered the telegram. Married. Long enough to have a child? He counted back through the months, and discovered it had been well over a year since he and Joaquín parted. Until Pablo came, he had not known for certain whether the boy's wound had killed him, or not.

"So much has happened." He thought of those evenings in Los Pobres when they sat in the tiny cocina after a long day in the fields.

Luis regarded him, just as thoughtful, at last saying, "Those were happy times."

"How do you always know what is in my head?"

"Not always. Only, when you think of Los Pobres, there is this look which comes into your eyes."

"Those days are gone."

He gave the pen and stationery a little shove. So far he had written nothing. In the morning, his intentions might be clearer.

It would be nice, he thought, getting into bed gently so as not to wake Anita, *if I could see Joaquín again.*

Married, but still thinking of Paz.

Ramón found himself wondering what had happened to her. Mariano probably knew.

Sereno looped the leather cord around his neck to free his hands from carrying the flute, made sure no one important was watching, and skimmed over the low wall of the mirador that bordered the forest.

Safe with the cover of stones at his back, he crouched on the descending embankment, excitement gathering. To his left, just visible past the corner, he could see the thatch roofs of village chozas. Señoras in dooryards knelt over metates, grinding the day's corn. Here and there, large kettles hung over coals, with frijoles, meat, and chiles simmering inside for the family's supper. He could smell the brown juice and fragrant spices.

Earlier, straddling one of the school benches, he'd helped friends struggle to make words out of letters. Domingo as usual had grabbed the best seat, where the morning sun wouldn't strike the back of his head. Out here in cooler air, bright sunlight was welcome, but the shady forest beckoned.

He slid to the bottom of the hill and hurried into the widebranching trees among whose depths lurked spirits of the dead, wild animals, and sweet-voiced parroquetos that reminded him of Mérida.

After a short distance, the woods gave way to rolling upland, cottonwoods and willows at the base of the western hills. Between the forest and llano, there was about a hectárea covered in thorny underbrush. He picked through the barrier and came to a low cliff, where he sat with legs dangling a moment before dropping to the mouth of a cave.

His cave, his secret place. Where Domingo was only an irritating memory, and notes from the flute echoed eerily like music from another realm. Having no torch to light the way, he had never ventured inside, but sat on the ground outside and played songs he'd heard village jovens strum on their guitars at night.

Other times he remained atop the cliff and played tunes of his own, of his heart, of his longing. He did not know what he yearned for, only that the feeling was there inside him, and came out of the flute just as they had from the cane whistle, only fuller.

In the afternoon, when everyone was observing siesta and stormclouds were building up for a hard shower, he retraced his steps. From the moment his head appeared over the top of the mirador wall, he knew he was likely to be seen and questioned about where he had been. Finding no face at the open windows, no one on this side of the house, he was over the wall in an instant and racing for the shelter of the porch.

Crawling into the empty hammock, he stretched out, trying to relax, but his heart thrummed. Undiscovered, again. Soundless, his mouth said, *Gatito*.

Now, in other mouths, gatito meant Bravo, not him—though the puma kit was not so little anymore. The meat Domingo fed it daily had taken away its gauntness and made the fur shiny and thick. The lost look in its eyes had changed to alert expectation.

Sereno was sorry the litter mate was dead, half eaten by scavengers. He missed having a furry creature to love, to teach to love him. Viento remained somewhat wary, unattached to him. Papá said it was because he didn't spend enough time with the colt.

"Mijo."

He hadn't heard anyone approach. He sat up, unsurprised that his father wasn't napping. "¿Sí, Papá?"

"Come with me. Your mother and I have something to tell you."

Chapter Eight

The way the words were spoken and the expression on his father's face put a cold sensation in Sereno's chest. Domingo was already there, sprawled in the stuffed chair. A glance assured him the older boy was as curious as he, but trying to cover the fact by showing interest in a book picked up from a nearby table.

Mamá sat on the edge of the big bed, and held out an arm inviting him to join her. *Better*, he thought, wanting to snuggle but feeling too old and proud to do that in front of his medio hermano.

Papá hunkered the way he did when laying wood on a campfire, and said, "There is wonderful news, and I hope you both will be as happy about it as we are." He took Mamá's hand and she smiled at him.

"What?" Sereno asked, prepared to be happy.

Mamá hugged him and then held him away. "There is going to be a baby. Señor Estrada says probably the middle of October."

Confusion flooded him. He knew the response he was supposed to make, the way he was supposed to feel, the things he was expected to say. Glancing at Domingo, he saw his own emotion reflected on his half-brother's face: someone else to divide their father's love. Only, for him, Mamá's love would now be divided as well. Overcoming the desolation this news had brought, he said, "If it is a niña, let us name her Violeta."

Mamá looked pleased, if a bit surprised. "It's a lovely name, mijo. Why that?"

"Because they are so pretty when they bloom." Also, it was the first thing which popped into his head that he could say aloud, and beat out Domingo in showing his parents how delighted he was with their announcement.

When Papá stood up, Domingo embraced him. "Good going, viejo." Mamá heard, and the blush on her cheeks made her look young and confused. Taking the jest with good grace, Papá laughed—embarrassed but seeming pleased—and slapped him on the back, saying, "Watch your bold tongue, muchacho!"

The exchange shocked Sereno. He scarcely knew what Domingo meant, but was sure he himself would never have said anything that hinted at the mystery which occurred behind their closed door.

The months which separated Domingo and him in age suddenly widened into an immeasurable gulf.

Most of Anita's dreams over the next few months were pleasant, recalled happily and cherished because in them she and Ramón were living in Los Pobres, her days absorbed by few chores that kept the house clean and stomachs fed, and visits with friends. In these dreams, she carried Sereno in her body, anticipating the day when she could hold him. Luis helped with the farm work, and nothing marred life on the rocky hillside.

Others, dark with fear and violence, gripped her in their power. They came seldom but lingered for days afterward, so the sudden slam of a door by the wind made her jerk and begin to tremble. Whenever she woke and sat up damp and uncertain, pulse thudding, she was always amazed that Ramón still slept, unaware.

Jarred to consciousness by dread, she groped in the darkness of her mind for images that caused this feeling of suffocation, of disaster—and found Ramón sitting up, too, his words harsh as he cried, "¡Diablos! I told him—" He was out of bed, scuffling into his trousers, before she realized the source of his anger.

Close—on the balcony, or in the house—came the yowl of el león de moñtana, piercing, wild, unexpected. Flashes of memories raced through her, chaotic, terrible. The moments just before she shot Fernando, when he challenged, 'You cannot hurt me. I drank the blood of el gran gato. I took his spirit. You cannot harm a spirit.' Those long night hours when she sat with Ramón while he held his dead caballito's mutilated head in his arms. The look on his face when she told him, *I had to shoot Fernando. He killed Mío.*

And the unspoken part: *He would have killed me.*

Now, she listened to Ramón's barely-controlled shouting as he upbraided Domingo for having the puma in his room. Their glass door stood open, letting in the chill night air, and she shivered as she heard them come outside on the other end of the balcony, the gato still making low-throated objections, Ramón promising, "You have not heard the end of this."

His bare feet made no sound as he came back inside, but she could see his silhouette against the moonlit sky beyond and heard the swish of trousers as he undressed. He took her in his arms. "I'm sorry. I never meant for that damned cat to be here this long—"

"It's all right," she said, smoothing the hair over his ear. "I had forgotten it was even here. He's been good about keeping it penned up."

"That's what I thought, but the truth came out. It's been sleeping beside his bed since the beginning. Only now it starts to feel the need of freedom."

"Easy to understand."

"¡Sí, ya lo sé! Yet you will be less understanding when you see what it did to the curtain over that door."

"Oh! My brocade? ¡Qué triste! You should be the one upset, as it cost a fortune."

"Domingo shall pay for it."

"Don't be harsh with him."

"Harsh? It's a good thing I didn't take my quirt out with me. You must know what that sound does to me."

She hugged him tight. "I know," she whispered.

Putting the young puma in its pen didn't prevent it from calling at intervals until dawn. Several times Ramón threatened to take his pistol and stop the racket, and tossed restlessly until the covers were all askew. After awhile the situation began to seem humorous but she suspected that if she laughed, his pride would be damaged and he actually would shoot Domingo's pet. Such an ending was certain to make things worse.

"We might as well get up," she said, turning onto one elbow and reaching for her robe.

But as soon as she stood on the woven rug, one arm sleeved, a warm wetness changed her mind. Dismayed, she said, "On second thought, maybe you should wake señor Estrada."

In the full moonlight she saw Ramón's panicked look and that did make her laugh.

"¡Ah, Dios mío, it can't be!" He jerked on clothing. "It's too soon. Isn't it? You said October—"

"In a few days it will be October. Don't worry, querido. I have not had any hard pains yet."

He fled, bootsteps racing down the hall toward Estrada's room.

She did worry, former doubts resurfacing and multiplying as she realized how soon it was, and that at best this was likely to be a long, difficult labor.

Estrada's presence, only minutes later, helped calm her. In the weeks since he joined the household, he had become a valued friend. When Ramón was overseeing the hacienda, or had gone into Culiacán for mail or news, it was Estrada who walked the gravel paths with her, whose quiet conversation about his boyhood in Nuevo León and over the border in

Texas, where his father's people lived, always made her forget there was a war, or that inevitably the day would come when the child had to be born.

She wanted this baby with a fierce longing, for it would complete the mending of her life's fabric with Ramón's; but lurking in her secret thoughts was the fear that it would not be perfect, or might be born dead, or die; or that she would die giving birth, leaving him with three children to bring up without her.

Two young women arrived carrying cloths, basins, kettles, and a shuck mattress so the bed would not be soiled. The mestizas were studying under Estrada with the intention of becoming assistants in the hospital he planned to build for Indios somewhere in a more southern place.

For a while nothing happened. Estrada read aloud from a newspaper, and Ramón was permitted to sit beside her and hold her hand. The boys came in for a brief visit before siesta. Broth, hot and bland, was brought and she managed to keep it down.

The afternoon dragged, Ramón fondling her hand while Estrada read aloud from one of their leatherbound books. When her pains advanced enough that she was unable to hold in the cries, Ramón started sweating and pacing, but returned to clasp her hand and rub her back. "You don't really want to stay, do you," she gasped, and he answered, "No, but if you want me to—"

She shook her head. "Better if you don't." He gave her a few kisses, smoothed her damp hair, squeezed her hand, kissed her again, and departed. She fell back on her pillow with a little laugh. "Now maybe I can relax."

Estrada grinned. "He did seem to be suffering."

"Men are so odd—" she endured a clenching that drew her over, and when it eased, finished, "they can fight wars, but can't stand watching a baby get born."

"The responsibility for wars is never so personal as that of creating a child."

"I nev— never thought—of that."

"I have," Estrada said.

Hovering in the hallway, waiting for Anita to have her baby, Domingo was glad Jefe was too distracted to follow up on his threat to be rid of the gatito.

When a criada announced breakfast, Domingo went and ate, but did so alone.

By the time for the next meal, Sereno's wide eyes had developed hollows beneath them which made him look like a little fantasma, haunting the upstairs in wistful silence. Ramón had put on a pair of soft leather shoes so his pacing wouldn't be noticed inside the room. "It's taking too long," he kept saying under his breath, as if he were not aware of speaking the thought which tormented him. Unaware, too, that his younger son was starving.

"Here," Domingo said, shoving a warm tamal into Sereno's sweaty hand. "Eat before you faint."

"I'm not going to faint. Señoritas faint." But he ate the tamal.

It was mid-afternoon when sounds from behind the door became alarming, yells that would have rivaled anything heard on the battlefield, had they not been muffled in a cloth. He tried to remember when Teo was born, but the only thing he recalled was tiptoeing to peer into the bundle Mamá held, and saying, "¡Qué feo!" How ugly. She forgave him, of course—he was only five, and the baby was ugly, though Teo might someday become rather handsome...if he didn't start looking like Pablo.

He felt shame. Pablo wasn't a bad-looking man, and had always treated him well. Only sad, with a hard glint in his eyes which hadn't been there in Monterrey. Yet, definitely not as handsome as Jefe.

He closely observed his father in the dim hallway. Women were attracted to him. Recalling doña Gloria in Hermosillo, he suspected there'd been intimacy between them, like Luis and the chica at Dos Corazones. Such thoughts disturbed him and he shook them off, saying, "I'm going to water the colts. Give a shout if anything happens."

Sereno nodded briefly. Jefe, leaning his forehead on the door, didn't respond.

Bravito prowled the worn path inside his pen, emitting annoyed *yeowrrrs* and reaching one front paw and then the other beneath the bottom pole. It wouldn't be long before he either leaped the thing, or dug a hole large enough to slip his lithe buff-colored body through. Then, little goats, beware. Then, Domingo, guard your ass, for Jefe will tear it apart.

Not a comforting thought. He opened the gate and latched himself inside, taking the weight of the puma on his chest as it greeted him with forepaws around his neck and a swipe of the moist tongue across his face. "¡Abajo! Down!" He made a slashing motion with his arm, and the kit sat on its haunches like an intelligent dog waiting for its supper.

He had fastened a short piece of rawhide around its neck, to assure having control on those trips before dawn when he returned Bravo to the pen after a night beside his bed. Until last night, everything had gone smoothly.

"Why did you have to ruin things?" Hugging the sleek body, he received another lick. "I thought you liked staying with me."

"Reerrrrrr," Bravito said, and tried to get into his lap the way he had only a few months earlier.

"You're too big for that. Settle for a good scratch behind your ears." Under my chin, too, said the tilt of Bravito's head. The golden eyes closed in enjoyment as Domingo complied.

When he had raided the storehouse for a shank with enough meat for a meal, he left his pet ripping at the flesh and went to a barn for grain. At the feeding station, the family mounts crowded and nuzzled, at last fixing on the portions he poured out for them. On grass all day instead of following an army, they required minimal amounts of corn. In the next lot, Gregorio and Luis were watering the second string of saddle horses; farther on, Martín and Lobo tended those belonging to vaqueros. "Hombre," he called. "When are we going to bring in more colts?"

Martín called back, "When Ramón decides."

"He's going to be too busy to think about caballos." He went to lean on the corral, and the men gathered to talk. "Anita is having her baby."

They already knew, Luis having told the news early this morning. "It seems to be taking a long time," Lobo ventured, foreboding in his tone.

"Nine hours," he said. "So far."

"A curandera might help her."

Gregorio's elbow punched the boy in the chest, and Lobo's frown answered. Martín said, "I am surprised she didn't want a woman. Who is this Señor Estrada, anyway?

We know only that he comes from Monterrey, and has the look of a gachupín."

For the first time, he was aware of how their guest appeared to hombres del campo, rebeldes norteños whose lives embraced war, matters of cattle and horses, fields, work done with the hands or from a saddle.

"He was the médico who delivered me." In the coming darkness, he sensed glances being exchanged. Estrada had patched up many wounds resulting from accident or quarrel; but he lived in the casa grande. "Pues, I'd better go back."

As he returned to the patio, he could hear his gatito muttering in discontent. Maybe he would take a bedroll out to the lot, spend the nights there.

Rounding a corner, he was knocked breathless and flung out his arms to regain balance.

Sereno bounced off him, wild-eyed. "It's here! I heard it cry! ¡Vámonos, anda!" He raced back up the stairs, Domingo close behind. But when they reached the shadowy hallway, the door was closed, and Ramón had disappeared.

Clutching each other's arms, they crept forward, and he laid his ear against the panel. Muffled voices, no cries. Sereno hissed, "¿Que está pasando?" and he motioned for silence, but caught nothing he could relate. Pushing him aside, Sereno strained to hear, and fell into his father's arms when the door suddenly opened.

Jefe came out, closing it. "Both are alive, and will be fine. You can see the baby as soon as it finishes eating."

He had a sudden picture of a baby attacking a steer shank as Bravito had done, and gave a nervous laugh.

"¿Niña o niño?" Sereno demanded, clinging to his father's shirt front.

"¡Niña!" Jefe cried. "Ana Juana Violeta Cordero La Barca, gracias a Dios." Then he seemed to go dizzy and felt along the wall until he found a bench.

Domingo punched his little brother lightly on the shoulder blade. "Señoritas faint."

"He's not fainting, are you, Papá. He's praying." Sereno peered into Jefe's face. "Aren't you, Papá?"

"Sí," Jefe said, raising his head. "Dios es gran."

Jefe agreed not to shoot Bravito on two conditions: that it stop disturbing their sleep, and if it escaped and killed even one chicken, Domingo himself would do the job.

Keeping the kit quiet was a puzzle until he hit upon the idea of taking it hunting. Their first outings were less than adventurous and, aside from providing new smells and flushing out a few quail, did little toward making Bravo independent. The puma didn't seem to know how to kill anything bigger than a field mouse.

His father's gratitude bore fruit in the foundation of a family chapel among the gardens and walkways between the casa and the south outer wall. Anita had desired it after seeing the one don Diego built at Dos Corazones for Tereza's mother. At the same time, Jefe conceded to the villagers' wish for a small church of their own.

"Who is going to be the priest?" Luis wanted to know at breakfast one morning. "The insurrectos have killed them all, or sent them into hiding."

"Listen to yourself," Jefe said. "Not so long ago, you were an insurrecto."

"Only because I had no choice, and I never harmed a priest."

"Neither did I."

"Yo sé," Luis nodded. "But it does not answer the question of where you will find someone."

"Who says we need a priest?" Jefe asked.

Seeing tension build, Domingo changed the subject. "Why not invite Mariano for Navidad?" he suggested, half expecting all the eyes to focus on him and see his real motive. "His hospitality last year deserves a return."

Anita cast him a grateful smile. "That's a wonderful idea. Only, travel might be dangerous, and they are still in mourning for Diego."

"If Villa is busy fighting in Chihuahua, what's to prevent a nice visit?"

Jefe pushed away a half-eaten flan, and Sereno claimed it. "Have you forgotten?"

Everyone glanced at each other, eyebrows asking for an explanation. Domingo searched his brain. "What?"

"Well, hell, if you don't remember, then maybe it is safe to have them here."

Like a small burst of light he thought of the burial, in the campo santo in the clearing, a quarter hour from here. "¡Ay! But no one would tell—"

"Tell who what?" Sereno asked, licking his spoon. Anita's eyes narrowed as she looked across the table at Ramón. "Tell—what?"

"How her father died," Jefe said, with a warning glance at him.

"How did he die?" Sereno wanted to know, kneeling in his chair.

"A river fell on him." He tipped the chair just enough to make the boy shriek.

"Domingo!" Anita gasped. "¡Qué insensitivo!"

"I'm sorry," he said at once, with sincerity. "Besides, it fell on me, too."

"You didn't tell us that." Sereno gazed at him. "How did it feel?"

He opened his mouth for another quick retort, but memory brought such a tangle of emotions that nothing came out. Jefe rescued him. Again.

"You don't want to know. I think, when the weather warms enough, you both must be taught how to swim."

Sereno looked pleased at the prospect, criadas who'd been waiting beyond the doorway appeared, ready to collect the used tableware, and the secret of don Diego's grave lay dormant.

Domingo constantly thought of Tereza, who answered Anita's letter with the customary polite phrases, accepting the invitation to visit. He was consumed with anxiety over what they might talk about. It kept him from sleep, so he was undisturbed by the muffled wails of his tiny sister, waking hungry. Anita followed Estrada's advice on nursing the baby herself rather than engage a suitable villager, thereby causing gossip among those women that circulated all the way up to the big house.

Estrada's handsome features, on top of his unChristian ways, made him doubly dangerous, doubly appealing; and Domingo once overheard two criadas discussing what they would like to do with the médico, if only he were not a pagan who bewitched gente bien like the doña Anita into behaving like a campesina.

Four days before Navidad, Bravo made his first kill. Fortunately, it was a rabbit and not one of the clumsy cabras awaiting the arrival of their kids.

He'd chosen the trail the mustangers traveled last year, rough country that offered game. Ramón let him carry a carbine in case he saw deer. He doubted he could shoot one even if the scent of a puma didn't send them all running before he came in range. It was the first time Jefe trusted him with a weapon, and he suspected it was in hopes that he might accidentally dispose of the kit.

He would have preferred wearing a belt gun, as did the other men. When he returned to the casa, he decided, he would ask Jefe for a pistol.

They didn't continue all the way to the earthen dam, though at the place where the new river was carving a channel among rocks and trees, he dismounted to walk about.

Bravo returned, jumping up and mouthing his arm. "Go away," he said. "You stink of blood, and will soil my coat." Pushed aside, the gatito looked hurt and puzzled.

Kneeling, he laid his arms around its neck. The fur on top of its head was as soft as a house cat's and the pleased noises deep in the furry throat sounded like a purr.

Half blinded by tears, for causing the gato sadness and for the loss of those innocent days in Monterrey, he was startled to see riders only a stone's throw from him, sitting on their horses, rifles at rest with barrels pointing skyward but fingers on the triggers.

"Hola," called one of them. Half a dozen. Travel-stained, bandoleers draped over their shoulders. Intruders, on Los Nuestros land.

He stood up, gauging the distance to his horse. "Hola." His carbine in its scabbard was on the other side. Bravo, gazing at the men, gave a yowl of disapproval which brought their rifles level. He grabbed the rawhide collar to restrain his pet. "No matalo, por favor." Please don't kill it.

The riders repeated his entreaty with amusement. The man who had greeted him said, "Noooo, joven. We kill Obregonistas. ¿Está usted un Obregonista?" They laughed. The leader dismounted and came toward him. "¿Dónde vives, muchacho?"

He made a vague gesture. "Mucho lejos." Very far. In fact, it was less than three hours to the lower gate. That uncharted, unguarded north border, he realized. They came through there. *Jefe will kick himself.*

"I am camping. Teaching my gato to hunt. His mother was killed."

A muttered exchange ran among the mounted men. The leader, wearing a coat with captain's stripes, said, "You're dressed like un hijo del hacendado, or some other kind of rico." He flicked Domingo's leather coat with the tassel of a riding crop. "I asked, where you live."

"In Cosalá," he blurted, thankful that he was familiar enough with that village to lie convincingly.

This close, he could see neglected teeth, and smell tequila as the heavyset capitán breathed through a slack mouth. Bloodshot eyes searched his face. "You are a pretty boy," the man said. "Who is your papá? I know people in Cosalá."

"He was killed fighting at Zacatecas with Villa. He sent me to friends."

"And, who are these friends?"

Racking his memory, he found he couldn't remember the family who had sheltered him and Paz so many months ago. "Señor Pedro Hernández," he said, grabbing a name out of the air.

"¡Ay! Pedro." The captain glanced over his shoulder. "He says he lives with you. Did you know that?"

The men laughed. Their horses were restless, having a gato so near, and the rawhide collar cut into his hand. For a moment he considered shouting out the truth and defying them to ravage a well-armed hacienda where half the men were ex-rebels. But how many more soldados lay back in the rugged hills? He did know Ramón wouldn't welcome visitors such as these. "Pues, there can be more than one Pedro Hernández."

"But not both in Cosalá, I think."

"Did I say Cosalá? I meant, Chacala. I have not lived there long—"

"You do not live there." The half-joking manner turned cold. "You're a stranger in this part of the Sierra. I have great curiosity how you came to be here, and what you are hiding. Why are you afraid? You have this gato grande to protect you."

"I'm not afraid of a bunch of damned Villistas," he said, "and I'm getting weary of your insults."

More laughter. Bravito let out a yowl. The horses pranced. The man didn't come any closer, but when he regained his breath, he said, "Villistas— Pues, sí, claro. We have been in Sonora, killing los soldados de Señor Calles, but the fight there has become indiferente. We decided to find a better enemy."

"Then, doubtless you are in a hurry to get to some other place, so I shall not keep you." He began dragging Bravo to the reata on his saddle. As he rode away, Bravito resisting and growling, they watched but didn't follow.

When he had put several hills behind him, he made a sharp turn toward home, keeping a wary eye on every arroyo or bosque where a dozen riders might conceal themselves. His heart slowly returned to its normal rhythm, but his brain raced, worrying over where they would end up and what might happen when they did.

Telling Jefe of the encounter, in private to keep from alarming the household, he finished, "As soon as I was out of sight I began covering my trail, so I don't think they could track me."

"Bueno." Jefe laid an arm on his shoulder. "Sharp of you, to do that. Yet, don't be surprised if we're raided." He gave a wry grin. "It's not exactly easy to hide a place this size. We must be ready to defend it."

Men were sent to guard the borders, especially the rivers on the trail to the earthen dam. "These patrols, and outposts at the estancias, will alert us." The majority of the fighting force, however, remained on home ground, and the women detailed to issue ammunition from the storehouse practiced running from doorway to doorway with bags weighing down each hand. School continued as usual, though Anita now used her time caring for Violeta.

When the day came to ride to Culiacán to meet Mariano and Tereza, he secured his gato in its pen and saddled Valiente. He had not been granted a pistol, but felt some security in settling the carbine in its boot. Ramón, Gregorio,

Silvestre, and Lobo made up the rest of the escort. They would hire a carriage in town, as the trip on horseback was too difficult for a niña of Tereza's class, and she was bound to have a dueña along to guard her honor. He wondered what had become of Paz. Would Mariano know—or care?

The train from the north didn't arrive until after midnight; so, when Tereza and her Tía Lola were safe in a hotel room with a tray of chocolate and dulces to hold them until morning, the men visited a cantina.

At the table with noisy rebels swapping news, Domingo sneaked drinks from Sylvestre's whiskey glass. It tasted vile, but after enough of it he started feeling good. From the glimpse he'd had of Tereza behind mourning veils, and her soft greeting, "Hola, Domingo," he could tell she was still brokenhearted.

Crawling into bed between his father and Luis, he tried to come up with a reasonable excuse to ride in the carriage with her tomorrow, but before he could do so he fell asleep.

Morning brought the din of a hundred hombres crashing about, finding boots and guns and making jokes, and sunlight stabbed all the way through his eyes and into the back of his head. "Ay, madre mía," he groaned. "Qué un duele en la cabeza."

Ramón's attention snapped to him. "¿Qué te pasó?"

He struggled to an upright position, hoping for a miracle. When he managed to open his eyes, however, there was Jefe waiting for an explanation. Carefully he shrugged. "I guess it's only the excitement of the fiesta."

"You have no business drinking," Ramón said. "And you know it. What will Tereza think of you?"

"I didn't drink that much. Un poco, muy poco."

He dressed in clean clothes and followed the others into the dining room, where, under the eye of the old señora, Tereza joined them. Seated across from her, he felt that everyone could see past the washed face and combed hair to his throbbing temples.

With food and fruit juice in his stomach, he realized she'd lifted her veil in order to eat, and in spite of great sadness and the passage of ten months, she was still Tereza, and more beautiful than ever.

Suddenly conversation ceased and he felt attention turn to him. Panicky, he wondered what had been said while he dreamed. Then Mariano spoke. "I know how much you value truth, Ramón. I'm glad you and Domingo can cherish each other openly now."

Tereza was staring at him, but he couldn't read anything on her face. "How strange," she said softly, "not to know your papá until you are grown."

His cheeks flushed hot. Reaching for his glass, he just missed tipping it over. Talk turned to politics, his ears cooled, his pulse slowed, and after a few minutes he was able to smile. She smiled back. As they left the dining room for the carriage waiting outside, he fell in step beside her. "How is the filly?"

"Wild. She needs someone to train her. Our best jinetes went with your father."

"If I may, I shall return to Dos Corazones when you go, and do that job for you."

"You would be welcome."

Then he had to untie his mount and ride ahead of the coche until noon. The day was cool and though they were making fast time on a dry road, the journey had never seemed longer. They were well onto Los Nuestros property when Ramón reined them in to rest and have a picnic at a shady spring.

Ignoring the teasing glances cast his way, he spread his sarape beside Tereza, reveling in her startlingly blue Spanish eyes, fair clear skin and well-kept teeth, and long curly black hair which she had not yet begun to pin up.

He had no appetite for his food, which required care to keep from dropping on his shirt, so rather than eat—and mindful of Tía Lola listening to everything he said—he told her about Violeta, and Bravo, and Valiente. She came out of her sadness to talk about the books she had read and the lessons in painting that her brother had given her for her saint's day.

As he assisted her back into the coche, her parting words were, "You haven't told me— How is Sereno?"

"As spoiled as ever," was all he had time to say.

At the casa there was a confusion of greetings and Tereza went off with Anita to see the baby. Weary, yet energized by having her under the same roof, he flung himself down on a cushioned wicker settee in the main patio and recalled everything they had said to each other.

She seemed older than before, quick and intelligent. The black mourning garb gave her a sweet lost air that haunted him. He looked forward to moments when they might talk without her tía present. He wanted to show her Bravo and discuss his next visit—had she not invited him, just like that?—and tell her his plans for taming the filly. He wanted to make sure she understood that he had been the one to choose it, that it was his gift to her.

"The part about Villa standing by while Fierro killed Urbina might be just rumor," Mariano told them at cena. "But it is a fact that Fierro the Butcher himself is dead, and I have a true report that the traitor Orozco was killed in September by Texas Rangers from the United States."

Ramón had mixed feelings about that. "I was sorry when he deserted Madero for Huerta, but if anyone had a right to kill him it wasn't the big dogs of the north. If they are going to intervene, dammit, why don't they cross the Río Bravo and fight."

"One day they will," Estrada predicted. "They are just waiting for all of our big dogs to kill each other first, so it will be easier."

Everyone laughed, but the sound had an uneasy quality.

The president of the United States had given official recognition to Carranza, a blow to Villista ambitions; the battles with Calles' troops at Agua Prieta, following the winter crossing of Villa's men into Sonora by way of El Púlpito, in the Sierra Madre, had left the Lion of the North incapable of sustaining the kind of drive needed for victories. No wonder men were deserting Pancho.

Mariano related the arrival of the bandit general and his army in Hermosillo, and their attempt to take that capital. "He fought General Diéguez' troops at Alamito before attacking the city. For more than a day and night they exchanged fire, and then Villa had to withdraw in complete defeat."

Normally, Sereno left the table when his mother did, but tonight he dawdled over a cup of chocolate, clearly hoping to remain while the men enjoyed more graphic conversation, coffee, and cigarettes; as Domingo had done since the night Pablo tried to take him away. Watching the older boy's gaze follow Tereza, Ramón realized how fast this son was growing up. May would mark his birthday.

When I was his age, he thought, *I had no awareness of girls.* María had changed that, a year later.

"Do you ever see Mano?" he asked Mariano.

His cuate poured another shot of whiskey before answering. "When we learned Villistas were coming our way, he joined us and helped defend the telegraph. There was a slight wound—in the leg, I think."

So the revolution had finally come to Mano in a way he couldn't ignore. With pride and regret, he said, "He will get himself killed at the last minute, and for nothing."

"Last minute?" Estrada scoffed. "If you think this thing is nearly over, amigo, you are mistaken."

"Obregón has Villa on the run." Luis glanced from one to the other, tentatively. "And in the north Lázaro Cárdenas has whipped Maytorena's ass at last."

"Do you realize," he asked, "that everyone on both sides believes in the same reform, yet the fight goes on. All because Carranza refuses to give up his claim on the government."

"Well, your General Obregón is his right arm." Mariano's smile removed any sting.

Domingo said, "And who is General Obregón's right arm? He needs a new one."

Their laughter was interrupted by singing from the main patio, where villagers had gathered for the posada. Ramón watched while others trickled out to take part in the distribution of useful gifts and special foods, and was puzzled when Domingo remained behind.

"Jefe."

"¿Sí?"

"Have you asked Mariano about Paz?"

"No. Have you?"

Domingo shook his head. "Where do you think she is? Tereza hasn't mentioned her, either."

"I wouldn't worry about her. Paz can take care of herself." He pushed back his chair and they walked toward the patio together, his arm loosely over the boy's shoulders.

After adoration of the Niño ended, about half an hour before midnight, Sereno chose to go with the villagers for the breaking of their piñata.

Tereza begged, "Tía, you must come. I wish to join the festivity, but doña Anita needs her sleep."

"And you think I do not?" her duena complained.

If the old lady didn't accompany her charge to the fiesta, Tereza would have no choice but to retire to their room. Ramón glanced about for one of Estrada's assistants, but all acceptable women had already left the house. "Sereno will take care of her," he said. "He's trustworthy, and like a brother."

Tía Lola gladly relinquished the hold she had taken of Tereza's arm, and the girl ran to catch up to him. Domingo followed as if reluctant or in deep thought.

Ramón had barely gotten settled into bed, after checking Violeta in her cradle, when shrieks and gunfire jerked him onto the cold floor and into his clothing. Anita tumbled out on the other side and picked up the baby in its blanket. "Is it Villistas?"

Buckling on his belt gun, he said, "Keep away from the windows."

In the courtyard amid scurrying people and flickering torch light, he saw Domingo kneeling, arms around Bravo and having difficulty holding the struggling young puma. Bravo screamed at being restrained and in apparent fury at the uproar his presence had caused. "¡Cállate!" the boy shouted. "You frighten him. Get away! Stop shooting!"

Martín and Gregorio forcibly steered armed cavalry men away from the house, while others moved the noisy children and women downslope toward their homes.

As soon as he could be heard, Ramón asked, "What the hell happened?"

Luis answered. "Bravo leaped over the wall of his pen, and scared everyone."

"When he's calm," Domingo said, voice shaking, "I'll put him in the little storehouse with the tools. He cannot escape that."

Ramón hadn't realized how big the gato had gotten in the last couple of months. If it really wanted to, he thought, it could easily get away from Domingo. The wild yowls set his teeth on edge. "You can't keep him in the little storehouse forever."

"Only at night, Jefe. When I take him hunting, he's all right."

"And when you're too busy to do that—what? He finds other diversions."

Domingo fixed his grip in the rawhide collar and they set off for the row of adobes which served the community as shops and warehouses.

He and Luis stood alone. Bravito's grumblings faded into distant silence, while in the village happy cries came from the plaza where the piñata was being pummeled by children.

"At least it was not Villistas," Luis said, starting back to the house.

Worse, he thought. If he had never allowed that gato to be brought here, he could have avoided having to do what he must do in the morning.

Chapter Nine

Domingo's cheeks burned when his father said, "What if he had attacked a child and killed it? All who live here are my responsibility. I cannot let you keep Bravo. Either he goes back to the sierras and stays, or he is shot."

Controlling anger and embarrassment, as they were at breakfast and Tereza witnessed the reprimand, he said, "I will leave within the hour."

Anita entered the comedor in time to hear. "Querido, can't this wait until our guests have ended their visit?"

Jefe was unyielding. "It should've been done months ago, and must be done before we live to regret delaying."

"I shall ride with you," Sereno offered, making him feel even more shame.

"No, you won't," Anita said firmly. "There are plenty of hombres who can go."

Tereza looked at Jefe. "How long will this take?"

"A few days." Domingo answered, wondering how he would manage to make Bravo stay in the mountains.

"A few weeks, more likely," Jefe amended. "The hunting range of a gato grande is wide. If you're thinking of leaving him at the estancia where we found him, I'd suggest more thought."

Two weeks from now Mariano would be on his way back to his hacienda—with Tereza. In desperation, he signaled her to wait when the women left for the sala and a morning's gossip.

"Is it possible you might remain here with your tía, after your brother goes home?"

She seemed startled, but pleased, and a smile encouraged him as she thought over the idea. "Perhaps. I can try."

Just then Lobo and Silvestre, who had been into Culiacán for the mail, brought three envelopes. One was for Jefe, from his mother. Another went to Sereno. Lobo handed the last to him.

"From Teo," he said in mild surprise, and Sereno glanced up, bright with joy. "Mine, also."

They sat on the stone steps to read what news each letter might contain. After polite greetings, Teo had written:

> Our hous has holes from sheling
> and thiefs carryed away almost everything.
> Papá's shop was all burnt so we took
> a train to Eagle Pass. That is in the
> United States. It is where Tía Marta
> and Dolores went on the train that night.
> Remember? Ther is much fiting along
> the Río Grande. Some times I fear
> we shall be killed but Gracias a Dios
> we found loved ones saf and soon
> shall return to Monterrey.
> We are all well and hav enof to eat.

163

> I saw El Primero Jefe Venustiano
> Carranza again and he looked just
> the sam. I miss you. Tell Jefe y Luis
> y Gregorio y doña Anita y Martín
> that I miss them to.
> Adiós de tú hermano quién ama mucho.

Domingo wavered between laughter and tears, as the pages brought his little brother so vividly to his mind's eye. Looking up, he saw Sereno sharing his message with Tereza. Their arms were around each other.

Comparing the letters, he found the only difference was the way Teo had signed them, using 'su cuate' for him, and 'tu hermano' on Sereno's copy. "Who is Dolores?" Tereza asked, and he answered, "Our—Teo's cousin. His father is her uncle."

It occurred to him that the girl he had always thought to be a relative actually was unconnected to him except in memory, and the house at the corner of Calle de las Flores y Matamoros did not and never would belong to him. It was strange to remember peaceful years spent there, never doubting that he belonged.

Sereno went to show his letter to his mother. Tereza stood up. To stop her from following, Domingo said, "Don't go. We have not yet talked about the filly. What did you name her?"

"Estrellita. She has a tiny star of white on her neck."

"She must be trained without delay, if you are ever going to enjoy riding her."

Tereza stepped toward him. "Instead of my remaining here, why not come and, as you said, do the job yourself?"

"Two reasons."

Her eyebrows questioned, so he explained, "Named Mariano and Ramón."

Laughing, she said, "I can manage one. ¿Y tu?"

"As you see, I am out of favor just now."

"If I were a boy, I could ride into the mountains with you."

Her smile took away lingering embarrassment caused by Jefe's rebuke. "Would you like to do that?"

Before she could respond, Tía Lola appeared at the patio doors and urged her inside. Leaving, Tereza turned to say, out of the dueña's hearing, "If I'm not here when you get back—hasta luego, Domingo, y buen suerte."

It wasn't much, but as he packed rations and saddled his gelding, the sound of her voice saying his name, and the hope of spending time at Dos Corazones, somewhat eased the pain of having to part with Bravo.

Ramón came down to the corrals where he and Sylvestre and Lobo were readying their mounts, and handed Lobo a box of shells, which the guide stowed in his pack.

"There is plenty of ammunition." He gave Domingo a belt filled with cartridges and a well-made .44. "If you see any bandidos, make sure you can whip them before you start a fight."

"Be sure of it," he said stiffly.

His father watched as he untied the tether rope from a corral post and Bravo rose from his haunches like a docile cur. Fed earlier, he'd licked his fur clean and would have preferred dozing in the sun. Domingo had often remained in the pen, watching the gato and marveling at its similarities to his lost mother cat.

Conscious of the unaccustomed weight strapped to his thigh, he swung aboard Valiente and gathered the reins. "Hasta luego," he said.

Ramón put a hand on his bridle. "Vaya con Dios, mijo."

The look which passed between them softened his heart a bit. Jefe was sorry for making him do this, and had bestowed the long-desired pistol. "Gracias."

Then he and his riders turned toward the eastern hills.

In his parents' room, watching Violeta while Mamá showed Tereza's tía Lola some embroidery stitch, Sereno was annoyed that he had to look up at Tereza when they stood side by side. At Dos Corazones, working on the piñata last year, they had been eye-level to each other.

"How do you like the flute your papá gave you for El Día de Los Reyes?"

"I'm playing 'Valentina' now," he answered, debating whether to attempt the rebel tune and risk making a fool of himself.

"Can you play 'Llorona'?"

"Sí, it was one of the first I learned."

"Will you play it for me?"

"Of course." He tugged on the leather cord at his neck, pulling the instrument from its customary place dangling against his back. Tereza laughed as if delighted, and propped her chin in her palms in anticipation.

The song seemed to fascinate Violeta too, for she stopped fretting and stared at the ceiling, waving arms and legs in an energetic way and then relaxing, until she nodded off like a little old woman. "Mira," he whispered, nudging Tereza. "She sleeps."

"If you had played 'Valentina,' she would be crying."

"She doesn't cry often, only when hungry, or cold."

"You love her, don't you?"

"Very much. Her skin is so soft. Feel her head."

Tereza stroked the sleeping baby's head, where the down was too pale to be easily seen. "You are all so blond, and Anita's beautiful eyes are the strangest color. Are yours the same?" She peered into his face.

He peered back. "Are they?" He thought better of reminding her that Papá and Domingo were not blond. The less she thought about Domingo, the better.

"Sí—like amber, until the sky reflects, and then they are almost blue. Or is it green?"

"Did your mother have blue eyes, like yours?"

"Sí, I think so. Of course, I don't remember, as she died when I was tiny."

"When I was in El General's town house in Mérida, I thought my father was dead."

"That must have been terrible."

"Sí. But, I had Mamá."

While he was softly playing 'Llorona' for the fourth time, Mamá and Tía Lola came in from the balcony and Mamá said, "Mijo, run find Lupe to stay with Violeta, and we can show Tereza and her tía the gardens."

"Let me take her," he said, starting to gather up the baby. Mamá said, "It's too chilly outside."

Tereza reached for her woolen rebozo. "These mountains are different from where we live."

On the gravel paths, Mamá and the old woman lagged behind while he and Tereza raced among the intricacies of lanes, walls, and corners. Ancient trees and vines established by former owners provided screens and hiding places among stands of evergreens and marble statues of saints. Bought, like most furnishings in the house and the farm and forge implements, cheaply from thieves who had raided the grand homes in Culiacán for the finery left behind by ricos fleeing the war.

Stopping outside the chapel, they leaned against its rock walls to catch their breath and laughed from the joy of having recaptured the easy friendship formed at Los Dos. "Play another," she challenged.

He filled his lungs and dashed off 'Adelita.'

"Traitor!" exploded a voice behind them.

Startled, Tereza shrieked. Luis frowned in the chapel doorway. "That's a Villista song. Don't play it here."

She pressed a hand over her heart. "For a moment I thought you were a deserter, hiding out from the army."

"We have guards," Sereno assured her. "Deserters, or anyone else unwanted at Los Nuestros, risk being shot."

"Anyone but a son of the hacendado would risk the same, if caught playing that song," Luis warned him, serious. "Some of our vaqueros hate Villa for the misery he has caused by not knowing when to quit."

"Mariano says those who distrust don Venus," Tereza told them, "hate Obregón for the same reason."

Sereno took her hand. "Let's forget the war. I have something to show you."

Leaving Luis sitting on a sunlit bench outside the chapel, they skirted a path where, shielded by shrubbery, they heard the women's voices chatting about flowers. When they reached the mirador, he remembered that Tereza was a niña, and her ankle-length dress was about to pose a difficulty.

"Damn," he said under his breath. "What I wanted to show you lies there." He pointed over the wall at the fringe of woods down slope.

"How do we get there?"

"I guess we don't."

She put her hands on his shoulders. "Help me up."

As gingerly as she had touched Violeta's head, he took hold of her waist and lifted her atop the rock barrier. In a flash of skirts and white petticoats she swung her feet over, and disappeared in a squeal of dismay.

Leaning on the wall on his stomach, he called down, "¡Ay, Dios! Are you hurt?" She had missed landing on the path and was lying on her back in a jumble of skirt and rebozo, giggling weakly.

Scrambling after her, he skidded to a halt, grabbed her arm, and tried to help her up, picturing what her tía would say if the dress were ripped or bruises became known. "¡Tereza, lo siento! I should have warned you of the steepness of the hill." Her giggles grew louder and tears ran down her cheeks. "Can you sit up? Did you hurt your back?"

Presently she grasped his shoulder and struggled upright. "You are not at fault," she gasped. "I was so busy wondering what you would show me, I didn't think of the hill below. I expected both sides to be the same."

"You're not hurt? Is your dress all right? Did you land in thorns?"

"No— Yes— No. That is, everything is fine." She looked around, noting the sheltered place where they were, where people in the house or yard could not see them. "No one will ever know." Then she leaned and kissed his cheek.

It was over so fast he had no time to react. She stood up, saying, "What secret did you want to show me?"

They began walking the narrow path toward the forest where his cave waited. "How did you know it's a secret?"

"It is, isn't it?"

"Yes. I come here when I want to be alone."

"Do you want to be alone often?"

"When I'm practicing a new song. Domingo laughs at me otherwise."

"Only then?"

He was spared having to answer as they reached the roof of the cave. "Don't fall off here. It's high enough to be dangerous."

Spreading his sarape for her, he felt the nip of wind through his shirt. They sat on the brink above the rolling grassland with its backdrop of crags that changed with the light. At this time of morning they were golden, rising sheer in the distance. "Some day, I am going to ride there, and look off one of those cliffs." He blew gentle notes on the flute.

Beside him, she breathed deeply of the forest and meadow aromas. "This is a lovely place. I'm honored you would share it with me."

He blew a few more notes, tender and filled with longing. "I like you," he said softly.

"I like you, too, Sereno," she said, even more softly.

A little silence. He ventured, "I thought you were fond of Domingo."

"I'm fond of both of you."

He was unable to voice the next question, Which do you like better? or the next: Have you kissed him? He found he didn't want to know that answer. Not just yet.

For quite a long time he played songs he felt confident would turn out well, until the wind made his fingers too stiff to execute them.

Another, longer silence. She said, "Perhaps we should go back to the casa now," and he reluctantly dropped the flute over his shoulder.

"Before we go," she added, "let me give you the Día de Los Reyes gift I have for you."

Gifts were supposed to be saved until tomorrow, put in a heap on the big table and distributed by Papá. This one must be special. Concealing his eagerness, he held out his hand and she laid a folded handkerchief in his palm. He drew back the corners.

It was a silver santo on a fine chain. "Who is it?" he asked, warm with pleasure.

"San Diego. I chose him because of my father, and because he is the patrón of our villagers."

"Gracias." He looped the chain over his head and arched his neck to look at the small medallion lying against his shirt. "I have nothing special for you," he said with regret. When he was in Culiacán with the family, buying presents, he had selected a tiny clay pitcher for Tereza. It cost only a few centavos, and beside the magnificence of the santo was poor indeed. She would receive it tomorrow.

"You gave me your music, here in your secret place. I think those are wonderful gifts."

They smiled at each other and he hoped she might kiss him again, but she returned his sarape and held out her hand. "Let's run. Your face is pale from the wind."

It is not the wind, he wanted to say. It is love.

171

II

Letting Bravo make his own kills, they worked their way eastward into the Sierra Madre. Lobo's campfire stories on moonless nights gave the younger Seri sueños malos, but Domingo's dreams had taken on a bizarre quality unrelated to the ghosts and demons of legend.

He thought he was back in Monterrey, searching the familiar yet unfamiliar house for something or someone. Objects he recognized were there, and furnishings, even to the portraits on the dark walls and Mamá's favorite chair in the sala. But no people, and the maze of rooms was endless, leading into and out of hallways and up and down sets of stairs he knew in the dreams but on waking found strange.

Always just ahead, something or someone urgently needed him, calling silently so his ears caught no sound, but his heart knew. He strained to hurry, to find whatever beckoned, yet a force held him back, making his legs heavy.

It was like being in the floodwaters of the earthen dam, only this impeding force was invisible, and there was no Jefe to rescue him.

Brooding over these night visions, he went about camp tasks unaware until the brothers approached him and Silvestre asked worriedly, "Are you angry with us, don Domingo?"

The title struck him as laughable, and he laughed. "When did I become an hacendado?"

Silvestre shrugged one shoulder. "You are a teacher in the school, and Lobo has told me about how you captured the caballo padre called Cimarrón."

He met Lobo's dark, brooding eyes. They made him remember how frightened Mamá had been to learn that their guide across the Sierras was a Seri, a tribe even more feared than the Yaquis. How long these last two years had been, stretching back into his other life.

"That was just luck."

Lobo's closed lips curved upward just a little. "Are we to believe it is luck which makes a gato grande, even a young one, obey you?"

"If he always obeyed me, I wouldn't be taking him into the hills," Domingo told him, and went to tend his gelding.

To avoid pueblos, they traveled away from streams and into high, rough country, where a dusting of snow lay on the north sides of the mountains and traces of silver mines had outlasted ravages of a hundred years and more: ore dumps in nearby barrancas, miners' jacales fallen to ruins, a large rawhide container in which peones carried rocks up from the depths of the shafts. Slipping his boot from the stirrup, he kicked at the basket-shaped thing.

"Lobo, tell me again the story of El Naranjal."

"¿Otra vez? There is another story, just as good. Let me tell it."

Wary of renegades, they crossed the Río San José de Viborillas and headed for what Lobo said was the headwaters of the Río Verde. They entered a mesa several kilometros wide, where they could ride abreast, and Bravo sallied forth happily like one of the bear dogs on some scent. "Ahh, muy bien. Tell it."

"In these nearby mountains," Lobo began, "there is another lost mine, like El Naranjal, only there is no casa blanca guarding it, named La Providencia. The owner, a rico of course, had taken much wealth from it, and expected to take much more, when a calamity struck."

Aware that Lobo relished these pauses, he waited without visible impatience.

"He was also don Domingo," Lobo went on, creating some doubt whether this part were true or fashioned to make things more interesting. "Como usted sabe, sometimes at this season of the year, there is hard rain, as in July. Pues, don Domingo the Rico started out for his mine after such a rain, but when he came to a certain spot on the trail, ¡Ay, Dios! everything had washed away. He saw rivers where before there had been none, and great boulders where once had been meadows."

Lobo lit a cigarette. He still carried a cartridge case with flint to make the spark, and as the breeze wafted his first draw of smoke away, he carefully put the case into a shirt pocket. "For the rest of his life, many long years, don Domingo the Rico searched for his mine. But La Providencia, with its veta de sueños dulces, was lost. To this day, it remains so."

"Muy triste," Silvestre nodded, though he must have heard the story countless times.

Domingo watched Bravo crossing the mesa, carrying something limp which proved to be a fawn. They skirted the spot the gato chose for its meal, continuing toward a cliff where Lobo thought there might be a spring. There was only a tinaja, but the rock basin was full and clean.

He stripped Valiente's gear and rubbed down the gelding with the cloth he kept in his saddlebag for that purpose. Indios seldom performed this service for their mounts unless the ride had been especially difficult, simply using dry grass in a careless manner. He noticed, too, that now the brothers waited until he had finished eating or filling his canteens before they would put food in their mouths or approach the springs. This behavior made him uneasy, for he both liked and detested the resulting feeling of importance.

If the Seris considered him macho, Tereza couldn't fail to see his merit. And with a pistol on his hip, his rank among the other jovenes increased significantly. It dawned on him that maybe the pistol was what finally set him apart from these mozos. Every afternoon since Jefe gave it to him, he'd practiced all the moves, from loosing the safety loop to hitting a target. Tender at first, especially in the wrist, the arm muscles daily grew stronger. Before long, unholstering should be smooth even if the aim lacked accuracy.

On the sixth night out from Los Nuestros, Bravo didn't return to their camp. Domingo dreamed of Tereza. Only a pizca, a scrap, but enough to keep him thinking of her as they dawdled over breakfast. It would be months before he would see her again unless somehow she had persuaded both Jefe and Mariano that the filly needed no hands but his for proper training.

"I think su gato has found himself," Silvestre said that afternoon, when the cat failed to return.

Domingo lingered at the spring. Though leaving the puma was the entire purpose of the trip, doing so was wrenching. Last night he had missed the warmth of the living creature sleeping against his back, and half hoped Bravo would lope into the clearing as usual, giving the horses a fright until they recognized him.

A few days ago he had removed the leather collar. Now he placed it over a broken branch of an evergreen growing near their camp. "Adiós, gatito," he murmured. Quickly they finished packing up and turned toward Los Nuestros.

The second night intensified his loneliness. He began to worry that another cat, older and bigger, might have attacked Bravito. The puma might be lying in the brush, bleeding and unable to hunt. Too, he must be confused, having been left in just the same way his mother had left him when the wild cow gored and killed her.

"Lobo," he said from his blanket, "do you think gatos have feelings like people?"

In the firelight the Indio's face was unreadable. "¿Quién sabe? Some ricos believe *they* are the only people who have feelings."

Into the silence, he pursued the idea. "What ricos feel that way?"

"All I have ever met. Except Jefe."

"He is no rico. Don Diego was a rico."

Lobo amended, "And don Diego," making him another exception.

Domingo tucked one cold foot into the crook of his knee to warm it. He would be glad to get home and learn whether a trip to Dos Corazones lay in his future. That rancho, down in the brush country, seemed ordered and civilized against the rawness of Los Nuestros and these mountains. Jefe had taken on a challenge, claiming this tierra. In a single year it was producing enough for the villagers to live well, though far from lavishly. As crews cultivated more and more of the original holdings, his home would take on that settled aspect; but he knew it would be a long time before the house acquired the graciousness of don Diego's casa grande.

Bravito didn't catch up to them in the days following his release in the Sierra, and by the time they rode onto Los

Nuestros property and stopped at the estancia guarding the eastern boundary, Domingo had given up looking for him on their backtrail. "It is best," Silvestre told him, sensing his emotion. "Otherwise, you would have had to shoot him."

He reached for the tin cup of hot coffee the young Seri handed him from the brasero. "I would die myself before I killed my own gatito."

"No, you wouldn't," Lobo said.

The outpost was manned by three Indios from Blanca Rosa, who gave them scant news. "Carranza and Obregón still have difficulties," the Opata said, dishing estofado from a pot in the coals. "The old Chief needs him to run Villa out of Sonora, but from the telegraph at Culiacán we heard that some Obregonistas are denied use of the wire and also the railroad."

"Did don Mariano leave for Los Dos Corazones?"

"Sí, we had word this morning, when Adolfo came with supplies, that your friends have made a safe journey."

Reassuring, after the other news; but knowing Tereza would not be there when he got home took away much of his eagerness to arrive.

Vida y Muerte. 1916

The winter evening landscape skimming by the dusty glass of the train window made Christine unutterably happy yet at the same time, unexplainably sad. Beyond the darkening plain, jagged mountains blended into deep blue storm clouds.

Crags of the Sierra Madre, where, on a night like this, spirits must haunt every canyon.

At thirteen, she had lately been reminded by her aunts in Kentucky that soon she would be expected to start acting like a young lady and give up playing ball with the boys who lived up the street, as well as rushing around town by herself to candy stores and the shoe repair shop.

Night thickened outside, so all she could see now was a dim ghost of her face and the shimmering pinpoints of light reflected from lamps in the grimy train car. Sliding onto her backbone and propping her heels in the opposite seat where her luggage was, she heaved a sigh.

She was eager to reach the ancient hacienda in the wilds of México, and though her skirt was rumpled and her stockings wrinkled at the ankle from bouncing around on the uncomfortable seat, trying to see everything at once, only her father and several dozen Mexicans were there to disapprove.

"Daddy, where are we now?" She had lost count of the times he'd answered that question.

Across the aisle, he leaned his head back and closed his eyes. "We'll be in a city called Culiacán in the morning, if nothing happens."

She observed his tired, irritable face, similar to her own with blue eyes and capped with fair hair. Mother, dead for nine years, had been dark. Not like the people Christine had seen in Mexico, but different from her and Daddy. "What do you think could happen?"

"In a revolution, God knows." His brown suit was creased and travel-stained, and somewhere he'd lost another hat, for it wasn't with the two suitcases beside him, which he guarded with a pistol in a shoulder-holster. At thirty-four, he seemed old. Six years ago he had gone to Mexico with two friends and bought a plantation, but had come home almost at once because of the war.

"If they're still fighting," she'd asked the day they boarded the first train, "isn't it dangerous to visit?"

"I've had word somebody's moved onto the property. If you leave these devils to do what they want, you'll never be rid of them. I can't let my investment fall into the hands of a thief."

Sights, sounds, and smells of foreign people, both in the train stations and as fellow travelers, interested her intensely, but Daddy had grown more short-tempered after they crossed the border and had to take a Mexican train. Soldiers in uniform and carrying rifles usually rode in separate cars, and so far they had not been attacked by any insurrectos, though she kept a sharp lookout for anyone resembling the faces pictured on wanted posters tacked up in the telegraph office in Nogales.

It was two days after New Year's when they finally got off the train in Culiacán and found a reasonably clean hotel. Daddy paid an old Indian man to carry in their suitcases, and arranged for food to be brought. Then he gave her the pistol and said, "Don't let anybody in unless you hear my voice. I'm bringing a friend of mine to stay with you."

Daddy's friend turned out to be a middle-aged woman named Greta, who lived in the hotel and smoked like a man. After a bath and meal, and with nothing to do but watch Greta read a newspaper, Christine grew drowsy supposing where Daddy was and how long he might be away. "A few hours," he had promised. A few hours of this kind of boredom threatened to kill her.

Back in Kentucky she had had many friends, cousins, school, parties, books, and a pony. Coming here seemed a risky thing to do, and her aunts—his sisters and Mother's—had opposed the move, but he'd convinced them in the end. Once established at the hacienda, he planned to grow guayule. He said the plant would make their fortune, as it was vital to the European war effort. She wondered how far the hacienda was from this hotel, and whether the place would be as noisy as the halls outside the door. At least there were no gunshots. "I haven't heard a single gun go off," she remarked, and Greta glanced up through a haze of cigarette smoke.

"You sound as if you'd like that."

"At least it would be exciting, as long as I wasn't the one getting shot."

"There is fighting beyond the mountains." Greta held out the newspaper, but it was in Spanish.

A knock woke Christine where she'd fallen asleep on the sofa. Morning sun gilded the single window pane.

She brushed hair out of her eyes in time to see Greta letting Daddy in. He wore his other suit, clean and brushed, and had shaved. "Get a dress on," he said, in high spirits. "After breakfast, we'll take a stagecoach out to my hacienda."

During the meal of scrambled eggs drenched in a hot green tomato sauce, and wrapped in the tough flour tortilla she had come to expect, Daddy told her he'd hired four armed men to escort them. "These people think I have money, so they treat me with respect," he said.

Greta was eating with them. She gave a shake of her head. "Don't appear to have too much money, or you'll end up robbed. Maybe worse."

"Even these barbarians would hesitate to hurt me while I have my insurance with me."

"Insurance?" Christine was confused. They had spent Mother's small death benefit long ago.

"Sure," he said, ruffling the hair over her forehead.

Greta's red lips turned down at the corners. "Don't count on it. Just because you still think she's a child—"

Daddy gave her the same look he used on plumbers or men who worked on his Buick when they overcharged. "Shut up," he said. "I don't know how else to do it, short of taking along an army, and I can't afford that."

Greta's eyes narrowed. "Did you ever think of going alone?"

"No." Daddy wiped sauce off his chin and stood up. "Let's go, Baby."

Dusk was gathering when the coach stopped and the driver unhitched his team. After a camp supper, they would overnight in the conveyance. She supposed the riders with them would have to sleep on the ground.

"This is all mine," Daddy said, waving his arm at the trees, crags, and canyons. He leaned to whisper in her ear, "I bought it on the deal that I'd raise guayule, and that's what I mean to do. But there's a secret."

She felt a surge of excitement. "I love secrets, Daddy. Tell me yours."

"Promise not to tell."

"I promise."

"On your mother's grave."

"I promise," she repeated, voice faltering. The grave, and a handful of photos, were all she had to remember Mother by. And memories that weren't all pleasant, owing to Daddy's temper.

He glanced at the mozos who were starting their own fire a little distance apart, and the driver, who was sharing the contents of a brown bottle with one of them. "There's a high grade silver mine on the property."

"Does that mean we'll be rich?"

He laughed, sounding joyful. "Well, there's plenty of money to be made in this godforsaken country, and no good reason why I shouldn't have my share."

Judging from his snores, he slept soundly, wrapped in blankets on the seat opposite hers. Rustlings in the brush, and low voices and occasional laughter of the men beyond the firelight, kept Christine awake for a long time. She could hardly wait to arrive.

Chapter Ten

Christine was relieved to hear their driver declare in English, "We shall reach the casa grande in two hours."

It was closer to three, but bright January sunlight speared through high evergreen branches, and morning bird calls filled the brisk air. Though the weather was warmer than it would be at home, she'd expected a jungle and parrots, and sweat dampening a muslin dress, so she was glad to have the flannel-lined coat and felt hat.

The stagecoach drew to a halt, and she leaned out of the window.

Ahead, the outriders had stopped at a massive stone wall. The huge wooden door had iron grating in the top third. Half a dozen men with rifles, obviously on a catwalk behind the wall, were visible from their waist up. Cartridge belts were looped over shoulders, and several wore the wide-brimmed hats she had seen in magazine pictures. Their voices were low and the streams of words coming out of their mouths made no sense to her, but Daddy, riding up top, asked the driver, "What are they saying?"

One of the outriders answered. "They want to know the purpose of your visit."

"I have business with the man in the big house," he snapped. "I don't discuss such things with hired help."

There was a conference among the Mexicans, both on the wall and on the horses, and the outrider said, "They will not let you in until they know why you are here."

"Dammit, I've spoken to grander men than the thief living in a house that belongs to me." Daddy stood up, and the edge of his coat trembled from anger. "Tell them I'm Mister Robert Allen Patrick Johnson, from Kentucky and points east, and I demand they open that gate immediately."

Christine felt prickles of fear that the dark-faced guards on the wall might shoot him. What on earth would she do if that happened?

There was mild laughter among the men barring the way. A few sentences passed between one of them and the outrider. "He says you must be lost, as they are not expecting guests."

"I'm not a guest," Daddy yelled. "This ain't no social visit. If I have to bring the law to get inside, I will."

Another conference. Then. "State your business, and they will send a messenger to see whether El Patrón wishes to see you."

"El Patrón, hell. I'm the patrón. This—"

"Daddy, don't fight," she pleaded, wishing Greta had come along. "Just tell them why we're here and let them send their message."

He whirled as if he'd forgotten her. Reaching down a hand, he said, "Come up here, Baby."

As soon as she opened the coach door, one of the younger riders was off his horse to help her. He grinned, showing nice teeth, and his grip on her arm was strong as he boosted her to the high coach seat.

"We want to be peaceable," Daddy continued in a more controlled voice. "I'll even give you my gun—" The instant his hand disappeared inside his coat six rifles clacked into readiness and all of them pointed at his heart.

Her throat closed on a scream. But they didn't shoot, and Daddy withdrew his pistol and dangled it out to the young rider.

The boy unloaded and returned the weapon. He said something to the crowd and many of them responded with laughter as before. Other riders dismounted and opened the coach doors. They took out all the luggage, sorted through it, refastened the suitcases and tossed them back inside. A wave of someone's hat signaled, and the huge gate slowly swung open.

"Jefe, there is trouble." Gregorio appeared at his bedroom door as he sat holding Violeta and marveling at her beauty.

Anita's head jerked around. "I have heard no shots."

"Not Villistas?"

"No Villistas." Gregorio's hat brim suffered between his hands. "Visitors. Chuco says bad ones. A man and a niña—probably his daughter. Señor Johnson, the gringo, claims to be patrón. He was armed, but no longer."

"Norteamericano."

"Sí. Y muy enojado." Very angry. "He had some campesinos with him, but they were kept out."

"How much time, before this hombre arrives?"

"Only minutes, Jefe. Chuco raced ahead, of course, but already they were coming through the big gate."

It was half an hour to the home compound gate here, where there was no guard, not even a lock. "Alert the policía and have them ready their mounts in case he needs to be impressed."

"Sí, Jefe."

Gregorio disappeared from the doorway, and Violeta smiled up at him. Anita waited for him to say something. He leaned to kiss the baby's forehead, and then stood up to put her into Anita's arms. "It will be my papers against his," he said. "With the war making everything in such a tangle, it can take years to prove ownership."

"Or," Anita said, "it will be his guns against yours."

"Don't worry. We can even pay him, if we have to. I don't take anything which legally belongs to another."

"What if he doesn't want money?"

He laughed and kissed her cheek. "What gringo doesn't want money?"

He went down to his office and poured two stemmed glasses half full of a sweet red wine. He took the papers he'd sweated weeks to obtain from civil authorities in Culiacán and the City of México, where the original land grants moldered in some government building. He laid out the envelope filled with receipts, official stamps, and signatures, which Luis kept neatly together. Then he locked his fingers over the buckle of his holstered pistol, and waited.

It was too cool to open the glass doors at his back, as they were on the north side of the house; but through them he could hear snaps of a whip and occasional sharp whistles as Sereno put his pony through a workout on the long rope. Before the arrival of Tereza, the gelding had been neglected until it was almost too wild to be ridden. Now, the boy seemed bent on impressing Mariano's little sister, who braved the shaded portales in her wool rebozo to watch.

Dios, he thought. *If Mamá had turned me loose in Los Pobres at that age, would I have been so prone to romance?*

Musings vanished at steps in the hall. Luis showed the visitors in. With them was a young Mexican whom he supposed had been brought along to interpret. "Good morning," Ramón said, standing and making a quick bow. "I hope your journey was pleasant." He offered his hand, but it was ignored.

Señor Johnson's face registered surprise. "Ah—you speak English." He nodded the little girl into the other chair and sat down. "I want to get right to the point, as it seems you've taken over pretty thoroughly. When I heard you'as squatting on my property—"

"Stop there," he said, disliking the man's abrupt manner and deciding to match it. "If you have a claim, I'd like to see the papers."

"Oh, I have papers." Johnson opened a leather case and extracted several pages of a closely-typed document. With them was a folded sheet which was undoubtedly a map. Ramón reached for it first.

Not exactly like the one he'd been given in Culiacán, but close, covering most of the area within the old rock boundary walls. More of the disputed land lay to the north and northeast. The south line cut off El Valle de Los Mesteños. If it came to a showdown, Domingo would be glad of that.

A stray thought intruded as he wondered what was happening with Bravo, and then he glanced over the rest of the papers. "I don't see any seals or signatures, except those of men who served under Presidente Díaz." He tossed the documents across his desk. "As you must know, many changes have taken place since then."

"In my country," Johnson said, his jaw so stern that his words came out tight, "once a contract is made, it's honored. I paid for this land, and now that my wife is dead, I want to live here. Your President Díaz knew how to treat investors."

He caught but didn't understand the startled look the little blonde girl gave her father when he mentioned his wife. It seemed his grief over losing her mother was long past. "Díaz knew how to do many things. Among them, how to make slaves of people in their own tierra."

"Tierra—what is that?" The girl leaned forward.

He regarded her. He sensed that she shared none of her father's arrogance. "Homeland," he explained. "The place where one is born, and belongs, and is happy."

She frowned. "Can someone not be happy except where he was born?"

Johnson laid a hand on his daughter's arm. "Be quiet. I want to get this settled today."

"Sir, even if you were dealing with Díaz himself, this matter cannot be settled in a day. You will be fortunate to have satisfaction in a year."

The cold blue eyes were slits. Muscles twitched. After a moment the man managed to say, "I hope you have a team of good lawyers."

Ramón let his palm rest on the butt of his holstered gun. "I have persuasive spokesmen, all around me. And I resent threats. We can settle this if—"

"No ifs. I don't intend to lose my investment. I—"

"Daddy." The girl tugged at his sleeve. "I'm going outside. I want to look around."

"Just on the porch," Johnson said. "There, where I can see you."

So norteamericano children were even more rude than his own. He hid a smile under the pretext of rubbing his face. The interpreter remained, looking uncomfortable.

To Johnson, Ramón said, "Do you care for wine, sir?"

"No, I don't. Now if you had bourbon, that would be different. But I guess that's too much to expect."

"Just what did you expect? To come here and order me away? That I would surrender stock, tools, furnishings, warehouses full of supplies? All the families in the village? I'm afraid I must disappoint you greatly."

"You should've known better than to settle here."

"I too have papers." He unfolded his map and spread out his documents with their colored seals and ribbons.

"According to what I could learn, this place belonged to an hacendado long dead, with no issue. No— ¿cómo sé dice? Relatives, to inherit."

"That was what I learned six years ago, when I paid good money and was given these papers in return. I'm surprised you didn't tell me you're one of those relatives."

Stiffly, Ramón said, "I don't lie."

"But you're damn willing to steal."

He was out of the chair before he knew it, yet the gun stayed holstered. "With respect, I have to point out, your claim is no better than mine. There were no owners or heirs left living for you to pay, so your money bought you worthless papers with dead men's names on them."

Johnson had jumped up, too, his fists clenched. "If you're saying the Mexican government swindled me, you might be right, but the fact is, I have prior claim and I mean to take this property, even if I have to bring the United States Army in here to clean it up."

"Clean it up? Your words are strange, but meaning is clear. Let me make things clear for you: until you are ready to talk without threats, and consider—"

"The only thing I'll consider is helping you pack up and leave. I have plans for this property, and they don't include a bunch of damned Mexkins who act like they own the place."

Gregorio passed back and forth in the hallway and Luis sat on the stairs and leaned on the banister. Tiring of such talk, they were impatient to escort this unwelcome guest all the way to Culiacán and onto a northbound train. Ramón didn't think he could be gotten rid of so easily. Anyone coming into a country at war, bringing a girl child, had some deeply important reason.

"Why did you wait six years?" He picked up his wine glass.

"I kept believing this revolution would be over. Then the war started in Europe—" Johnson gathered up his papers and shoved them into the leather case. "I'm staying in Culiacán. When you come to your senses, send me word. I don't hear from you in a week, don't blame me for what happens."

He marched out through the glass doors to collect his daughter, and Gregorio and Luis followed to make sure he did in fact leave. Ramón went to prepare Anita for the unpleasant and inevitable conflict ahead.

On the veranda the air was cold, though the sunlight drenching the road and corrals and tile-roofed buildings opposite made the day seem warm and glowing. Christine saw a dark-haired girl about her age sitting on the low stone balustrade, arm around a roof post, watching the activity of a dozen men and some beautiful horses.

Looking around at her, the girl smiled and said, "Hola."

"Hello." Ready to make friends, she felt uncertain. "I don't speak Spanish."

"I know a little English."

"Do you live here?"

"No. I am señorita Tereza del Ortega, visiting from La Hacienda Los Dos Corazones, in Hermosillo."

Christine stared at her light skin, black hair, very blue eyes, and thought, *All those words, and not more than half of them English.* "My name is Christine. I'm from Kentucky. That's in the United States." She perched beside Tereza, looking out over the lawn toward the men. "Those are lovely horses."

"Yes. They were wild, but the Corderos tame them."

"Corderos?"

"The family who own this hacienda."

Rather than get into an argument, she kept watching the riders and was intrigued when a blond boy younger than herself swung into a saddle and came through a gate opened by a peon. She knew that's what men in baggy white pants and sandals were called.

The blond boy rode up to them, tousled curls falling over his forehead, tan trousers dusty from the clouds kicked up by hooves. He wore leather boots without spurs, and appeared more comfortable on that horse than she was on this stone wall. He reined in close and looked down at her. The animal pranced and tossed its head, dribbling slobber onto the sidewalk.

"Tereza, ¿quién es tu amiga?"

"Cristina, de Kentucky. Ella es una gringa de los Estados Unidos y no es mi amiga."

Hearing their easy exchange, knowing it was about her but unable to guess what they said, made her shy for the first time in her life. She recognized these as a high class of people, almost white and surprisingly civilized. A contrast to the rough-looking men casting glances her way but going about their business, or the soldiers on the trains, or the señoras and vendors who tried to sell fruits, meats, and tortillas through the train windows at every stop. Daddy wouldn't let her touch any of that food, though how it might be different from what they were served in restaurants, she didn't ask.

While she stared at the boy, as beautiful as the horse he rode, he and Tereza carried on more conversation which she didn't understand. Straining to read in his face whether he made fun of her, or if by any chance he felt the same interest in her foreignness as she felt for him, she was disappointed when he reined away, out of sight behind a retaining wall covered in thick vines. "Who is he?" She yearned to know everything about him.

"Don Sereno Cordero, son of the hacendado."

The sentence rippled out of the girl's mouth like cool water from a spring. She knew from reading about the Spanish culture that 'don' was a title and not part of his name, and also that 'hacendado' meant the landowner. "Your language is wonderful," she said. "I must learn it."

The girl regarded her without comment.

"What a gorgeous shawl. May I try it on? Here, try my coat, so you won't be cold." She slid her coat off and held it out. Tereza hesitated briefly before taking the garment in one hand and unwrapping her shawl from her shoulders.

"I read about those in the guidebook," Christine said. "Say the word for me, please."

"¿Qué, esta?" Tereza looked at her shawl as if she'd never seen it before, and passed it to her. "Rebozo," she said, then, twice. "Mi rebozo para el frío. Esta tierra es fría."

"Tierra! I just heard that. What do you mean by it?"

"This month is cold here." Tereza made herself shiver. "But your coat is warm." She ran her fingers over the soft lining.

Before Christine could untangle her confusion, the boy—Sereno—galloped back into the yard and jumped out of the saddle. As soon as reins touched ground, the lathered horse began grazing the winter-brown grass beyond the paving. Sereno threw himself atop the wall and wiped his forehead on his turned-up sleeve. He wasn't cold. "¿Dónde está mi papá?"

"En su oficina, con su padre." She nodded toward Christine. "¿Chucho no dijo?"

"No, solamente que hay un malo norteamericano con una pistola vacia."

They laughed, and looked at her, but the boy gave her a friendly smile. "Cristina. That is a nice name."

"Oh! You speak English, too—thank goodness."

"A little. My father is a teacher."

"Your father—Señor Cordero."

"Sí. Yes."

There was a silence as she sorted through the dozens of things she wanted to know. Before she could settle on what should be first, Sereno asked, "Would you like to see my little sister?"

"Ella está una bebé," Tereza added. "A sweet niña, a baby girl."

"Yes!" she cried, jumping off the wall. She followed them down the porch to another set of glass doors.

They had just entered a sunlit room when she heard Daddy shout. "Christine!" Fear and fury in the single word sent a dart of ice through her stomach.

She nearly knocked Tereza over as she leaped back outside and saw him at the other end of the patio, leaning over the wall, ready to explode. "Here I am, Daddy."

"What do you think you're doing? I told you to stay in sight." He started toward her, and with an apologetic backward glance she ran to meet him.

"I was just going to see the hacendado's baby."

Daddy took her by the wrist, still breathing hard. "He is not the hacendado, dammit, and you should know better than to go into some other part of that house while these people

193

are in it. You didn't leave anything like a purse— Good God, what are you wearing?"

She had forgotten the exchange, and as she turned to find Tereza, she bumped into the girl again, following with her coat. Wordless, they passed the clothing between them. Sereno stood at the far glass door, one hand resting gracefully on the framing. He waved, and she waved back. Then Daddy pulled her toward the waiting stagecoach.

II

"You missed all the excitement," Sereno told him the moment he hit the door, dirty and tired, and feeling sick.

"What excitement?" Domingo tossed down his hat, shucked out of coat and gloves. A criada gathered them up and took them upstairs. He'd trusted Silvestre with tending his pony, and part of his mind was occupied by that decision. When he had bathed and eaten and rested, he probably should check to make sure things had been done right.

"What excitement?" he repeated, as Sereno calmly gnawed a chunk of piloncillo left from the Navidad and El Día de Los Reyes, fiestas which had gone on without him. He wouldn't see Tereza again until some arrangement was made about the training of her filly. Sereno's words jarred him into attention.

"... americano malo here to take away Los Nuestros from us. Papá sent him running back to Culiacán, but he said he was coming here again in a week—that will be day after tomorrow—and I bet there's a damn big fight."

"Don't let Jefe hear you talk like that. You're too young to use crude words." He grabbed Sereno's wrist and tried to take the last bit of sugar out of his hand, but Sereno crumbled it so he couldn't. Most of it spattered on the floor, and a criada waiting in a corner glided forward with a rag and wiped the tiles.

Hearing their voices, Jefe came out of his office. After an abrazo, Domingo said, "Well, I did it. Bravito stayed in the high mountains."

"Let us hope so." One hand lingered on his shoulder. "The beef is almost ready."

"¡Bueno! I'm tired of pinole and stale tortillas."

"Lobo didn't get a deer?"

"That, too. Somehow, none of us can cook venison over a campfire like Luis."

Joining them in the hall, Luis greeted, "You missed me, did you?"

"Your skill, solamente. Not your ugly face."

There was a good-natured tussle, after which he went to the baño to bathe and change for the evening meal, while Luis finished the month's accounting.

They entered the dining room behind Jefe and Sereno Anita and Estrada were already there. He wondered how long the médico would continue living with them. "I trust that Violeta is well?"

"Sí." Anita added, "It's good, having you home."

"Gracias." He didn't expect further discussion about the americano malo until after most of the meal had been eaten; but while he savored the juicy beef and fresh bread, his thoughts worked on what Sereno had told him.

There was less food than usual. He supposed the expense and lavish dinners over the holidays had caused shortages. Too, Anita had persuaded Jefe to send wagons loaded with supplies into Culiacán, to be distributed among the starving poor.

"So long as no one knows where it came from," he had said. "I don't want crowds of beggars finding their way to my gate."

"Most of them would die on the way," Anita had rebuked, "as they would have to walk for weeks."

Beneath the glow of lamplight with a mug of frothy chocolate in his hand, Domingo thanked Dios for the comforts of home. Having this familia, this tierra, eased the pain of losing his gatito; yet he dreaded going into his room and stepping on the rug where Bravo had spent many nights. Dreaded seeing the shredded curtain where on more than one occasion the puma had tried to claw its way through the glass door. *You are free now*, he thought. *Make the most of it.*

After he'd checked his horses to be sure they had been properly tended, he went upstairs with one of Jefe's books under his arm, hoping to occupy his mind until he could fall asleep.

He'd gone inside and was reaching to light his lamp when Anita came to his door, her bare feet soundless on the polished floor of the hallway.

"Tereza left this for you." She handed him a small object wrapped in a silk lady's handkerchief bordered in colorful embroidery. The design seemed to be birds and flowers, but he was too overcome to be sure.

"For El Día de Los Santos Reyes," Anita explained, and with a little smile of understanding, she left him.

Clutching the gift, he fumbled with the lamp wick and shade, closed the door, then opened the folds of the cloth. A silver crucifix, as finely done as Mamá's which Ramón had given him months ago and which he wore around his neck. This chain was of similar length and heaviness, and of superior workmanship. Even before the war drove prices skyward, it would have been expensive, and likely had belonged to the wife or daughter of a well-to-do Creole in Hermosillo, sold when they left the country, or taken by soldiers looting for valuables.

He undressed and got into bed, pondering what significance Tereza's gift might have. Last year at Los Dos Corazones, their Día de Reyes presents had been childish, handmade tokens of friendship. The four of them—Sereno and Teo, also—had fashioned Ojos de Dios, Eyes of God, the twine and bamboo symbols of prayers for good health and long life used by the Huichols of Jalisco. His hadn't been very skillfully done, but it was amusing to make them.

What had become of those given him, he was unable to say. Lost in packing for the journey to Los Nuestros, no doubt. In the morning, he would ask Anita if she knew. It would be interesting to see what colors and design Tereza had used in the one made for him, and he wanted now to put the gifts together, in a little box. Wearing the medal was out of the question, as it would draw comment and teasing from the men.

... he was in the house in Monterrey, and it was evening but no lamps were lit. The high-ceilinged rooms echoed with each boot step and pieces of furniture were missing or misplaced. Somewhere in the labyrinth ahead he sensed a presence, waiting for him. From faraway, up the stairs it seemed, there came a soft wailing, like Bravo in distress. Heart chugging, palms leaving dampness on the banister, he ran up the steps to the bedrooms. In the upper hall, darker than below, he searched the rooms but found nothing alive, not even Tía's periquitos in the gold-wire cage. *I turned them loose*, he remembered. *I set the birds free, and they flew away.*

Then he heard gunfire, and froze, thinking, *Villa is taking the city.* Where was Mamá? He tried to hurry down the stairs, but a crowd of strangers had filled the house and were rushing about, their wide eyes and silent screams from open mouths sending terror into his very soul. Several jostled, knocked him against the walls. A door opened behind him, where no door had ever been, and he was suddenly in a narrow, dark room. Outside, the clamor went on, but inside was quiet. He knew no one had been in this room for a long, long time. There was a small, dusty glass window high in the far wall, and out of the dimness, from among stored boxes and pieces of unused furniture, came Bravito. The warm furry little body crawled into his lap; holding it brought comfort.

But the gunfire continued.

A pounding on his door jerked him out of the dream and onto the cold floor. "¿Qué lo es? ¿Qué pasa?" he shouted, and Sereno flew into the room more excited than Domingo had ever seen him.

"It's the Americano! He's brought an army and attacked the guards at the gate, and our men have gone out to fight."

Chapter Eleven

"Damn him, he's two days early." Ramón searched under the bed for his other boot, where it had somehow been kicked.

Anita handed him the cartridge-filled gun belt. Her eyes were wide with apprehension and she seemed not to hear Violeta's screams at being wakened by the shooting.

"If I've told them once, I've told them a hundred times not to waste ammunition," he complained, buckling on the pistol and kissing her near the mouth in the same motion.

The firing and galloping hooves of thirty or more men finished passing the house, and Sereno dashed into the room, Domingo close behind, still stuffing in the tail of his shirt, his own gunbelt over his shoulder. "Oh, no, macho mío," Ramón said, snatching it off and tossing it onto the bed. "You are not going."

"But, Jefe—"

"No! Anita, keep him here if you have to tie him by the neck."

He put on his short coat on the way downstairs, where Luis waited with two rifles and a bag of shells secured at his waist. Estrada joined them in the zaguán, also with a rifle. "Médico, stay out of the fighting," he said. "We'll need you afterward."

The boys trailed them into the yard and across the road to the corrals, where Martín and Gregorio had horses ready. Lobo and Silvestre had gone with the noisy ex-rebels, now out of hearing though dust from their mounts hung in the still air. "Vaya con Dios, Papá," Sereno said, hugging him.

Returning the embrace, he was surprised how tall the boy had grown. "Gracias, mijo. Don't worry, and encourage your mother."

Turning to Domingo, whose face was stormy at being denied, he said, "If I am killed, you must run this place. Never let that maldito americano get his paws on it. It is Los Nuestros, now more than ever."

Leaving his firstborn speechless, he leaped into the saddle and led his riders through the home gate, which had been thrown wide to admit the defending force ahead of them; there was no delay in reaching the battleground, less than half an hour from the casa.

The guards at the entrance had been overrun and the fight was hotly engaged all over the road and extending into the forest on both sides. The reinforcements—all three of them—got off a few rounds at a run before landing in the middle of the confusion.

The old fear of accidentally shooting one of his own men gripped him as he slid out of the stirrups and to the ground, his horse pounding on to trample down an unwary hombre. Combat was too close for the rifle now, but he didn't dare throw it aside as an enemy would surely grab it. With the pistol he shot three men he didn't recognize, all in civilian clothing.

From old guns, powder smoke filled the air, stinging his eyes and nostrils and bringing images of those first battles at Juárez, when the revolution belonged to Madero and a mere handful of loyal rancheros.

Yells of fright and anguish mingled with lusty shouts from both sides and squeals of horses, and everywhere was the crackle of gunfire.

The wooded terrain, thick with downed leaves, limbs, and combatants, made running difficult; but standing still got a man killed, so he ran about, alert for an opportunity to fire.

Presently all the horses had fled, the clamor lessened and then stopped, except for the sobs and groans of the wounded.

Lobo strode from body to body, shooting each in the head until he called, "¡Alto! ¡Alto! That is not necessary."

The young Seri looked at him with surprise. "You do not want to fight them at a later time, do you?"

"Besides," Martín added, coming to where they were, "most of them would not live anyway, from the wounds."

"Let Estrada decide that."

The men who heard him glanced at each other, and Gregorio said, "Jefe, surely you're not thinking of taking these villanos to the house. Eso es loco. Waste medicines and bandages on men who came to kill us? Muy loco."

His riders were helping their wounded onto caught horses. Luis called, "Patrón, some of ours need transport. I have sent for a wagon."

"Good work." He met Lobo's eyes again. "Bueno, get on with it, and bury them outside the wall."

Two of the attackers were not seriously wounded and began begging for their lives. They tried to climb over the still-barred gate, weeping in fear. Ramón stayed Lobo's hand once more. "Let them go. I don't think they will ever return, for any man's money."

The Seri shrugged and holstered his gun. "As you wish, Jefe." Then he grinned. "I was out of ammunition anyway."

As soon as the victors rode through the gate, doors were flung open and windows unshuttered. Dogs barked from excitement and villagers streamed into the plaza. Leaving Luis to tend his horse, Ramón crossed the patio and was met by his entire household except for Estrada, who had gone to his clínica to prepare for the wounded.

Congratulations rained around him from the people who worked in the house and those who tended the gardens. Sereno gave him another hug, and Anita finally had a chance to cling to him and whisper, "Gracias a Dios, mi vida."

At the foot of the staircase, his older son waited until everyone else had drifted away. He slowly took off his hat and coat and pistol and discarded them. Domingo stood watching, at last blurting, "Did you mean what you said? That I would run this hacienda? Not Luis, nor Gregorio, nor even Sereno?"

He laid his hand on his son's shoulder. Their arms went around each other as they began walking though the house toward the long porch where the hammock swung gently in a fitful wind, and morning sunlight warmed the paving.

Stopping at the edge, he focused on the mirador across the grassy space before them, "Domingo, you are becoming a man at an age when I was still a child. The life you have been forced into is largely the cause, and I regret it; for there is much to be said for remaining innocent. But I think you have in you what you shall need to meet a future so uncertain that tomorrow we might all be dead. If I can't trust Los Nuestros to you, there is no one in all the world worthy of my trust."

The words came from his heart, and from the somber look on the boy's face, had lodged in his.

They stood for a long while, listening to the corridos being sung to celebrate the victory. Several wounded, a few seriously, but none lost. This time.

He didn't think Johnson would give up easily, and made a mental note to check further into the history of this property, to learn, if he could, what made it so valuable to a foreigner.

Jefe's words moved Domingo almost to tears, so he didn't try to say anything. No one had ever burdened him with so great an honor and responsibility, and the importance of it threatened to crush him.

What confidence his father must have in him, to trust him with all that lay at their feet, including whole families from Los Pobres and Blanca Rosa, and grown men who had been soldiers under Ramón's command. He still couldn't quite believe he'd heard the declaration straight out of Jefe's mouth. Los Nuestros, his!

And where did that leave Serenito? Just as Ramón turned toward the door, he found the courage to ask. "What—What about Sereno? I know you must mean to divide what is here, when the time comes."

"Dividing Los Nuestros is not my plan, though that might become necessary, God knows, with drought, a hostile government, and Señor Johnson all ready to destroy us. Part of what I'm depending on you to do, whatever the situation, is to be fair."

Another heavy burden—worse than the one Mamá put on him the day she died, when she said, *Be good to Teo.* Now Jefe expected him to be fair to someone only half a brother to him. In a burst of clarity that took away his breath, he realized that Teo, too, was only a medio hermano.

"Jefe," he said, gripping his father's upper arm, "I will do my best."

Ramón smiled. "I know you will."

They went in to discover what might be salvaged of a breakfast cooked more than an hour earlier. Sereno was dawdling over a bowl of champurrado. Unaware, childish.

While they were eating, Estrada came through, clothing stained with dried and fresh blood. "After I have washed and changed," the doctor said, "I shall give you a full report."

"Bueno," Ramón nodded, and held his cup to the criada for more hot coffee.

"Papá, you have not said— Was Señor Johnson in the fight?" Sereno was frowning down at some small object, held in his fingertips.

It was a medal, on a chain around his neck. As Domingo watched he tucked it into the front of his shirt. Was that the replacement which Anita had promised, for the one bestowed as a parting gift to Teo? Or—his ears grew hot— A present like his, from Tereza.

He missed the rest of what was said, until everyone was rising and Sereno invited, "Come see what I can do with Viento."

Hoping for a chance to learn whose gift encircled the younger boy's neck, he followed Sereno to the corrals and climbed to a perch on the top pole, along with a crowd of amigos from the village, who frequently left chores and games in order to watch whatever was happening in the horse pens. Martin's stern voice sent a few of the older ones back to work, but Sereno had a sizable audience when he led out his pony. Light mountain saddle, colorful blanket, bitted bridle. Impressive.

He saw the medal swing out and glint in the sunlight as Sereno mounted. If Tereza had given it to him, how had it happened? Had she placed her package with the rest of the gifts, or did she hand it to him directly? What had they said?

A burst of cheering from onlookers snapped him out of his reverie. Sereno had made the pony rear, forelegs curving prettily, and hold the pose long enough to encourage shouts of praise.

It galled him that he had never attempted to do that, but concentrated on getting quick turns, pivots, and clean stops. He was still trying to teach Valiente to back.

A few metros away, the pen where he'd kept Bravo was full of grunting pigs. Sickened by the idea of those creatures living in the same space once occupied by his pet, he dropped off the corral pole. So far he'd shot rabbits, squirrels, and a couple of quail, which Bravo had eaten, thereby saving him from having to handle the little dead bodies.

Now, he felt a driving need to kill something. A javelina, maybe. It was a pig. Fitting. The villagers could roast it over coals for a community supper.

While he was saddling Valiente, Gregorio came up behind him. "Ramón says it's time to go for the mesteños in the cañon, while they're full of new grass and the foals are small. He wants us to leave in a couple of days."

Tucking the leather strap into the cincha, he said, "I'm ready. Who else is going?"

"Martín, of course. Lobo, Silvestre, myself, Luis, and Sereno."

The casual way the young man spoke didn't reveal any awareness of the tension that existed between the Cordero boys. Domingo tried to keep his resentment hidden. After all, had not Jefe granted him, the firstborn, the highest of honors?

And the trip would give him an opportunity to slyly question Sereno about that medal.

He rode across the compound and among the village casitas toward the northeast, the same trail they would take in a few days to reach the sealed valley. Several niños ran out, asking where he was going, and seemed excited by his answer. "¡Buen suerte!" they called. Good luck.

Without Bravo, the ride was lonely. His eyes kept darting here and there as they had when he was pressed to keep track of the gatito, blending as it did into the buff-colored brush and rocky landscape.

He missed watching the cat stalk something unseen in the chaparral, each movement controlled, energy concentrated into the swift, precise pounce. He could almost see the shake of the sleek head, the triumphant emergence into the open with limp prey dangling from powerful jaws.

It was like those days in the patio of the house in Monterrey, watching the mother cat lurk at the base of a wall where thick grass eluded the scythe of the gardener. She almost always caught a mouse, sometimes a rat.

Once, she'd even gotten a squirrel that had for days tormented her with its scolding. He remembered being awed by the contempt she made plain by chewing off that squirrel's head and leaving it uneaten, walking away from the broken thing with an air of having settled a long-standing grudge. For the first time he'd understood that animals possessed emotions, that the apparent love she had for him was real and not simply an interest in the food he gave her, the stroking of her fur or pleasurable scratching beneath her chin.

Bravo, too, had been all that, and more.

Dismounting, forehead resting against Valiente's warm shoulder, he let the tears come. When he had cried away the emptiness and from force of will filled it with resolve never to be so hurt again, he shucked the rifle from its scabbard and walked, gateando, toward a cedar-thick bosque near a stream, where javelinas might be holed up.

Tales of their ferocity swirled in his head, making his palms sweaty. Foolish, to approach on foot; but a surge of recklessness pushed him onward. Close enough, he picked up the biggest rock he thought he could throw effectively and sailed it into the shady scrub. It *thunked* against something and he thought he'd hit a tree. A startled squeal and the explosion of pigs from the weeds made him jump back, too amazed at first to run or lift the rifle.

But they weren't coming at him, scattering instead to the left and right, three one way, one in the opposite direction. He fired at the last pig to leave the thicket, heard it scream, and, running sideways, squeezed off another shot that brought the animal down.

Trembling all over, he sank to his knees, gripping the rifle to steady himself. The sound of something rushing toward him spurred him into action. He'd barely levered another shell into the chamber before the wounded javelina struck his left shoulder, knocking him backward. Valiente's screech sent shocks through him.

Struggling upright, he saw his pony galloping for the edge of the forest, head held high and to one side to avoid stepping on the reins.

A couple of wagon lengths away lay the pig, its legs jerking. Then the quivering stopped.

Panting, he made three attempts before he was able to whistle loud enough to make the caballo hear and respond to his signal. Valiente halted, whirled. Seeing no pursuer, the horse stood wild-eyed, flanks heaving, ears pricked.

Weak with spent emotion, he fell back against the earth and laughed. Presently he felt a nudge on the arm resting over his eyes to keep off the sun. "Hola, caballito. Did that give you a scare?"

Faced with transporting the kill back to the village, a distance of three kilómetros, he realized he'd brought no knife for dressing the javelina, no machete nor rawhide for making a drag. "Damn," he muttered, sitting on a boulder beneath a leafing acacia. Pack it out whole, admitting he'd come unprepared? Or deny the success of the hunt and leave the pig for scavengers? After some minutes he unsheathed the puntilla, a short dagger, the silversmith had made for him. He located and cut out the scent gland. If left, it would ruin the flavor before he got it home.

Then he went down to the stream to wash his hands and face, and take off his shirt to view the damage to his shoulder. His jacket had cushioned some of the impact, but a rip a handspan in length went through the leather, the pig's tusk tearing a similar hole in his shirt and leaving a bleeding but shallow gash in the flesh, beginning just below the point of his shoulder and ending at his elbow. Bathing it until the ooze of blood stopped, he hoped there would be enough of a scar to show Tereza.

His caballito was unhappy with having to carry the dead pig, though he made the chore less distasteful by anchoring the carcass behind the saddle and away from the horse's sensitive nostrils.

When he rode into the village and loosed the thongs, women caught the kill and carried it toward a pit already dug. Niños danced about, chanting some victory song in their dialect, and several of the young girls—a few pretty mestizas among them—patted Valiente, a hand or two finding its way to his thigh as if touching him somehow satisfied a need.

Unsure what it meant, he was embarrassed and as soon as he could without being impolite he rode on, escorted by dogs sniffing the bloody wild scent lingering on his gear. In the corral, he instructed a stock handler to wash saddle and blanket. "Pay attention to the seams," he added, giving the boy a few tattered Carrancista bills.

Anita was sitting on the long porch with Violeta, both enjoying the mild day. "I watched you ride in," she greeted. "Will you attend the barbacoa tonight?"

He sprawled in a chair facing her. "Maybe. I've never eaten that meat."

"If cooked properly, it is supposed to be good."

Leaning his head on the back of the chair, he retraced the hunt, trying to find points where he might enhance the adventure. Violeta sat bobbling and cooing on her mother's lap. He envied her fresh new skin and wisps of fine, shiny hair, her cheerful manner which knew nothing of death, but celebrated in the security of loving arms that prevented a fall to the paving.

"Tell me about it," Anita suggested.

Without enhancement, he described flushing the quarry, Valiente's fright when the pig recovered from the first two bullets, and how close it was before he could fire again, ending with, "Is there some medicine for a cut?" He showed her the slashed jacket.

"¡Madre de Dios! You are hurt." She handed the baby to a waiting niñera, and made him strip off his shirt right there on the porch. While she was exclaiming over the wound, Ramón came up from the stables. "¿Qué te paso?" he asked, joining them for a look.

"Nada, Jefe, the pig just scratched me a little."

"Pig?"

"The one I shot for the villagers to have a barbacoa. I washed this small cut in a stream, and Anita is going to put on medicine."

"You brought in that javelina? You are lucky not to be ripped to shreds. Next time you want to do such a thing, at least take someone with you."

Ramón's stance and tone were angry; not the reaction he had hoped for. "It ended all right, Jefe."

His father's hand reached to pick up the medal at the end of its chain, not Mamá's crucifix but Tereza's gift. "You have a powerful saint watching out for you, hijo. Thank him."

"I didn't think you believed in saints."

"I don't. Angels, maybe. Jesucristo, certainly. But Tereza has faith in them, and clearly it is justified."

Embarrassment heated his ears. Jefe wasn't fooled about whose gift had replaced Mamá's rosary. At that moment Sereno appeared around the corner of the house.

"What is all the excitement in the village?"

"A barbacoa tonight," Anita answered. "Domingo killed a javelina."

His glance taking in the naked chest, the medal, the rip from the pig's tusk, the younger boy cried, "¡Maldito sea!" and Ramón gave him a disapproving tap on the head. "Watch how you speak in front of your mother."

Domingo hissed, "Didn't I warn you?" To Anita, he said, "May we get the medicine now?"

They went to the storeroom where household herbs and spices were kept, and she sorted bottles, tins, and fragrant packets of paper until she found what she wanted. He allowed her to tie on a clean cloth, and, to get the most attention for his wound, he tore off the sleeve of an old shirt so the bandage would show.

"It binds, otherwise," he explained, seeing Jefe grin.

The saddle maker promised to mend the jacket.

In the end, Domingo decided not to attend the barbecue. The touches of muchachas' hands on his leg had made him uneasy. If one of them invited him into a dark casita while villagers partied in the plaza, he wouldn't know how to respond. Of course, he could always ask Luis

That evening at cena, he learned that Ramón didn't plan to accompany the mustangers on the roundup. "But, Jefe, you must go with us. Otherwise, who will be the boss?"

"Martín is el jinete mejor, and knows better than I what should be done. I can't leave the casa while Señor Johnson is in the area."

"Is he in the area?" Anita asked, forehead furrowed.

"Soldados at headquarters, who are watching him, sent a message with the mail that he is still trying to hire another bunch of bandidos for a future assault." Ramón pushed back his chair and wiggled his fingers at Violeta. She squealed and lunged forward against her mother's arm, wanting his lap.

After the transfer was made, he went on, "I am more worried about what he might do legally than about a few hired guns getting themselves killed in his employ."

Estrada leaned his elbows on either side of his empty plate, chin on locked fingers. "Can he do harm, legally?"

"That depends on who finally sits in the great chair in the Capitol. If Carranza and Obregón can stabilize the country, I have little worry. If Villa recovers from his defeats, or someone else rises up with an army and takes over the government, my claims might be worthless."

If that happened, Domingo knew there would be nothing to inherit, and the possibility chilled him. Los Nuestros was more than dear—it was his future.

"You have papers," Anita said defensively, but Jefe said nothing.

"Papá, we can whip any gringo devils that are stupid enough to fight." Sereno mashed his patty of frijoles into a mush. His mother made him quit.

"But those who fight are not gringos." Domingo hadn't forgotten the men he'd seen while out hunting with Bravo. "I bet some of them are Villistas who deserted."

"They could work," Anita pointed out. "They don't have to keep fighting and killing."

Violeta began to fret, and the parents rose and went toward the sala, Sereno and Estrada following.

Domingo and Luis continued sipping their coffee, while criadas hovered in the hallway, waiting to clear the dishes. Pensive, Luis said, "I have decided not to go with the mesteñeros."

"First Jefe, and now you. What kind of trip will this be? A failure, sin duda."

"I am more needed here. Besides, the last time I went mustanging my horse nearly broke his leg, and mine too."

"Take a sure-footed one from the mountains. I can pick it for you, if you want."

Luis shook his head. "I appreciate the offer, amigo, but truly, I prefer to stay on the rancho. Martín has already chosen someone else, and Ramón approves."

"Who? No one can take your place. Even before Martín, it was you who taught me about horses."

"Gracias. But you'll like this hombre. He is brother to the señorita who was looking at you this afternoon."

"What señorita?" Already he knew it was the girl whose glance had held his longest when he delivered the javelina to the villagers. "Where were you, that you saw her? Not that there was anything to see—"

Luis laughed at him. "The rider's name is Máximino. He's a mestizo of great integrity, and can be a valued friend. But—" He stood and clapped Domingo on his uninjured shoulder. "in your place, I would beware of his little sister. I know that look well."

"Paz?"

Luis stopped in his tracks. Then, eyes averted, he said, "No. Not Paz."

Domingo remained, experiencing curiosity, mild fear, anticipation, and a great physical lassitude. Noticing criadas scuffling in the dim hallway—some pushing the others forward and those being pushed resisting, all giggling—he lifted a hand to them to enter, and they did. Three rather plain girls, several years older than he. They piled the used plates, glasses, and cups on trays and bore them out without a word. In a minute they returned for bowls, silverware, dirty napkins, and the tablecloth. He watched them leave and heard little explosions of laughter as they rounded the doorway.

What did it mean? He examined himself in Anita's gilt-framed mirror at the entrance to the dining room, and found nothing amiss. He'd even worn a whole shirt, to avoid being teased about showing off his battle scars. The glint of silver chain was visible at the throat of the garment, but the medal itself lay hidden under the fabric, next to his skin, where he could feel it respond to his movements.

Deciding the criadas were just being silly, he went to prepare for the trip into the mountains.

II

Christine chafed at being left alone with Greta, who did little except read newspapers and complain about the hotel service, which was careless, though the food was good. The dishes of beef and chicken, smothered in red sauces and accompanied by green ones, weren't as spicy as she'd been led to believe. Fresh fruits and flowers whenever she wanted them seemed a luxury, but the lack of butter was a hardship.

"Aren't you going to eat your flan?" she asked, noticing the untouched dessert

Greta pushed the bowl toward her without missing a line.

"What is so interesting?"

The woman didn't answer, but peered over the top edge of the newspaper. "Honey, did your father say when he was coming back?"

She shook her head, savoring the custard on her tongue.

Greta took a cigarette from a case and struck a match. "Is he always so desperate? I don't remember him being that way when he was here before."

The woman wore more makeup than Christine was used to seeing on a face. It drew attention to the wrinkles and sour expression, although the squint caused by smoke added to that effect. Raised eyebrows reminded her to answer the question. "Truthfully, I don't remember him ever being any different. Maybe, before Mother died."

Greta said *mmmmmnnn* with her lips closed, and a little gray puff came out her nostrils.

He'd been away from the hotel for two nights. She had learned not to look for him until he was standing before her, radiant with success or glowering with rage. It was peaceful here in the patio, despite the pockmarked plaster which a mozo had told her in broken English was due to the artillery shelling. "Many months ago," he'd hastened to say, seeing her fright.

"I must learn Spanish," she declared. "If Daddy wants to live in this country, we ought to know what people are saying."

Greta said, "Mmm," and turned a page.

The sun moved to angle beneath the patio roof, and a growing quiet in the streets, signaling the time for siesta, made her drowsy. She had not been sleeping well since the visit to the hacienda. At night her mind raced about, filling her with restless energy and leaving her exhausted during the day. *What is the matter with me?* She half feared some deadly jungle disease that would result in her being shipped back to Kentucky in a boxcar, to lie beside Mama in the Ridgemont Cemetery.

She didn't mention her feelings or fears, neither to Greta nor Daddy when he came in the evening and ate a supper of chile con carne and beer without telling them where he'd been. He would never trust a Mexican doctor, and going back to the States without settling the dispute over the property wasn't a choice. If she were sick enough to die, then she would just have to die.

Daddy probably wouldn't miss her much after a few months anyway. They had never been close, though he kept very strict control of everything she did. "For your own good, Baby," he so often told her. "I'm doing it all for you."

Now, she wondered exactly what it was he was doing. The secret silver mine lay at the center, of course. Daddy had come from a large family, none ever well off, and only his marriage to Mother had given him a middle-class house and the small saddlery shop that made them respectable and prosperous. For a while he'd wanted to own a horse farm. They'd visited many wealthy stock breeders, where she had picked up some of the terms and much appreciation for the animals grazing and frolicking in the lush pastures enclosed in neat white fences.

"The fencing alone would cost more than I can get out of another mortgage," Daddy complained bitterly.

Then while going through a drawerful of old papers he'd come across something that made his eyes glitter. "By God, this changes things. It was a joke when we bought into it, but I always had a feeling— Crawford gambled away his part to me on the train back, some place out in Texas. He'd be mad as hell if he thought I'd cash in on it."

The handsome Señor Cordero put a kink in Daddy's plans. He had papers, too—one of the developments that made Daddy moody. If Greta expected anything different, Christine thought, she'd be disappointed. It looked like a fight ahead. Daddy had used the courts before, sometimes pleading his own case; mostly he didn't win, but once in a while he did. Just enough to keep him confident in his own powers. She groaned. She didn't like the shouting and arm-waving that was a part of these episodes. If only she had stayed with one of her aunts . . .

Then she would never have seen Sereno Cordero.

"When are we going back, Daddy? Couldn't you and Señor Cordero talk more and make some kind of deal?"

"I'm working on it, Baby. Believe me. You don't see what I'm doing because you don't need to. There's things to be done, before I go back with nothing but talk."

Chapter Twelve

The fire-bell woke Ramón in the middle of the night. He was out of bed and into his clothes while Anita was still saying, "Madre de Dios—what now?"

Flickering orange shadows on the bedroom wall made him feel sick, but coming as they did through the glass doors, he knew it was the village and not the casa which was burning. "Go calm your women" He stamped into his boots. "and send Estrada to help."

Luis joined him on the paving at a run and they flung open storehouse doors and parceled out buckets and wide-mouthed ollas to the men who gathered, barefoot and shirtless.

From a dozen houses flames and smoke spread through the thatch, and to each house raced a man and his sons and cousins who lived with him, carrying water from the earth reservoir Ramón had seen completed and filled less than a month ago. *Thank God I had the foresight to do that.*

A pity, however, to have lacked foresight to make the villagers wet down their roofs. Above the noise of flames and shouts and barking dogs, he yelled, "I should have known the bastard would try something like this."

"Villa?" Luis panted, scooping up a bucketful of water and passing it to ready hands.

"No—that maldito gringo, Johnson."

"Why, Jefe. You have no proof of that."

"All the proof needed is in his manner."

It took more than half an hour of hard, dirty work to stop the fires. Lampposts at the end of each lane seemed feeble in contrast to the brightness of the flames. Resting on the tank rim, he wiped his face on a soaked shirt sleeve. "Was anyone injured?"

Estrada answered. "Some of the babies and smaller children, and the old ones who had to be helped out of their beds, suffer from breathing smoke. But no one was caught in the blazes, and I have treated those burned from getting too close."

People were milling about, the lower half of many faces protected from the night air by rebozos or rags. Children clung to each other and to their mother's skirts, older boys raced among the smoldering ruins, exclaiming over any spared object.

Ex-rebels came at him in a group, Refugio as their spokesman. "Jefe, we are ready to go after the devil who did this. Only give the word."

After a moment Ramón said, "If we fight, he will think there is something more valuable here than land to defend. Get some rest, if you can. Tomorrow we begin rebuilding. If homes are too damaged to stay in, put those families in the new storehouse, and be sure everyone has enough blankets."

He started up the road to the casa grande and saw his household in the yard, watching. He was glad the boys were safely on the way to bring back a new string of potros to be gentled. Criadas, fearful for relatives, detached one at a time and came past him. Anita waited until he was close, and they hugged each other.

When they were in bed, unrelaxed and far from sleep, she said, "You think Señor Johnson did this, don't you."

"Paid to have it done. Maybe one of my own men."

"None would ever betray you like that—especially not by destroying his village."

"Money is powerful, when one has been poor."

Anita laid her cheek on his chest, one arm across him and their fingers clasped. "I feel sorry for the little girl. Sereno says she is pretty."

"I suppose she will be, one day. Her hair is light and curly, and her eyes are still innocent." He rubbed his chin against the top of her head. "I thought he liked Tereza."

She was silent, though not asleep.

"What do you know?" he asked, suspicious. "They're too young, for it to be much."

Anita raised her head enough to face him, though the moon had passed and the room was dark. "It isn't much. Only, his heart is tender, and Tereza gave Domingo a silver santo like the one she gave him."

"Does that bother him?"

"I think it does, very much."

"I wonder how they're getting along on the roundup."

She snuggled back into her former position. "I would feel better, if you had gone."

"If I had, there wouldn't be this." He caressed the silky skin of her thigh.

II

Sereno gave up trying to be friendly after the first day. He concentrated on doing everything right so Martín would have no reason to rebuke him. Domingo was watching him like a hawk, waiting to pounce on any mistake.

When they had finished a supper of venison roasted over coals, Máximino kicked up the campfire and the Seri brothers began telling stories of ghosts, lost treasure, and silver mines, concealed during the last century by Spanish owners forced to leave the country.

Domingo leaned over and took hold of Tereza's medal with thumb and forefinger. "It's not exactly like mine," he said, satisfaction in his voice, and Sereno heard the unspoken part: it is inferior to mine.

He'd never gotten a close look at the one she had given his medio hermano, as it usually hung below the closure of the boy's shirt. *Had* Tereza given himself an inferior gift? Yet…she had kissed his cheek. Surely that meant something. Worrying in the long night hours, he tried to recall any time when she might have been alone with Domingo long enough to kiss him.

He studied the older boy, envying the ease with which he guided Valiente with almost no visible move of hands or legs. His own achievement in teaching Viento to rear and pose on command had brought praise from everyone except his brother, but after awhile the trick was old, as people only smiled and nodded when he did it. He wished he had opportunity to show Tereza, or the blonde gringa named Cristina. She had seemed nice.

"¡Mira!" Domingo had lowered the field glass, and was waving them forward to the brink of a stream. "It's Cimarroncito!" He would have ridden right down the bank had Martín not reined in front of Valiente, saying, "That is not our purpose."

In the distance, Sereno could see several dots, horses grazing on new grass. He had heard of the great stallion called Cimarrón that lived in El Valle de Los Mesteños. He'd heard more than he wanted to about how Domingo had got a rope on the caballo grande. Clearly, this was a different animal.

"Don Diego caught him," Lobo explained while they rode along the stream, "and gave him to your papá. After don Diego was killed, most of the mesteños we had captured were set free."

"Jefe made me leave Cimarroncito." Domingo kept the field glass focused on the distant manada, reins careless between the two last fingers of one hand. When he turned, his eyes were filled with an intense light. "Now he's even more beautiful than his padre. Why not these? Jefe would be happy to have them."

Martín took the glass and studied the herd. "There are only half a dozen, and no young. He wants ten colts."

"He never told me that."

"He told me," the arrendador said with finality.

Sereno fought to keep the smile off his lips. El hermano mayor might get his way with Papá, but Martín took authority on this trip seriously.

They continued for three hours before making camp in a cottonwood bosque at the base of a cliff. He went with Silvestre to gather firewood, and when they returned, Domingo was still trying to gain permission to capture Little Cimarrón and rejoin them tomorrow or next day.

Martín's swarthy face was firm. "I cannot allow it. The country is too wild for you to risk doing something so dangerous."

"I've ridden far in the countryside alone many times with Bravo. Cimarroncito was tamed by my own hand. And did I not kill the javelina without help?"

"Mesteños are more dangerous than a wild pig. That caballo will not remember you. Además, hay las pumas peligrosos."

"I'm not afraid. I have weapons and a fast horse."

"You should be afraid," Martín grunted, and tossed out the dregs of his coffee.

"También," said Lobo, "Villistas are hiding in these mountains."

Máximino laid another stick on the fire. "And bandidos worse than Villistas. You must have heard how they ride into villages and take even the women."

Domingo was silent, gazing into the flickering bright orange tongues of flame.

Sereno wrapped himself in his sarape, turning his feet to the warmth, his head filled with unpleasant thoughts of

Domingo and Tereza. She was older than either of them, thus closer in age to the firstborn. Suddenly he remembered something which made him jerk upright. Domingo had mentioned going to Los Dos to train a filly brought home from the last horse hunt.

"¿Qué te pasa?" Martín asked. "Did a scorpion bite you?"

"No—está nada." He lay back down. If Domingo talked Papá into letting him go north, Sereno meant to go along.

... he sat on the roof of his cave, playing 'La Llorona' flawlessly. The sun lay soft and bright on the valley beyond the pines. In the distance he could see the border of forest, backed by rugged brown peaks which gradually turned lavender and then purple as the sun moved to the west. He felt secure and happy.

Then something changed. Panic filled him. Glancing about for the cause, palm sweaty against the wood of the flute and his heart thumping hard enough to hurt, he saw nothing worthy of alarm. Periquitos in the branches above chattered and fluttered in the usual way. But far across the plain he spotted something moving. Something shapeless, dark, advancing swiftly. In moments, he knew, it would overcome him, attack him. Scrambling down the bank, tearing skin from palm and knee, he turned for the opening of his cave—and encountered a closed door that was not supposed to be here. Silent shrieks burst from his mouth as he beat upon the weathered wood. Who had done this? Blocked from safety, he whirled to face the awful unknown thing—

"Dios mío," came Domingo's irate voice, "¿Qué es lo que te pasa ahora?"

Fingers pinched his shoulder and he came to himself in the dark of night, campfire coals like demons' eyes glowing red near his unbooted feet, Domingo close beside him and Martín hunkering at his other elbow. Gregorio, Máximino, the Seris, all asked, "What is happening?"

Awash with relief, he said, "Un sueño, solamente."

"A nightmare, from the sounds you were making," Domingo accused. "I thought you were being strangled."

"I screamed?"

"Only noises," Martín said. "Are you all right now?"

"Sí—" He lay back down and they returned to their places. Fragments of the dream—and the fear he'd felt— kept him awake for a long time, wishing he were home.

At first light, he was aware of compañeros tossing greetings and joking about whose turn it was to bring fuel and water. He rubbed a stickiness out of his eyes and sat up. A small piece of paper was pinned to his blanket with a long thorn.

Blinking, he freed it and read the scrawl.

> Do not worry. I will join you
> here in a few days when you come
> back through with your horses.
> DRC

"¿Qué es ese?" Silvestre asked, pausing to look down.

He handed the note to the young Seri, who shook his head. "I cannot read enough yet. Tell me what it says."

At that moment Martín discovered Domingo was gone and exploded in a stream of cursing.

"He left a note." Sereno jumped up and offered it before remembering Martín couldn't read at all. "He says not to worry."

"I don't worry about him," the horseman said, his scowl boding trouble when he caught the older boy. "It is my pelt which don Ramón will send to the tannery."

They ate pinole and leftover meat, no coffee, and packed up for the day's journey. When Martín led out, it was to the east, and Gregorio followed. The rest glanced at each other, then at Sereno. He shrugged and took his place in file behind the older men. Leaving Domingo in this manner gave him a queasy feeling in his stomach.

Throughout the day, his thoughts returned to the dream, unremembered except for that great fear of his sanctuary being threatened by something unseen but very real. From time to time, when he wasn't occupied by the rough footing of the trail, he wondered what Domingo was doing.

If something bad had happened to him....

He assured himself that of course he didn't want a bad thing to happen. Losing Domingo would crush Papá. But, with no older brother, Los Nuestros and its wealth someday would be solely his. His and Tereza's.

"Ahí lo es." Martín pointed. Thornbrush-covered cliffs formed steep walls of the valley, still at a distance.

Gregorio dismounted and gave Sereno his reins. "Stay with our horses. We must be sure the herd is away from the entrance, and that no one is using this place as a refuge." He left a loaded pistol and the field glass.

Carrying only canteens, reatas, and side arms, they set out, Martín in the lead.

Sereno watched los jinetes grow smaller as they used available cover in moving toward the canyon. He raised the glass and adjusted it until they came into focus. Nimbly they scaled the barrier of boulders that kept the horses in, and disappeared over the top.

With nothing to do, he grew bored, sleepy. Cinchas and bits had been loosened, the ponies staked. Pack mules dozed, tails lazily at work against the flies. He shook himself, went to Viento, unhooked his canteen, lifted it for a drink.

A pistol shot in the distance made his hand jerk and drop the container. Through the field glass he saw the mesteñeros at the gate, waving him forward. Quickly he readied their geldings and rode to where the others waited, sweating, telling jokes. Any worry about Domingo vanished in the work at hand.

The basin stretched in an irregular oval about three kilometros at the widest part, with a deep stream running through the middle from east to west. Cottonwoods, willows, and lush grass drew all sorts of wild creatures, mostly birds, though Lobo took a half-hearted shot at a coyote which unconcernedly ghosted into the weeds.

His belly was cramping from hunger when, just at dusk, they located the yeguada. The last band of sunlight gilded west-facing cliffs. Supper smoke and roasting deer meat, the cool evening, and the sight of grazing mustangs gave a sense of contentment. He'd never liked camping out due to the inconveniences; but tonight, soft laughter and relaxed movements of friends around him, and a purpose ahead in the rounding up of the colts, made him glad to be part of a brotherhood, un hombre del campo.

Gregorio and Martín had their heads close together. Straining to hear what was being said, he wasn't surprised when they gave each other a nod and Gregorio went to saddle his horse. "Is he going to find Domingo?" he asked, and

Martín said, "I cannot rest as things are. We shall have to do this job with fewer hands."

The job began at daylight, after a meal of tortillas wrapped around cold meat. He heeded Martín's order to leave behind anything that rattled, clinked, or reflected sunlight. The silver santo, however, he could not bring himself to trust to a pocket. To conceal the shiny medal, he wore a shirt which laced at the neck with a cord. To protect his hands from the reata, he put on supple gloves. If Domingo could rope a mustang, so could he. In two months he would be thirteen. Un hombre. No? Even if Martín had taken back the pistol.

They rode over the tussocky grass in a wide circle, getting behind the herd, intending to nudge it toward the gate. As soon as the mustangs were through, it would be secured again to hold the yeguada with their stallion Bandera, for another year of breeding, unchallenged by younger stallions.

He pictured Papá, sitting down to a hot breakfast and big mug of chocolate, unaware that anything was amiss. If Gregorio didn't find Domingo, or discovered him dead from a fall or wild animal attack, Papá would blame all of them. Such a thing would raise the older boy to the level of a saint, all faults forgotten.

Sereno began to fume. Tereza might become like one of the women Mamá had once read about, devoting the rest of her life to prayer for Domingo's soul, forgetting about him...

"¡Cuidado!"

The shout ahead snapped off his daydream; at the same instant Viento leaped sideways, nearly unseating him. Horses bore down upon them, enveloping him in choking dust. When he could see through it, he kicked his heels into his mount and raced to bring back three escaping colts. That accomplished, he reined close to Lobo, who was nearest him. "Where is Bandera?"

"Back there," the young man answered, gesturing. "Martín is keeping him away, just to be safe."

From talk around the campfire, he knew that Bandera was tame compared to Cimarrón Grande, the caballo padre in El Valle de Los Mesteños. Still, Papá, Martín, and Gregorio had warned him to be watchful of stallions, which could be dangerous if crossed. "Do you think Domingo can capture Cimarroncito?"

Lobo shrugged. "Perhaps. When that one was first caught, don Domingo worked some with him. But it was months ago, and now el joven has yeguas."

He considered what that might mean. Like Papá, stallions defended their families against any enemy. If not for the threat of Señor Johnson, Papá would be here, riding back and forth in the swirling dust, giving orders.

Doubt crept in. Maybe he would be with Domingo, chasing Cimarroncito.

After an uneventful hour they brought the selected colts to the opening. One by one, as Lobo and Máximino roped them, he and Silvestre tied three to a line. Martín divided responsibility, putting Silvestre in charge of the mules, Lobo the remounts, and one of the strings into his care. The arrendador himself took the wildest ones and set the pace.

All afternoon they pushed onward, so there was no noon meal, no siesta. He was ready to drop when they came to a place to camp. It was beside the stream where Domingo had first spotted Cimarroncito, but now no mustangs grazed in the valley, and there was no sign of him, or of the man who had gone to find him.

Writing a note in the dark wasn't easy. Domingo pricked his fingers thoroughly in finding a thorn suitable for pinning his message to Sereno's blanket.

As quickly as he could, he dressed and packed his gear, trusting in the bond between him and Valiente to keep the horse quiet while he fumbled with cinchas and bit. The moon had set, but there were plenty of stars and he knew that once he was on the trail back, Valiente would keep him from getting lost. Walking beside his mount, he circled the camp and finally eased himself into the saddle. He mentally checked to be sure he had enough food, ammunition, his knife and pistol.

By midmorning he was well along, and by afternoon he was back at the stream, where he let Valiente drink. Crossing, and with cliffs rising on his right, he rode toward the grassy flat where he had seen the stallion.

Tracks were everywhere. Cropped grass, manure, places where they had rolled. He wished he had brought the field glass. Riding in wide circles, he scanned the arroyo-cut plain, watching bosques of cottonwoods for movement. Having grazed, they would hole up in shade for hours. Full of water and likely suffering from having gorged on new grass, they would find running difficult. No colts, so the mares were probably a mix of old ones and those not yet fertile. Half a dozen, Martín said, an estimate confirmed by the glass.

He headed northeastward on the trail that appeared freshest, raising his eyes frequently to scan the rolling grassland, scattered with boulders the size of the casa at Los

Nuestros. Groves of trees at this altitude had received rains and were leafing. Deer, wild turkeys, small families of javelinas, a couple of coyotes. No mustangs. He rode with the rifle across his saddle, ready for defense.

Rounding a forested ridge, he saw spread before him yet another grassy, well-watered valley. By the sun, he was two hours from the first stream, and closer to the sealed cañon than before. He began wondering if he might make a short cut and meet the other mesteñeros—providing Cimarroncito chose to cooperate. Wiping sweat from his forehead and hatband, he sat enjoying the solitude.

Valiente's ears pricked. Domingo's hand fell on the action of his rifle.

"¿Qué es?" he whispered, feeling the horse's chest expand and relax in small sniffs as it tested for scent. Eyes and ears alert, he tickled the flanks with his spurs and they moved forward. Around a cluster of boulders they came into the dooryard of a hut. Dismounting, he called out, "¡Hola! ¡La casita! ¿Quién vive?"

The lashed-pole door hung slightly open. Cautious, he stepped inside, rifle first. Dimness, dust, and little else except for a worn-out broom lying forgotten. A rag which turned out to be part of a shirt, a boot heel but no boot.

At the back was a rock boundary wall higher than a man's head. Climbing up, from its top he saw a distant mountain range. Quite near, grazing, were Cimarrón el Joven and his six fillies. They didn't look bloated or tired. They looked sleek and fast.

"¡Guau!" He shivered from a thrill of anticipation. Last year, using juicy pieces of cane to make friends, he'd petted and talked to the horse in the corrals at Los Nuestros; yet

Jefe was the one who had spent the most time with the stallion, putting on the jáquima, providing food and water, and it was Jefe's rope to which Cimarrón would yield. He couldn't expect an animal to remember the tears he'd shed the day Jefe forced the release.

But his voice. . . . With just enough force to be heard, he called, "Cimarroncito— Yo soy aquí, amigo. Venga, por favor."

The mares paid no attention, their caballito marido raised its head to stare at him with mild curiosity.

"Let's be friends. ¿Bien? Would you like a treat?" He dropped off the wall and got his food sack from Valiente. He'd brought enough tortillas to last several days. Carrying three between his teeth, he scaled the boundary wall again. Then he repeated the call, adding, "No tengas miedo. Don't be afraid. I'm coming to meet you."

Ears forward, the stallion watched his approach.

Then, head extended, nostrils flaring, it jerked back with such a sudden shrill warning that he jumped at least a handspan off the ground. Being afoot was dangerous. More dangerous, Martín had warned, than stalking a javelina. One hoof pawed out a crescent of dirt. The hindquarters danced, restless. This didn't look good.

Holding out the tortillas, he kept talking despite a waver in his voice. "You remember me, don't you? Mi muy guapo caballo, I would give you a sweet if I had it, but these poor tortillas are the best I have. Why don't you try them? You like corn, I remember. These are corn. Taste."

The stallion trotted back and forth on an invisible line, snorting, whirling, but issuing no further challenge.

"You are not wild, you only think you should be. Remember don Diego? He was kind to you. And Jefe, who

231

fed you grain. I shall be kind, also. Remember how you used to let me put on the jáquima sometimes? Allow me to breathe into your nostrils again. Come, mi buen amigo. Taste these nice tortillas—"

Cimarroncito gave a short lunge but stopped, looked uncertainly to where his band grazed without alarm, and swung his attention back to the food.

"Can you smell the corn? Do you remember? It was I who set you free that day we left. If Jefe knew you were here, he would want you at Los Nuestros. You will make beautiful colts for him, given yeguas which are strong and well-formed, like yourself."

He held out rolled-up tortillas, and Little Cimarrón took a bite, just as if the offering were a stick of cane. Over his shoulder the coils of his reata were useless, but his free hand reached for the length of lead rope he'd brought for this purpose. He rubbed the face and neck with the rope and succeeded in looping it behind the ears. Making a temporary halter with one hand was difficult, but as the last bite was swallowed, he got a second loop over the stallion's nose and secured it. A large knot in the end of the rope dragged on the ground; stepping on it for a day or two would reaccustom the horse to the feel of a restraint.

Alert for any change of mood, he slowly began backing away, still saying whatever came into his head. "¡Qué caballo! ¡Qué un buen amigo! Tu eres muy muy guapo y tranquilo. Ah, Cimarroncito, surely Jefe will give you back to me, for bringing you home."

Of course they were far from home, and the next decision was whether to rejoin the mustangers or wait for them to come to him. Going, he might lose this small bunch in the cañons and arroyos, but staying would increase Martín's anger.

Already this afternoon was past, and evening had come. Tomorrow, or next day, he could meet them. Traveling slowly to keep their mesteños from losing confidence, they might reach the first stream in two days. Trailing him here would require another, and take them off their route. He reconsidered the idea of a short cut, discarded it.

After a supper of leftover venison and stale water from his canteen, he spread his bedroll on the packed earth just inside the choza door. Turning and twisting to find comfort among inconveniently placed depressions, he tangled his feet in the end of a blanket more than once. However, having the rifle gave him courage, his gelding outside assured him of being wakened should anything intrude.

… he was riding Cimarrón Grande through a valley of yellow grass, wind at his back, the steep cliffs at Rincón rising on his right, El Valle de Los Mesteños stretching opposite to familiar blue mountains. He'd never been more content. Everyone at Los Nuestros was happy. When he returned from his ride, there would be music, dancing, a feast of delicacies. Maximino's sister waited with a little gift for his birthday. Wondering what she meant to give him, he reined Cimarrón up the rugged path toward Rincón.

Then, a perplexity. He didn't know her name. Who could he ask, without feeling foolish?

Something brought him awake, disoriented but with enough sense to grab the rifle and skin out of his bedding to wait in a darker corner, soundless, unspeaking.

Peering through the open doorway, he located against the night sky the silhouette of his horse—and a man standing beside it.

Chapter Thirteen

Jefe always said, *Make the first shot count.* Domingo couldn't shoot for fear of hitting Valiente. A bullet would blast right through the flimsy wall of the shack, if his visitor chose to fire. Palms sweating, he held his breath and heard the man talking quietly. He crept to the door.

"Pues, caballito, he can't be far. But, where? In the casita? Or, more sensibly, in the brush..."

He called, "¿Quién es?" and dropped to the floor, warning, "Yo estoy armado."

"¡No dispare!" cried a voice he recognized. "Dammit, Domingo, I ought to leave you to the wolves."

"Gregorio?"

"Who else?"

They met in the dooryard and the man gave him a grudging abrazo. "Martín is very angry with you."

"I know. But I had to try, and, ¡hombre! I got a rope on him so easy. Tomorrow, I bet I could even ride—"

"*There,* I draw the line. If we can, we'll take him and his lady friends with us. But more than that and I won't help."

"I didn't ask for help."

"You shall need it, in any case, when you start to drive him from this tierra. Escuche, it's almost dawn. Get a fire started so we can have coffee. I don't wish to delay."

By daybreak they were circling the stallion and his band, pointing them in the direction of a rendezvous with the other mesteñeros. He was confident of his ability to train young Cimarrón. Under Martín's supervision, he'd done much of the vital early work on those introduced to the bit by the arrendador, and he'd watched the process countless times. More important, he had been assured he possessed the nameless quality which Martín said was born in all great horsemen.

They were having difficulty persuading the band into the first stream when a shout behind them undid all their efforts. Fillies scattered, the stallion disappeared over a low rise, and Gregorio swore profusely.

At a gallop ten riders broke from a jumble of rocks and surrounded them with a wall of dust and jaded horseflesh. His heart suddenly felt too big for his chest. "These are the men who stopped me once when I was out with Bravo."

All wore what appeared to be the same clothing as three months earlier, faces grimed with dirt, gunpowder, sweat and tobacco. The leader grinned at him. "Ah, el chico rico. Today you have a gun, I see. And a friend. May I ask what you are doing on my land?"

"Leaving it," Gregorio said, "as fast as we can."

"Oh, this little stream is not my boundary, if that is what you mean. My tierra reaches all the way to the Río de Las Viborillos. A long way from here."

"Then, we shall go a long way."

"I think not until you have explained your business."

"I came to find this boy. He was lost."

The bandit leader feigned surprise. "This boy? Lost? Unbelievable. He hunts with a gato grande. I saw, with my eyes. Don't you, joven?"

"Not any more. I set him free."

The man laughed, coughing and catching his breath with difficulty, then said, "Panchito, come here." One of his riders walked his mount forward. "Is this your gato? We set this one free a few days ago." He jerked a stiffening puma hide off the shoulders of the rider and tossed it to the ground, striking Valiente's forelegs. Valiente reared but Domingo controlled him.

"Madre de Dios," the leader yelled, "he is a jinete, too. Rico, we need you in Villa's army. Can you shoot?"

Domingo swung up his rifle and shot off the bandit's sombrero. The other men shouted with laughter. Their leader bent to pick up the hat, face muscles working as he decided whether to take it as a joke or fight.

"Now you, señor." Domingo offered his rifle, butt first. "Although my hat is smaller."

Another burst of laughter, in which the bandit joined. "Not today, muchacho." He shook his head. "We have urgent business, so must say adiós. But—" He spoke over his shoulder. "Do not come this far again, or I might be less friendly."

When they were out of sight, Gregorio leaned on his saddle horn and said, "Nice shot," though his face was drained of color.

"They talk about Villa, but I think they are only cowardly bandits. They enjoy a jest."

"Did you look into their eyes? If I had done what you did—or if your bullet had hit flesh instead of felt—we'd both be dead now."

Domingo stepped down from his horse and knelt to examine the puma skin. There was no way to tell whether it was Bravo, as he found no marks by which it could be identified. The feel of the fur, even dry and lifeless, brought back rich memories.

He shook them off. "Let's go after our horses."

"Are you loco? Those bastards will shoot us if we cross them again."

"Cimarroncito, if no other, is mine, and I intend to have him."

Gregorio gave a shake of his head. "I understand now what Ramón has to endure."

On guard, they followed the stallion's trail in silence. Before long the scattered band had come together and by midmorning they found it grazing in a cañon sweetsmelling with blooming acacias. Working out the timing and the angle at which they were most likely to meet their compañeros, they used reatas to turn the band in the direction chosen.

He fought the temptation to make a loop and settle it over the young stallion's head in the same way he'd once snared El Cimarrón Grande. "Tomorrow," he said, "I'm going to take off the drag rope. It's skinning his nose."

"It is keeping him respectful." Gregorio struck a match for his cigarette and grinned. "But you know little about being respectful."

"If you are referring to Señor Bandido, he deserves no respect."

"You nearly made me soil my pants when you fired at him."

"He made a joke at my expense the last time we met."

"And that is not a wise thing to do, eh, muchacho?"

"Life is too short to submit to someone's boot."

"Spoken like a true revolutionario!"

When they came to the trail that led to Bandera's stronghold, Gregorio studied the ground, finally saying, "The others have not passed. Probably tomorrow, God willing."

There was a bit of grass to hold their small band, and the presence of their geldings seemed to have a calming effect, so they made camp. As soon as Domingo lay down he knew no more until his friend woke him for guard duty. Under the starry night sky, he smoked one of the cheap cigarettes Gregorio used when there was no money for white paper ones, and made plans. What to say if Jefe objected to his intention to train this Cimarrón himself. What would result if Gregorio told Jefe about meeting the bandits again?

In the silence just before dawn, he remembered his interrupted dream and wondered whether Maximino's nameless sister ever thought of him.

II

In the hotel patio, waiting for Daddy to join them for lunch, Christine overheard excited conversation among a party of men who looked like soldiers; with fewer than a dozen words of Spanish at her command, she could only guess that the revolution had broken out again close by. If so, why weren't they off somewhere, fighting?

"Greta," she hissed. "Listen to them. Tell me what they're saying."

Still holding the day's newspaper in front of her face, Greta strained to untangle the exchange. In moments she leaned to whisper, "They said that one of their friends, a rebel officer named Ramón, was attacked the other night and the village at his hacienda was burned."

She felt the blood leave her face. "What hacienda? Was it the one belonging to Señor Cordero?"

She could see the big white house going up in flames, brownskinned people rushing about with sloshing buckets of water; Tereza trapped in an upstairs bedroom, and Sereno running into the roaring flames to save her.

"Oh, Greta, did they say who the attackers were? Was it Pancho Villa? But, he's a rebel, too." She sat back, perplexed by a war which had many sides. The property Daddy was fighting over would be less attractive without the casa grande and the finery she had glimpsed on that brief visit. There was a baby sister, she recalled. "I wonder if anyone was hurt."

Greta made shushing motions, her ear still pricked toward the soldiers' table, but then returned her attention to the news. "They've switched to something else, now."

"But, do you think it was Señor Cordero they meant? How can we find out? Daddy will be upset if someone has destroyed the house where he wants to live."

Greta's voice came through the pages of the paper. "Don't worry about your daddy."

Lately that was difficult to do. He was gone most of each day and far into the nights, and she'd caught whiffs of liquor on his breath. The hard glitter in his eyes was always a bad sign. She had to be careful bringing up a topic that might cause a bad reaction.

When Daddy finally arrived, he ordered broiled fish with a gray sauce. She filled up on buñuelos and frothy chocolate. As soon as he finished telling about the farm machinery he was having sent down by rail, she asked, "Is Señor Cordero's first name Ramón?"

"Why, yes, Baby. Why?"

"We overheard some soldiers." She glanced at Greta, who explained, "Someone started a fire on that hacienda. They believe it was Villa, because Señor Cordero was an officer for Obregón."

"A warning, do you think?" Daddy's eyes glittered up at the woman, then fastened on his plate.

Greta shrugged. "Probably. Are you going to do anything about it?"

"Why should I? Let Cordero fight off the bandits. If he gets tired enough he'll see reason."

Christine watched them, a knot of suspicion starting in the back of her mind. If Pancho Villa wanted to strike an enemy, he wouldn't stop at destroying a few huts. The homes of the wealthy had been his target before. What kind of man could burn a village?

Someone desperate. Like Daddy.

"Did you enjoy your morning, Baby? Go shopping again? Need money?"

So far she and Greta had shopped every day, bringing back baskets, linens, a pair of sandals which bruised her feet, a rebozo woven too heavy for spring in the lowlands. Greta complained over the scarcity and poor quality of the foods, high prices, and insolent soldiers who made remarks as they passed. She wanted to go to Chihuahua.

"I bought a pair of silver filigree earrings," Christine said, "and some little silver figures of arms and legs that I put on a necklace chain."

"Milagros," Greta supplied, closing her lips against saying more.

Christine showed the milagro necklace to Daddy, who pretended interest with the same studied look she'd always gotten from him just before he said things like, "Well, girls, I've got a meeting in a few minutes. Have a pleasant siesta."

She felt like shouting, I don't want to siesta. I want to visit the Corderos and see the baby sister. I want to sit on their cool veranda and listen to Tereza and Sereno talk Spanish. Instead she said, "You will be back for supper, won't you?"

He turned at the edge of the patio pavement and smiled. "I'll try. Tonight, for sure."

III

Ramón watched while Estrada bandaged the hand of a young mestizo who had gotten the worst of a knife fight over some girl in the village. The absence from work for a few days wouldn't be felt, as the fields, corrals, shops, storehouses, and ranges were well manned with ex-rebels and youths who were growing into that time when they lusted for women and a good fight. Guards had been tripled since the night the village burned, and already homes were restored, even improved.

The mustangers were due back today.

"No more tepache," he suggested, as the young man turned his hand this way and that, admiring Estrada's work.

The injured one smiled and shook his head, but when he had departed, Estrada said, "You know such an expectation is unreasonable."

"I know." Tepache was the homemade wine of the Yaqui, in some ways preferable to pulque but the source of endless bickering and wounds that required the médico's services. For other ailments, Anita and the midwives, along with the village curandera, had taken over the former vegetable plot near the house for an herb garden. One of the storerooms was pungent with bunches of cures tied to the rafters with string, in baskets lining the walls, or on tables covered with petates laden with drying blossoms, leaves, stems, and roots. "At least it's not aguardiente."

"No sé." Estrada shook his head. "At least with that, one expects the outcome. Tepache tricks a man into feeling all is well."

"Too much peacefulness does the same thing," he said, and went back to his account books. Something else which bothered him was Luis's absence. The boy—no longer a boy—had asked to go into Culiacán last week, adding, "I am not sure how long I must stay."

"You don't need my permission," he' told Luis, irritated. "You are free to do as you please, even if I can't break you of calling me Patrón."

"Sometimes, when I remember, I call you Jefe."

Domingo still called him that, too, another irritation. Leaning back in his chair, desk littered with papers needing Luis's attention, he wondered how Sereno had fared on the trip. The child—no longer a child—was tough, resilient, stubborn. Qualities also possessed by Domingo. Under his breath, he cried, "¡Ay, ay, ay, *AY*! Dios help us if they ever want the same thing."

Anita leaned around the door casing, Violeta in her arms. "Are you speaking of our sons?"

He went to take the baby, kissing her smooth little cheek with affection. Anita tiptoed for her share, and when they parted he said, "If they don't ride in today, I think I shall be crazy tonight."

"See? I told you, you should have gone." She pinched his earlobe playfully. He caught her hand and bit her fingertip, playfully. Violeta waved both arms and let out a happy shriek.

Bootsteps racing down the corridor startled them; Luis's sudden breathless appearance in the room brought terror. In that instant Ramón vowed to have some of his rebel friends put, if not a telephone, at least a telegraph line to Los Nuestros, even if every inch of it had to be watched over by armed guards to keep insurrectos or animals from disrupting it. Rumors had been circulating since Villa's daring though foolhardy attack across the border last month, and he would not have been surprised to see the gringo general Pershing himself at Luis's heels.

"¿Qué? ¿Qué paso?" He handed Violeta to her mother, who, fearful-eyed but silent, shielded the baby's face with one hand.

Luis halted, sombrero brim crushed in his grasp. "Don't be frightened," he gasped, sinking into the visitor's chair. "There is no danger to us."

They waited for him to catch his breath. Through the glass door Ramón noticed a mozo leading his jaded horse toward the corrals.

Calmer, the young man glanced at Anita as if he wished she were elsewhere. Alert to the gesture, she left the room but listened from the hallway.

Hunkering at Luis's knee, he gently removed the broken hat from tense fingers and laid it aside. "Ahora. Tell your news."

Softly, as if he knew Anita lurked behind his back, Luis blurted, "Paz is married. To Mariano!"

The shock rocked him back on his heels, only the desk preventing a fall. "Madre de Dios, I don't believe it. He would never—" He bit down hard, remembering Luis's deep attachment for the girl, but his thought continued: *marry someone so beneath his class.*

Luis gave a self-conscious nod. "You can say it, Jefe. The idea stunned me, too. Why do you suppose he didn't tell us?"

"Why indeed." He stood slowly and, pushing objects to clear a space, seated himself on the desk. "I wonder what Tereza thinks of her."

"I also wondered."

The words implied a desire to elaborate, and when he lifted encouraging eyebrows, Luis continued, "Will not she and the niña talk of—intimate things? Things señorita Teresita would never dream of otherwise. Jefe, hadn't you better warn Domingo?"

"Tereza is barely fourteen," he said uncertainly, knowing Paz was younger when she became Joaquín's soldadera; the same age at which Anita had fallen in love with him. "But I was older than Domingo," he muttered, with even more uncertainty.

"When you married, sí, but before that, if I recall, there was María—"

"I never slept with her."

Luis drew breath to say more, but abruptly closed his mouth.

He knew what was in his friend's mind, however. Before Anita, there was Serafina. Just audible, he mused, "Do we ever stop paying for our sins?"

Standing, Luis picked up his hat. With the other arm he hugged Ramón and said, "You have paid enough, compadre. Now you must forgive yourself."

Light footsteps in the hall betrayed Anita's retreat. At the office door, Luis paused to say, "Domingo could do worse than Tereza. But I think they are not right for each other, even if don Mariano would allow a union."

"Why wouldn't he?" He frowned, cut by the insult, though it was unintentional. "We are like brothers."

Gently, the reply came: "You know why, Ramón."

After Luis had gone, he sat brooding. In a family of predominately Spanish blood, Tereza would never be allowed to marry beneath her class, even if her brother chose to do so.

Anita came and leaned against him, resting her chin on his shoulder, arms around his ribs. He breathed in the clean scent of her hair. "You heard?"

She kissed his neck. "Yes."

"More to worry about."

"Yes. But, not the way you suppose."

He held her apart enough to probe her eyes. "What do you mean?"

"It's Sereno who is in love with Tereza."

"You told me that was innocent."

"For now. Years pass, even when they seem not to."

He enfolded her in a jealous embrace, realizing he had waited for her to reveal, by hints or brutal clarity, the details of her captivity in Mérida. He believed her assurance that El General was not capable of the marital joining. He sensed now that he would never know what humiliating things the old man had been capable of, and done. His own secrets, despite how heavy they weighed, also should forever remain unsaid.

"Forgive me," he murmured, and kissed her on the mouth. The sweet stirring of desire began flowing and he allowed himself a few moments to enjoy it before suggesting, "Let's go upstairs."

Arms around each other, they walked along the hall, where a criada was leisurely mopping. A fresh breeze blew through the open doors, and with it came a shout.

"¡Los mustangos están regresando!"

He made a disappointed face, and Anita laughed. "Later," she promised. Fingers entwined, they went to greet the riders.

Both boys appeared older than possible after only a few weeks' absence. Stepping down from saddles, dust swirling to cling to skin and garments, they tossed reins to horse handlers standing ready, swept off hats, and came across the dry brown grass.

Sereno visibly resisted running into any welcoming embrace his mother might have bestowed. He allowed her to kiss his forehead, leaning a bit so she could reach him.

Dios, I must notice things more. Ramón gave his younger son an abrazo. "No broken bones, I see."

He and Domingo slapped each other roughly on the back. By Navidad they would be eye to eye. The prospect shook him. In May the older boy would be fourteen. He looked sixteen. Was this what war could do?

After receiving Anita's kiss on his cheek, Domingo said, "I brought home Cimarrón el Joven." He gestured to where Martín and Gregorio were supervising in the separation of the mustangs into small lots. Alone in a high-walled pen, the stallion trotted round and round, head high, nostrils flaring.

Ramón said, "Doesn't surprise me," though it did.

"Will he be mine?"

Hesitating, he was conscious of Sereno going into the house with Anita, ready for a bath and clean clothing. Weeks with the Zapatistas seemed to have left as little mark as those years in Mérida. Sereno never liked being less than tidy, while Domingo often forgot to change his shirt and frequently went about with knees or elbows ripped from encounters with thorns or any other sharp object that happened to be in his way. Did living in rebel camps cause this? Or, was it the loss of his mother . . . .

"Jefe? Will he?"

The eyes frowning into his were like looking into a mirror. Needlessly, he reminded, "You have Valiente."

"He's a gelding."

"I know that."

"I can handle Cimarrón, if that worries you."

Filling his lungs with the sweet, dry air, he blew out a sigh. "Much worries me, hijo. Don't add to it."

"But, Jefe—" Anger tinged the protest.

He turned away, calling over his shoulder, "I shall consider it. Bastante. ¿Bueno?"

He would listen to Martín's report later. Anita was waiting for him in their bedroom.

Domingo kicked a fist-sized rock out of the road. It bounced up the gravelly bank, narrowly missing Luis's ankle as that young man rounded the bougainvillea covered wall.

"Cuidado, muchacho," his friend cried, joining him. "Did the trip go badly?"

"No. The trip was fine. But the return so far has been less than satisfactory."

"¿Cómo? I see Jefe's little stallion. Did that not please him?"

"When was he ever pleased about anything?"

Luis leaned beside him on a corral rail. "Ah, Mingo, your father has responsibilities. Have you not heard?"

"Heard what?"

"The village was burned just after you left. Jefe thinks el señor gringo is responsible."

He climbed on the corral for a better look. He'd noticed the new thatch, but supposed it was because the rainy season was fast approaching. "Was anyone hurt?" Maximino's sister lived in one of those huts.

"Not your little sweetheart, never fear." Luis jerked his chin toward the plaza, where villagers had gathered to watch the work of the horsemen. "See—she awaits you."

"She is not my sweetheart. I don't even know her name, hombre."

"She's called Mina. Why not go and say hello."

"Loco, I am not ready to die."

"Caray, niño, I never suggested that you carry her off. Just make friends. Máximino likes you well enough."

His heart seemed to lodge throbbing in his throat, suspending talk for a minute. When he glanced toward the plaza again, Mina was gone. Disappointment and relief mingled. Walking back to the casa with Luis, he asked, "Señor Johnson. Does Jefe think he is a threat?"

"Any man who tries to burn up people in their homes is a threat," Luis answered.

At supper, Jefe finished an account of the incident with a warning. "No one is to leave the rancho compound without full escort. At least ten guns. There is something here that the man wants badly. I'm going to Culiacán in a day or two, to see if I can find out what it might be."

"What might it be, Papá?" Sereno asked. "Treasure?"

"Lobo and Silvestre have been filling his head with stories," Domingo teased. "He believes there is a lost mine on Los Nuestros." He watched Ramón closely, and was a bit surprised to see a guarded look come into Jefe's eyes.

"Luis, perhaps you should tell everyone your news," Jefe said, holding his plate for a second enchilada. "There's no reason for it to be kept secret."

Face flushed, Luis choked, coughed, tried a drink of water, and turned away to cough some more.

Estrada pounded him on the back and Anita leaned to rescue his half-eaten tortilla from the baby's reaching fingers. Jefe stared at him in concern. "Lo siento—I didn't know you still cared for her—"

When able to draw breath, Luis stared back at him for several moments before saying, "Oh, you mean about Paz."

"What did you think I meant?"

They waited out a tense little silence while he drank deeply of the water.

Then Domingo had to say, "What about Paz?"

Eyes all around the table glanced at him and then fastened on Luis, who said at last, "She and Mariano married. The cabo Valdéz in Culiacán heard it from his cousin, who is a sergeant in Hermosillo."

Paz, married. To Mariano! Well, it should not have been so surprising, he thought, remembering that night she left Dos Corazones with their friend. Cutting his eyes toward Anita, he sensed a lifting of her spirit. Then, she too had suspected a connection of some kind between Paz and Jefe.

"What did you think I meant?" Ramón repeated.

Luis lifted his chin as if defending himself. "I went to the city to learn what I must do to become a priest."

It was as if one of the bombas had landed in the room, and the diners sat motionless, waiting for it to explode. At last Anita said, "¡Qué magnífico! The chapel has been so empty, with everyone afraid—"

Estrada laid down his fork.

Ramón slid back his chair as if he meant to stand up, but remained on its edge.

"Why is everybody acting loco?" Domingo asked. "Don't we need a priest?"

"No," Jefe said.

"I shall stay out of this." Estrada tossed down his napkin and left.

Sereno said, "Luis, will you wear robes like the padre from Blanca Rosa used to do?"

"You remember him?" his father asked, astonished.

"I remember he carried a staff, like the goatherder, and a boy ran in front of him with a little gold pot on a chain. The smoke that came from the pot smelled good."

Anita speared Jefe with a look. "We need a priest."

Jefe finished leaving his chair and followed Estrada.

The food grew cold as those left pushed it around their plates in embarrassed silence.

Finally Luis said, "I never meant to cause division between you." Laying her hand on his arm, Anita answered, "He is only surprised. Give him time."

Domingo wondered how much time must pass before something changed Jefe's opinion.

Leaning on the parapet overlooking the mirador, Ramón told Estrada, "I always knew he was devout, but had no idea there was any desire to become a priest."

It was too dark to see the line of trees at the bottom of the slope. The médico's elbow touched his. "The boy's heart is good. He wants to help his people."

"Without doubt. But if what has been is any sign of what is to come, he could be killed by men who rode into battle at his side."

Calles was now the governor in Sonora, and with Obregón's approval was making that state unsafe for priests. Sinaloa was no safer; already the clerics had fled or been imprisoned or killed. The past abuses of the Church had won it no friends.

Estrada said, "You are aware, I believe, that for many years I have been a Protestante, and have suffered for my faith. In Monterrey, before Madero, I opposed the injustices of the national Church, and even though I hate killing for any reason, I can understand such men and their need to be rid of that yoke." He turned, a sad smile touching the corners of his mouth. "Pablo hated me, for he saw no evil in the practices of his religion. Clearly, you do."

Ramón shook his head. "From the day a loco old priest shot my father, I have had nothing to do with the Church. Anita and Luis are sustained by their prayers and santos, and I respect that. But I do not believe those things are necessary to feel the presence of God."

"Nor I. Yet most of your villagers yearn for the structure of the Mass and the guidance of a priest. So long as Luis remains pure-hearted, he can be of great service."

"So long as he remains alive. Is it possible to become a priest without embracing the evils of the Church?"

"I suppose we shall find out."

They walked back toward the house, where the glow inside beckoned. A mozo was lighting the patio lanterns. "They are not my villagers," he said, belatedly.

Estrada gave a short laugh. "If you're not responsible for them, amigo, who is? Someone must be."

"If that is so, why in hell did so many die for the ideals of the Revolution? Nothing has changed."

"Much has changed. I'm unsure what it means."

In bed later, Anita said, "Amado, if you didn't want a priest, why did you build me a chapel? Or restore the little village church? And who better to give us spiritual assistance than Luis?"

Chewing on the innocent insult, he didn't answer. Life at Los Nuestros was failing in what he' hoped for: continuation of the peacefulness he'd experienced in the City of México when Anita came back into his destiny. Responsibilities weighed heavier each day.

Faltering, she went on, "You have never thought of allowing Estrada—"

"No. He's the médico, and a friend. Nothing else." He turned restlessly, sat up and punched the feather pillow, lay down and adjusted the blanket. "If Luis feels this is a thing he must do, I'm glad. Sereno surprised me, though."

A lengthy silence.

Then she said, "Are you going to let Domingo go to Dos Corazones to train Tereza's filly?"

With Luis's warnings nagging, he said, "Let's try to avoid that. Besides, he will have both hands full with Cimarrón."

In the mornings, Ramón played with the baby on the roofed galería, impatient for the day when she would stagger across the lawn unaided, dreading the time when her fond glances and smiles turned from her Papá to sweethearts.

Nearby, Anita lounged in a cushioned wicker chair with a mug of chocolate and a book, having given the household her instructions for meals and chores. She had settled into the position of señora del hacendado with ease. He'd even heard her reprimand one of the girls for not dressing Violeta warmly enough.

Hugging his daughter until she squirmed, he watched Domingo in the first corral, working up a sweat on himself and the young stallion. Martín perched on the top pole, his Indio face shaded by his sombrero, keenly watching for any misstep such as a flare of temper on the part of either caballo or boy. None came.

"Where's Sereno?" he asked, sure Anita would know. She looked up, expression hazy from being interrupted.

"I think he took his flute into the forest to practice."

For awhile now he had been aware of the path his son had worn in the grass beyond the paving, terminating at the corner of the mirador wall. Carrying Violeta, he went to peer over and discerned the rocky trail leading into the trees bordering the slope. How far might the boy go, on foot? Was he safe alone, without the armed guard to fight off renegade Villistas, bandits, hired guns working for that maldito gringo? Although men were stationed at likely points, the boundary of Los Nuestros covered vast deserted stretches.

As he was pondering whether to call out, follow the track, or trust Dios to protect his family while he made good his plan to ride into Culiacán for information about the possibility of treasure or ore on the property, a rider on a lathered horse reined it to a dusty halt in the road and ran into the house by way of the glass doors leading to the office.

Before he could transfer the baby to Anita or prepare her for news, the messenger burst into their midst. "El Señor Johnson is on his way, Patrón. He is not armed, and the little girl is with him, so Chuco said we should let him in."

"Bueno—only, send heavy reinforcements to every guard post, in case we're attacked at a point of weakness."

The boy leaped over the low wall bordering the yard and in minutes, the pounding of hoofbeats announced bands of defenders scattering in all directions.

Putting his daughter into Anita's arms, he said, "Go upstairs and don't come down in spite of what you might hear."

Domingo joined him in the sala, face streaked with trickles of sweat and dust from working with the stallion. Needing no talk, they strapped on gunbelts which always hung ready in the zaguán. He welcomed his older son's presence, even if the sight of a pistol on his hip was disturbing.

"Rifles, too," he said, and they went out to wait for the unwelcome guest.

Chapter Fourteen

Christine was excited to be returning to Hacienda de Cordero. The ride in the coach was as bumpy and endless as before, but anticipation made the discomforts bearable.

"Daddy, please don't argue with Señor Cordero this time." He'd been moody for days, probably putting the finishing touches on his plan, so she had tried not to say anything; but the sight of guards on the wall and the closed gate ahead forced out the plea.

"Stay out of this. And quit worrying. I know how to handle Mister Señor Cordero." He gave her a sharp look. "And for God's sake, don't go wandering off. You stay with me. These people could take you hostage."

She didn't believe they would do anything of the sort, yet an uncertainty amounting to fear made her palms damp. She was surprised when the armed men opened the way to them as soon as Daddy let one of them search him and the coach and found no weapon. The young one she had noticed before grinned at her as if he would have liked searching *her*, but nobody tried that.

Passing through the second gate, which was open, she saw the gleaming casa grande through the coach window.

The two-story structure with rust-colored tile roofs and paved patios, unexpected low rock walls and old trees, and freshly whitewashed, gave her spirit a thrill. It felt almost like coming home.

"Oh, Daddy, I'm so glad the house didn't get burned." Still troubling was her suspicion that he might have been behind the setting of that fire.

He was out of the coach almost before it stopped, leaving her to help herself to the ground and follow him toward where the hacendado and a handsome dark-haired boy stood at the edge of the paving, gunbelts on their hips and rifles in their hands.

"Buenas díaz," Daddy said. "I'm sorry I didn't get back to you as soon as I said I would, but I had other business to tend to. Them guns look mighty unfriendly. Maybe you misunderstood my intentions before—"

Christine hated the tone of Daddy's voice, and the falseness must have grated on the Mexican's ear as well, for Señor Cordero's reply was cold. "Then state your intentions, quickly."

Her attention shifted to the boy. His heavy-lashed eyes were narrowed, alert for any move which might give him excuse to level the rifle and pull its trigger. He didn't appear to be much older than the one named Sereno, whom she had hoped to see again. A bit taller, heavier. Yet his manner—hostility held in check—separated him from the almost childish blond boy who had caught her attention with his expert riding.

This one looked like the hacendado.

Señor Cordero hadn't budged during Daddy's ornate explanation of the delay in returning, his rock-solid claim to the disputed land, his desire now to negotiate. When a silence fell, they all stood staring at each other, though the dark boy's eyes skittered past hers and lodged somewhere in the distant trees behind her.

Then Ramón Cordero said, "I've listened to what you came to say. It changes nothing. Please get in your hired coach, go back to your tierra, and think twice before sending more men to die for a useless cause."

Sending men to die? She tried to read their faces and saw only the stiff mask of unwillingness to give in. Then the hacendado, too, believed Daddy was to blame for the fire. With a tingle of awe at her boldness, she said in a voice strange to her own ears, "I would like to see la niña, por favor."

The fragment of Spanish acted like a spark on the Mexicans. The boy's eyes widened as if he hadn't heard right, and the faintest of smiles touched the hacendado's lips. Señor Cordero stepped aside, gesturing with the arm not burdened with a gun. "Mi casa es suya."

He said other things to the boy, who moved only to ready his rifle with a nerve-jarring clack and point it at Daddy's heart. Daddy jumped as if he'd touched one of the wires at the back of his crystal set. For once, however, he had the good sense to keep his mouth shut.

Christine followed Señor Cordero down a wide hall floored with some highly-polished wood, across a section of tiles, and up a staircase anchored by a carved lion on a post. Her fingertips brushed the flowing ridges of the mane.

The upper floor was airy and light from open rooms with French doors leading onto balconies. He led her into one. Seated in a stuffed chair was a young woman, light-haired as

Sereno and certainly his mother, who held a girl baby about nine or ten months old, dressed in a loose-fitting cotton shirt that reached past its feet. Her face was startled, her blue eyes wide but trusting as Señor Cordero spoke gently. Then, in English, the woman said, "This is Violeta. Would you like to hold her?"

She had never held a baby in her life and trembled at the thought that she might drop the little one on its head, sending its parents into a rage.

"Sí," she whispered. "I would."

Señor Cordero motioned her to sit on the edge of a large bed, and the woman laid the baby on her lap. It stared at her, its face wrinkling to cry. "She can sit up," the woman said, taking a place beside them and fondly smoothing the child's dark hair.

Bracing the little back with her arm, Christne tried to take in the furnishings—few—and ornaments—foreign—in the room, to be mulled over later. She marveled at the baby's skin, darker than hers but light compared to many of the Mexicans she had seen in Culiacán and most of the workers on this hacienda. "She is beautiful."

She was glad it had not cried after all. "Sereno was going to show her to me the last time we were here, but Daddy made me leave." She paused for one of them to reveal where Sereno was now, but when neither did, she went on, "I met Tereza then, too. Is— Is she still here?"

Making the baby's hair into curls around her finger, the woman shook her head. "She returned to her home in Sonora."

Señor Cordero went out, his sudden departure leaving her feeling a little awkward. Daddy was going to be livid. After

Mother's death, he'd whipped her on a couple of occasions, once with a limb off the willow tree, once with his belt; and she expected a real row as soon as they got back to the hotel. Greta wasn't likely to take her side. She could only hope he did it before he started drinking and still had a measure of self-control.

She wondered what was happening on the patio, and how much longer she should stay. Balancing Daddy's short temper with what might appear rude to her hostess, she smiled at the pretty mother, smelled of the baby's clean skin, and listened for any hint of a fight outside. All she heard were sounds of someone making horseshoes, pleasant voices calling to each other, and, nearer, birds twittering in the large trees beyond the balcony.

"I would love to stay here forever," she said, on a sigh.

"You are welcome whenever you wish to visit."

"Thank you. Gracias." She placed her hands on the baby's ribs and boosted it into its mother's lap. "I guess I'd better go."

She stood, turning slowly round, noting a chest of drawers, velvet curtains that could be pulled over the French doors, woven mat rugs on the wood floor. The patios were either glazed tiles with colored insets, or plain dust-hued unglazed ones.

On the way downstairs, she stuffed images into her memory. Many dark wood doors lead to other rooms, several servants stood about with rags or cloth mops, staring at her from dusky corners. Against cream-tinted plaster walls, the furniture was all dark and heavy, mostly chests and tables with carved panels and legs, a few chairs that looked as if sitting in them would make one's back ache. Brass wall sconces holding candles. Oil lamps with colored glass shades. Gilt-framed paintings of people dressed in old-fashioned clothes.

Then she was back in the courtyard with Daddy and the handsome boy. Neither seemed to have moved, but Daddy's hands had clenched into fists.

At the side of the circular clearing where carriages turned, the coach horses dozed beneath overhanging trees. Señor Cordero leaned against the vehicle, chatting with the driver who lounged in its open doorway.

Fortunately the sun hadn't yet moved to this side of the house, so Daddy wasn't roasting, though sweat trickles on his face and ice in his eyes told her he'd almost reached his breaking point. "I wasn't gone long, was I?" She tried to cover her nervousness with an apologetic smile. "Her name is Violeta, and she's the sweetest little thing—"

Daddy grabbed her arm and strode toward the coach. The driver jumped up, gave a nod to Señor Cordero, swung onto the perch, gathered the reins. She looked back. The hacendado bowed low and when he straightened, the corners of his eyes crinkled with good will.

"Vaya con Dios, señorita."

Domingo watched them leave, the throbbing in his temples having increased until all he could think of was a large mug of Anita's cooling herb teas—and the weak sensation in the backs of his legs. Slowly he lowered the rifle. Jefe came toward him. "Did you believe him, when he said he would stop trying to take our land?"

Jefe glanced over his shoulder at the departing coach. "No. Men like that are dangerous."

He laid a hand on Domingo's shoulder. "Let's have a drink."

In Jefe's office, they toasted each other with a sweet red wine, and strolled out to the porch where the morning sun had lately left.

Sereno lay in the hammock, gently swinging it with one foot. "Papá, if Señor Johnson did pay someone to set that fire, what do you think he will do next?"

Their father stared out across the mirador. "Quién sabe, mijo." After a minute he added, "I wonder if the little girl has any idea."

"Did she like Violeta?" Domingo asked.

"She finally saw Violeta?" Sereno sat up, smiling.

"She held her." Jefe drained his wine glass. "A pity her father is not a good man, instead of a loco."

Sensing Jefe's strained nerves, he teased, "Who, the gringuita, or Violeta?"

In the following scuffle, one of the wine broke on the tiles. A criada came out with a broom, Sereno began playing 'Valentina' on his flute, and Anita leaned over the balcony railing to call, "We must decide how to celebrate your birthdays. Is it to be a fiesta, or a día del campo?"

Because of the work necessary for moving into Los Nuestros, last year the occasions were marked simply with useful gifts of books and clothing, and the preparation of a favorite meal. Jefe didn't approve of keeping one's saint's day; and as he and Sereno were born only a couple of months apart, the plan was to honor them both with one large celebration. It meant he had to wait, and Sereno was given his treats early.

He suspected that his medio hermano disliked the idea of sharing as much as he did, but accepted the situation in order to please the parents.

Sereno suddenly voted for the picnic, adding, "Let us go right now. But, where?"

Anita laughed. "Tomorrow is soon enough, if you wish to invite friends and have the whole day to play games and eat enough rich food to make you sick."

Though he kept silent, he wanted a fiesta, with music, fireworks, dancing. Shy glances from Mina. A chance to speak to her without drawing attention. Perhaps he would even try to kiss her, to see how it felt.

They settled on going to a falls two kilometres from the casa, at the end of a winding trail through the south forest. Choosing friends to share in the festivities was difficult, but those left out were made happy with the promise of a huge fiesta for Jefe's birthday in November.

The morning of the picnic, a village Opata boy drove a wagon into the kitchen patio. Anita, Violeta, the niñera who helped care for the baby, and the niñera's two small daughters and three older nieces who would serve and pack up afterward, all settled themselves among filled baskets and piles of blankets brought to soften the jolts. Anita carried a parasol to shade herself and the baby from stretches of meadow sun. Domingo had lacked the courage to invite Mina.

Riding in front were Estrada, Jefe, and Gregorio, with a guard consisting of Lobo, Silvestre, and Máximino. Behind the wagon, he and Sereno rode with their two favorite amigos, Marcelo and Rosendo, mestizos only slightly older and valued for their sharp wit, agility in games, ability to learn at the school, and respect for horses. A rear guard was made up of their older brothers, already skilled horsemen and weapons handlers under Martín's guidance.

Domingo wished he could have ridden Cimarroncito, but knew the stallion needed further training. If lucky, by the time Jefe's birthday came round he'd have the horse ready and could show off. He imagined Mina conquering her shyness enough to compliment him. Thinking of her turned his thoughts to Tereza and his unfulfilled promise to train her filly, Estrellita. Thinking of Tereza, his hand strayed to her gift of the santo on its chain around his neck. He realized Sereno was really fond of her, and wondered which of them she liked better.

Unexpectedly, the face of the gringuita flashed into his mind. Something unsettling had occurred the moment they looked at each other, so he'd avoided meeting her eyes afterward. He sensed her intense interest, in itself enough to make him uneasy as an object of curiosity, such as the Indios were to him.

She seemed to think she belonged here, having boldly invited herself into the casa. He felt vague disappointment that her father was such a loco hombre that there could be nothing but trouble if he remained in México.

The outriders reported that the clearing near the falls was safe, and guided the wagon into some shade. Anita and the girls went to throw sticks into the water for a bit, before the niñera called her nieces to spread the blankets.

He dismounted with the other riders and loosened bits and cinchas. A cool breeze fluttered slender leafing branches, dappling the grass. The ex-rebels warned the little ones against rattlesnakes that might hole up under rocks, and as soon as the mounts were comfortable, the men and boys divided into teams for a ball game.

Anita had her hands full keeping the baby from creeping off the blanket, while the older girls helped roll stacks of tortillas around fillings of meat or vegetables. For dessert, there would be polvorones, flavored with cinnamon for Sereno; empanadas of pineapple and coconut for him.

After the game ended and the men lay resting in the grass, Sereno said, "I miss Luis. I wish he had waited, before going to the city."

He missed Luis, too. The only priest he had known, in Monterrey, was old and somewhat absent-minded, but kind. Mamá had been quite firm about making him spend hours with the padre, learning the rules of the Church, which for the most part had left him more puzzled than instructed. Maybe Luis would explain things, in time.

When everyone had eaten to excess and were relaxing beneath rustling trees, lulled by the water pooling at the base of high rocks, he was shocked out of his doze by a scream.

The men leaped up with exclamations of surprise, women and children ran screeching for the wagon, and Ramón darted toward the falls. Domingo had worn his belt gun but, like the others, had removed it for comfort. Another hand grabbed the weapon from its holster beside him, and fired. He was astonished to see Sereno holding the pistol.

Beside the pool, Anita stood rigid, shielding the baby, both crying. Reaching her, Jefe put his arms around them.

A buff-colored puma stretched dead on the ground. Domingo rushed to it. The familiar pattern of a few darker spots scattered in the creamy fur on the back of the haunch forced out a cry of anguish. "¡Bravito!"

"You cannot know that—" Jefe began.

Sereno had come to a stop beside him. Unleashing a fist into the boy's face that knocked him down, Domingo yelled, "Damn you! You've killed Bravo!"

Blood flowed from one nostril. Sereno wiped it with his arm. "I couldn't let a gato hurt my loved ones."

"You didn't have to kill him." He struggled to be free of Gregorio's hold, ready to strike again.

Not getting up, Sereno insisted, "There was no time, he was going to jump!"

Into his ear, Gregorio said, "It was necessary. ¿Comprende? The gato would have bitten Violeta."

Anita was sobbing too hard to say anything and the baby squealed with fright.

Embarrassing tears of rage nearly blinded him. "I could have called to him. Bravo always listened to me."

Jefe took hold of his shoulders and Gregorio let go. His father hugged him hard against his chest, shielding his face from the staring crowd, his dead pet, the brother he hated.

Sobs began pouring out and he wished he had died on that morning in La Puerta del Sol when enemy fire took Mamá, or in the floodwaters that claimed the life of don Diego. Anything, to have escaped such pain.

After a minute he gained control and pulled away, and Ramón released him. The others were returning to the picnic area. Wiping his matted eyelashes, he stumbled the few paces and knelt by the limp body. His trembling hand hovered over the tawny fur but jerked back without making contact.

Helpless to stop a fresh rush of tears, he cried, "¡Oh, this hurts too much!"

Cradling him in a looser embrace than before, Jefe murmured, "Yo sé, mijo, yo sé. Lo siento mucho, mucho."

Presently they sat apart and stared down at the creature which in life had been so dear to him. The small bloody spot where Sereno's bullet had entered seemed innocent, incapable of causing death. "He could have frightened Bravito," he muttered. "He could have done that."

"Maybe you could have done that," Jefe said softly. "But in the excitement of the moment, who knows?"

I know, he thought. Swallowing past the tightness in his throat, he said, "I want to bury him." Already flies were gathering on the fresh blood.

Ramón stood up. "I'll send Silvestre for a shovel."

Waiting in the glade, fanning away flies, he heard Silvestre's horse depart at a gallop. Sporadic conversation from the picnickers filtered through the drone of the waterfall.

In a little while Sereno came up behind him and said, "I'm sorry, hermano."

He answered without looking around. "I'm not your brother."

After a few heartbeats the little swish of boots dragging through tall grass told him he was alone.

Sereno's nose began bleeding again. When Mamá saw it, she said, "Into the wagon, hijo," and wet a cloth with their drinking water. Reluctantly, he surrendered his reins to Rosendo and climbed in among the women. Mamá made him lay his head in her lap, and applied the cool rag on the bruise. Even with blankets beneath, bumping over the rough trail seemed likely to do worse damage than the blow from Domingo's fist.

In their dialect the girls chattered about their fright, increasing the throb in his temples. "You must forgive him," Mamá said quietly. "He loved Bravo very much."

"Forgive him? He is in the wrong." How could she defend someone who ranked an animal above family?

Yet, reviewing the event, he began to have doubts. Perhaps he could have fired a warning shot. Two seconds before Mamá screamed, he'd seen the puma crouching on the high rocks beside the falls, only the width of the little pool between it and his mother and sister. Had her scream caused it to pounce? Or…had his shot made it fall.

The girls grew quiet and he removed the cloth and opened his eyes to find the reason. Riding up to the wagon, Papá said, "You did the right thing, mijo." Then he reined about in the direction of the picnic ground.

"Mamá," he said after a while, "I'm nearly as good with horses as Domingo. Why don't I go to Dos Corazones to train Estrellita? That filly is going to become so wild no one can ever use her." He held his breath, tense for her answer.

It was long in coming. At last, gazing somewhere distant as the forest moved by them, Mamá asked, "Do you want to train the filly—or visit Tereza—or get even with Domingo?"

The soft words pierced him. He laid the cloth over his eyes and pondered. Presently he said, "All of that." Then he added, "How did you know?"

"I am your mother. It's my business to know." Her voice held a smile.

They traveled the rest of the way to Los Nuestros in an easy silence. He sensed it was better not to press her for consent. She always talked over every little decision with Papá. Something this important might require a week or more to achieve, yet he was confident that she was on his side and the visit would take place.

Burying Bravo was the hardest thing Domingo had ever done, other than walking away from Mamá's grave in La Puerta del Sol.

Silvestre and Jefe waited with the horses, respecting his feelings and the need to cry. Having seen how cruelly some villagers treated their own stock, as well as curs who scrounged for food and belonged to nobody, he was sure that giving a Christian burial to a dead puma and shedding tears like a woman marked him as a loco.

He dreaded returning to Los Nuestros. He must go without delay to Dos Corazones.

Jefe came slowly toward him as he was tamping the final shovelfuls of dirt. He pretended to wipe sweat on his shirt sleeve.

They stood side by side for a moment, looking down. Jefe laid a hand lightly on his shoulder. "Remember when I told you about Mío?" he said. "Believe me, I know what you are feeling."

"Is it wrong," he whispered, distressed, "to hurt like this, for a creature?"

"It is not wrong to love," Jefe said. "Only unwise." There were tears in his father's eyes though they didn't spill over.

"I know. Every time, I think, never again, but my heart does not listen."

"Pray that it never does."

Arms around each other, they walked to the horses.

II

Christine counted herself lucky that Daddy was too involved in his alternate plan to punish her for making friends with the hacendado's family. Days passed agreeably enough. Sketching, eating, shopping in Greta's company. She scarcely saw Daddy.

Alone, she tried out the few Spanish words she'd learned by listening to waiters, vendors, soldiers, and clerks, and eavesdropping on the better class of Mexican families who came and went in the hotel. She studied a phrase book to get the shape of the words into her head along with the sounds that came to her ears. After three weeks, she could say, "Gracias" and "Por favor" and "¿Cómo sé llama?" as well as "Buenos días" and other greetings suited to the time of day.

A favorite, "¿A dónde va usted?" meant, Where are you going? For awhile she had difficulty with "Quisiera que ser su amiga," I want to be your friend. Tables of verb endings made sense as long as she was looking at them, but as soon as she laid the book aside they all became tangled in her head and refused to come out properly when she needed them. Greta practiced with her five minutes at a time before finding another pursuit. Daddy—when he was around—brushed her aside and launched into accounts of the problems he was having getting machinery from the States for his guayule plantation.

"But, Daddy, if you can't use the land, what good will machinery be?"

"Quit your infernal doubting. This is going to happen. Remember that secret I told you? Well, keep it that way. I'm not licked yet."

One afternoon in August she began to believe him. He came in after the usual downpour had stopped, and told her, "It took my last penny, but these people work for peanuts, and giving them a piece of land makes them think you're rich. Pack your duds, Baby. I've got a little surprise for you."

Daddy's surprise lay at the end of a wearying journey through countryside less wooded but probably more suited to crops than the Cordero hacienda. On all sides of a wide valley rose great rolling uplands, with groves of trees here and there, scattered with outcroppings of rocks and cut by rain-swollen streams.

In the valley was a low plank house sheltered by wide branching old trees and weathered into a dark unpainted brown. Corrals and sheds—though there was no stock of any kind—and a few stick-and-thatch huts huddled at a distance from the main house; and in a clearing between them stood about two dozen dark skinned people in plain country clothes.

"I've had a devil of a time getting things ready, but even if it's not all you'd like, we'll be comfortable. These Indians raise unbelievable vegetables, and I've found the best cook in the state. She's called Mokee or Tokee, or something like that. And I know how you hated to leave your pony, so go look in the corral there—that's your horse."

The carriage halted in the yard and Daddy jumped down. "Don't bother with your suitcase, let one of them get it. We've got servants now, so you don't have to lift your hand to do a damn thing you don't want to do."

The house was built in an L with two bedrooms, a sitting room, and a kitchen, which she had learned to call a cocina.

Crude furnishings compared to the finery at the Corderos home, but the rooms were spacious—if dark, despite oil lamps without fancy globes—and the floors were wood instead of the packed dirt she had feared.

Altogether, the place gave her the feeling of an old-west bunkhouse, with trunks and wardrobes, hewn tables and chairs, and a kitchen cabinet straight from a mail-order catalog. At least, it was like the pictures she had seen. Heavy shutters over the windows promised security on dark nights when owls called eerily in the cottonwood grove, and coyotes howled before dawn.

At first she was glad Greta had chosen to remain in the city, but after a few days she had to admit she missed the woman's company and fluent English. The Indians knew very little Spanish, but communicated with each other in their own dialect, regarding her with smiles on their faces each time she spoke to them.

Daddy was away from the ranch all day, though now he did come home at night, and if he was drinking, she saw no evidence of that.

Tokee wasn't the cook Daddy declared her to be. No matter what the dish was called, nor the manner of its preparation, it was always beans and beef with peppers, or beef and peppers with beans, or peppers and beans with beef—with pieces of tomato and onion, and an occasional squash cooked in.

Hens were kept solely for their eggs. Also unvarying was the hot red sauce that somehow she began to crave. And, of course, tortillas, usually of corn but sometimes larger ones made with flour. For snacks there was goat cheese, melons if she was lucky, or piloncillo; the latter being great cones of brown sugar that had to be hit with a piece of iron like a railroad spike in order to break them into manageable chunks. She could have spring water or goat's milk. She began sneaking Daddy's coffee, which he insisted on making himself, as there was never any cream and without it he said the Mexican brew was "strong enough to float a locomotive."

Whenever she went for a ride on the gelding she'd named Jump, she was supposed to take three of the Indian men along for protection. They were all as old as or older than Daddy, and not very skilled in the saddle, making complaints and groaning when she stayed out more than half an hour at a time. Under threat of severe punishment if she disobeyed, however, Christine accepted their company and gradually lengthened the radius of her travels.

One thing which kept her from losing her mind in the solitude was the extra trunkful of books which Daddy had acquired somewhere. Most were in Spanish but a few were in English and occupied long hours when she otherwise might have given in to despair.

With the afternoon rains came masses of wild flowers of all kinds, bright pinks and yellows mingling thickly in the ungrazed grass, or orange and red trumpets on vines similar to those at home. Also familiar were carpets of blue, lavender, and white morning glories. Sweet aromas rode on the breezes, and unhurried bees and other insects, and birds singing morning and evening, all made her glad she was in México.

One morning while eating Tokee's blanquillos revueltos, which were like scrambled eggs in a tomato and pepper sauce, she said, "Let's call this rancho Las Flores. That means The Flowers. I wonder if hollyhocks grow here?"

"Did the mail come yet?" Daddy scooted back his chair and tried to light a cigarette with one of the wax fosforos the Indians used. "Damned if I don't have a barrel full of real matches sent down from Tucson, soon as I remember to do it." He got the end glowing and drew a deep breath of smoke, exhaling it with the words, "What about the mail?"

"Hasn't come." Daddy didn't trust the mountain letter carrier, who was an Indian on a mule, and rather than use one of his men to ride to Culiacán after it, he had arranged with Greta to send a messenger from the city. "Are you expecting something important?"

"Could be. Could be. Let me know if he gets here any time soon."

He left the house without telling her where he was going, but she dawdled at the table instead of rushing after him to find out. When the messenger did come a couple of hours later, she was pleased to receive an envelope with her name scrawled across it in Greta's handwriting. She gave the boy a few centavos—all she could find lying about—and went to the spring to read the news.

Among trivial things like what was happening on the revolutionary front, Greta had written

> You might be interested to know I
> learned from Soldiers that señor Cordero's
> place—don't tell your Daddy I called it that —
> is known as Los Nuestros but I think it was
> Casa Blanca in the old days. When indians made
> raids on the Hidalgo who Built it. Until
> he took his Family back to Spain. At least
> that is the story Here.

P.S. the older Boy is named Domingo

When Daddy came back just before dark, he didn't mention the mail and Christine neglected to tell him about Greta's letter. But she went to bed with it under her pillow, and tossed half the night hearing *Domingo* in her head and seeing his proud stance at his father's side, ready to do battle for Los Nuestros.

Chapter Fifteen

"Pershing's Expedition killed our General Gómez and eighty of his men," Estrada read from the newspaper with some concern, as they sat in the darkening patio waiting for the boys to finish changing for supper.

Anita made a wordless sound of dismay. Ramón realized it wasn't for the dead men, but because Violeta's tottering steps had landed the baby face-first on the tiles before her mother could intervene. He scooped her up, jounced her a few times so she stopped crying, and said, "No damage." To Estrada, he said, "Where? And when?"

The médico glanced at the date of the newspaper. "Chihuahua, two months ago."

"Why kill Carrancistas? The gringos are supposed to be chasing Villa."

Estrada shrugged. "Evidently if they can't find him, they will fight us instead."

Domingo and Sereno presented themselves to Anita for her approval, and everyone went into the comedor.

Ramón ate with little notice of the food, thoughts occupied with his sons. Since the fight at the picnic they had kept out of each other's way. Both worked with the horses though at different hours. Sereno frequently disappeared with his flute, and Domingo spent much of his time in the village.

Each had requested a visit to Los Dos Corazones. Aware of their growing interest in Tereza, Ramón had postponed a decision. Innocent and harmless as the attraction might be now, the tangle of complications arising from Mariano's marriage to Paz, and the boys' rivalry and dislike of each other, made the choice of what to do a heavy one. Anita left it to him, saying only, "I am praying for you, querido."

Well, her prayers were potent. He waited for the answer. Finishing his coffee, he watched her lift the baby into the arms of its niñera, who brought Violeta to him for a kiss before bed. He cuddled his daughter, savoring the peacefulness of his household and wondering how long it would last. "Has anyone heard from Luis?"

Anita watched them depart. "He sent a message by Lobo last week, to say he was studying under a priest who used to teach in the seminary at Culiacán."

Lobo was the only one to whom the long ride into the city for mail and telegrams, rather than the monthly excursion for supplies and shopping, never grew stale. Ramón had also set him to listen for any news about Señor Johnson. The man along with his daughter seemed to have dropped off the earth, for inquiries to the soldiers at Hermosillo brought no record of his passing that way, and probes sent to Mazatlán—a long shot—resulted in similar reports. Where had he gone? More important, what was he doing? "Nothing good, you can be sure," he muttered, and everyone looked up from the final course of frijoles.

He realized that his companions had not followed the thread of thought from Luis to the gringo, and hastily said, "I was speaking of our enemigo blanco."

"The little girl is charming," Anita mused. "A pity that her mother died, leaving her with—him."

Sereno excused himself, followed in moments by the others.

Except for Domingo.

"Jefe," he began, a small crease of frown between his eyebrows, "if Sereno wishes so much to go to Dos Corazones, then I'm content to stay here."

Ramón poured himself another cup of coffee before finding anything to say. Then, he couldn't help asking, "What made you change your mind?"

"Cimarrón. We're working on some special things for your birthday, and if I stop now, he won't be ready."

Something about the boy's answer bothered him. Truth, to a point; but tainted with more unsaid. "Sereno will thank you."

"He won't, but it doesn't matter. I know you've been trying to choose the fair thing to do about this—"

"¡Ya lo sé! And all I had decided so far was not to let either of you go."

"That is your privilege, but I thought I would tell you my side." He left in the direction of the village.

Climbing the steps of the central staircase, Ramón thought, *I should speak to Máximino in the morning.* He went out onto the balcony, and in the faint glow from a distant lamp post saw Anita come toward him in a pale flowing robe. Behind them, sets of glass doors opened into their bedroom, the hallway, Domingo's room. The first two were softly lit, the latter was dark.

"Violeta is fast asleep."

He slid one arm around her and drew her near.

"Ramón."

"What?"

"Estrada says Mina is fifteen."

"Small, for her age."

"Old, for her years."

Like Paz.

"I saw Domingo going into her house."

"Lamps are lit, and her family is there. Máximino will keep him in line."

"I hope so," she said, her voice troubled. "He is… easily hurt."

"He told me he prefers to finish training Cimarrón rather than go to Dos Corazones."

Anita's palm moved up and down along his spine, a gesture he had long ago learned meant she was thinking deeply. "I don't want Sereno to go, either."

"Too young?"

"They must not run away from this anger. It's not about Tereza or even Mina. It is about them, whether they begin to love or hate each other."

Turning toward their room, he said, "How long does Luis think it will take for him to become a priest?"

"Ah! You have changed your mind about that, then?"

Since the long-ago day Luis moved in with them in their casita in Los Pobres, the boy had grown into a young man at his side. Simple, pure, loyal. Enduring the abuse of an older brother, fighting with the rebels in a bloody and endless war, suffering wounds and heartaches, losing his head and his virginity over Paz—despite every trial, Luis had remained devout. With him, the corrupt nature of the Mexican priesthood and the Church in Rome were unconnected with Dios and morality.

"If anyone can become a true man of God," he said, "our Luisito can."

Domingo's courtship of Mina had barely passed the warm-glance stage when Máximino invited him to their house for a gathering of ex-rebels to play monte. The small room filled with men he knew: Martín, Silvestre, Chuco—who had finished his turn at manning the main gate—and Marcelo de la Cruz, almost sixteen and starting a mustache, as all mestizo boys did to set them apart from the smooth-faced Indios.

The salsa Mina's mother set out with refreshments was more picante than he was accustomed to, so before long he was dying for a drink. Others were swilling beer, a dark bitter variety he didn't like. When Gregorio and Lobo joined the crowd, he gave up his space and went outside, as much to escape the cigarette smoke as to get a drink from the olla suspended from a roof viga. He knew water would increase the burn, but would allay his thirst.

"Hola," said a soft voice from the starlit darkness. His hand jerked, spilling water from the gourd down his chin. He wiped it with his hand. "Hola."

Mina came to stand beside him, fingers holding her rebozo close about her face. She was pretty. Maybe prettier than Tereza, in a different way. Darker-skinned, long black hair worn in a loose cascade down her back whenever she allowed the rebozo to slip off. Her rich brown mestiza eyes held a sparkle of joy instead of the cool sadness he felt in Tereza.

Unfortunately, she was a villager and would never fit into the station of patróna at Los Nuestros. Marrying her would be more loco than burying Bravito and crying over the gato's death. Lately, he'd given much thought to his future as Jefe's heir. He would be just in dealing with Sereno, of course; his conscience demanded that. But there was plenty of time to figure a way to be rid of his medio hermano, short of cheating him.

"What are you thinking?" Mina said. "You are so quiet."

For several months she had come to Jefe's school and he'd hardly noticed her; however, since the day he killed the javelina, and Luis pointed her out to him, he had paid more attention.

"There is thunder deep in the mountains," he said. "Hear it? There will be more rain tonight."

"I like night rain," she said. "It whispers secrets to the earth."

They stood listening to the faraway rumbling in the Sierra Madre.

"I am sorry about your gato," she said softly.

He wished she hadn't brought that up. "Thank you." What had she heard? That he'd cried? That he was strange, grieving over a wild animal? Yet—she was here, so near he could detect a faint odor of mesquite smoke lingering in her clothing from the supper fire.

"Some of the Indios—" she began, then stopped as if she'd had second thoughts.

Mina leaned against the roof post, not looking at him; but he felt a connection to her, and in the lamp light coming through the doorway of her house he could examine the curve of her forehead, nose, and chin. Very pretty. "What?" he urged, curious to learn what villagers were gossiping about him.

"They believed Bravo was your nagual, until he died, and you did not."

"I don't know what that means," he admitted.

"Nagual," she repeated, as if he would understand the word if she said it again. "Your guardian spirit."

He searched his mind for anything Mamá or the priest in Monterrey might have told him, but he was sure neither had ever mentioned such a thing. He recalled having to memorize endless responses to the padre's questions, and being drilled until he knew a hundred saints, all gradually forgotten over time. "Angel," he said. "Is it an angel?"

Mina shook her head, turning a little toward him, and the rebozo slid to her shoulders. Before she drew it over her lower face to keep out the dangerous Los Aires, he noted the precise part in her clean-smelling hair.

Muffled by the cloth, still her voice was clear. "No. Different. A spirit, yes, but of the earth, not the church."

Ideas tangled like Anita's embroidery thread after Violeta found it unattended. He hoped Luis would return soon with proper teachings that would make clear the things Mamá and Anita and the Monterrey priest had tried to explain.

He knew Indios had their own set of beliefs, which Jefe respected but considered inappropriate for mestizos. Of course, Jefe was not yet convinced that the mestizos had it right, either. Estrada—well, he was a Protestante. Domingo remembered how furious Pablo and his tía used to become at the mention of that word and the concepts which lay behind it.

"Tell me, what is meant by nagual. Why should they think I would die, just because Bravo did."

Concentration narrowed her eyelids so long lashes prevented his reading the intensity of her gaze. Before she could answer, the vague sounds of conversation inside rose into distinct voices calling his name. "Domingo, hombre. ¿Dónde estás?"

Mina stiffened with alarm and in a moment she was gone, vanished into the dark beyond the ramada.

Gregorio appeared in the doorway, blocking the light. "Mingo, are you out here? Ay—come amigo, and be my luck even if you don't wish to play."

Luck? he thought. Which was right? Luck, fate, Dios, or a nagual, which inhabits animals, and takes your life when it dies. Maybe, in some strange way, all were right.

Maybe not.

Taking his place among the men, he knew one thing: tonight, he belonged here, alive, senses full with fumes of rank tobacco and pulque and the moist air of a rainy summer night, family safe, friends happy and joking around him. And Mina—or Tereza—in his tomorrows.

Tiptoeing up the stairs to his bed, he remembered la señorita Johnson and experienced again that spark of unnamed emotion when their glances met. As if she belonged here, too.

I don't even know her name, he thought. *And she does not know mine.*

"Perhaps you may go next year," Mamá said, trying to cuddle him as she used to.

Sereno shrugged free of her embrace, upset but too proud to show it. "¿Porqué no?" He heard and hated the childish note in his voice which he was unable to control. "Mingo said he doesn't want to go, and I do."

They were alone in her bedroom, a place where he had hoped to gain some advantage after being told at the breakfast table she and Papá had made up their minds, and no one was going to Dos Corazones.

Mamá rested her palms on the bed, on either side of Violeta, but looked up at him. "I have many reasons, mijo, besides the fact that you are so young—"

"I'm older than you think, Mamá. Did I not manage well when you sent me from the house of El General, to send Papá that telegram? And then I was only a baby!"

A smile tugged at the corners of her mouth. "Sí, but, oh, the worry that caused me! I prayed that if ever we were together again, I would treasure you with all my heart. And" She stood up. "that means, Dos Corazones *next* year."

"The filly will be worthless by then."

"There are more fillies in this world. Mira, Violeta wishes you to hold her."

He took his sister and carried her onto the balcony, where cushioned wicker chairs matched the ones on the porch below. The clear morning air was a balm, and through open doors below came voices of criadas at their chores. One began 'Rayando el Sol' and others joined in.

"Listen, Violeta, they're singing a little song for you."

In one of the larger corrals across the road, Domingo was putting Cimarrón through a stiff program of paces, stopping and starting, wheeling. In the near corral where the saddle horses waited for use at a moment's notice, Valiente and Viento, along with Teo's Volador, switched their flowing tails at flies and stamped restless hooves.

"I miss Teo," he confided to the baby, and she cooed and babbled at him. "I wish he was my brother."

A second letter from Teo had come last week, with its twin addressed to Domingo, but aside from the usual polite phrases expressing affection and good wishes, and a brief account of the progress don Pablo was making on restoring the family home, Teo had said nothing to show he missed those days of friendship spent in Sereno's company.

He'd made a number of false starts in trying to answer, before shoving aside the paper and pen.

Confined to his lap, Violeta became fretful. He left her with Mamá and set off for a ball game with boys in the village. At this time of day, most of them worked in the fields with their families, so he had to play with niños too young for the labor of crops and cattle. Like Violeta, he soon grew fretful with boredom, and tossed the ball to a good-natured Opata.

Passing the corral where Domingo was grooming the stallion, he felt regret that they had never overcome the poor start which marked their meeting in the City of México two years ago. Domingo glanced up, the horse brush momentarily still, before returning to business.

Sereno changed his course and went to lean on the corral pole. After awhile he said, "Cimarroncito is looking good."

"Sí. He learns quickly."

A silence. The sun grew hot.

Domingo put away the brush and unfastened the tether. He turned the horse into the large pasture with half a dozen mares and some burros, and came back to pick up his hat and spurs. "So why are you hanging around watching me?"

He resented being spoken to as if he were one of the peones, but kept his voice mild. "I can watch if I care to."

Domingo joined him beneath the scant shade of a blooming acacia. They lounged elbows on the top corral pole, an arm's length apart. Eyes on the distant eastern mountains, his medio hermano asked, "When are you going to Dos Corazones?"

"I'm not."

Domingo's head spun around, a question in his eyes. It failed to reach his lips. He jerked his chin toward a group of hopefuls getting their mounts and money ready for a race on the track lately built after Papá had given consent. "Cimarrón can beat any of those caballos de carga."

"Viento could do that, easily."

Their eyes locked.

"¿Quieres apostar?" Want to bet?

He shook his head. "Not if you ride Cimarrón. Now, if it were Valiente—"

Domingo was already heading toward the rack where he'd placed his saddle. "¡Vamos, chico! Get your caballo warmed up. I'm going to beat your ass."

"Like hell!" He ran to the gate and whistled for his gelding.

In the time it took for them to ready their horses, two other races had goaded riders and spectators alike into fervent betting. The appearance of the hacendado's sons, mounted and clearly intending to compete, brought a round of *¡Viva!* and fresh wagers. Martín and Lobo held the centavos and kept a paper tally.

Getting a drink of water, he asked, "Is anybody betting on me?"

Martín grinned. "It's about even, muchacho."

Domingo's compañero, Marcelo, said, "Those who put their faith in Viento are hoping you do not fall off."

"See if I do!"

Swinging into saddles, he and Domingo rode onto the track and, on the mark beside him, waited for Gregorio to give the starting signal with his hat.

The instant it came, heels dug into flanks and with a leap Viento hit a gallop as if the caballo knew they must cross that line first. Mane whipping his face, knees clinging, he gave as much rein as possible without losing control. *¡Demonio!* he thought, realizing only now that the older boy had placed himself to have the first inside bend.

That was how those in the know won their pesos! Which to do? Chance winding his mount to stay even, or slack off and gain the lead in the next turn which bent in the opposite direction?

He cut behind Valiente, got a mouthful of flying dirt, heard Domingo laugh as they thwarted his attempt to slip between them and the inside edge of the track, bordered with rocks and low brush. Almost to the turn. If he remained blocked, there was no hope of gaining the lead.

Kicking Viento mercilessly, slapping the horse's neck with the reins, he felt a spurt of effort in the churning muscles and, though they went a bit wide in the curve, they began the return even with Valiente, if not ahead. For a breathless minute he believed he was going to win. Then Domingo's left hand brought a quirt down hard on his mount's shoulder.

Surprise dropped his lower jaw. His concentration faltered, and so did Viento. They crossed the hoof-cut rope marking the finish line nearly a full wagon length behind, to the cheers of those who had won money and the jeers of those who had bet on him.

While his horse was still moving, he was out of the saddle, shoving through hombres who were hurrying to slap Domingo on the back, and, too quick for anyone to realize his intention, he hit the older boy with his fist, in the exact spot that had resulted in a bloody nose for him that day of the picnic. However, Domingo didn't go down. Instead, the hand with the quirt still looped around the wrist shot out to smack him, cheek and ear, and before he could land another blow of his own, vaqueros were pulling them apart.

"¡Ay de mí !" Gregorio cried, holding him around the neck. "Your papá will not like this."

"¡Ya lo sé!" He jerked free. "See how much Domingo thinks of his caballo, to cut welts in order to win."

Martín bent to examine the marks on Valiente's shoulder. "He didn't bring blood."

Others were muttering, taking sides, little arguments springing up. Lobo brought Viento and gave him the reins, saying, "He needs to be cooled."

"So do you," Gregorio suggested, trying to lead him away.

Facing Domingo, who wore his stubborn look, Sereno said, "Valiente did not deserve that," and turned to end the spectacle.

"You're just sorry you didn't think of it," Domingo called after him.

He whirled, wrathful. "If I had, I would never insult my horse by using a whip."

Walking beside him, Gregorio reminded, "Martín said he caused no injury. That is not why you are angry, admit it. You hate to have him beat you."

"To win unfairly—sí, I hate that. Valiente wouldn't have won, if not for the quirt."

"Maybe. Maybe not." Gregorio tugged the reins out of his hand. "I shall walk him awhile and tend him. Why not go somewhere and quiet yourself?"

"You mean, where I won't be in the same corral with Domingo."

"¿Una idea luminosa—no?" Gregorio gave him a friendly grin, and they parted in the road.

After a few paces, he turned to ask, "Did you lose much?"

"It is only money," his friend answered, with a wave.

To you, he thought, skirting the wall of the mirador.

If he went into the house for his flute, he likely would run into Mamá—or worse, Papá—who by this time would have been told about the race and the fight. Best to avoid both parents until the incident lost some of its importance.

The secret place in the forest always soothed his temper, though it felt strange to be here without his flute. Breeze-tossed branches overhead murmured and sighed, like lonely voices in a language long dead. "Indio voices," he said aloud. "Or—spirits."

He lay prone on the low cliff above the cave, without benefit of sarape. Although the sting of Domingo's slap had faded, in his memory a tingle remained, causing him to touch the place gingerly. Burrowing his face in the curve of one arm, he muttered, "I should have known we can never be friends."

He woke pelted with rain, flashes of lightning in the cloud-dark sky, reverberating thunder claps. Scooting to the edge of the cliff, he dropped to shelter in the cave, glad there was no locked door as he had once dreamed. The unnamed Thing his sleeping self had feared didn't exist; so the pitch black interior held no terror. Arms clasped around his knees, he sat in the entrance, watching a curtain of rain advance across the valley.

Behind it, in a clearing sky, an enormous rainbow arched over the encircling mountain range. Three deer left the forest and browsed the freshened grass. As beautiful as Los Nuestros was, he often thought of those sun-drenched patios at the townhouse in Mérida, and wondered what had become of the parrot Pájaro and his young friend Victor. He thought of the summer storms lashing huge trees between the house and the high rock wall that had kept Mamá prisoner. Sometimes, he found himself longing for that wall, that safety.

Sometimes, he felt he did not belong here.

As he leaned against the side of the cave, something sharp poked his shoulder. Investigation revealed a corner of a sawn timber sticking out from between two stones. What was it a part of? He backed off and studied the placement, noticing too that attached to the wood was a bit of what seemed to be an old leather hinge, such as countrymen used to hang—"Madre de Dios," he breathed. "There was once a door."

Aside from assuring himself at the start that no wild animals lived in his cave, he had neglected to explore past the point where light entered. Now, he cautiously stepped across the packed floor, alert for any living thing, natural or supernatural.

When the passage became dark, then made a turn, he hesitated. He ought to bring a torch, or at least matches with which to light a brand of ocote to light his way. Yet his feet resumed moving forward, nerves taut, breath suspended. In the blackness, his outstretched hand encountered something and he bit back a cry.

A rough, flat surface filled the narrow opening. Planks, wide ones. Another door, deep inside the cave, one which had no latch, and did not budge when he pushed against it with all his might.

"Papá—come see!" Sereno burst into his office, breathless. He closed the door before coming to lean over the desk where Ramón had been struggling with the account books Luis used to keep straight. "It's not a cave. It's a tunnel—the entrance to a gold or silver mine. I bet that is what Señor Johnson is after."

For a moment, brain still filled with columns of figures which didn't balance, he looked at the earnest face and saw the excitement without understanding the cause. Then, *mine*, and *Johnson*, registered. "You found a mine?"

"¡Sí, Papá!" Sereno rounded the desk and gripped his wrist. "Come with me. Let me show you." He seemed to have second thoughts. "Only—don't tell Domingo. It's connected to my secret place."

Picking up his hat, Ramón warned, "If it is a mine, likely it has been worked out, so if you are thinking of becoming rich from it, don't get your hopes up."

Like thieves they stole out of the house with an unlit pine torch, and ran down to the corner of the mirador wall. Clambering over, landing on the path below, he thought, *I'm getting too old to go charging about like this*. But he kept his footing on the path and soon entered a canopy of trees. He felt privileged to be here, even if the invitation came simply because it could not be contained.

Sereno showed him traces of a door that had been removed to make the opening appear natural, then led him into the a tunnel to the unexpected barrier. "How does it open?" he asked, and Sereno answered, "It doesn't. That is what I cannot figure out."

Their searching hands located no lever, spring, or knob by which the thing could be fastened. "It goes that way," he concluded. "And is barred from the other side."

"Then— There is another way in!"

In the glow of a pine torch, he looked at his son with amusement and respect. "Sharp of you to think that, instead of supposing someone locked himself in to die with his treasure."

"Papá, I'm not stupid. That happens only in stories. Where do you suppose the entrance can be?"

"¿Quién sabe? Rather than spend time looking for it, why not chop down this door?"

The idea fired Sereno, who would have raced all the way to the storehouse for an ax. Ramón held him back. "If you plan to keep your secret, wait until tomorrow. Siesta is ending, and we're sure to be seen."

Throughout the evening, spent with Estrada, Anita, and the baby, he considered the possibility that the sealed tunnel was an old mine. "More likely, a root cellar," he'd pointed out to Sereno, to keep the boy from becoming too hopeful. But it would explain what the gringo Johnson sought on Los Nuestros land.

Sereno barely slept. In his mind he enacted a return to the cave—no, tunnel—and Papá chopped a passage through the planks. They followed a flickering ocote light deep into the earth, where rich veins of silver glistened and sacks of ore lined timbered dirt walls. Domingo would explode with envy when everyone heaped praise on him for this discovery.

With wealth from the mine, Papá could buy needed machinery for Los Nuestros. There would be more goods in the storehouses, items of finer quality for everyone to enjoy. And, put aside until now as impractical, the restoration of Papá's northern hacienda, Casa Vásquez, could go forward.

He remembered that Mamá had never been to Casa Vásquez, though during their stay in Mérida, she often spoke of the place, making it seem magical, a haven. If not for the fighting in Sonora and the chance finding of this casa grande, the family would have gone to live there. Pondering the twists his life had taken, Sereno watched the sky grow paler until criadas opened windows and sang their morning devotions.

Jumping out of bed, he pulled on comfortable old clothes and hurried to breakfast. Quelling his impatience, he waited for the others to straggle in, take seats, murmur greetings. Papá carefully kept from meeting his eyes. It seemed the servers took longer than usual in bringing food; Violeta was cranky and delayed Mamá's finishing her meal; Estrada dawdled over extra coffee.

Only Domingo appeared the same—moody, putting away beef and eggs and pan blanco with efficiency.

When it was polite to do so, Sereno excused himself and strolled onto the east patio to wait. He blew a few notes on the flute, an unsettled feeling in his stomach preventing anything more. The line of sun had moved the width of a finger over the tiles before Papá came out of the house. Carrying an ax. "¿Listo?"

"¡Sí!"

Inside the tunnel, he held the torch and Papá swung the ax. The planks began to splinter, pieces dropped to the floor; but the wood was thick, and making a hole big enough for a man to crawl through took awhile.

At last Papá stood back and said, "Give me the light."

He would have liked being first, yet handed over the torch and waited until Papá called, "Ven."

Stepping through the jagged hole, he stood beside Papá and gazed at the dim walls. In the glow, he saw ends of roots, mine timbers, a dusty broken shovel, a rag that likely had been a workman's handkerchief. No shining traces of silver threading rocks and earth. Papá led the way into the winding passage.

"It is a mine, is it not?"

"No doubt of that. But you know this country is full of old mines. Those abandoned like this are useless."

When he was silent, Papá glanced over one shoulder, "I warned you not to be too hopeful."

"But, Señor Johnson believes there to be wealth, else why would he send men to fight and die?"

Papá moved the light in an arc, peering at the ceiling. "Greedy men often do stupid things, mijo."

At intervals, vents had been made to the surface, to admit air for the miners. At intervals, other tunnels led right and left. "Maybe one of those contains the silver," he suggested. "Or, gold."

"This leads somewhere and is easy to follow. We ought to mark the passage to avoid becoming lost." Papá handed him the ax. "Here."

Every few paces, then, he hacked a chip from a timber or made a cut in the earth wall. Deeper into the mine, the torch light began to pick up shiny patches, some as thick as a man's arm. "Diosito," Papá said in mild wonder. "It looks like silver to me."

Containing excitement, Sereno said, "To me, too."

Presently, walking required more care, for chunks of ore lay scattered about, and they paused to pick up several. Papá turned a large piece this way and that. "I suppose it wouldn't hurt to have this assayed. We should have brought a sack."

Sereno stripped off his shirt and they tied it around several kilos of rocks. He fastened the sleeves to his belt, the weight at his hip promising great things.

"That is heavy. Why not leave it until we come back?"

"I like carrying it."

The close, damp air soon gave a sweaty chill to his skin, and he wished they would locate la veta madre—the mother vein—and have the fortune assured. Instead, they reached the end of the tunnel. "Papá, what now?"

At the same time, they glanced upward and saw the under side of a trapdoor. With the ax, Papá pounded the thing until it loosened. "I'll boost you up."

He undid the burden of rocks and, lifted on his father's shoulders, pushed aside the panel and wriggled into the darkness above.

Chapter Sixteen

"What do you see?" Papá's voice below sounded hollow.

Sereno crouched on the lip of the hole, sensing space before him. "Send up the light, por favor."

With the torch, he found himself on a landing of earth, a rope-and-pole ladder leading up to another small opening covered by a plank trapdoor. Driven into the dirt was an iron pipe, to which was fastened a coil of knotted rope. He tossed the length down to his father, saying, "Can you climb this?"

"¡Ah, que Dios me ayude!" Papá muttered, but in moments his head cleared the rim and he looked about. There was nothing on the landing except a sandal with a broken strap, its coating of dust evidence that its owner probably was dust himself.

Sereno's shirtful of ore tied round his neck, Papá pulled himself onto the landing. Testing his weight on the ladder, he reached the second trapdoor and knocked it open. The briefest of silences. "¡Madre de Dios!"

Jumping up and down in agony, he shouted, "¡Qué es, Papá? What?" then scrambled to see for himself.

They stood in a small storeroom, its walls lined with big ore-filled leather sacks. Putting more samples in his own shirt, Papá said, "We might as well be thorough."

Across the room was a regular door. Half afraid to turn the brass knob, he was disappointed when he did and nothing happened.

Papá tried it, peered at the fixture and swore softly. He stood back, measuring with his eyes, and gave a kick that broke the latch and sent the door crashing against a wall. Crossing the main patio toward the cocina, two criadas screamed and dropped the platters of soiled breakfast dishes they had been carrying. "¡No tengan miedo!" he yelled. "¡Es solamente yo!"

The sight of their hacendado's bare chest was enough to send them fleeing even after they realized who had startled them.

Papá shut the cracked door just as Mamá and Estrada rushed to discover the cause of the crash.

"¡Ay! ¡Qué un lío!" Mamá cried. What a mess! She and the médico picked their way among broken plates.

"What is going on?" Estrada asked.

Sereno controlled his giggles long enough to say, "Mamá, I found—"

Papá covered his mouth with a less-than-gentle hand, and told her, "We frightened the girls, that's all. I was merely unsticking this door."

Mamá gave him a slightly annoyed look and went in search of someone to clear away the damage.

Estrada lingered to say, "You both find it necessary to remove clothing in order to unstick a door?"

Giving his head a little squeeze in the circle of his arm, Papá released him and said to the doctor, "Sereno and I were just playing a game. Mijo, run get us each a fresh shirt while I repair this."

After months of allowing the man to live with them, it seemed Papá didn't trust the médico entirely. Belatedly, he realized that Mamá wasn't to be let in on the secret, either. The knowledge produced a tickly feeling in his chest. When he returned with the shirts, Estrada was watching his father bolt on a padlock.

"You and your papá play rough games," the médico remarked.

"This one got a bit out of control." Papá stood and examined his handiwork.

"Breaking doors is somewhat extreme. I recall it has always been stuck, but now to put on a padlock intrigues me."

"There is a hole in the floor. I don't want anyone falling down it." Papá gave them a one-sided grin.

"Then, why not patch the hole?"

With a quick frown, Papá said, "Mind your own business."

"Ho, Ramón, you are touchy. You trust me with the lives of your esposa and niña, but not this."

"If you insist on believing I'm hiding something, do me the favor of keeping silent." He went to his office and started laying out folders of papers.

Bursting to tell someone, Sereno followed. "Everyone will know, as soon as we start to work the mine again."

"We are not going to work it."

He couldn't believe he'd heard right. "But it can be the way to restore Casa Vásquez for Mamá."

They stared into each other's eyes. Then Papá's features gradually relaxed. Coming from behind the desk, he took Sereno in his arms and hugged him close. Another long moment passed, during which he saw his medio hermano pass the window at a distance, mounted on Cimarrón. Then his father released him and sighed. "Siéntese."

Sensing a confidence, he sat down in the visitor's chair, and Papá poured a glass of white wine before seating himself.

"A long time ago," he began, "when I wasn't much older than you, I found a treasure map—"

"¿En serio? ¡Qué maravilloso!"

"Don't interrupt." A smile softened his words, but he was instantly serious, gazing inward as he remembered. "It belonged to my grandfather—your bisabuelo—and I'm sure, had I followed, it would have led to a fortune."

"¡Chispas! You didn't follow?"

Papá shook his head. "I almost did. But in the Sierra Madre, oh, far north from here, I saw my father. He died before I was born, so it was his espíritu, understand—that warned me against using blood money to—" He broke off, sought and found the proper word, "—to gain the love and respect of other people. When you spoke of Casa Vásquez, you reminded me of myself, and my intention to find that treasure for my mother. But I have learned that money, whether bandit treasure or wealth from the ground, is not what brings peace. Nor even happiness."

"But surely, having our fine casa, and the horses, and the silver given me by don Miguel when he was dying in Vera Cruz, we're happier than those Indios and other villagers who live in huts and own nothing. Already we are comfortable. Think how much better, if we are rich!"

The corners of Papá's lips curved up. "Observe them closely, mijo. Not one of them worries as I do."

"They are too stupid to worry."

"Never think that! It's not lack of intelligence. It is lack of responsibility. With wealth comes the necessity to know what to do with it."

"I would know what to do."

Papá laughed softly. "That is exactly what I once thought." He sipped from the wine glass.

The discussion at an end, Sereno stood up, but his father stopped him.

"Keep our secret, mijo. When the revolution is over and the government is stable, we can plan. Then—and only after I am convinced el maldito gringo is far from here—we can do as you desire. Restoring Casa Vásquez has always been in my heart, and I don't give up my dreams easily."

Domingo learned of the rumor among the villagers when Mina said, "My cousin told me she was there when El Patrón broke open that door which has always been stuck, and then put a big lock on it."

Her expression said she wanted him to explain the mystery of what Jefe was guarding. He was ashamed to admit that he didn't know. Angered, too, to suspect that Sereno did, and wasn't telling. Since coming to Los Nuestros he'd never felt so left out, mistrusted.

He closed the lesson book they had been studying. Anita was walking in her gardens with the younger pupils, leaving him with Mina in the cool classroom. Since the roundup, he'd spent most mornings gentling horses, but Mina's request for help had brought him back to the school. Beside her on the bench, he was aware he would never have a better opportunity to kiss her.

He wiped sweaty palms on his jeans. Since Jefe and Anita were married, the embraces they shared—playful pecks on a cheek or intimate caresses when they believed themselves unobserved—didn't count. Neither did the displays he noted among caballeros and their sweethearts, for such men were experienced. "Mina—"

She was looking at him. Waiting.

He hesitantly touched a strand of her hair. "You like me, don't you?"

"No." Smiling, she laid her arms on his shoulders and leaned to whisper close to his mouth, "Te amo, Domingo."

Startled, he grasped her wrists. "I don't want you to love me." She tried to peer into his face but he turned away, hurt by his glimpse of her pain and confusion.

"Then, what do you want?"

Unable to answer, he started to rise. She grabbed his shirt sleeve and would have torn it if he hadn't stopped.

"I thought you were sweet," she said, low and controlled yet clearly angry, "but you are no different from the rest."

"We're too young to think of love," he told her, feeling hot all over.

"But not too young to think of—other things!"

He did get up, and she let go of his shirt but blocked the aisle so he couldn't leave without leaping over a bench. Her laugh was shaky. "Ay, jovencito, no tengas miedo—I know my place."

"What do you mean?"

Mina tossed her head, her lips curving downward. "Sons of the hacendado take their pleasure, just as always. My uncles died in a worthless fight. Things are never going to change, so long as some are ricos and others are their peones."

"You sound like Paz."

A blaze of jealousy in her eyes amused him as she demanded, "Who is Paz?"

"Someone I never kissed." He put his hands on either side of her head and she let him draw her close. She clung to him, her mouth soft beneath his, yielding…then she began kissing him, in a way he hadn't expected and wasn't ready for.

Voices outside, people on the walkway leading to the schoolroom, made them step apart. He snatched up the book he'd laid aside and pretended to study it. But his heart thudded and long moments passed before his face cooled. By that time, Mina had left for the village.

II

Bored to distraction, Christine put on the riding dress Greta had found in a thieves' market in Culiacán, and ordered one of the mozos to saddle Jump.

All summer she had kept within sight of the ranch, afraid of encountering some of Pancho Villa's soldiers with only three old men to defend her.

Not for the first time, she wished she had stayed in the United States with one of Mother's sisters. Tokee made efforts to please, even to serving supper at a reasonable hour. Crates from Greta occasionally arrived filled with books and pastries.

But Daddy always took the Indian interpreter with him, leaving her struggling to communicate her needs in the few Spanish words she'd learned. Resorting to gestures caused much amusement among the servants. She suspected they didn't know any more of the language than she did, for they spoke their own dialect, punctuated by frequent laughter.

During the rainy season, amusements here were few. Sketching and painting scenes of the rancho, coaxing the old cook to teach her how to prepare different Mexican and Indian dishes, riding Jump to the stream, reading books sent from Culiacán— These palled after awhile. She felt she would go insane if something exciting didn't happen. Today, she felt reckless enough to take on Señor Villa himself.

Packing a cloth with tortillas, two oranges, and a chunk of piloncillo for desert, she filled a water jug in case no spring or tinaja was handy where she chose to have lunch, and found her wide-brimmed hat.

She had stopped leaving notes for Daddy. He seldom came home during the day to read them, sometimes not appearing until after dark. He was full of talk about the progress his plan was making, but on examination what he said contained no substance. She still had no idea what guayule was, beyond his claim that the crop was needed in the European war effort, and would make money. If he had planted any, the fields didn't lie within range of her excursions.

With mozos trailing, she put Jump into a lazy canter southward, toward a line of trees that bordered a stream. Earlier in the summer she'd explored the near bank for some miles in each direction; today she meant to cross. It was barely dawn—she would have hours to fill before the threat of afternoon rains forced a return. The mozos hated getting wet.

Here and there on the rolling grassland, she saw knots of grazing cattle owned by Daddy's Indians. Beneath trees along the watercourse she often found them holed up in the cool shade at noon. The mozos warned her against dismounting, the beasts being somewhat wild and prone to running over a person on foot.

Wildlife, glimpsed from time to time, fascinated her. Songbirds, hawks, owls; rabbits, an occasional skunk, foxes; deer, even beavers. She wished she hadn't lost her camera, though buying film might have been a problem. She had to make do with her pencils and sketchpads. Already she'd filled two of those, and twice had asked Daddy to find a tin of watercolors when he made the monthly trip into Culiacán for supplies. "Sure, Baby, sure. Watercolors," he'd say; and then forget.

This month, no matter if he insisted the long ride was too difficult, she intended to go. Nothing was available at the market in Huajupa, the nearest village. She had exhausted its delights in two visits.

Reaching the stream, she rode along the bank until she came to a place where a sandbar and pebbles visible on the bottom seemed to indicate shallow water.

"Señorita—"

She glanced over her shoulder. One of the men waved his arm in a languid arc. "¿Qué quieres?" she called back. What do you want?

"Vengas acá, por favor."

Another added, "Vamos a su casa ahora."

"I'm not ready to go home!" she answered, sure that they had no trouble understanding what she meant. Kicking Jump's belly, she urged the gelding across the stream, and the mozos followed, complaining among themselves.

She usually led them in a big circle. This time, her course continued southward. Maybe something would happen.

Not dangerous, only exciting, like seeing a band of rebels in the distance. Or even Carrancistas, the current brand of Federales. Her grasp of the politics of this revolution remained hazy, though thanks to Greta she was aware that General Obregón had been fighting Villa and seemed to have gotten the better of him.

Daddy said the war in México was almost over. She wondered what differences that might make in their lives.

The mozos were shouting at her again. She waved at them. Loping over a rise, she thrilled in the freedom of a sweeping expanse. Across a mountain-rimmed valley was a bosque of tall, broad-leafed trees. As she drew near she saw a break in the foliage, the mark of a trail or road. "It must lead somewhere," she said aloud. But where?

Resigned, the mozos had ceased to beg her to turn around, but followed, still arguing back and forth, likely predicting disaster if one of them didn't do something.

Beneath the trees there was no underbrush such as she was used to seeing at home. Dense shade and a park-like atmosphere, as well as the angle of sun which said it was close enough to noon for a picnic, lured her off her horse. Looping the rein over a limb she could reach, she untied the oilcloth and spread it on a level spot.

At a respectful distance the mozos dismounted, still carrying on a debate, their speech a garble of Spanish which she still didn't comprehend, and their own dialect which she couldn't hope to decipher. Without loosening cinches, as she had, they squatted and unwrapped their tortillas and chiles, hats laid aside.

She was peeling an orange when they stretched out on the bare ground and gave themselves up to siesta. This was the hour she always spent drawing whatever was in sight, including them. In an hour, however, she and Jump could cover a lot of new ground. The prospect of an unexpected community, with its modest cornfield and naked children, or a waterfall in a glade of wildflowers, was irresistible.

I can be back before they wake up. Rising, keeping an eye on them, she secured the cinch and eased herself into the saddle. Walking the horse away, she looked back a couple of times, but the mozos continued to slumber.

Riding several times a week in various directions, she had never chanced upon Daddy or any of the men he'd hired to plant and cultivate fiber. Where did he go? What did they do? All at once she remembered the secret. The one she had taken so lightly that she'd forgotten all about it. Used to Daddy's schemes, and hearing daily about guayule, she hadn't been impressed by the notion of a fabulously rich silver mine.

Now, his promise of wealth made her consider his absences in a fresh light. Of course! He was searching for the mine. Maybe he'd already found it, and men were working to smuggle the ore out of the country.

Señor Cordero's ore, she thought with a pang. Daddy was stealing someone else's silver.

It hurt her to think of her father being a thief; yet, after suspecting him of burning the village at Los Nuestros, she found the probability less than shocking. She wished she were back in Kentucky, getting ready for school, spending her small allowance on stick candy and books, and going to the Presbyterian church with Aunt Olivia.

Shrubby hills had sprung up around her, and she came out of the reverie with a mild sense of alarm. The rocky ground showed only criss-crossed paths made by wild cattle or game. Jump kept walking as if he knew where he was going, so she gave him rein and hoped he would either find the road again or take her back to the picnic ground.

In a few minutes they hit a faint track that appeared used, if infrequently, and Jump followed it. Though she felt they were still heading away from the ranch, whatever lay ahead beckoned.

When the trail began to climb, Jump kept his pace, carrying her among low cliffs, greater ones all around. Just ahead, on the crest of a chaparral-covered ridge but beside what was passing for a road, stood a dead tree. Its few broken branches reached out in silhouette against the blue sky. Once there had been a twin trunk, long ago chopped off a couple of feet from the ground. A hole in the stump halfway up looked like a good place to hide things—or find a tarantula, scorpion, or rattlesnake.

Reining in, Christine looked about her. From this vantage point beside the dead tree, she had a dizzying view of brown hills, smoky green vegetation, blooming cacti. Ringing her at distance were almond colored bluffs and beyond those were blue and lavender mountains.

To the east—away from the arcing sun—lay a branching ribbon of sparkling water. Rivers, for which she knew no name. She hoped the smaller ribbon was the stream on which Las Flores was situated. She couldn't see the rancho or determine which bosque of trees concealed the picnic ground and the sleeping mozos.

Her heart gave a little leap of fear before she assured herself that all she had to do was head straight north—or maybe slightly northeast—and she'd come into country she recognized. Perhaps the mozos had wakened and were on her backtrail. If she retraced her route, she would see them, soon. Wouldn't she?

Mina's caresses had intensified feelings of attraction, curiosity and unfulfillment, and Domingo avoided her, afraid if he went to see her she would manage to get him alone. Already he felt in over his head, floundering as he had in the floodwaters of the broken earthen dam, his imagination and urges scaring him more than a little.

Too, those flashes of jealousy, bitterness, and strong will in Mina had showed him a different image of her. Before that day in the classroom, he had seen only her lowered lashes and shy smile, heard the soft, musical way she spoke. Her unmusical accusation, that he was no better than countless gachupines who took advantage of their people, cut his pride.

Still, it was after that accusation that she kissed him.

Sometimes, he daydreamed it was Tereza who had kissed him so warmly, and he tried to imagine what might happen when he visited Dos Corazones again.

"¡Cuidado!"

Martín's sharp warning jerked him back to the sweat and dust of the corral, where he had allowed one of the colts to become entangled in a neglected length of rope. While they freed it, Martín said, "Enough for today. Your mind is not centered."

His mind was centered. But not on taming horses.

Riding northeast, he followed the winding course of the Río San Lorenzo with no destination in mind. He had packed food and bedding in case he decided to camp. When Anita hugged him she murmured, "Come back safe, hijo." Jefe's reminder about renegade Villistas only made him grin and pat his pistol. The suggestion to take Volador as a remount was a sound idea, which he heeded.

It was afternoon when he stopped at the outpost manned by four Mayos who'd fought under Jefe all the way from Sonora to the City of México. Sharing beans and tortillas, he asked, "What lies north of here?"

They talked among themselves in their dialect and one who knew some Spanish answered, "Our patrolling takes us west and east. Sometimes we go over the mountain to Los Remedios to visit the women. North? We don't go that way."

Then the youngest added, "Traders from Huajupa and Soyupa say that a gringo has moved onto the rancho upriver, on the north fork called San Juan y Los Camarones. Many of the Indios are working for him."

"Gringo!" Domingo's hand jerked, spilling coffee down his chin. Wiping it with his shirtsleeve, he prodded for more information, but that was all they knew. "You did not find out his name? Hell, it must be El Señor Johnson, and Jefe must be told. How far is this rancho?"

The answer was vague, ranging between all day and half a day. By the time he came to the place where the rivers forked, San Gregorio and Los Remedios branching to the east, it was well into the early evening.

Mid-August, and rains seemed already to have ceased. He hoped it wouldn't be the beginning of a long drought. Villagers depended on the rains. Jefe had tried to persuade them to put in irrigation ditches for themselves but somehow it never was done.

Coming to a sandy place where the river pooled beneath acacias, he let his horses drink lightly and tied them in the shade. Then he pulled off his boots, hung the pistol on a

307

handy limb, and was just taking the shirt over his head when a child's voice called from the rocks above, "Por favor, necesito ayuda—"

Shading his eyes against the westering sun, he saw someone small clinging to a boulder and leaning down in such a way that he yelled, "¡Retrocede antes de caer!"

Then he realized it was a pale-haired girl in a light blue riding outfit—Señorita Johnson—and repeated in English, "Get back, before you fall."

His eyes sought a way up among the rocks, even while his mind told him this could be a trick. Alone, she certainly had no business here. He was nearly to the top of the cliff when he remembered the pistol, useless on that branch below. *Damn. If they kill me, it will be my own fault.*

She had moved back to stand beside a solitary dead tree, both figures silhouetted against a round-topped mountain, above which were clouds tinged with pink and gold from the sunset. A quick glance showed him no one was with her. "How did you get here?"

"I rode my horse." She pointed to a gelding down the trail. "But he seems to have gone lame."

He walked over to examine the roan's legs, and she fell in step, saying, "I was looking for my mozos when I saw you, and since you have two horses, I thought—" He picked up the off front, which had some swelling. She bent down to see his face, and finished, "perhaps you would let me ride one of yours."

Pressing the gelding's leg from hoof to knee, his fingers found a tender spot around the blunt end of a thorn embedded in the flesh. As he released the hoof and straightened, intending to get pliers out of his gear, the girl offered her hand. "You remember me, don't you? I'm Christine Johnson."

"I remember you." He flung back over his shoulder, "I remember your father, as well."

She caught up to him at the brink and he whirled, thinking she meant to push him over. Her blue eyes were stormy. "I'm not my father! Don't judge me by what he does."

Without reply, he went back down to his horses. Paz, Mina, and now Cristina—all ready to defend themselves against any offense, whether justified or not. Was Tereza as headstrong as the girls he had the misfortune to know?

He got the tool and medicine from his mochila, and returned. "I am doing this for your horse." He jerked out the thorn, making the wound bleed.

"¡Caray!" she cried, "no wonder he refused to go—that thing must be two inches long."

"Keep to the trails, or it can happen again."

"I was on a trail—sort of."

"Also, it is very dangerous to be out here alone."

"Well, my mozos were asleep, and I thought they would catch up to me, but they didn't."

He couldn't help noticing the sheen of sunlight on her hair. It was much fairer even than Anita's. She must look like her mother. Who, Jefe had told them, was dead. "I'm sorry." He didn't intend to say it aloud, and she looked puzzled. Dousing the wound with medicine, he bound his pañuelo around the animal's leg. "How far, to your casa?"

She shrugged. "I left early this morning, but stopped for lunch and to sketch. Then Jump came up lame and I've been here for hours, waiting for him to get better, or for the mozos to find me."

"He was only going to get worse, with that thorn in his hoof."

"I didn't know it was a thorn. I thought it was only a sprain."

"Do you know which way?" he said, half in jest until she shook her head and her lostness became worrisome.

"By the Río San José—but from here I could see three rivers, and I was afraid if I followed the one I thought was right, it would be wrong."

"Were you frightened?"

"A little," she admitted. "Until I saw you."

"You are lucky it was I and not a Villista." Untying her roan, he knew his horses could not come up that cliff, nor could Cristina and her mount safely descend, so it was necessary to search out another path.

At his elbow, she said, "Didn't General Obregón defeat Villa?"

"Is Villa dead? No? Then he is not defeated." Still barefoot, he swung into her saddle so its tapaderos would shield his skin, and urged the horse into motion.

"What are you doing?" Cristina shouted, fear and anger in her voice. "Don't leave me here!"

"I am going to get my caballos," he flung down at her. "Stay there."

Glancing back he could tell she didn't believe him. At the base of the hill he found a break in the chaparral and collected his things. Her relief when he reappeared at the other side of the cliff made him grin. He changed her saddle to Volador and helped her up. Giving her the reins, he said, "I'll take you within sight, but you must not tell your father you saw me."

"Why not?"

He neglected to answer; but when the ground leveled enough to allow them to ride abreast, he asked instead, "Do you know why he wants Los Nuestros land so much that he would burn our village?"

"You have no proof that he did that."

"The proof is in your eyes when you think about it."

Cristina was silent. Then, "I think he might have hired someone to frighten your family into leaving."

"So, what he wants is valuable. As he has not the look of a farmer, it can't be land. If it is not land, it must be ore. Silver—or gold, perhaps."

Her startled glance rewarded him. "Is that what your father believes? That Daddy is trying to take away a mine which belongs to your family?"

"Isn't he?"

Her eyes held his. "Is there such a mine?"

He laughed. "If so, would everyone break his back to grow cattle and crops?"

"Then, you're saying there is no mine."

"I'm saying, Do not tell him you saw me. He will suspect that I am a spy."

She smiled, tilting her head to look at him. "Are you? What else could you be doing out in this wilderness?"

"The same as you, no? I like being away from so many people, and the responsibilities of the rancho." And, it put a comfortable distance between him and Mina.

It was nearly dark when they came to a bosque which Cristina said was her picnic spot, empty now except for many hoofprints leading in different directions. "They seem to have made a search without bothering to think," he said. "I could have tracked you, easily."

"They are old men whose eyesight is probably poor."

"Not the sort I would put to guard my daughter."

"I hope nothing has happened to them." In the dusk, her face was troubled. "Should we call out?"

"No—unless you can find your way from here and want me to leave."

Quick, she said, "Don't leave. It's another hour or more to where I can see the house."

They rode through the bosque, crossed the stream, and followed the river. "What place is this, where you are living?" He meant to find some indication of it penciled in on Jefe's map.

"I named it Las Flores, because there are all sorts of blooming vines and flowers there, especially around the spring."

"What is the house like?"

"Low, in the shape of an L. There's a porch across the front, and big trees nearby. It sits in a grassy basin, with hills all round that make it shady in the morning and evening. But it's not nearly as nice as your home."

The tremor in her voice touched a chord in him, the same feeling he had every time he returned to the casa grande with assurance that Anita and the baby, Jefe and everyone else who made up his household, would be there, safe.

"I get lonely, with no one except the Indians and Daddy to talk to. In Kentucky, I had a dozen cousins and dozens of friends, and there was always somewhere to visit."

"You have no brothers or sisters?"

"No. Only Daddy." A short pause. "I wish I had a family like yours—complete. Violeta would be such fun, and Sereno—"

She broke off. What had she started to say? "Believe me," he advised her, "Sereno is no—fun?—to me."

"Oh, cousins used to say that about their brothers, but they loved them, all the same."

"I don't love him."

Her head jerked around. "You sound jealous."

"He is favored."

"I'll bet he thinks the same about you."

"He is often mistaken in what he thinks." Glad it was too dark for his face to show clearly, he lifted Valiente into a faster trot, despite the limping roan.

A quarter hour from the house, they rode over the rim of the basin and saw its lights. Although there didn't seem to be anyone about, extra torches had been lit on tall poles in the yard. "If there were people it would look like a fiesta," he said.

"Daddy must be frantic—" Cristina started forward.

"¡Alto! I want Volador back." He drew alongside, leaning to return her gelding's rein.

"Oh—I forgot—"

To make the exchange he had to dismount, re-saddle her horse, and help her up. Before he could finish, riders were upon them, and he silently cursed himself for being taken off guard. They had not come from the house, but some point at an angle, looming out of the dark on winded mounts, and a harsh voice demanded, "Christine! Where the hell have you been? I've got the whole damn place out looking— And who's this with you?"

On foot, he had the sensation of being run down by her father's horse; and at his shoulder, Volador snorted and plunged, almost pulling the bridle out of his grasp. But Johnson halted short of a collision, glared down at him in the torch light, and cried, "You!" in a tone of disbelief and disgust.

Far from calm himself, he managed to swing into his saddle and retort, "See to the roan, before its leg becomes infected." Then he spurred Valiente into the darkness.

Christine resisted calling a farewell. Daddy was sure to accuse him of spying, or worse—though what might be worse was vague in her thinking.

"He helped me find the way home," she shouted, her words plowing through a stream of Daddy's ranting, mostly about Domingo's doubtful parentage and the likelihood of his coming to a bad end. Suddenly she was too tired to defend herself. "Did my mozos make it back all right?"

"They came with some tale about losing you in the hills. You won't see them again. Baby, what happened? Did your horse run away? If it did—"

"Jump doesn't run away, Daddy. But he did have a huge thorn—"

As they descended the hill toward the house, she explained about riding too far, being unsure of the route, the roan's injury, and Domingo's coming to her aid. She felt that, now she was back, Daddy only half listened. "Don't send the mozos away. It wasn't their fault. And I won't do it again."

"I'll think about it." He got off his horse and tossed his reins to one of the riders. He strode into the house.

Reminding one of the Indios about tending Jump's injury, she lingered to gaze beyond the flickering torches that ringed the yard, into the night which had swallowed up Domingo.

A few weeks later, while loitering over the task of straightening papers Daddy had left that morning, she idly unrolled one of the maps. Her eye fell on the winding course of the Río San Lorenzo, and she leaned to locate their house. Penciled in Daddy's hand, the label read 'Temp - livable.'

To the east, up to the forks, she saw mountain ranges named Cerros Espinazo del Diablo—roughly translated as Spiny Hills of the Devil—and Cerros Los Zapotes and Santa Rosa. Far to the west, a penciled X over the small printed words 'Casa Blanca.' Beside it was 'Cordero' and beneath that, 'here', and '10 millions in old record' and 'mother lode untouched.'

Jump had long been recovered. The distance between the ranchos couldn't be as much as it looked. Domingo had ridden it, easily. If she didn't waste time with drawing or eating, she could ride there in less than a day. Hadn't Señor Cordero said, My house is yours; and hadn't his wife said, You are welcome whenever you wish to visit.

She dreamed about doing just that, seeing again in her mind's eye the plain but elegant staircase with its carved lion post, gloomy portraits on the walls, the airy upstairs bedroom with its French doors opening onto a roofed galería. She imagined undressing for sleep in just such a room, instead of this cramped, dark cubbyhole, and waking to the calm voices of the Corderos instead of Daddy's complaints.

One morning at the end of October, he announced, "Baby, I've got to go into town for a few days. Send some orders off, and a few telegrams. You'll be safe here. Unless you want to go and visit Greta?"

She shook her head. "I'd rather stay, Daddy. You go ahead, and don't worry about me."

Chapter Seventeen

Estrada climbed the stone staircase to the balcony where Ramón and Anita were directing Violeta's toddler steps across the space between them. The médico said, "Why are you not enjoying the fiesta? There's talk among your villagers that the hacendado's family is becoming too grand to mix with common people."

"Who has been spreading that rumor?" Ramón was in their plaza, shops, homes, all the time. He'd bought all sorts of articles from vendors, and so had the boys. Of course, Anita was busy with the baby, so seldom left the casa except to walk in her gardens. "Some of the women?"

Estrada shrugged. "Who started it, I don't know; I have heard more than one household voice the sentiment."

Was that the source of his unrest? An enemy, under his elbow. Looking him in the eye and smiling, even doffing the hat with a respectful bow, calling him Patrón despite his efforts to make them use his name. Most of those under his former command called him Jefe.

He labored to recall who might have shown signs of guilt. "There is a damned traitor in this place," he said, sure that it was the same person who had lit a torch and set the thatch roofs ablaze a few months ago. "trying to turn everyone against me."

"That may be," Estrada said. At the same time Anita cried softly, "Surely not, Ramón. They all love you."

"You love me," he said. "Not everyone does."

When the médico left with Violeta riding on his shoulders, Anita hugged him. "I shall always love you, mi corazón. Even if you are going to be thirty-two tomorrow."

He promised, "Just wait until your birthday, mujer," and swept her into his arms. With a little shriek she clung to him and he carried her into their bedroom.

Luis had returned for the celebration, which included observances for the Day of the Dead, with an exchange of sugar skulls and toy skeletons, the placing of marigolds on the graves in the new campo santo beside the village church, and a candlelit vigil over the deceased ones. He had not the authority yet to conduct any rites, but delivered a short homily and gave out small gifts.

When he and Luis were alone, he asked, "Do you believe a man can know something before it happens? Without any apparent reason for knowing."

"Sí, Jefe, of course. If the heart is open, important events are often foretold in order for us to choose rightly." After a silence, he added, "Have you had a revelation?"

"I wouldn't call it that."

"What, then?"

He brooded awhile. "I'm not sure."

Domingo put Cimarrón through his routine one last time in the clearing near the old campo santo. The fenced spot where Tereza's father don Diego and the ancient owners of Los Nuestros were buried, with the graves of their peones separated by a wrought-iron barrier, was far enough into the trees that no one could see them from the compound.

The nearest boundary wall was only a couple of wagon-lengths from where he reined the stallion in a tight circle and finished off the program with the feat which had taken him months to accomplish.

Today was Jefe's birthday, celebrated with his favorite foods, family gifts of books, clothing, a pocket watch, boots, and a new saddle bestowed this morning, to be followed by entertainments and music this afternoon, a community feast in the plaza, and fireworks just before midnight.

Pressure with hands and knees lifted Cimarrón into a rearing posture like the one Sereno had been so proud of. Then a jab of both heels brought the hind hooves up in a kick while they were still off the ground. The landing, jarring when training began, now was smooth. Ready.

It was early evening but still quite daylight when the last hill fell away behind Christine and she halted Jump at the rim of a grassy valley to take in the scene before her. Her legs were numb from the long ride though she'd stopped several times to rest, and the sight of festive canopies within hailing distance lifted her spirits.

Crowds of people—several towns full, it seemed—milled about, and smoke rose from many cook fires. More than one band blasted the air with fast-paced music and groups of men were singing at the top of their voices. To one side, feathers flew in a cockfight. Walking her horse at the edge of a cornfield, she skirted that spectacle, and none of the men betting on the outcome noticed her.

As she rode into more thickly packed people, however, Indian and mestizo faces lost their laughter and stared. Niños punched amigos to draw attention to her, and little girls hid behind their mothers. Should she get down and introduce herself? But she feared such a mob, and dared not lose control of her horse.

Worriedly searching over their heads, she saw the casa grande on its little hill and turned toward it. The peones moved aside for her. She rode past vendors in the plaza and had just spotted the largest canopy of all in the middle of a grassy slope below the house, where a few people were seated facing the road, when a figure caught her eye.

Down the road trotted an almost silver-coated horse with dapples of dark spots on its haunches. Its black mane and tail were flowing, and saddle and bridle were black leather studded with shiny medallions, exactly like an engraving out of an old book. But the thing which took her breath away was the rider. Domingo!

He was dressed in tight black trousers, a white shirt that on close inspection would surely prove to have pleats down the front, and silver-spurred boots. His head was bare, and a fitful breeze whipped the dark hair off his forehead. Coming to a stop in a flat, grassy arena, he began to do tricks. A series of quick stops and starts, tight turns, and a pirouette at the end of the gallop.

Beneath the canopy, the family—along with some men she didn't know, and villagers who were watching—clapped and cheered. While Domingo took a bow—and made the horse bow, too, just like in a circus act—she realized that Sereno was absent from the spectators.

Then drumming hooves snapped her attention back to Domingo. His show wasn't finished. Shoulders erect, chin carried proudly, he seemed scarcely to move either hands or feet as the pace and direction changed. It was as if the horse did everything without any signals, but read his mind. Was that possible?

Reining to a stop, Domingo made a little speech which she couldn't hear, as he was turned from her. He patted the spotted horse on the neck, spoke to it, and straightened.

Then the animal reared, held, and suddenly kicked in such a way that all four feet were high off the ground at once. Cries of wonder came from those watching. She had seen riders in Kentucky—even jockeys who raced horses for a living—yet none with such flair. She shouted, "Splendid!" and saw Domingo's head jerk around.

Sereno had endured his brother's performance from a seat on the flat rim of the plaza fountain, Viento's reins slack in his hand and a grinding, like intense hunger, in his stomach.

Friends jostled him, clapping, their ¡Viva!s deepening the frown he could feel between his eyebrows.

Worse was the warm approval he could see on his parents' faces. He and Viento could do the same tricks which drew such applause, but the fact that Cimarrón was a stallion made those accomplishments special. Then came that damned leap into the air, as if horse and rider were suspended above the earth for more than a heartbeat.

"Splendid!" The shout came from a voice strange in this place, but familiar.

Standing, he saw the gringa Johnson on her horse, surrounded by villagers and ex-rebels, though in the next instant she was dismounting and out of sight.

A wave of dismayed exclamations made him push through the crowd, which smelled of pulque and sweat and smoke. Some of the women were lifting her but she seemed unable to stand. "¿Qué paso?" he demanded.

Apologetically she looked up and said, "I think I must have been in the saddle much too long."

He would have carried her to a comfortable seat, if he hadn't feared she was too heavy for him. Just then Papá appeared. "You are not hurt, señorita?"

She shook her head, seeming embarrassed to be the focus of such attention. "Only numb. If I could just sit here awhile—"

Papá ordered everyone to move back. Picking her up, he carried her toward the casa. Mamá and Estrada and Luis and the house criadas followed with Violeta and some cushions they had in their hands.

Cheated of his own riding demonstration, Sereno glanced at the older boy, watching from the saddle. Mina ran forward and Domingo leaned to receive her kiss. Some of the ex-rebels made low gleeful comments and gestures, and a few señoras tossed their own jabs at so bold a girl.

Over Papá's shoulder he caught the look on Cristina Johnson's face. Unsure whether it expressed distaste or disapproval, he was even more uncertain when her eye fell on him and she gave him a smile and wave of her hand. Trusting Viento to Marcelo de la Cruz, who had to be shaken to get his attention, he said, "Count me out of that last ball game, amigo. I have a roaring headache."

"Yo, también," Marcelo said, turning away to stable the gelding. So have I.

In the sala, Mamá was ordering criadas to bring herb teas, damp cloths, and fans, and plumped cushions at Cristina Johnson's back as the girl rested on the only comfortable piece of furniture in the room, a stuffed sofa once belonging to a deserted estate near Culiacán.

He tossed aside his hat and, taking the cup from the server and placing it in Cristina's hand, knelt beside her. "Did you ride all the way from the city? No wonder you are exhausted."

She tasted the liquid, lashes shielding her eyes. "This is wonderful. What is it?"

"Mint, and a few other things," Mamá answered. "To help you relax. I drink it when I have had a long day."

"I could use one of those," he said, pulling up a footstool nearer Cristina. His parents glanced at each other. Estrada introduced himself and offered his medical services. Luis left, and Domingo came in.

"You cannot stay out of trouble, can you?" he said, shucking off his riding gloves.

Together Mamá and Papá cried, "Domingo!" in shocked tones.

Cristina gave him a haughty look, then turned a friendly one on the others. "I don't mind what he says. I wanted to visit but didn't realize how far it would be." Her smile faltered. "I— I'm afraid I'm going to have to ask you if I can spend the night—"

"Of course." Mamá gestured to a criada who hurried out, narrowly missing the one coming in with Sereno's tea.

"You are welcome," Papá said. "When you feel better, perhaps you will care to have supper with us in the plaza. This fiesta is in celebration of my birthday."

"Oh! a birthday—what fun. I've been in México for months now and this will be my first fiesta. I've read about them—"

Sitting on the sofa arm where he could see her, Papá said, "How did you get past our guards?"

Domingo leaned over the back of the sofa. "I should like to know that, too."

She shrugged. "There was no one on the trail. A rock fence about three hours from here is down, and the sha— the cabin was empty."

Papá left without a word. Sereno knew if those guards had come to attend the fiesta, they would regret that decision. He sipped the tea. His headache had eased.

In the dusk among crowds, Ramón searched for the three men whose duty it was to guard the north. As assignments shifted every three months, he was unsure who was supposed to be there, but Gregorio swore only trusted hombres were ever sent to that important outpost.

"Jefe, I'll ride up there tonight. Máximino and Lobo can go with me."

"Better do that. And don't use any lights, or fires."

"We won't. Do you think the girl was sent to turn our attention?"

Ramón gave a shake of his head. "Who knows? In the morning, check for bodies."

Dios, he prayed, *don't let there be any bodies.* "Maybe they did indeed come in—but you'd best not delay."

He didn't find the guards, and relatives were certain that their men would never desert. The bad feeling he'd harbored for days thickened.

Long tables held every sort of dish, waiting the arrival of the hacendado's family, who would be served first. When Anita and the boys, accompanied by Luis, Estrada, and the señorita Johnson, came into the lamplit plaza, he hurried to them. "I think we'll be more comfortable in the casa. Go back to the dining room, and I shall have our food brought."

Anita clutched his wrist. Before she could speak, or he could reassure her, there was a sound like firecrackers, a solid blow made him stagger and go down, and Anita's scream and fingernails ripped into his consciousness. A jumble of noise, pinpoints of light swirling in the darkness, rushes of words in voices he knew but couldn't untangle, a hot pain running up and down his side. Hit, but where?

He tried to get up, without being sure which of his limbs still functioned, and in a moment of clarity realized he was being laid onto something flat, and too narrow, and damned hard.

Firing all around now, and the sensation of jostling over uneven ground, soft thuds of running booted feet on either side. Screams and hoarse shouts faded behind them.

In moments, hours, maybe days, he was transferred to something soft—the sofa—and he was trying to say *Domingo* when darkness overwhelmed him.

Unarmed, Domingo leaped for the rifles that had been stacked by men anticipating supper. In the panicky crowd he'd spotted someone he expected not to know, but knew— and fired, knocking down the shabbily-dressed hombre.

He fired again at another who was shooting into former rebels scrambling for weapons. More enemies bobbed up from behind the low rock fence of the home pasture, but a heavy return by several marksmen routed, then finished them.

Martín hunkered beside him and said, "Are you hurt, muchacho?"

"No— Did we get them all?"

In the quiet, babies shoved under tables by their mothers softly wailed. Here and there men with the bearing of soldiers cautiously stood, eyes busy, bodies tense.

Marcelo leaned against a storehouse wall, holding his arm above the elbow. Mina ran to him.

No more shots. He looked around for Sereno, but none of the family had stayed. Slowly he stood up, rifle sliding out of his limp fingers.

On the way to the house, he asked Marcelo, "¿Cómo estás?" and his friend answered with a slight grin and nod. Mina glanced up, but was busy binding the injury with her hair ribbons and someone's white handkerchief.

The sight of his father lying pale and still on the sofa made him feel sick. He stumbled forward, pushing aside Anita and Cristina, and knelt. "¡Papá!"

Jefe's eyelids flickered but didn't open.

"Where is Estrada?" he yelled, jumping up, frantic. "Why don't you do something?"

Anita tried to take him in her arms. "He's bringing his medical bag. All of you—Sereno, Cristina—will be better, upstairs. Or outside, if the shooting has stopped."

Followed by Luis carrying blankets, Estrada hurried into the room. They moved Jefe onto a low table.

"I'm staying," Domingo insisted.

"So am I," Sereno declared.

Clasping Ramón's unresponsive hand, Anita tried not to faint. Cristina took a few steps backwards, eyes wide with fright, then perched on a footstool. When Luis and Estrada began stripping off Ramón's clothing, however, the girl fled.

The wound was in his hip, entering high at the back. The slug had not come out. "I've seen worse," Estrada said softly and she murmured, "Sí— But—did they live?"

Sereno held a folded white cloth over Ramón's nostrils. Moistened in a liquid, the fumes of which made her giddy, it was freshened periodically while Estrada probed. Domingo was instructed to put his fingers on the pulsebeat and give an immediate report if it faltered. Luis chafed her hand and silently prayed. She supposed that was what he was doing. It was what she was doing. She tried to believe that Diosito couldn't be so cruel as to take Ramón now, when life was so sweet.

After a few minutes the nurses who helped Estrada arrived. One tied a fresh sweat cloth around the médico's forehead. Another stood at Ramón's side to keep him from jerking suddenly and falling off the table. A third mopped at the blood.

Watching was difficult; not watching was impossible. In shadowy corners, criadas in their white aprons hovered, whispering and waiting. The loyalty of the house girls touched her. They had sweethearts in the village, and might have been tending wounds or sharing delicacies instead of being here.

Though Anita longed for the boys to turn to her with comforting hugs, neither did. They were too absorbed in their father, barely keeping out of the way. The first assistant handed the médico new instruments. When the second threaded a needle, she felt sick; Luis's hand on her elbow gave her strength. "It is nearly over."

But it was a long time after that before Estrada stepped back, bloody to the elbows, and said, "Now it is up to God."

"It always was," she whispered.

Sereno's knees were like the spongy pieces of chicle that his little friend Victor in Mérida had sometimes carried in a pocket for chewing and later bouncing on the pavement. Drawing deep breaths, he watched Luis and Estrada place Papá on a clean shuck mattress on the floor. One of the criadas brought another, and a pillow, for Mamá, who lay down beside him.

Luis lowered the lamp wicks. The médico went to the cocina for refreshment, his helpers remaining behind in case of alarm. Domingo flopped onto the sofa as if he'd traveled a hundred kilometres.

Drained, Sereno went into the hallway and found Cristina sitting hunched on a bottom staircase step, one arm around the carved lion, half asleep. He sat down beside her.

"Is he going to be all right?" she asked, wearily.

"As God wills."

There was a lengthy silence. Their eyelids drooped. A quiet knock at the back patio doors was answered by one of the criadas. He peered down the dusky hall and saw her talking to Martín. The horseman left.

Domingo slumped over on the sofa cushions and slept. Estrada returned to wait on the most uncomfortable chair. Luis sat near him. The time for the fireworks came and went in silence.

Cristina's head nodded, and he moved closer, putting an arm around her so she could rest against his shoulder. "You do not have to stay up," he told her gently.

"I want to. I'm very tired, but I don't think I can sleep."

He laid his cheek on the top of her head, adjusted his balance so he was more relaxed, his arm braced against the lion post. He was almost dozing when he realized that Domingo had finally called their father Papá.

"What happened to the gringo's daughter?" Ramón asked as soon as the sedative wore off.

Anita answered. "Domingo and Martín, with five outriders, are escorting her home." He sensed there was more and raised his eyebrows. She bent and unbent his fingers, her lashes downcast, then said, "They're not in Culiacán, but living at an old estancia called Las Flores. It used to be part of this place."

"I know."

"You do?"

"Domingo told me. I bet it is still part of this place. Have Luis bring me a map, por favor. He will know which one."

"Estrada says—"

"Estrada can go fight with Villa. I want that map."

He learned from studying it that he was correct; but, no matter. The Indios who had come from that area said the land was poor, and he didn't intend ever to use it. When Gregorio returned, he asked for a report.

"Her father wasn't there. None of the people knew where he'd gone, yet thought he would be away for another two days. She said he told her he had business in Culiacán, but Lobo's friends never saw him."

"And the guards at the north outpost?"

"We found two of their bodies. We think the third either ran away or was one of the enemy."

Enemy. He was certain Señor Johnson was at the root of all his misery.

"Those men who attacked us," Gregorio said, "were the ones Domingo and I met that time when we brought in Cimarroncito. The ones he saw once when he was out with Bravo."

He lay back, weary but free of the thing which had haunted him for weeks. The bandits had made their attack, and been beaten.

On the day-long trek over the hills back to Las Flores, Christine tried to talk to Domingo, but either worry over his father's wound or the presence of the mozos accompanying them to provide protection kept him from responding any more than he had to.

Daddy returned the following day, and as none of the servants cared to admit carelessness in letting her ride off, she was confident he would never learn of her trip to Los Nuestros.

His scowl and sharpness with the cook gave evidence that something major had gone wrong. She shrank from guessing what it was.

"Nothing but a damned waste of good money." He slammed down his coffee cup so hard it cracked.

She watched liquid seep out and form a little pool on the table. "Does—does that mean we're going home?"

Seeing the Cordero boys again—plotting a way to do that—had become her intense desire. Everything about their lives, so remote from anything she'd experienced, intrigued her. A thousand questions thronged her brain, demanding answers. Leaving now would kill her.

Daddy ignored the one she had posed to him, forking in mouthfuls of breakfast.

"I suppose it's not a good time for me to want a camera," she said, getting a rag for the spilled coffee and another cup.

"Camera? I thought you had a camera."

"It disappeared on the train."

"Damn Meskins! They'll steal a person blind—"

"Somewhere in Texas. Or possibly Oklahoma."

"Well, I'll see what I can do. There's plenty of our American reporters still down here, covering Pancho Villa's war. Maybe one of them will know where to get a camera and film for it."

Every day she watched southward, hoping to see one of the Corderos approaching. She felt torn over which boy she preferred. Sometimes it was Domingo, with his flashing eyes and dark good looks. Sometimes it was Sereno, so brave the night his father was shot.

Daily, she took pains to wear clean clothes and brush her curly hair until it behaved, and insisted Tokee clear the dishes and sweep immediately after Daddy left. She spent a lot of time washing herself and her hair to get rid of the fine dust that filled the air whenever the wind blew.

The rainy season was long over, and the countryside turned brown. The garden plot yielded a few late ears of corn and some pumpkins, no more. Meals heavy with venison, beef, and quail made her long for those jars of berries, tomatoes, green beans, and home canned vegetable soup that her Aunt Martha used to send over after Mother died.

"Tokee," she said one evening as they sat listening to a dove calling its mate to roost in the acacias at the spring, "you ought to taste the soda biscuits we had. You'd never eat another tortilla."

As usual, the Indian woman smiled and nodded, not understanding a word, Christine was sure. "I'd try to make some myself, if the stove had an oven." It didn't, only the two eyes and a fire box. Tokee cooked over a charcoal brazier, her distrust of the stove clear in her avoidance of it.

"I wonder how the Corderos' cook manages? Does she feed them the same things you give us? No wonder Domingo is surly, if he burns his insides with chiles all the time. Sereno must dine on honey, he's so sweet."

Tokee nodded and grinned. Christine was thankful that the chubby cook had no idea what confidences she was missing by not knowing English. It was better than writing in a journal, for then there was nothing Daddy could find and use to shame her.

Christmas week was dismal. One by one the Indians had all disappeared, having muttered something about 'mi tierra.' Daddy stayed in, reading newspapers and jotting down things in one of his little notebooks. She cooked his suppers, not without trepidation. He cut down a cedar and nailed it to the floorboards.

Using her scissors and some of the precious sketch paper, she made decorations. Snowmen, snowflakes, stars, candles, angels. Placing them was no fun, for the needles pricked her hands horribly. The yellow paint in her tin barely stretched to complete the star that drooped on a top twig, and she hoped the single present Daddy had put under the tree for her would be the much-requested set of watercolors. It was in a box big enough to hold several items, and she suspected boots to replace the ones that were now too tight, and jewelry chosen by Greta with Daddy's name on the tag.

On Christmas morning, he woke her while it was still pitch dark, singing 'Jingle Bells.' She covered her head with her pillow but he pulled it off, and her covers as well. "Come on, lazybones, don't you want to see what Santa Claus brought you?"

Groaning, she chided, "Daddy, you know I don't believe in Santa Claus," rolled out on the other side of bed, and slid into her wool robe. The desert night chill required it, though by noon she would be in a cotton dress with her hair making her neck sweat.

The big box held all the things she had expected—and at the bottom a final thing, wrapped separately. The square knobby shape, inexpertly concealed by Daddy's fumbling efforts with paper and twine, made her heart skip. "Oh, Daddy—" She ripped off the covering. "My camera!"

"I don't know why you're so surprised. Doesn't Daddy always get you what you want?"

Not always, she thought.

Chapter Eighteen

"How can I be sorry for killing a man who was trying to murder my father?" Domingo and Luis were standing in the sacristy of Anita's chapel. When next they stood thus, in a few months, Luis had told him, it would be possible to observe a proper confession.

He wasn't sure he wanted to take part in that, though Luis was a trusted confidant without becoming a priest, and Anita expected him to. Jefe also was having difficulty accepting the idea. Domingo had overheard him telling her, "I can make my peace with Dios directly through my prayers, so why should I need anything more?"

"You sound like Estrada," Anita had reproved.

"You adore Estrada."

"I value him, as do you. I also respect him, but the Church considers him a heretic."

"Even Luis stops short of calling him a heretic."

"Luis is a kindhearted soul." Her smile showed she adored Luis as well.

If she entreated, Domingo suspected both he and Jefe would end up on their knees in the confessional, blurting every sinful thought to Luis, whether they wanted to or not. That was going to be damned embarrassing, since lately his thinking encompassed courting Tereza, Cristina, and Mina, all at the same time.

Such an admission would surely shock Luis, who had purified his thoughts by force of will once he discovered how indulging in pulque and women only made him miserable. Domingo was also miserable and found himself bringing up the killing of the bandits in the plaza. Taking any human being's life was a mortal sin. "It weighs on my mind," he admitted.

Luis pondered before saying, "Even if you cannot feel sorrow for the killing, you clearly feel regret that they drove you to do it."

He pondered before answering. "Well, sí, claro. I never even meant to kill him—only stop him from shooting anyone else."

"There were two of them, no? Which you shot?"

"I shot at two. Gregorio said more bullets than mine finished the second one."

"Murder was not in your heart when you did it."

"Of course not."

"Then, put your worry behind you. Dios is just."

"Luis, how did you become so wise?"

His friend smiled. "You like that answer? It is not mine. It is wisdom, from God."

"Oh. I thought it was from the priest in Culiacán—or from being a soldier."

"Soldiers often learn this. Have you never talked of such things with your father?"

He shook his head. "Wars cause much killing, don't they."

"Men cause much killing," Luis corrected. "In their lust for power."

Lust occupied much of his thought, but not for power. He spent hours exhausting himself working with the frisky potros so he could sleep at night; but dreams disturbed his rest, and he was troubled that in many of them the person who made love with him was not one of the girls, but another man's wife. Tereza's sister-in-law. Paz.

For this reason, when Jefe offered to send him to Los Dos Corazones after Navidad to salvage what he could of Tereza's wild filly, he fled to his sanctuary at El Rincón and stayed for three days. When he came back, Mina and Marcelo de la Cruz were engaged, and Sereno wouldn't speak to him.

"What the hell is wrong with him?" He put the question to Gregorio, the only one in his circle of friends with whom he felt comfortable discussing his medio hermano.

They shared a cigarette. "You don't know? ¡Ave María! You are thick in the head."

"So I'm thick. Tell me."

"You are older, bigger, you beat him in races—unfairly, he thinks—you have your father's ear, you bewitch wild animals, you work with a top arrendador and earn his respect, you make the stallion Cimarrón do tricks, Anita loves you, and you saved Jefe's life by killing two men. Good God, Domingo, what more can you do to him, to make him unhappy?"

After a moment he said, "You left out something."

"I did?"

He started to walk away, but Gregorio grabbed his sleeve. "There is more? Unbelievable. What else?"

Grinning, he twisted out of the young man's grip and went into the casa. Not even Gregorio could be trusted with his deepest feelings. He had decided to test himself by going to Dos Corazones. He dreamed of Paz, but daydreamed of Tereza.

"Did I give you a big scare?" Ramón joked, now that the danger was past. But Sereno refused to talk about the shooting. It was after Navidad—a subdued celebration in light of his confinement—that his younger son asked, "Papá, am I too young to be in love?"

Treading carefully, he answered, "Do you think you are? In love, I mean."

A pensive stare at something beyond the glass balcony doors. "Sí . . . for a long while now. Since last Navidad."

He had to bite down hard not to ask, Who? even though he thought he knew that answer.

"I think about her all the time."

"Usually one of the signs. But a strong friendship can do that, too."

Sereno fiddled with the silver santo on its chain. "When her letters come, I always wish they were longer."

"And, that they came more often."

Glancing up, the boy gave a relieved smile. "You do understand." Then, restless, he got up and went to stand at the closed doors. "I can never write in my letters what I wish to say."

Softly, Ramón asked, "Why not?"

The response came out harsh. "Because of Domingo! I think she loves him."

After a long moment of held breath, he blew it out and wished he had not given up cigarettes. He had no advice. "You're young," he said tentatively. "But love comes when and where it will. Sometimes we have to be strong, to take all that comes with it."

"I'm not strong, Papá. Not like Domingo."

The quiet anguish touched a deep chord. "My first sweetheart made my head spin in just the same way."

"Mamá?"

"No. María. You met her. Manoleto's wife."

Sereno's eyes widened as if he suspected a joke. "She is so feo, next to Mamá."

Repressing a smile, he said, "She was pretty to me, when I first saw her. I dreamed about her night and day for months. She had come for her abuelo's burial, and a few minutes of talk was all we had before she returned to Hermosillo. I didn't see her again for three years."

"Did—being apart—ever get easier?"

"Oh, yes. I had Mío, and friends, and my feud with Francisco, to keep me busy."

"When you saw her again, did you still love her?"

Cast back into that time, so long ago, he was silent, remembering.

Sereno persisted, "Did you?"

He answered, "I thought I did … until I met Anita. And maybe a little bit afterward, but it didn't last."

"Was it the same?"

"Was what the same?"

His son frowned at his stupidity. "Loving Mamá. Did it feel the same as when you thought you loved María?"

He sighed. "Perhaps you are too young to hear this after all. But—well, some of it felt the same. Some was different. I can't explain any more than that. Ay de mí, where is Luis when I need him?"

"You don't need Luis," Domingo remarked, leaning against the door framing. "You need Gregorio."

Sereno's face flushed with alarming suddenness. Yet he was capable of stalking past his brother, chin in the air, and down the stairs with a defiant clatter.

"How long were you lurking?" he asked, as Domingo dropped into the bedside chair.

"Jefe," Domingo said reprovingly, "I don't lurk. I came to visit, only."

"You could have made your presence known."

"I did, and my advice was good. Besides, the door was open. Anyone in the hall could have heard."

"What, exactly, did you hear?"

Domingo shrugged. "About when you loved María." He grew serious, sitting forward, elbows on knees and hands loosely clasped. "Did you never love Paz?"

"¡Qué sinvergüenza! I don't owe you that knowledge. But—no, not in the way she wanted me to."

"And doña Gloria?"

"What do you remember about her?"

"She made good estofado." Domingo grinned. Then, after a pause during which he became somber, he asked, "Jefe. Did you love my mother?"

Something in the way the morning light struck the wall at the corner, the faint sounds of community outside, brought a flood of emotion tied to memory. If he shut his eyes, he would be in the casita in La Puerta del Sol, and if he opened them quick enough, he would see Serafina, her long black hair streaming over her shoulders, eyes joyous. "More than I realized," he said softly.

Domingo gave him a closed smile, and left the room.

Ramón spent the rest of the morning going over the accounts and praying Luis would train someone in that chore before deserting him completely for priestly offices. At a soft knock, he said, "Pase usted." Expecting someone with his food tray, he was surprised when Máximino leaned his head around the door post and waited for further assurance that he was meant to advance.

"Is something wrong?"

"It is the matter of my sister, Patrón."

He nodded at the guest chair. As Máximino perched on the edge, the movement took him back years to Casa Vásquez just after Manuelo's death left him burdened with the operation of that hacienda. His boyhood friend, Tonio, not seen for half a lifetime, had entered the office there and called him Patrón. Tonio, dead in the revolution. Despairing afresh, he cried, "What was it all for? Is not this Los Nuestros?"

Máximino looked startled. "Have I come at a bad time?"

He gave a short laugh and shook his head. "What about your sister, hombre?"

"She is engaged to Marcelo de la Cruz."

"Yes, I know."

"But she is in love with don Domingo."

Don Domingo. Well, wasn't that what he imagined, when he made plans to leave his firstborn in charge? Someone had to be the boss. "I cannot tell her whom to love, nor to marry."

"That is true. But this is causing problems. If you will—talk to him? To your son, that is."

"You mean, make him stay away from her."

"Sí, Patrón. If you will."

"I would. But if she loves Domingo, his staying away can only make things worse."

The face tensed again. "I have nothing against him, in fact I like him, but you understand that Marcelo intends to marry her."

"Shouldn't you be talking to your sister? I think the choice of a husband is up to her."

Máximino stared at him, seeming not to know what to say next. Finally he blurted, "But Marcelo will make a good home for her, and she cannot marry don Domingo."

Shifting his position in an attempt to ease the dull throb in his hip, Ramón said, "Well, he is a little young."

They exchanged stares for a minute, Maximino's eyes full of uncertainty. At last he laughed. "Patrón, you jest." He stood up. "Por favor, I would be grateful if you speak to him today. In order to keep everything friendly."

"I understand perfectly. Cease your worry."

Sending Domingo to Los Dos Corazones was the best solution. He expected to give an account for his move, both to Sereno, who said nothing but swiftly left the room, and to Anita, who asked in an aggrieved tone, "Why will you let Domingo go" she gave him no time to reply but went on, "when you know how Sereno longs to see her."

"Don't be angry—"

"Do I sound angry? Maybe because I am. I thought you understood how important this friendship is, and what damage can come from throwing Domingo into the middle of it."

"Damage to him, too. You don't seem to realize that he is also in love."

"With Domingo, not Tereza, or even Mina."

"That is cruel."

"That is true." Her stormy eyes and pouty mouth reminded him of Violeta, and he couldn't hold back a laugh.

She whirled, indignant. "Oh, you take this lightly? What would you do if I sent Sereno to fight for his sweetheart? He deserves the chance."

"He would suffer as much there as here—maybe more." All this talk of romance heated his blood, and he snared her into the bed, upsetting the empty supper tray which he had failed to remove.

She gave a little squeal of surprise and surrender, and he thought she was warming to his caresses when she drew back. "Should you be doing this?" she whispered, concerned. "Your wound—"

"We can be careful," he said, one hand clearing the dishes while the other cupped the back of her hair, directing her mouth to his.

A criada on her way into the room for the tray halted, tiptoed out. He saw her close the door.

Estrada had allowed him to limp about the upstairs for a couple of weeks now; but warned that a return to his usual activities would require a vague amount of time stretching for months into the rainy season. Since the attack, the birthday books had all been read, the pocket watch looked at a hundred times a day, clothing worn; but new saddle and boots remained untried.

This is one thing I won't let Estrada take away, he thought. The release and pleasure were worth the pain it cost.

Sereno made a point of being elsewhere when Domingo, Luis, and four outriders left for the train at Culiacán, so he didn't have to pretend good will. Mamá had seemed upset by the whole thing, but only said, "I'm sorry, mijo. Maybe when he gets back. We cannot spare both of you at the same time."

He knew that was an excuse, and for days could do nothing more than lie in the hammock, too downhearted to raise the flute to his lips. Anger, disappointment, and frustration overflowed. If Mamá wouldn't stand up for him, there was nowhere to turn. *Dios*, his heart cried. *Are you there?* He waited, breath held, listening. His pulse throbbed in his temples. Muted noises of corral and village.

Then, in the house, Violeta's musical chatter followed by her joyful laugh. He missed playing with his little sister, and longed to rejoin the once-close circle.

But remembering how Papá had betrayed him, how Mamá had failed him, he hardened his heart and squeezed a couple of tears from the corners of his eyes.

The older brother of his friend Rosendo happened to pass the porch. Hector had been one of the outriders to escort Cristina to Las Flores. Sereno called to him.

"¡Hombre!"

"¿Sí, niño?"

"You are good with that pistol, no?"

The outrider grinned. "Yo creo que sí."

"Saddle our horses. We are going for a ride."

While that was being done, he searched for Mamá and found her instructing a seamstress in making a dress for Violeta. As soon as she finished, he blurted, "Domingo is always allowed to camp out whenever he feels like it. I would like the same courtesy."

Her eyes took on their worried look, the set of her mouth promised refusal, and she reached for his arm to draw him to her. "Hijo, you know the dangers—"

Resisting her hug, he hurried on. "He didn't even take anyone with him when he was gone all last week, and I have Hector, brother of Rosendo, who can use a gun much better than Domingo."

She seemed to mull it over as she put sewing articles into her basket. "Bueno, if you did not go too far . . ."

He gave her a hug and a kiss on the cheek. "Mil gracias, Mamá."

"But only if Ramón says you may—" she called after him, for he was already rushing out the door.

He packed a mochila with two changes of clothing and instructed the cocinera to fill a fiber bag with tortillas, dry beans, chiles, pinole, and fruit.

Unsurprised when Papá appeared in the doorway, he was surprised when his father said, "You might need this," and handed him a belt gun. Seeing the crutches, he had swift second thoughts and hesitated before taking the weapon. "Gracias."

"Your mother will worry the whole time you're gone."

"But the bandidos were all killed, and Hector is second only to Lobo as a compañero."

"Bandidos are never all killed." Papá's half smile was rueful. "Take Rosendo and Pedro as well, and make your journey to the south."

He failed to answer, having no intention of seeking peace for his spirit in the area where he'd shot Bravo. Giving his father a gentle abrazo, he said, "Tell Mamá not to be concerned. Dios will take care of me."

"Sometimes, hijo, Dios lets us make our own mistakes."

It was nearly an hour before his bodyguards were mounted and ready to ride out. Mamá had kissed him again and then gone to her room with a cup of headache tea. He had played with Violeta on the shady patio. Then Hector gave a shrill whistle and he turned his little sister over to her niñera.

At the corral, Papá leaned on the top pole, along with others who had gathered to wish him a safe trip. Partly, he knew, to make sure he headed in the right direction.

However, as soon as a few hills shielded them from sight, he turned the course northward. And because of his position as son of the hacendado, despite Papá's denial of that honor, none of the riders questioned him.

A sense of freedom and power engulfed him—until he remembered that Domingo was at Dos Corazones, with Tereza, who had given both of them a silver santo. Kicking Viento into a gallop, he called over his shoulder, "¡Andale! ¡Andale, muchachos! ¡No estámos burros!"

II

Getting off the train in Hermosillo, Domingo was shaken by memories he'd believed had been left behind. It was here, by chance, or fate, or the will of Dios, he first saw Jefe.

Even then he'd sensed that more than friendship bound the man to Mamá, and at her burial in La Puerta del Sol he had known somehow that his own destiny was linked with that of Major Cordero. Her words, "Thank God I've found you!" haunted him now as he stood in the cool bright sunshine of a February morning, the bustle of the city flowing around him.

"How strange," he murmured, "that while everything has changed, nothing is truly destroyed."

Beside him, Luis nodded. "This place holds recuerdos for me, also."

"You are going to see Paz?"

"No. My purpose—besides promising your father that I would accompany you on the way—is to fulfill the last requirement of my study under the padres. I shall not be visiting Los Dos Corazones."

They went to the hotel where Mariano was to meet him. In the adjoining café, they were only a little surprised to find Mano, Luis's older brother and formerly Jefe's best friend in Los Pobres, at a table with the young hacendado. After greetings and inquiries into each other's health, and drinks of norteamericano whiskey which he wasn't allowed to have, the hermanos left together and Mariano turned to him. "Ramón tells me you can tame this wild filly which Tereza calls Estrellita."

"I plan to try."

"She has been neglected far too long. I hope you don't break your neck trying."

The ride out to the hacienda was pleasant, recalling his first journey there in a wagon, when he was trying to avoid being sent back to Casa Vásquez. "I wonder what happened to Jefe's place in Sonora." He didn't expect an answer, but Mariano gave one.

"The casa grande has been looted, but otherwise left alone by the Villistas. Of course, there is no stock, and fields have gone to chaparral, being untended. It will take much work and time to make it live again."

"How do you know this? Have you told Jefe?"

Mariano shook his head. "It would divide his mind, to think about Casa Vásquez now. As for how I know, remember some of the families at Dos Corazones came from there, and have relatives in the north who sometimes make the trip."

They caught each other up on ranch news, Jefe's difficulties with Señor Johnson, the progress of his health since the birthday attack. Then they fell silent.

Nearing the front gate, he wasn't sure who he wanted to see more, Tereza or Paz. He began to tremble and his palms grew sweaty. He wished Gregorio had come along, or that Luis hadn't been so bent on receiving his priestly instruction.

Mariano, riding at his stirrup, was handsomer and older than he remembered. It stretched his imagination to think of the ex-rebel as Paz's husband. He wondered if she had told about the episode in the hills when the Indio attacked her, making her with child. Gradually untangling much of the puzzle, he'd suspected her loss of the baby was not the accident everyone assumed. If Mariano had known, would he have married her? "How is Paz?" he asked, embarrassed that his voice was hoarse.

"You will see some changes, I think."

The first change was immediately apparent as they rode into the yard. Paz and Tereza lounged on the long porch, waiting for them, and when the girls stood up Domingo was startled almost to the point of tangling his boot as he dismounted. ¡Prenada! Paz was pregnant.

He accepted her cheery "¡Bienvenido!" and awkward hug, then tried not to stare as she laughed, adding, "How tall you are, Domingo! ¿Casi un hombre, no?"

"What do you mean, 'Almost'?" he retorted, all thoughts of romance flying out of his head. Judging from what he had learned from Mamá's carrying Violeta, she was far enough along to give birth right on this porch. "Caramba, Paz, I can't picture you as a mother."

"Then you had better start. Josefina and the partera tell me they are twins."

How easy, to fall back into their old habit, bandying mildly barbed words.

How difficult, to look into Tereza's eyes and grasp her offered hand with the shadow of Sereno between them. Had she wanted the medio hermano here instead? She said, "I trust that everyone at your home is well."

"Sí—although I suppose you heard about Jefe's being shot."

"Yes. Sereno wrote to me. And your mother."

She seemed to want to say more, but the others were urging them to enter. Mariano showed him to a room where a niño provided a basin of hot water and towels for refreshing himself. Afterward everyone sat on the patio with plates of buñuelos and mugs of champurrado.

Seated between the girls, he leaned and whispered in Paz's ear, "See how wrong you were when you told me you did not belong in a place like this?"

Calm, she murmured back, "That was a long time ago, hermanito." The waist-length braids were now caught up with silk ribbons that matched her dress.

"In another life," he agreed.

Tereza asked, "Do you wish to see Estrellita now?"

He set aside his empty dishes and stood. "Sí."

Mariano came with them and leaned on the top corral pole, indifferent to the possibility that they might want to be alone. "She is quite wild."

"But she seems placid." He caught Tereza's glance. "And is as beautiful as ever."

"Careful she does not break your—skull," Mariano said, in a tone that left some uncertainty whether the words meant more than they said.

"You know to keep her without food or water until tomorrow afternoon. And then put her in a smaller pen."

"I have instructed the mozos to that effect."

As they strolled back to the house, he asked, "Why did you not become a horse tamer, as was your father?"

"Perhaps I had no patience. Or was too lazy. ¿Quién sabe?"

Or, perhaps, Domingo mused, *you feared being injured.*

Entering the sala once more, Tereza excused herself, saying, "After so long a journey you must be tired. Until later." Her brother said, "I must go over the accounts," and disappeared into his office.

Paz was nowhere in sight, and doors along the hallway in the sleeping wing were closed. The big house was silent. Far away in the village, he heard strains of guitar music and voices singing. Feeling lonely, he chose to return to his room and try to rest.

Thinking sleep was impossible, he was disoriented to wake in the dark, roused by a tapping at his door which was Jesús calling him to supper.

In the comedor, the long linen-covered table gleamed with silver, and place settings glowed in the halos of a dozen candle flames. When he had eaten at this table before, don Diego was alive and his own family filled the extra chairs.

Paz clapped her hands, signaling criadas to begin bringing in platters. Paz presiding over serving girls was as strange as being here without Jefe, Anita, or Sereno. He couldn't decide whether he felt more childish or more grown-up; either way, the sensation was anything but comfortable.

Mariano informed them that the gringo Pershing and his troops were leaving Mexican soil. "As Ramón would say, 'It is all politics' from now on. Don Venustiano is going to be presidente and landowners and priests will find life more risky than facing enemy fire."

Domingo paused a forkful of carne asada halfway to his mouth. "In what ways?"

"Sources in Hermosillo told me those attending the convention created a thing called Article Twenty-Seven, which gives the government all rights to land, water, and minerals. This ideal of an equal distribution of land to every Mexicano is going to hurt, if some cabrón in power decides to give his relatives property which belongs to people like your papá and me."

"If that is so, you and Jefe better make plans."

"Short of starting another revolution, there's not much we can do."

"But you are Carrancistas!" Paz said. "Surely what you fought to keep will never be taken from you."

"Many of us have come to doubt Señor Carranza. And with Obregón as his secretary of war, we can no longer depend on him for justice."

Domingo's head swirled with fears as the old names and faces of war returned. "I thought all we had to worry about was the Villista traitors."

"Villa is finished." Mariano helped himself to a tortilla and piled it with beans. "You can stop worrying about him."

"That has been said before."

"Sí, but now he has few followers. Pancho can never become a strong leader again even if there is a rebellion against the government of Carranza. He lost many friends by fighting Obregón."

Tereza had been listening. "Papá once said it was Carranza's fault that Villa and Obregón became enemies."

Surprised that she was interested in the conversation, he asked, "Do you know why he felt that way?"

She shrugged delicately, her eyes like dark pools reflecting pinpoints of candlelight.

Mariano said, "It was Carranza who controlled the supply, and kept Villa's army from reaching the City of México first. A humiliation Pancho couldn't forgive."

He recalled the long march down the west coast with General Obregón's rebels. The triumphal parade along the Paseo de la Reforma, bearing the flag and riding beside Major Cordero, had thrilled him beyond anything he'd ever experienced.

How unaware and ignorant he had been then, not knowing that Major Cordero was more than Mamá's friend. How jealous of Sereno, his resentment stretching back to that first meeting in the City when he realized they would have to share Ramón, and had believed himself at an enormous disadvantage, not being a son.

One thing which remained constant was the bitter rivalry between him and his medio hermano. Gregorio had listed the grievances Sereno held against him. Now, he counted those he felt justified in clinging to.

First, Sereno still had two parents, married to each other, a true family. What had made Mamá marry Pablo Valente, instead of the father of her unborn child? Clearly they had loved deeply, to have remained in love after so many years. When he returned to Los Nuestros, perhaps he would ask Jefe what had gone wrong.

Second in his list was the killing of Bravo. He grudgingly admitted that, had he not been dozing, he might have done the same thing. Violeta was dear to him, in a distant sort of way. Yet he wasn't entirely convinced that Sereno failed to recognize Bravito, or that the shot was a killing one only by accident. Sereno had always been jealous of the bond between him and his pet.

As for the mesteños, Sereno also possessed the light touch and long patience needed to become a first-class horse tamer. If his attention should ever focus on the horses, it would be easy for him to match—or even surpass—the skill which had brought praise and a little glory to Domingo. That was not to be borne.

Finally, and certainly not least, was Tereza. Except for a few letters, she had always treated them more or less equally. The santo was proof of that. Had he answered in his own hand instead of sending messages in Mamá's letters, he didn't doubt that he too would have had a packet tied in string to hide under his pillow.

After supper, the evening was warm enough in the sheltered portico to lounge in cushioned chairs, belly full, Paz asking about life at Los Nuestros. He told her of the mustangs, the bandidos and their supposed connection to Señor Johnson, the burning of the village and how it had been rebuilt. He avoided mentioning Bravo, or Mina.

"And Violeta? She must be walking now."

While he related little incidents, he wondered if her questioning held a measure of longing to know about Jefe.

After all, she had been so in love with him that she risked her life in the Sierra Madre to find his patrol; so in love that she rejected the devotion of Luis and caused him much misery. Growing silent, he lapsed into a reverie. The nature of love was too complex. It filled the heart with both joy and pain...the two sometimes intertwined so he had difficulty separating those emotions.

Long after midnight he lay awake. Subduing the filly would increase his worth in Tereza's eyes, and any dreams she had of Sereno must surely fade.

At Dos Corazones, as in other upper class homes, criadas brought breakfast trays of chocolate and dulces to each bedroom, so he didn't see Tereza until he had been in the corral for half an hour, working up a sweat-streaked film of dust on his face. Estrellita was wild, but she remembered him, and after he'd spent time talking softly and breathing into the flared nostrils, she let him begin at her head and rub his palms over her whole body except for her back legs.

He had the filly on the short rope and was leading her around the enclosure when he saw Paz and Tereza coming to the gate. Neither covered her head with a rebozo, though the shawls lay ready on shoulders. The breeze whipped Tereza's long curly hair. Stopping a few paces away, he tied the filly in some shade, and joined them, saying, "All this flying dust will soil your dresses."

Tereza gave a careless little laugh. "¿Qué da? We want to watch." Paz leaned on the pole fence. "Besides, washing our clothes will give the lavanderas something to do."

"You spoiled girl," he cried in mild reproof. "I seem to recall a time when you were not too proud to wash your own dresses in the Río Culiacán."

"And I seem to recall a time when you had decent manners. Does being a Cordero give you an exalted opinion of yourself?" Her tone was less sharp than it might have been.

"Ah. Then you know about that. Who told you? Mariano?"

"I should have realized it without being told."

"Were you surprised?"

Paz grinned. "Let us just say, I'm glad things worked out as they did. Being your madrastra would be a pain." She and Tereza laid arms around each other's necks. "We are comadres. So watch your step, muchacho."

Unsure what he read in Tereza's sparkling eyes and amused smile, he turned away, tossing over his shoulder, "I'm busy, muchachas."

The filly snorted and drew back when he approached her, and it took him nearly a quarter hour to undo the mistrust which resurfaced because he was unable to hide his irritation. When he allowed himself to look, the girls were no longer watching. He gave Estrellita a rubdown and a drink of water, and turned her onto grass.

Then he renewed friendship with some boys in the village and they all went to a pond to swim. After siesta, a ball game, another swim, idle swapping of news. He smoked half a marijuana cigarette, and returned to the casa grande feeling jaded.

The girls were on the long porch, watching for Mariano to return from an outpost between here and Hermosillo. Tereza said, friendly, "You're very good with horses. She bit one of the mozos last week."

"He must have done something to provoke her."

"I think she only needed someone she respects to show her what to do."

Paz gave him a wink, which Tereza pretended to ignore. "That is all any girl wants, Domingo. No?"

"Cállate," he advised. Hush. Being married had made her bolder than ever. Or maybe she considered him old enough now for such frank talk. He wished he knew.

III

The third night out, Sereno had difficulty sleeping. The ground was hard, the night was cold, and the camp food tasteless. They had traveled in a loosely northern direction, chiefly because the trail led that way, though he found himself curious about the estancia which had been taken over by Señor Johnson and his daughter.

Dawdling so none of his outriders suspected he had a destination in mind, he considered what approach to use for seeing Cristina again. If her father were home, the venture would prove dangerous and must be abandoned. Otherwise, he meant simply to ride up, hail the house, and say Buen día. Perhaps she would invite him in for a cool drink. He might even ask a few harmless questions and learn information that could be valuable to Papá.

They came to a ridge overlooking the house in the basin below, and quickly dismounted off the skyline. "Wait here," he said, giving his reins to Rosendo. The others squatted in the thin shade of acacias.

Careful of crevices where scorpions might lurk, he crouched near a boulder and studied the scene. Indian women ground corn on metates in front of their huts. Two old men dozed beneath a ramada, rifles propped against the outer wall of the main house. No wagon or carriage. The horse in a small corral was the one she had ridden to Los Nuestros. He and his party mounted and continued into the yard.

"¡Hola! Estámos amigos. Cristina—are you here?"

Several things happened at once. The old men woke, leaped up with cries in their dialect, and ran over each other trying to get to their rifles. His outriders—amid warnings and curses in Spanish, horses kicking up dirt as they spurred about—drew pistols and someone fired into the air, whether accidentally he couldn't tell.

And Cristina appeared in the doorway, alarm on her pretty face, her blonde hair streaming in curls over her shoulders. "Don't shoot!" she screamed, rushing in front of the Indios. Then she turned a beaming face on him. "It's Sereno!"

Chapter Nineteen

Commotion ceased, riders jerked their horses to a stand, pistols unholstered but suspended. The Indians retreated, muttering, and Sereno swung down and came toward her.

He was taller, blonder, slimmer, and better-looking than Christine remembered. His pleated white shirt, and tan trousers above black leather boots reaching nearly to his knees, made him seem like an illustration out of some magazine. "Hola, Cristina," he said, smiling.

"Hola," she said, finding his eye-level slightly above hers. "Welcome to Las Flores. I'd offer you lemonade if we had any lemons."

She backed into the tiny front room, ashamed of its dimness, crude furnishings and lack of paint. He came in, glanced around, tossed his hat onto a slat chair, propped his hands on his hips, elbows akimbo. "A drink of cold water would be nice," he said.

The riders with him remained outside. She glimpsed them through the window, being led to the spring by her mozos. Thankful that Daddy wasn't expected back for another day or two, she filled a tin dipper from an olla, conveyed the water to him, and watched him satisfy his thirst.

His accent fascinated her, especially the way he said her name, so precisely, so musically. The r and i came out of his mouth different from the ordinary sounds, and he replaced the silent e with a soft little a. Cristina.

"This is the strangest country," she remarked. "Those men were ready to shoot each other moments ago, and now they're laughing like relatives."

"Maybe they are."

He returned the dipper and, when she gestured at an easy chair draped with a Mexican spread, relaxed into it. She chose one of the chairs at the table, glad she'd cleared Daddy's maps and papers away. Glad too that Tokee stayed in the kitchen, with no more than an occasional peep into the room. "What brings you visiting?"

Sereno gave her a closed smile. "We are neighbors. It would be unfriendly not to visit."

"I—trust your father is—recovered?" How terrible, if he had died! But she must ask.

"Not completely. But the médico says, in time."

"Was anyone else hurt? It was all so frightening—"

"Several of the villagers." His smile flashed beautiful teeth. "All well now."

She felt giddy with pleasure at seeing him again. After weeks of having nothing but insubstantial memories, she had begun to doubt she had ever been to Los Nuestros, or gone to sleep against his shoulder with his arm around her, to be wakened by Domingo, who had said roughly, "You should eat something. It is a long way to your house."

Unwilling to risk being fired at, her escort had left her on the ridge. She wondered if Sereno would have been such a coward. He was wearing a businesslike belt gun.

Into a silence, she said, "Daddy gave me a camera for Christmas. Would you let me take your picture?"

His eyes were mildly questioning and she thought for an instant that he didn't know what a camera was; but he shrugged and said, "¿Cómo no?" one of the first phrases she had learned. Why not?

The best place for good snapshots was at the spring, and when they walked down there, all the men wanted their pictures made, too. She placed them in a group— with Sereno in front—beneath shade, and maneuvered to shoot from different angles.

For several exposures, she moved close enough that only Sereno would appear in the finished picture. Her heartbeat made her hand tremble so much that she had to steady first against a sapling and then on an outcropping of rock.

While she was loading fresh film, some of the Las Flores women and children ventured from their huts and were entreated to join the activity, but with energetic cries the señoras pulled their little ones away as from danger, and the men drifted to a game of chance in a dooryard.

"You have more film?" Sereno asked, coming to her and watching her fumble with the latch and sprockets under cover of her shawl.

"Yes—as soon as I exchange it." Dropping the used film into her pocket, she said, "Now, you with your horse."

They walked around to the other side of the house where the animals were tethered, and he swung into the saddle. She backed against a porch post and clicked the shutter on what surely would develop into a pleasing remembrance of this day.

When he made the horse rear and hold the pose, she exclaimed, "¡Viva!" though excitement jerked her hand enough to ruin the shot.

Two more—one of him dismounting, another as he turned toward her—and he said, "Let me take one of you."

"Oh—no— This dress is old, and my hair—" She let him have the camera.

"Muy bonita—very pretty— Do I press this?"

He backed off and before she was ready, had done the deed. Then he called to one of his riders, and the boy jogged across the yard. Sereno showed him how to work the lever and came to stand beside her, one arm around her, his hand lightly laid on her shoulder.

Gingerly, she put her arm around him, her hand scarcely touching the fabric of his shirt over his ribs; yet she felt the contour and warmth of his lean body. After the click, he drew away, going to retrieve her camera.

Returning it, he frowned and said, "We should have done another, so I might have a picture also."

"I shall instruct the developer to make two of each."

While they sat beneath the ramada, she resisted the urge to snap more, loathe to use up all of the film in case Domingo should happen to come by in the future. "How is Violeta? And your mother?"

"Both are well, gracias a Dios."

"And—Domingo?" She strove to make her question blend, as if the older brother's well-being were of no special interest.

"He is visiting friends in the north." Sereno's voice suddenly took on a harsh quality, and from the look on his face she dared not push him for an explanation.

"Do you think you might stay for supper? Tokee's cooking isn't good, but it's better than mine." She liked the level way Sereno met her stare. The fleeting irritation sparked by her mention of Domingo gave way to his customary easygoing expression.

"Your father might not approve."

"Daddy won't know. He's not supposed to be back before tomorrow."

"Not supposed to be; but might be."

"Unlikely. He took extra food and horses."

"Where did he go?"

She shook her head. "He never tells me, exactly. Out to check on the guayule crop, I guess."

"Guayule?"

"He says it's used somehow in the war effort, though he means the one in Europe, not your revolution. Mex— I mean, people have been known to steal the crops right out of the field, to sell."

"You think he's guarding his fields?"

This conversation was heading in the same direction as the one she had had with Domingo. "Do you think he's doing something else?" she asked curiously.

"Have you never followed him?"

She shook her head again. "I've thought about it, but if he caught me—"

Sereno waited. When she failed to finish, prodded, "If he caught you—?"

"Well, Daddy can make everyone miserable when he's angry, and if he thought I was spying on him, he would be very angry."

Sereno gazed out across the sunny yard. "Do you not trust him, Cristina?" he asked softly.

"Not entirely," she answered, on a sigh. "I reckon Domingo told you that."

"Domingo and I don't tell each other anything." Again his words were edged, but he swiftly changed the subject. "Bueno, if you think it is safe, I would like to stay for supper. Con permiso, I shall inform my riders."

She watched him walk the length of the porch and cross the yard to where the men were still gambling. He remained talking with them so long she wondered if he would come back to her; but presently he did. The mozo who had made a snapshot of them led away the horses to be tended. An evening breeze sprang up, bringing aromas from the kitchen to where they were sitting. Beyond the spring, doves called to each other.

She brought out her sketch pads and watercolor pictures to amuse him until the food was ready. He liked a street scene in Culiacán so much that she gave it to him.

"After we eat," he promised, "I'll play a few little songs for you on my flute."

"Oh, I love flute music."

They were finishing a rice dish cooked in sweetened milk, when another of his riders came to the back door and delivered a short urgent-sounding message before vanishing. In a smooth motion. Sereno rose, plucked his hat and belt gun off a chair, said, "Hasta luego, Cristina—y gracias," and kissed her cheek.

Then he was gone, leaving her with too many dishes and the sound of hooves approaching the front of the house, fainter sounds of horses departing at the back, and the sensation of his lips against her skin.

When Daddy came over the threshold he looked so weary she jumped up, concerned. "Poor Daddy, have you ridden all day?" But part of her mind was occupied with blocking his view of the table as Tokee hurried to clear it.

He sat down and took off his boots, pulling at them and his socks as if the effort were almost too much. "Well, if getting in and out of the saddle a hundred times and climbing over hellish boulders since dawn counts as riding, I'll say I've ridden all day. Tokee, stop whatever you're doing and tell Arturo to fill up that tub. I want a bath, not supper." He groaned as he stood up and tottered barefoot to lean in the front doorway.

Behind his back, she glanced at the cook, who gave a little nod and smile. The table was clean.

When she sent her film to Culiacán by Daddy to be developed, she never expected him to look in the envelope. She had supposed he'd come in and hand her the sealed package with his preoccupied air, freeing her to pore over the images at her leisure, choosing which were good enough to send to Sereno while devising a way to get them to him.

Now she stood shaking and trying not to cry or blurt out any defense, while Daddy strode back and forth across the small room, waving his arms and scattering the prints, accusing her of things that made her ears burn. She didn't really hear half of the words, only the volume, anger, and wounded pride, and sensed that he was calling her bad names and comparing her to her mother.

It was some minutes before she realized what he was saying: not different, but alike—both a disappointment and not worth the aggravation they'd caused him. She hadn't known he felt that way, but fuzzily recalled similar scenes before Mother's death. She had always thought his tirades were directed at something outside the family.

In a lull during which he glared down at the single picture left in his hand, others trampled underfoot, she swallowed against the choking sensation in her throat. "Since you hate me so much, I'd best go live with Greta."

"You're not even going to deny it, are you?" His eyes glittered with fury and too much to drink.

Deny what? She couldn't deny that Sereno had been here. The photographs plainly showed the spring, their mozos, the ramada, their porch furniture.

And the one Daddy had waved beneath her nose at the start. Her, self-conscious and grinning stupidly into the lens. It was embarrassing.

"How many nights did he stay? Or did you go out in the brush? My God, I didn't think I had an ignoramus for a daughter. Consorting with my worst enemy—and to flaunt it at me with pictures!"

Clutching the corner of the table, she shouted, "I don't know what you're talking about. He never stayed one night and we never left the yard. Ask anybody!"

"You think I'd believe anything these damned Mexkins told me? If they could be trusted, I'd've had that mine by now. You don't realize—

"Then you should believe *me*." Hovering tears spilled over and ran down her feverish cheeks. She hated that her voice shook, hated more that her trembling had increased until she had to fumble for a slat chair and sit down. In the past, Daddy's scenes had been stormy and painful, seldom justified, but soon over. She felt this one marked a turning point, though she was too upset to define why.

His voice went on, harsh and endless, while she blew her nose on Tokee's dishrag and wished she dared gather up the photographs before his boots damaged them further.

Remembering her pleasure the day they were made, she found with surprise that her misery was dissipating even while Daddy ranted. The negatives were still in the package, safe on the table, within reach of her hand. And Sereno was safe at Los Nuestros.

Her numbed mind began working again. If Daddy no longer loved her, or maybe never had, and didn't want her around, she didn't have to live with Greta. She could seek refuge with the Corderos.

IV

Domingo wasn't surprised when Paz went into labor one evening at the end of his second week at Los Dos. He'd just come in from the corrals, anticipating a bath, when a criada rushed past with an armload of clean towels and the cheery information that la patróna required all of the hot water.

In the hallway outside her door, he found Tereza and Mariano, one seated tense on a cushioned bench, the other pacing.

"Amigo, you look like Jefe when Violeta was being born." Tereza made room for him, but he shook his head, not caring to offend her with smells of sweat and horse. "A swim will do us both good," he suggested, but Mariano said, "I cannot leave her. You go on."

"It might be hours before anything happens."

Tereza said, "The partera thinks it will go swiftly. She has been hurting all afternoon."

Domingo took clean clothes with him to the pond and remained in the village for the meal. Lounging beneath a ramada afterward, sounds of an Indio household at his back, a desert vista silvered by moonlight before him, he let his thoughts wander. The birth of his little sister. Progress he was making with the filly. Memories of a younger Paz. Mina. He shut out images of Bravo, and tried to shut out those of Cristina; but the latter kept returning. When he entered the casa again, a crowd of women had gathered in the hallway.

Tereza ran to him, excited. "Twins!" She grabbed his hand to lead him forward. "A girl and a boy. Mariano is with her, and everybody is so happy."

Just like Paz, to finish with unpleasantness as soon as possible. He said, "Gracias a Dios, for sparing them."

"Gracias a Dios." Tiptoeing, she kissed him on the mouth.

Simple as the gesture was, with no overtones of passion, it set his blood to racing. Giving a quick look to be sure none of the servants had noticed, he grasped her shoulders and pulled her into the shelter of a turn in the hallway, where he kissed her. Unlike Mina, she kept her lips closed and after a moment she drew back, as if she regretted allowing him the liberty. But he had felt her response and knew she wasn't angry.

Then the bedroom door opened and Mariano came out, holding up a naked baby, his face alight with the joy of creation.

Following him, a smiling Mayo girl held a second, smaller baby. "El es Diego Ramón," the father declared. The criadas cheered. "Elle es Angelita Luz," he said, and kissed the girl-child. Another cheer.

Tereza hurried forward to see the twins up close, and Domingo said to Jesús, who hung on the fringe of well-wishers, "Bring glasses and some wine."

When the tray was brought, he filled two goblets and gave one to Mariano. "Long life and health, amigo," he said, and they drank, eyes meeting over the rims.

"And an end to this damned revolution," Mariano added, "so that my children may live in peace."

A few days later, news came that Carranza had been elected Presidente of La República. "It is as we expected." Paz was sitting up in bed, an elaborately embroidered garment covering her above the sheet. The babies were asleep in another room under the eye of their niñera. Mariano held her hand in both of his, touching her knuckles to his lips in a thoughtful manner.

Domingo recalled what the hacendado had said about the possibility that lands owned by the Ortegas—and the Corderos—might be broken up and granted to others. "The new constitution could give Señor Johnson the wedge he needs to ruin us."

Mariano frowned. "If Ramón wants help fighting this man, all he has to do is ask."

"Gracias. But I think the gringo will think twice before attacking again. Jefe believes the danger now is from illegal claims and lawyers."

"Why does Señor Johnson want Los Nuestros?" Paz yawned and reached for a glass of juice on a bedside table. "I thought gringos were after oil."

"Sereno has the foolish idea that there is a lost mine on the property. Perhaps Señor Johnson has the same idea."

Mariano gave him a sharp look. "Not so long ago, weren't you the one talking about El Naranjal and how legend says the mine is in the mountains somewhere close to your casa grande?"

His face flushed uncomfortably. "I was a niño then. I've grown up." He went out to the corrals, mostly to cool off, partly hoping Tereza would join him.

Estrellita was tame enough for him to ride now, so after waiting a few lonely minutes he saddled the filly and set out for the far reaches of the hacienda. Sometimes he didn't feel at all grown up. He wished he could go back to being the boy for whom mustanging and taking Bravo hunting were the chief excitements of life. Yet...the feelings surging in him brought a confusion both pleasant and dreaded. He wished he could go forward and share his nights with... Which?

Mina's flashing eyes and eager mouth held promise, even if she did try to make him jealous by becoming engaged to one of his friends. She reminded him of Paz. Paz, a couple of years ago.

With pale Spanish skin, blue eyes, and curly black hair, Tereza had always attracted him. Since his first sight of her at Dos Corazones when they were children, he'd been awed by her beauty. Accustomed to living in a casa grande and having criadas to boss around, she would make a more suitable match than anyone from Jefe's village.

Unbidden, another face appeared in his mind's eye. Eager, irritating. Out of the question, with Señor Johnson for a father. Besides, as heir to Los Nuestros he had no business thinking about a gringa who could be nothing but trouble for his family.

With some effort, he turned his attention to the not-too-distant time when he would present Tereza with a gentle filly. He was glad the death of don Diego had not tarnished his gift for her. Riding past the family campo santo, he noted the carved stone marker Mariano had erected for their father, and wondered what she would do if she learned the hacendado lay in Los Nuestros land, instead of here beside his wife.

When he had stabled the filly and entered the back patio, he found the girls basking in the balmy air of late afternoon, the babies sleeping bundled in rebozos on their laps. Down wide hallways, aromas wafted from braziers and ovens, and he could hear the muted conversation of the cook and her helpers preparing the evening meal.

"There's a letter from Ramón," Paz said, holding out an opened envelope to him.

He saw it was not addressed to him, but to Mariano. A pang of disappointment clouded the lines. His father's familiar handwriting expressed good wishes for the family on the occasion of the births, concern over the direction Carranza's policies would take in implementing Article Twenty-Seven, and tidbits of news from Culiacán.

Then there was a message for him.

> Do not be alarmed when I say that
> circumstances here will soon require you
> to come home. The need is not yet urgent
> but when you read this, make plans to
> return at the end of the month.
> Anita sends her love with mine.
> > Jefe.

No good wishes from Sereno, though he didn't expect any. "It's the end of the month now," he remarked.

Tereza was staring at him gravely. As their gazes met, she seemed to turn shy and began fussing with the nearest baby's blanket.

"Oh, not for another two days," Paz said. "Mariano thinks he should accompany you, and he cannot go before Sunday."

"The filly isn't ready," he said.

"You've been riding Estrellita for at least ten days." Paz observed.

"Ten days is nothing. She is still unbitted, and too wild for a woman to handle." The importance of this grew as he considered it. "All my work will be wasted."

"What do you think is happening at Los Nuestros, that you must leave?" Tereza asked.

He tossed the letter onto the cushion beside Paz. "I can only guess. But it had better be important."

Feeling the pressure of so little time, he found it difficult to sleep. At last he rolled out of bed, put on his jeans and went down the moonlit hall in his bare feet.

The great silent house, the cold muzzle of the yard dog in his palm, the restless shadows of horses in the corrals, reminded him of those nights when he stole out to check on Bravo in the pen. He shoved those memories aside, as the loss was still painful.

He knew guards were on duty at intervals along the outer walls, though not even the glowing tip of a cigarette nor the odor of smoke betrayed their presence. He swung to sit on the top pole of the corral where Estrellita and half a dozen yeguas milled and snuffled. She butted her face against his knees. Using both hands he scratched below her ears. "Hola, Little Star. If I had one more week, just one—"

"What else would you do? She is tame already."

The voice startled him almost into falling. As he grabbed at the rough pole, the filly threw up her head and stepped back. Tereza moved toward him out of the dense dark cast by the stable. She wore pants and boots and her hair was tied back.

Climbing onto the bottom rung, near and facing him, she said, "Please don't tell Mariano."

His pulse slowed, though not to normal. "You shouldn't come out here by yourself at night. She is not tame enough. Didn't you believe me?"

A trace of amusement in her voice, Tereza said, "My Little Star and I have an understanding, don't we, niña?" She laid an arm around the filly's neck as it pushed between them. "I have ridden her these last three nights. Jesús helped me with the saddle. Feel how damp she is? He did not have time to rub her down before you came."

The corner of his eye caught movement as the old man came to the stable opening then shrank back inside.

"You might have been hurt," he said, stern. "Your brother would forbid me at Dos Corazones forever if he thought I had put you at risk."

"That is why you must not tell him."

A soft rattling of the oat bucket summoned Estrellita into the stable, two of the others following. Moments ticked by in uncomfortable silence. He was aware of gripping the railing on which he sat, bare to the waist in the moonlight. Tereza stepped onto a higher rung. "I wish I could go with you," she said. The side of her hand touched the side of his. The night breeze failed to cool his face. He felt as sweaty as the filly. They had never been completely alone together before. "Why not do that? Paz has plenty of help, and you would be welcome."

Tereza gave a sigh. "I already asked. Mariano says, not while there is a chance of danger."

"It couldn't be serious, or Jefe would have sent a telegram."

"If it were not serious, would he have wanted you to come home?"

He mulled that over. "I suppose not." He watched Jesús ghost out of the corral and cross the dappled yard.

With a movement as unthreatening as any he'd ever made in taming the wildest mustang, Domingo reached to lightly grasp Tereza's chin. It felt silky to his fingertips. Making no objection, she let him draw her toward him and returned the caresses of his lips; but, uncertain of her reaction, he kept himself from becoming too bold, as he had with Mina. After a few kisses, inhaling the faint sweet aroma of her skin and hair, he murmured, "I love you, Tereza."

Close to his ear, she said, "I love you, too, Domingo."

The warmth and strength of male arms around her, the touch of his naked skin and seeking lips, his soft voice and the texture of thick curly hair in her hand at the back of his head, made Tereza's heart race.

He had certainly grown up in the years since her first sight of him in the kitchen at Dos Corazones, fearless even then when he was alone and still dazed from the death of his mother, not knowing he had a living father, riding on campaign with the rebel army, his life out of his control. She had never imagined anyone so handsome and romantic outside one of her books.

Now, his skill with horses fascinated her, for she sensed that he loved them as much as she did.

He gently disentangled and said, "We'd better go inside." They walked into the house together and he left her at her door with a squeeze of her hand, whispering, "Buen sueños."

Her senses were so filled with Domingo that she had undressed and was tossing sleepless on her bed before she remembered Sereno. The little gifts they had exchanged, her pleasure at hearing him play his flute, the letters they had written—his tied in a packet and secreted beneath her underthings in a drawer—in which each hinted of tender feelings for the other.

The day he took her to his secret spot overlooking the plain and played his flute so sweetly, affection spilled over and she had kissed his cheek. The expression in his eyes told her he loved her. And she had loved him. Did she still? She didn't know.

But how exciting, to find out!

"Hermano," she said, at Mariano's side as he packed his clothes for the trip, "if Los Nuestros were not safe, wouldn't Anita and Violeta be coming here? And if they are safe there, why can I not go?"

He paused, a badly folded shirt in his hand, as if finding a way around her logic. Then he said, "Perhaps I can send for you later."

"I'm surprised Paz made no objection to your leaving so soon after the birth of the babies."

He finished with the bag. "I wouldn't leave my family for anyone except Ramón."

"He has a hundred men to fight his battles. And you are sending an escort with Domingo to keep him safe. Why do you feel you must go?"

Mariano's dark eyes met hers briefly. "I think you know why."

Curious, Tereza followed him down the hall toward the storerooms. "She told me she once loved Ramón. But all that is over, no? Since she met you." She watched him fill a food sack.

"She still worries about him. It is natural."

"Are you not jealous?"

Mariano paused again, with the same penetrating look, this time allowing himself a little smile. "So long as she is here and he is there—no. Besides, Ramón and I are blood brothers. I trust him."

"You were very angry with him a few months ago. Why?"

Mariano hugged her, kissed her forehead, and said, "A misunderstanding, only."

She followed him to the corrals where riders were readying their horses. Domingo had taken Estrellita out one last time. "And—Domingo? You trust him, too, don't you? And you like him?"

He whirled as if suddenly realizing the basis for these questions. "I thought you had feelings for Sereno."

In some confusion she admitted, "I do— How did you know?"

"Hermanita, as hacendado of Los Dos Corazones, and your older brother, it is my duty to know."

While he was saddling his horse, Paz came out to say buen viaje. They stood outside the corral, shading their eyes with their hands. "Domingo is returning," Paz said.

Her heart began to pound.

He and the filly covered the distance at a slow lope, and when he dismounted he handed the reins to her. "Ella es tuya."

"Muchas gracias." She managed to grasp his hand for an instant as she took possession.

Paz hugged him, and standing apart, he gave her stomach a playful pat, saying, "The last time we embraced, was not so comfortable."

She laughed and slapped his chest. As he started for his own mount, she called, "Give my love to your family."

He cast an understanding look over his shoulder. "I shall."

"Vaya con Dios," Tereza cried, and he waved from the saddle.

Then the riders circled for position, a mozo opened the corral gate, and in a rush of hooves they departed.

*   *   *

Don't miss the conclusion of Tierra del Oro!

Book Nine, *TESORO*

First published in November, 2012

Chapter One

Ramón sat in the dark porch alone, aware of others in the house … muted voices, shadows moving in the light cast through tall barred windows, criadas snapping fold-wrinkles out of a tablecloth and chattering in their dialect, the *clunk* of silverware as they placed it for cena.

It had taken years to accustom himself to eating his supper late. How long, to accustom himself to a life without the ability to swing into the saddle and ride wherever he chose? With a sigh he rested his head on the cushioned back of the chair, eyes closed against the yellow-orange squares of village lamps, the street lights leading down to the deserted plaza.

"What kind of defense can I put in motion if I am like this?" he had demanded of Estrada at their last meeting.

Turing away as if placing instruments into his bag required concentration, Estrada had said, "You have many capable armed men under your command. And Domingo is older than his years might suggest."

Domingo. On his way home from Dos Corazones. Despite skill at taming mesteños and accuracy—luck?— with firearms, yet a boy. Judgment had come late to himself. He couldn't expect his firstborn, Serafina's child, to possess it in any great quantity.

Hell, I still find difficulty knowing which of my decisions will turn out right.

✻✻✻✻✻✻✻✻✻✻✻✻✻

To order the Tierra del Oro novels,
go to the author page of RLB Hartmann at
Amazon

To contact the author, email *rlbhartmann@gmail.com*

The Cordero Saga -
One story, one family, one continuing adventure.